House on Butcher Harbor

Butcher Harbor Series

Book One

Lisa Lewis Moon

ISBN:978-1-935636-16-8 Second Edition
PUBLISHED BY: Lisa Lewis Moon
Cover Photo Courtesy of Ron Chapple Studios/ Dreamstime.com
Printed in the United States of America.

DEDICATION

To my children Michael Moon and Trevor Moon for always pushing me to finish the book. They are constantly saying "shouldn't you be writing?" Yes! And THANK YOU SO MUCH. I love you both beyond words.

ACKNOWLEDGMENTS

This book would not have been written without the inspiration of the Genesis song HOME by the SEA and my husband, who disconnected my internet so that I could stop playing games and focus on writing. The following people have assisted with editing and beta reading this book: Teresa Overton, Jeannette Brasher, Angie Barnett, and Mary Angel. A huge Thank you to all of you for your contribution to keeping me encouraged and on track.

CHAPTER ONE

The summer storm battered Templeton House set on the end of Butcher Harbor Peninsula. It was the only house that stood on the peninsula of this tiny North Eastern town. Rain pelted the glass windows and the weather worn roof as gale force winds shook the very foundation of the beach house. Inside, sixty year old Elizabeth Templeton stood in the living room in a crazed state, a carving knife in her trembling hand. Her striped house dress hung loosely on her tiny frame, not unlike the skin on her aging body. Her eyes were as wild as a wolves. She moved the blade of the carving knife from side to side as if to hold off her attackers. There was no one in the room with her, at least no one living that is.

"I asked you to stop this ruckus for just a while- STOP! Is that too much to ask?" Distress wrinkled her face. Tears streamed down her cheeks unchecked.

"Listen to us," hundreds of ghosts said in their own way.

"We live because you hear us."

"Don't desert us," the needy voices called out to her. All the noise made her head ache and grated on her last nerve.

"Go ahead and do it," the haggard old woman with the knife hissed at her from the corner of the room.

"Yes, join us," others said. Each one of the hundreds of souls trapped in the house needed her in one way or another to help dispel the torment and anguish of their lives. Dead or alive they knew she would listen to them.

"Do it," the old woman cried out again.

"No, wait!" cried the soft pitch of a young boy. "Don't listen to her," he pleaded. "I need you. I miss my mommy. Please stay with me. I am scared." The boy looked around the room at the other ghosts, panic on his face.

"Haven't I been here for you all these years? All of you?" Elizabeth pleaded, her eyes wild with fear and pain. All these years she had delighted in listening to their desperate stories. They had become her friends, her family. They were all she had left in her world since her husband passed on and her daughter Claire had fled the house of ghosts after high school. But tonight, with the storm raging outside she needed quiet. The years had taken a toll on her and she could no longer meet the constant demand on her attention. They required too much from her these days. Was it too much to ask for a break to recharge her frail body and mind?

Each time the house was slammed by the insistent wind she was afraid it would crumble around her. There was no need to worry about the house. It was sturdy as ever. But what if on this treacherous night, like her, it too might be weary.

"Yes, join us," cried many voices from all around the room, the voices came from the very walls of the house itself.

"Can't you be still for just one night and give me a little peace?" Elizabeth cried out.

"No," the room shuddered with the cry of many voices in many languages as yet another gale force wind assaulted the house.

"Nein."

"Non."

"Never."

Tears streamed down her face. She was tired. They were not about to give her the rest she needed. They were sucking the life out of her. Exhausted, Elizabeth held the carving knife to her throat in one last attempt to quiet the voices for just this one night.

"I'll do it. I swear I will," she threatened.

"Yes," hissed the haggard old woman's voice again, "Do it you weak bag of bones."

"No please," the little boy pleaded, "I'll be quiet. I promise."

"Do it!" the old woman hissed yet again. "Do it you filthy whore."

Elizabeth took a deep breath. The voices grew louder, fighting to be heard over one another.

"I can't take this anymore." She fell to her knees between the sofa and the coffee table. She sobbed into her trembling hands, still clutching the carving knife. She didn't want to die, but the voices wouldn't stop. She knew they couldn't. It was too much for her.

"Join us," they whispered at once.

"STOP!" she screamed as she lost what little as left of her mind. A sharp thin pain was followed by warm flowing blood as the cold metal blade slit first her left and then her right wrist. A flash of light was followed instantly by a thunderous boom. The house shook from top to bottom. Tears ran unchecked down her cheeks and mixed with the warm blood as it ran down her hands and onto her striped house dress. This was not the outcome she had planned on. She believed that they would care enough about her to let her rest. She had given them all so much. Surely they could have given her this one thing.

"NO!" the little boy screamed as he rushed across the room and hugged her.

"That's right you stupid bitch. Leave it to you to bleed all over the clean floor. Claire will love cleaning up that mess," the old woman scolded her.

"Someone please help her!" cried out a German Sailor in uniform.

Outside the endless waves beat upon the shore. The rain pelted the rugged exterior of the house, drowning out the voices inside. Only a quick flickering of the lights betrayed the secret the beach house held within its walls as the life ran out of gaping wounds. They look like tiny desperate mouths she thought as everything went black.

CHAPTER TWO

Tires crunched along the crushed seashell covered road as Deputy Raymond Dogg drove his police SUV into the cul-de-sac at the end of the Peninsula Road. This was the only place the deputy could find peace during the busy summer months on Butcher Harbor. Summer season was in full bloom and the natives were restless due to the summer storm. It had trapped them inside their homes, rental cottages, town restaurants, and bars for several days. He anticipated a lot of calls tonight. There would be bar fights, cooped up husbands lashing out at tired wives. Then there was the summertime fights over parking spaces made worse by everyone's desire to park closer to the door.

The deputy glanced across the peninsula toward the harbor and the town. Lights dotted the beach and surrounding port. It was a sight he never got tired of, even while the rain pelted his windows and the wind buffeted his cruiser. On the opposite side of him was the ocean, black and rolling. Fierce waves spewed sea water up onto the peninsula. The heavy spray hit the cruiser even though he was parked twenty feet from the rocky edge.

He turned his windshield wipers off, allowing the rain and sea water to wash across the windshield freely and placed the cruiser in park. He reached over to the passenger side floorboard for the cooler that contained his lunch. A thermos was on the seat next to him. He poured himself a cap full of his mother's famous coffee; roasted with just a bit of her secret ingredient- cinnamon. Coffee breaks like this one were the highlight of his night. The taste and the smell of the coffee brought back wonderful childhood memories of his dad sneaking him sips of coffee when his mom wasn't looking. Enjoying the aroma of the spiced coffee, he scanned the peninsula to his right. The only thing on the peninsula was the Templeton House, a quarter of a mile away. To add to the oddness of the dark, stormy night, the widow Templeton appeared to have left every light on in the house. Perhaps she was using the light to ward off the loneliness the storm seemed to bring with it.

He knew from previous breaks here that Elizabeth Templeton rarely kept more than one light on at night. She was probably on a very tight budget. That could be the only reason anyone would be foolish enough to burn only one light in that house at night. Raymond had heard stories about the ghosts of Templeton House since he was a toddler. Mrs. Templeton was said to be loony from all the ghosts she allegedly kept company with within those walls. He remembered her daughter Claire had left shortly after her husband had passed on. Claire couldn't get out of that house fast enough.

All the stories started with pirates who landed on the peninsula and built the house upon the craggy shore from parts of boats they shipwrecked during storms just like this one. Boats they themselves had scuttled. The harbor was named for the blood bath they created out at sea and on land. His father told him the story about the mob from town that gathered and finally drove the pirates off, extinguishing the lights of the house, and saving countless seamen a brutal death. Tales of strange sights and sounds followed the house to this day. The list of the missing and the dead grew with each telling, yet for some unexplained reason he could not understand the house always remained occupied.

Templeton House captivated Raymond as he stared at the two story structure. He wondered what it must have been like to grow up in that house. Remembering the teasing Claire had taken in school, he decided maybe he didn't really want to know. He had put up with his own hazing with the name Dogg. Now that he was a deputy, his friends gave him shit about his name all the time. And when it came to names, the name- Butcher Harbor- was a thorn in the town's back side as well. The town hated the house and anyone crazy enough to inhabit it.

He ate half his sandwich, saving the other half for his next coffee break later in the night. He drank the last sip of his coffee in his cup, placed the cap back on the thermos and put the canvas cooler back on the floor next to him. He turned the windshield wipers back on. A huge gush of salt and rain water whooshed across the windshield and was wiped clear only to be filled quickly by new rainfall. When the windshield cleared, he pulled the cruiser back onto the road.

"You have a good evening Mrs. Templeton," he said out loud as he passed the house headed back into town. He gave a little salute to the brightly lit house as he passed by. Before him awaited the chaos of the night. The deputy smiled. He loved his job.

As he drove toward town he took one last look at the Templeton house in his rear view mirror.

"What the hell!"

The wheels of the cruiser locked up nearly sending it off the road. Dogg fought to bring the cruiser back under his control.

"Harbor Two to base," he called in to the station.

"Base. What's up Dogg?" the soothing woman's voice of the third-shift dispatcher teased.

"I'm not sure. The lights of the Templeton house are flickering on and off."

"Maybe the ghosts are having a hurricane party of their own like the rest of the town," she said. Dogg thought he could hear a giggle in her voice. Chances were more likely that some drunken tourist were playing a prank on the old widow.

"I'm going to check it out," he said. He threw the cruiser into reverse. Of course there was always the possibility that the house itself, and not the townsfolk, was the cause of the trouble at Templeton house tonight. He thought about this for a moment. He didn't believe in ghosts, but the rich history of the house, and the endless disappearances and deaths contributed to it made him leery. Just in case, he called back to base.

"If you don't hear from me in ten minutes, send backup.

CHAPTER THREE

Claire Templeton stood at her station in a sea of drawing tables and sewing machines at the J & B's fashion house. She was wearing her favorite gypsy style outfit. The layers of fabric were bright and delicate. On her wrists were golden chains filled with charms. A bright red ribbon was wrapped several times around her long brown locks. A model stood before her wearing her latest creation, another in the gypsy line for the fall. Around the models waist Claire grabbed a handful of fabric and put a pin in it. The model flinched.

"Emily, you should know by now that I won't stick you. Stand still or you'll make me mess this up and we'll have to start all over again."

"Sorry. It's a habit."

"Have I ever stuck you before?"

"No."

"Then why do you never trust me?"

"Most of the others do," Emily said dipping her head so as not to be heard by those around them.

"There's always a first time," Grace Noble winked at Emily as she walked up. Grace picked up a pack of fabric samples and leafed through them. Grace and Claire had come to J & B together straight out of high school. They had fled Butcher Harbor the day after their graduation party. With an eye for fashion and some experience creating summer clothes for the tourist trade, the girls convinced the owner of J & B, Charlie Baxter, to let them work. He agreed as long as they both worked for one salary and produced clothing that would sell.

The girls jumped at the opportunity and soon had a line of summer clothing that flew off the racks. The girls seemed to know which fabrics worked best in the heat and humidity of the east coast; they liked fabrics that breathed well and dried quickly. They also knew how to uncover a body without exposing too much. The buyers caught on to the girls' line of clothing, and the summer business at J & B doubled the next summer season. Even though both girls seemed lost at winter fashion, Charlie kept them on, knowing that a few years in New York would teach them about fashionable winter wear.

Starting out with one paycheck between them, the girls made a cozy apartment out of a storage area in the old warehouse. Charlie helped them out allowing them the use of the warehouse kitchen and bathroom facilities which luckily included a shower for the models. Soon the girls were sewing their own clothes out of leftover scraps of material. Charlie reaped the benefits of the design and sewing skills the girls picked up while dressing themselves. They soon learned to dress in high fashion. Claire preferred the gypsy style of layering bright colors, while Grace chose more professional attire of a New York business woman. Within six months the girls each took home their own paycheck and they moved into an apartment together on the lower east side.

"Anyway, of course I told him no," Grace rambled as Emily continued to fidget under Claire's steady hand. Claire did not respond. Grace was not surprised. "Listening Claire?" she said.

"Yeah?" Claire asked.

"So, then he beat me in the face with his fists and raped me right there in front of everyone." Grace blurted out in frustration.

"That's nice," Claire said without looking up from her darts.

"Son of a Bitch," Grace slammed the book of fabric samples down on the work bench. Claire jumped, sending the straight pins in her hand spilling all over the floor. Emily leapt away from Claire, afraid she might get stuck.

"I did it again, didn't I?" Claire asked, as she picked up the pins from the polished concrete floor.

"Yes, yes you did."

"I'm so sorry."

"Damn it Claire- this is important to me. The least you could do is pretend to listen."

"Grace, you know I care. You are my-" Claire started.

"-best bud," Grace finished, still angry with her friend, "But you could at least try to listen when it's this important."

"You're right. I'm sorry. I just get so task oriented. I promise I'm all ears," Claire said, placing the pins on the work bench as Emily stripped out of the outfit, tossed it at Claire, put on her robe and fled the area. Claire's face burned with embarrassment.

"I am so sorry. Forgive me?" Claire asked and put on an exaggerated pout for her friends' benefit.

"Of course I do," Grace said, hugging her friend.

"Quince wants me to move in with him," Grace said.

"Wow." Claire rested against the work table and stared at her.

"Yeah, wow," Grace repeated.

Claire took a deep breath and stared blankly at her best friend. Fear settled in the pit of her stomach as she realized what that meant for her. Grace will move out. There was no way she could live alone. Grace's room would have to be rented out. That would mean living with a complete stranger. We have been inseparable since grade school. Can I even live with someone else? Grace made good noise and kept the bad noises away. Who else could do that for her?

"Can you think about me for just a second?" Grace cried out, making Claire wonder if she had spoken out loud.

"Of course, sweetie." Heat rose up in her face again. When did I get to be so self-absorbed? The thought made her heart ache. Grace was the best friend she ever had. Claire would never intentionally do anything to upset her.

The phone on the work bench rang. Both girls jumped at the sudden sound. They each grabbed for it at the same time, but Grace got to it first. They giggled like school girls.

"Yes, I see," Grace paled as she placed the receiver gently into its cradle.

"You're wanted in the Principal's office," she said quietly.

The Principal's office was a term the girls used for Charlie's office. If you were called in there, it was bad news; he had a short fuse to match his short round body. Claire took a deep breath and headed for his office wondering what she could possibly have done to make him mad at her.

Tears formed in the corners of Grace's eyes as watched Claire leave. Bad news awaited her in Charlie's office, news that would change both of their lives forever.

CHAPTER FOUR

Charlie's office was all glass overlooking the work floor. He's watching me. I know he is. She glanced across the warehouse toward his office. The blinds were closed. His blinds were never closed. He had to keep a close eye on his employees or else all work would cease, and wild, rampant parties would ensue. Today was the first time she had ever seen his blinds drawn.

Giggling nervously she glanced around to see if panties were sailing through the air, or to perhaps catch bits of confetti flying about. But it was as she expected, everyone was hard at work making J & B's next season of amazing clothing a smash hit.

Claire took a deep breath and wondered what she could possibly have done to be sent to the Principal's office. The last five outfits she had submitted received great reviews. Two of them were slated for the fall line. None of her designs had ever made the fall line. She knocked on the door marked Charles Baxter. Like every other time she had entered his office she walked in without acknowledgment. Charlie was speaking to a tall, thin man dressed in a police-issue brown uniform. The man towered over Charlie's short round frame.

"I'm so sorry, Mr. Baxter, I didn't realize-" Claire started to apologize for barging in.

"It's quite alright. Actually Chief…"Charlie fumbled for the name of the police officer.

"Harris," Claire finished for him. She recognized the face of the man towering over her boss.

"Ah, yes, Harris," Charlie smacked his hands together. He seemed delighted to have that out of the way.

Chief Harris reached out and shook Claire's hand a bit longer than she considered normal. It made her feel uncomfortable. This is not going to be good news.

"Is it…" She attempted to speak, but found her mouth had gone quite dry.

"Your mother? Yes." The Chief answered, finally letting go of her hand.

"Is she…" Claire tried again, but could not seem to finish this sentence either. Her legs suddenly felt weak, and the room seemed to fade away.

"Dead? Oh no. Sorry to scare you. She is in St. Anthony's in guarded condition."

"A heart attack?"

"No." Chief Harris blushed. He seemed to be having trouble reporting the news of her mother's condition.

"She- your mother- it appears that she slit both of her wrists sometime last night. My deputy found her when…" Chief Harris paused. He seemed to not want to go any further.

"When Chief? He found her when?" Claire was sure the answer had something to do with her mother's blasted house.

"During his rounds," Harris finally said.

"I see," He's hiding something, but he is not going to say anything in front of Charlie. She was sure she would find out later whether she wanted to know the truth or not.

"I'm sorry for notifying you so late, but your work address was the only contact information we could find," the Chief said.

"I understand. No need to apologize," she stated. Then more for Charlie's benefit than the Chief's she added, "My mother and I didn't exactly keep in touch."

It took great effort to speak. Just standing seemed to be quite a chore. The world seemed like it was miles away, and she felt like she was falling.

Charlie caught her arm and led her to the nearby sofa used to entertain buyers in the office. Then he pushed the intercom button on the phone that sat atop the end table.

"Yes, Mr. Baxter?" the secretary inquired.

"Could you ask Miss Noble to join us in my office?" Charlie requested.

"Yes, Mr. Baxter."

The line went dead. The three of them sat in silence unsure of what, if anything, to say. Charlie was probably afraid to say the wrong thing; the Chief most likely felt he had said too much; and she was afraid that all of this meant going back to that horrid house.

CHAPTER FIVE

Grace and Claire rode in the front seat of the rental sedan in silence. Crammed in the back seat was Quince Johnson, a tall lanky man with shoulder- length brown hair. Quince liked to dress in blue jeans and polo shirts. He sat behind Grace on the driver's side of the car. Vincent Baldwin was of average height. He wore his black hair so that it was not really parted at all, and was longer in the front than the back. He wore his usual black skinny legged jeans and long sleeved black tee-shirt. He sat behind Claire on the passenger side of the car. Scrunched between them was Ethan Parks. He was an elfish looking man, who looked more like a boy than a man, and had a head full of blond curls. Ethan wore his favorite gray slacks and a light pink shirt.

The receptionist had told Grace the reason for Claire's meeting with Mr. Baxter when she sent for Claire. Grace immediately called the boys and put them on alert. It was Friday morning so when Grace called the boys they each agreed to take the rest of the day off and go back to Butcher Harbor with Claire to support her through this ordeal. None of the boys had any idea how hard this was going to be for her.

The girls had met the guys in New York City after they had fled Butcher Harbor. Quince and Vincent were both photographers hired by J & B to take photos of the girl's outfits on fabulous NYC models. Ethan was a graphic design artist trying to break out on his own. He had done odd jobs for J & B as a freelance artist and got along well with the others immediately.

"Turn around," Claire demanded, breaking the silence in the rental car. Grace looked at her concerned. They still had at least 95 miles to go before they reached the Harbor. It was way too early in the trip for this.

"I said turn the fucking car around," she screamed. Grace continued to drive. The boys who had never heard Claire talk like that, sat up taller in the back seat.

"Settle down. You can do this. We'll help you," Grace spoke slowly and softly, glancing in the rear view mirror to the boys for support.

"Screw that. You know I can't do this. And you know why," Claire ranted.

"It's alright, Claire," Quince said from the rear seat, "we're all here to help get you through this."

Vincent grabbed her shoulder and squeezed it gently. Ethan reached over the seat and stroked her hair.

"You can do this," he said.

"You don't understand," Claire said turning around in her seat to face the boys. "None of you understand except for Grace. She was there. She knows why I can't go back there. Not for my mother. Not for anyone."

"We'll take this A.A. style- one step at a time. Step One- we all go to the hospital and face your mother with you. Step Two- We get a motel room and rest. Step Three – we plan the rest of the steps. Okay?" She should never have broached that as a question.

"Not okay. And no matter what, I am not going back to that house!" Claire yelled pulling herself away from the others reach. She huddled against the window, cold and shaking.

"Claire," Grace said firmly, "Chief Harris is waiting for you at the hospital. He is expecting us. Remember, he said he needs to see you when you get there."

"We'll call him," Claire snapped, "From the apartment."

"It doesn't work that way," Quince told her.

"Why not? What if she had no family? What if there was no one to come to the hospital? What then?" Claire cried.

"But there is someone," Ethan said, almost to himself.

"Harris saw you this morning with his own eyes. Ever wonder why he showed up instead of just calling the local police? He knew this would be hard for you, but he knew you had to come," Grace told her as she continued to drive toward the Harbor.

"Coulda' been an impostor you know," Claire said.

"Harris? He looked the same as ever to me," Grace was confused.

"Not Harris," Claire said. She slapped Graces arm almost playfully, "Me, you idiot."

"Oh," Grace said stunned. She didn't know what else to say. This wouldn't be the last of Claire's outbursts. Grace was not accustomed to Claire acting like this, and it threw her, but she understood the motivation. She wondered how far they would get before they had to have this same conversation again. It was only a two hour drive to the harbor, but it was going to be a long one.

CHAPTER SIX

Chief Robert Harris returned to the Harbor and went straight home. He parked his police cruiser in the driveway and went inside. Later he would have to meet Claire at the hospital, but right now he needed a shower and something to eat. His house looked like all the other houses on the Harbor: small house, clapboard siding, tiny yard. Like most people, he entered the house through the back door.

As he walked around the corner of the kitchen island the room seemed to get fuzzy. He grabbed the island counter- top to steady himself. Ever since that awful night when he had made Deputy with the Butcher Harbor Police Department, he couldn't walk around the island from the back door without feeling faint. It was supposed to have been the best day of his life. He had returned home anxious to tell his wife, Becky, about his big news. When he came around the corner of the island he found her lying on the floor in a puddle of blood, salad greens on the floor all around her, the salad bowl upside down next to her. Becky had to have a hysterectomy that night, and she would never be able to have children. She loved children and they had talked about raising a big family. He pushed the memories out of his mind, took a deep breath and released it slowly. It didn't seem to help much. The room was still swimming around him.

He cursed himself for coming home when Becky wasn't there. Usually she got home before him. The evening meal would be cooking, and she would be humming along to the radio, songs from the fifties and sixties, her favorites. How he loved to watch her light up when he entered the house. That was the highlight of his day. He almost never came home when she wasn't there first.

The phone rang, bringing him back to the present.

"Harris," he said, hoping it wasn't business. He really needed a shower and his stomach growled.

"You're home. I was afraid you might still be in the city, so I didn't want to bother you on your cell. I was just checking to see how things went," Becky said.

"I'm fine. Shouldn't you be in class?"

"The kids are at recess, and I got Sarah to watch them for me while I called you."

"I just got back, but I need some rest. I have to meet Claire at the hospital tonight when she gets in. Not sure how that's going to go."

"Surely she and her mother will put aside their differences considering."

"The Templeton's are a hard headed bunch."

"Yes, I know. Not unlike someone else I know. Do you want me to come home and fix you something to eat?" His wife had never called in sick a day in her life, and he was sure they would let her leave, but it wasn't necessary.

"How would it look if people found out that the Chief of Police couldn't fix himself a tuna on rye?"

"Still, you've had a rough night. The kids would understand," she said. The children in her class had become her surrogate children since she couldn't have any of her own. He loved that she had been able to surround herself with children and not become bitter or angry. Instead she became their teacher and helped shape their lives through education. Each year she got a whole new group of kids to mother, she loved that.

"I'll be fine. Good news is, I should be here, asleep, when you get home. Wake me. We can have supper together before I have to go."

"I have to tell you something. Promise you won't get mad," she said.

"What have you done now?"

"Raymond let me in the Templeton House after you left this morning."

"Why?" he asked, getting angry now, but more afraid for his wife.

"I couldn't let that poor girl come home to all that blood on the living room floor," she said.

That was Becky, always worried about someone else.

"You should never have entered that house," he scolded her.

"Raymond was with me. You know he wouldn't let anything happen to me."

"Still. I want you to stay away from that house."

"Don't tell me you believe all that rubbish about ghosts?"

"You know I don't believe in ghosts, but that house has a reputation. People disappear. Things happen there."

"Yet I am fine and so is Raymond."

He knew he could not win an argument with her.

"Okay, well I have to get a shower. I will see you when you get home. You want me to put that roast on to cook?"

"That'll be great. I'll see you then. Hugs and kisses," she said.

"Hugs and kisses."

When he hung up, he put the roast in the crock pot and made a quick sandwich. Then he took a long hot shower. Life on the Harbor was about to get crazy. Claire would be a handful all by herself. The struggle between her and her mother was common knowledge, but when the town folk realized Claire was back, things would get dicey. There was no sympathy for the down trodden. How much did Claire remembered about her childhood? He only wished Elizabeth had waited for the off season to attempt to take her life. He brushed that thought away, embarrassed that he had even thought of such a thing. At the same time, he knew he was right.

Later that night, after a quiet dinner with his wife, he stood in the stark hospital waiting room looking at Claire Templeton. She looked exhausted and distracted. Claire had not seen her mother or anyone else on the Harbor, for that matter, since she left. This was going to be hard for her. He hadn't expected her to show up at all. The fact that she stood in front of him now said something about her, and about the friends that had gotten her here. He approached her and took her hands in his. They were cold and trembling.

"Only one person can be in the room at a time per hospital policy. I tried to get them to make an exception, but they were firm about it." He spoke to Claire slowly. This had all been quite a shock to her and he wasn't sure she was hearing anything he said. She would needed her friends too, especially Grace, to get her through this, but this was one thing she was going to have to do on her own. He could feel her trembling hands and just about hear her knees knock. He had never seen anyone so shaken during his entire career as a police officer.

"You ready?" he asked.

She shook her head no and then slowly yes. Claire and Grace were still holding hands as the Chief led her toward the ICU ward doors. Grace let go of her friend reluctantly. Both girls stared at each other for a moment before Claire turned and faced the locked doors.

"We'll be right here when you get back," Grace called. The boys all assented in unison.

A buzzer sounded and Chief Harris led Claire through the double doors toward her mother's room.

CHAPTER SEVEN

Grace was sure Claire needed her, and she wanted to argue with Chief Harris about hospital policy, but she knew he was right. This was one thing Claire had to do on her own. It was painful to be separated from her best friend at a time like this. Grace physically ached for her as she watched Claire walk through the ICU doors. Claire could be tough, but never here in Butcher Harbor and never around her mother.

But the forced separation gave Grace the first opportunity to fill the boys in on the situation between Claire and her mother and bring them up to speed on what was in store for them over the next few days. It was hard to rehash the old memories. Even after all these years, the girls never spoke of Butcher Harbor.

"Claire grew up an only child. And she lived in the only house on the Peninsula," she told them. "Her house was supposedly built by pirates. Legend says they lured ships to shore and raided them. They used the wood from those ships to build the house. Later they used the house to lure in more ships during the worst storms. They stole the cargo and scuttled what was left of the ships that they couldn't use. It makes for great reef diving off our coast. Great for the tourist trade, but it wasn't so great for Claire growing up. People around here hate anyone that lives in that house, and they hate the name of their town. It was named after the brutality of those pirates."

Ethan squirmed in his seat. He didn't seem to like this story very much.

"According to town legend, every fifty years or so a mob gathers and tries to take the house down. The house always wins. Once, they even set fire to it. The house didn't burn down, but some of the people were burned badly when the fire got out of control. The town believes the house turned the fire back on the mob."

"How did it do that?" Ethan asked, scooting up to the edge of his chair.

"No one knows for sure. That house is pure evil. Growing up there made life a living hell for her. The other kids were forbidden to play with her. No one would share a seat with her on the bus to school. I was the only one brave enough to approach her. We moved here when she was six years old. I had always been a rebel at heart, and I took to her right away when I saw how the others treated her. She was a lost and lonely soul for a six year old. It broke my heart."

Quince smiled at her, obviously proud of her. He truly was a hopeless case.

"I tried to protect her from the other kids at school. But kids can be so cruel. At home, her mother and father got along well until her ninth birthday. That was when Claire started to see things."

Grace paused to let these words sink in. Her friends had never been told about Claire's haunted house or that Claire could see ghosts. She watched their faces for a reaction. When no one fled the room screaming she continued.

"At first, she just saw shadows in the corners of the room. Then the shadows became faces. Seeing them made her jumpy. Her dad asked her what was wrong. Up until she saw the ghosts herself, Claire had been able to ignore the ribbing she had gotten at school about her house. She thought that none of it was true and that the kids were just superstitious fools. Now she questioned everything that she knew about her home and weighed it against the rumors she had heard all her life. She told her dad what she was seeing, and he hit the roof."

"He got mad at her?" Vincent said.

"No, he was mad at Elizabeth. He started to argue with her mother. He wanted to get Claire out of the house right away. Elizabeth refused to leave. He loved his wife so much he stayed and tried to convince her to move into town, or at least take a vacation away from the house. Once he got her to leave the house, he planned to trick her by not bringing them back. Elizabeth found out about the plan and refused to leave the house for any reason. She and Henry barely spoke after that."

The boys stared at her in silence.

"He became so depressed; he even lost interest in Claire after a while. Scorned by her mom and now dejected by her dad, Claire fell into a deep depression. I was the only one she could share her frightening ghost stories with, or speak about the painful rejection by both her parents. When she was twelve, she awoke to a terrible scream from her parents' room. She rushed in to find her mother hugging her father and rocking him in her arms. He didn't move. 'You did this to him, you took him from me,' she screamed at Claire."

"Holy crap," Ethan said

"Claire repeated those words to me so often they seemed etched in her twelve year old brain. She was crushed. The official report stated that her father had died of natural causes. None of that mattered to Claire. Her mom accused her over and over again for so many years; Claire now believes that she did kill her dad. She believes she broke his heart, and he died from it." Grace took a deep breath. "The resentment from her mom never subsided; their relationship was severed forever. This started the countdown to our great escape. The only thing that kept Claire going throughout high school was our plans of leaving Butcher Harbor and Templeton House forever."

"That's when you guys came to New York?" Quince stated.

"Yeah, Claire stopped talking about the ghosts in her house, even to me. The only thing that mattered was getting out. She left Templeton House and her mother the day after our class graduation party. She never returned and never called or wrote to her mom. And now she is about to see her mother again for the first time in seven years."

The boys stared at Grace in disbelief. They had never heard her or Claire speak of Butcher Harbor, their families, or of any time before they arrived in New York. Like most New Yorkers, the boys never really paid much attention to life outside of the city. Grace knew that this information would rattle them and make the girls seem like strangers to them. They would have to get to know the girls all over again.

CHAPTER EIGHT

Every muscle in Claire's body trembled as she walked down the hospital corridor with Chief Harris at her side. She forced herself to take deep breaths Her body betrayed her; nothing seemed to work without constant attention. Mixed up thoughts crept into her mind: What if my mother dies? Will I be sad, or happy? Will I cry? How sad is it that I even have to ask myself these questions? Chief Harris slowed and pointed to the next hospital room on the right-Room 308.

"She's in there. Do you need a minute to pull yourself together?" he said.

"Yes, Thank you," she answered. She tried to pull in fresh air, but her chest felt tight and full. Her entire body trembled visibly. It felt as if she would fall over any second. Standing took all of the energy she had. The last time she saw her mother they had a terrible fight. Claire had been planning her great escape. She was sure her mother had no idea of her plans. Yet days before she was to leave, her packed bags were found unpacked. The empty bags were in the bottom of her closet. Her packed clothes were stacked neatly in her chest of drawers. Her jewelry was in the tiny chest on top of her dresser. Her favorite photo of her father was stuck back in the mirror- top right corner- where it had always hung. It was as if she had never packed at all.

Claire became furious. Her mother hadn't said a word to her when she entered the house. She acted as if it were just another ordinary day in Butcher Harbor. She obviously knew Claire planned to leave since she had unpacked all her bags, but she never said a word to her. Perhaps she thought that by unpacking Claire's bags it would be enough to make her stay. She couldn't have been more wrong.

Angry, Claire threw her clothes back into the bags, stuffing things all haphazard in her rush. She grabbed the photo of her father and tucked it carefully in the side pocket of the packed bag. The next day, when she returned home from school, the bags were unpacked again and everything was back in its place. Enraged, Claire repacked her bags to spite her mother. The next day her bags were gone completely. She searched her room, but there was no sign of them; no bags, no photo, no jewelry, even her clothes were missing.

20

Claire barged into her mother's room and headed for the closet. She threw open the doors and searched for her things. They weren't there either. She searched under the bed; there was nothing. She rummaged through her mother's drawers, still nothing. Her mother came up the stairs and found Claire rummaging through her stuff. She too became enraged.

"What on earth are you doing?" she screamed.

"Getting my things back mother," Claire stood her ground.

"What things? What are you babbling about?" her mother asked, putting her own things back into her drawers as quickly as Claire pulled them out.

"Don't act like you don't know. I want my bags back. I want my clothes, too. And Dad's picture," Claire demanded.

"I assure you I know nothing about this. Why would you have your bags packed?" her mother asked, acting confused.

"To leave, Mother. To leave here. Look, I am leaving, with or without my things. I am out of here. Do you hear me? No more shadow people. No more voices I don't understand. No more crack pot mother trying to keep me locked up in this loony bin of a house. No more people laughing at me everywhere I go."

Elizabeth turned pale. She looked shocked by Claire's outburst.

"Dad tried to leave. He tried to take all of us out of here. He's dead now. Is that what'll happen to me, too? Will I die in my sleep or perhaps mysteriously fall down the stairs on my way out the door?" Claire ranted as she headed for the stairs, terrified that her accusation might prove true.

"What a terrible thing to say, to suggest such a thing. You know I would never do anything to harm you, Claire," her mother cried. "Come back, you are not thinking clearly!"

Claire slipped out the front door and bounded off the porch steps. She turned back to face her mother, now standing on the porch watching her.

"I am thinking more clearly than I ever have. It is the events of my entire life that brought me here. You will never see or hear from me again," she had told her mother, "None of you will ever see me again, you hear me!" she screamed at the house and all its unwanted occupants huddled in every window. She grabbed her bicycle and was gone before her mother could say anything else.

Until graduation day, Claire hid out at Grace's house in the shed behind her home. Grace gave Claire some clothes and went with her to the thrift store in town to buy more. Claire and Grace both had small pay checks from the local boutiques for designing and selling summer wear. It wasn't much, but they didn't need much at the time. They had been saving for their great escape for years, so Claire made sure they didn't waste any more money than they had to on replacing her clothes. She would do without to get away. Nothing was going to stop her from leaving.

Julian Laws, Claire's boyfriend at the time, knew that Claire was hiding out at Grace's, so he sneaked over to see her during the long summer evenings. Graduation was only a few days away, and they would be leaving the Harbor together forever. Grace was furious that Julian was coming along with them, but she didn't fight Claire about it. Claire and Julian were as inseparable as Claire and Grace had always been. After the graduation party, Claire and Grace fled Butcher Harbor immediately. Julian, who had always been there for her, and promised to leave with her, never showed up. Claire told Grace they had to go to his house and steal him away from his mom. She must be keeping him from leaving. Grace dragged Claire onto the big bus kicking and screaming. In the end, Grace and the need to flee Templeton House won out. Claire boarded the bus without him. She never heard from him again. Her body and soul felt as battered as her mind as she boarded the bus for New York City.

Claire wasn't sure if her mother had even shown up for graduation. If she did, she never tried to see Claire. Grace and Julian had tried to distract Claire from looking for her Mom, but it didn't work. Angry as she was at her mother, Claire felt that at least she could have shown up for something that important, especially since Elizabeth knew she was leaving right after the party. But her mother never came. And Claire had never seen her again… until now.

CHAPTER NINE

Slowly Claire inched toward the hospital room. The smell of antiseptic burned her nostrils and turned her already upset stomach. She could not even fathom how to face her mother after this long of an absence. Her mouth was dry. Her tongue was thick and stuck to her teeth and the roof of her mouth as she tried to speak. Her body still betrayed her as her muscles trembled out of control. Part of her hoped she would pass out, but she knew she wouldn't be so lucky. She had to face her mother.

Will she be angry at me? Ignore my presence? Laugh at me? Blame me for her attempt to take her own life? There was no way telling how she was going to react. Chief Harris tugged gently on Claire's arm, pulling her into the hospital room. The first bed was empty. The second bed was hidden by a curtain that stopped just short of the end of the next bed. Claire crept further into the room. Chief Harris waited by the first bed, letting her greet her mother on her own. Claire felt small and frail.

She cleared the curtain and followed the bed sheet up to the withered hands of her mother. She dared not look into her face. The hands were old lady hands: thin, pale, and spotted. Tubes and tape were attached to them, the wrists wrapped almost to the elbow, arms strapped to the side of the bed. Claire took a deep breath and moved her eyes up the sheet to the face, familiar, yet not. Her mother's eyes were shut. She looked old, tired, and sad. It was hard to believe this was the same woman who had raised her. The same woman who had chosen a haunted house and ghosts over her own flesh and blood, those same ghosts that had somehow driven her mother to try to take her own life. Claire was sure they had something to do with this. Her mom was unconscious. The plastic clip clamped to her finger measured the oxygen content of her blood. Monitors kept track of her vital signs, sending stats to the nurses' station. The beeping of the monitors grated on Claire's last, frazzled, nerve.

"She's been like this since we found her," Chief Harris spoke from somewhere behind her, startling her from her thoughts. Claire felt like she was in a tunnel; everything seemed so far away, and nothing seemed clear or made sense to her.

"Will she wake up?" Claire asked, her tongue thick and dry. She needed a glass of water.

"We don't know yet," Harris said. "We just don't know." His words sounded too concerned and sad for an officer doing his legal duty. Perhaps it was just her, feeling so out of whack with the rest of the world right now.

"I don't know what to say. I'm not even sure how I feel right now. Does that sound crazy, Chief?"

"After the day you've had so far, I'd say it seems quite natural. Why don't you catch your breath?"

Okay, I have come. I have seen. Send me a post card. Drop me a line. A phone call would suffice. Let me know how all this turns out. Just let me out of here. Now please! She glanced at Chief Harris, hoping she had not spoken out loud. His tight smile did not offer her any comfort.

"I know how hard this is, Claire."

One step at a time Grace had said. Grace, who was waiting for her just a few hundred feet away in the waiting room- Grace, who would be there for her when she came out of this room.

"I'm sorry your friends couldn't be with you. Hospital policy," Harris seemed to be able to read her mind.

"Hmm," Claire thought that sound came from her lips, but she wasn't sure of anything anymore. She felt as if she were about to drop to the floor at any moment. The room seemed to move away from her. Her head felt light and ached. Breaths were not automatic anymore; she had to concentrate to breathe. She forced yet another breath in, a small, tight, barely helpful breath. Perhaps she needed a breathing machine of her own.

"I'm alright," she said out loud. I will get through this. But she wasn't sure how that was going to happen.

"I'm going to check with the nurses and see if the doctor is available to see you," Harris said and slipped out of the room.

Claire walked closer to her mother's bedside. There was a pitcher with water and a cup on the table beside the bed. Claire filled the tiny green cup and gulped it down. She was so parched; the water seemed to slip down her throat without hydrating her. The ice water made her brain freeze. Being so close to her mother bothered her. She glanced at her mothers' frail face. She looked so old. How could anyone be afraid of such a delicate creature?

Suddenly her mothers' eyes blinked open and stared at her. Her face twisted as she snarled at Claire.

"You did this to me," her mother said, her voice raspy as she spoke through the oxygen mask. She raised herself up from the pillow, lunging toward Claire. This set off all the monitor alarms as they screamed their warnings in Claire's ears.

Claire jumped back from the bed, dropping the cup and knocking the pitcher of water crashing to the floor. She was afraid her mother would reach for her despite the fact that her wrists were tied to the sides of the bed. Her mother fell back down on the pillow and went silent as Harris and the night nurse ran into the room.

"What did you do to her?" the nurse asked as she pushed past Claire and checked Elizabeth's various wires and tubes.

"I didn't do anything. She just..." What? Had that just happened? Claire wasn't sure if she should even tell them what had just happened. Just like everyone else on the Harbor, they would just think she was crazy.

"I think she should leave," the nurse told Harris as she checked Elizabeth's pupils with a pen light. The nurse turned off all the alarms and called for the doctor, all the while glaring angrily at Claire as if she had caused harm to her invalid mother. No, she won't believe me. Tears burned her eyes as she turned and fled the room. Chief Harris was hot on her heels.

CHAPTER TEN

"The rates are cheap and you can walk there from here," the nurse offered Grace and the boys a phone number to a local motel. "People from out of town use it whenever they have someone in the ICU."

"Thanks, we appreciate it," Grace said, checking the number on the slip of paper in her hand.

"Just dial nine to get out," the nurse instructed, pointing to the phone on the wall.

Grace walked over to the phone and dialed the number. It was tourist season already. Grace was certain the hotel would be booked through the fall, but she had to try. It beat the alternative.

"Butcher Harbor Motor Lodge, how may I help you?" A man's voice came over the line.

"My friends and I are visiting a sick relative at the hospital and wondered if you might have a room or two available for the night," she asked.

"Sorry but we are booked through the summer. All the motels in town are booked solid." Her heart sank as he confirmed her worst fears. Since she'd left the Harbor her parents had moved away. She had no family or relatives here, or nearby, anymore. Push come to shove, they were all going to have to do the unthinkable. They were going to have to stay at Templeton House.

"Thanks anyway," she told the man and hung up. She dialed a few more numbers in the phone book attached to the wall. Everyone had the same answer to her request. She wondered how in the world she was going to break this news to Claire. When Claire came out of the ICU she looked dazed. Grace called her name several times to get her attention without any luck. Harris led her by her elbow over to where they were seated.

"Is everything okay?" Grace asked Harris.

"Things did not go so well," he stated.

"Isn't her mother in a coma?" How could anything go wrong when the woman is unconscious?

"Yes, she is. But there was some sort of ...incident." Harris didn't offer any more information, and Claire just stared blankly at the floor.

"Well, I'm afraid I have even more bad news. All the motels in town are booked solid for the summer," Grace paused to let that thought sink in. Claire did not seem to get what she was saying.

"There isn't a room for at least a hundred miles," Chief Harris said.

"We will probably have to stay at the house," Grace said, waiting for Claire to have another meltdown over Templeton House. Claire didn't seem to hear what she said. She just stared at the polished floor, lost somewhere in her own mind.

"You want me to go out there with you?" Harris asked Grace.

"No. We'll be alright. You look like you could use some sleep yourself." She took Claire's arm and leading her out of the waiting room.

"She blames me," Claire said without looking up.

"No she doesn't. You'll see. She'll be glad to see you when she wakes up," Grace tried to calm her, but it was not working.

CHAPTER ELEVEN

The rental sedan pulled off Peninsula Road into the driveway of Templeton House. The setting sun provided a picturesque view for the boys, but for Grace and Claire, it did nothing to cheer them up. Claire sat in silence while the boys oohed and aahed over the house and the sea. Grace tensed and prepared for possibly the worst night of her life. She had never stayed at Templeton House overnight before, and she had heard enough stories to never want to set foot in there again. Claire only let her in once after she started to see the ghosts to see if Grace could see them too. When she didn't see anything out of the ordinary, Claire forbid her to enter the house again. Claire was afraid because Grace could not see the danger around her. Claire said she wasn't sure which way was worse: seeing or not being able to see the ghosts.

The driveway wrapped around to the back of the house. On the harbor all houses faced the sea, so the back porch was actually the front porch. Grace pulled around the small circle drive and parked. The boys got out still amazed at the view. Due to the remnants of the hurricane, the expanse of sky was made dramatic with the gray, black, and the most amazing blue Grace had seen since she left the harbor, mixed with a hint of pink.

"Wow, can you imagine growing up and looking at that every day?" Ethan said as he slid out of the back seat of the sedan. The wind, still strong after the storm, batted his blond curls into his eyes. He brushed them aside only to have them blown right back again.

"Yeah, a gay guy would think so," Quince said.

"Come on, tell me that is not gorgeous," Ethan insisted.

"I was just messing with you Ethan. Yeah, it's nice," Quince said, his own long hair blowing in his face as well.

Vincent stepped out of the car on the passenger side. He concentrated on stretching his legs and avoiding the conversation about gayness and sunsets. He knew Ethan was gay. It bothered him even though he never let on in front of his friends. He liked being part of the crew and did not want to get bounced out because he didn't agree with Ethan's sexual preferences. Besides, Ethan wasn't a flaming gay, so Vincent felt he could tolerate him. He knew if his father ever heard him say that a gay guy was tolerable, he would roll over in his grave.

"The sky didn't look like that every day. It's because of the hurricane that hit Florida. Hurricanes don't happen every day," Vincent said.

The girls still sat in the rental sedan. Grace looked out across the ocean acting like she was getting ready to get out. Claire stared at the floorboard frozen in place like a statue. Was she even breathing?

"Let's do this thing," Grace said to Claire.

"Okay," Claire answered, but did not move. Not knowing what else to do Grace popped the trunk of the car and got out.

Everyone pitched in grabbing their bags from the trunk. Grace grabbed her own bag and Claire's as well. When she looked up from the trunk she was pleased to see that Claire had dislodged herself from the front seat and was actually standing outside the car. Claire stared off across the ocean, still not turning to look at the house. Realizing that she too had not turned to look at the house, Grace forced herself to turn around and face their demon.

The house looked the same; grey shingled, two story house she knew as a teen. There were no neighbors. The isolation gave Grace the chills. The covered porch was massive with large wicker chairs still waiting for occupants to watch the beautiful sunsets. The hanging swing she and Claire always sat in moved gently in the wind. Claire had always said the porch was safe, like home plate in baseball. Apparently, the ghosts could not get out of the house. That was hard to believe, but she believed in her friend, and that was all that mattered. Claire slept on the porch at night and hid out there on nights when her mother thought she was upstairs in her room.

"Let's get this stuff inside," Grace hefted the bags and headed for the porch. Quince had his bags and was already at the door looking through the window.

"Hey babe, how are we supposed to get inside? The door is locked," Quince called to her.

"And it has one of those police thingy's," Ethan added, pointing to the Police caution tape across the door.

Grace reached up over the door jam, grabbed a key, and then used it to slit the police tape before unlocking the door. The boys stared at her in silence.

"What? Harris told me I could cut the tape to get into the house," Grace said as she pushed the door open, grabbed both bags, hesitated for a brief moment, and then stepped inside. She didn't know what to expect, but it all seemed so harmless, like it always felt when she was here: vacant, devoid of life, not a home at all. The house had always felt empty to her even when everyone was home. Grace never minded being exiled to the porch. Claire was right, the porch was safe; it felt like home. She wanted to go back outside, but she had to put up a good front for the boys. She didn't want them afraid of what they could not see and didn't want to poison how they felt with her own fears.

"Hey, watch it," Grace called as Vincent pushed in behind her.

"Where's the bathroom in this place? I've got to pee," Vincent stated, no apology offered.

"Upstairs," Grace motioned toward the stairway at the back of the living room. Everyone else had piled into the house and began looking around; everyone that is except for Claire.

"Doesn't seem so bad," Quince noted.

"To us," Grace took a deep breath, turning to look out the open door toward the sedan and Claire, who still stood looking out over the ocean. "It's different for her."

"Right," Quince stated in disbelief. "It all seems pretty normal to me, Gracie. The airs a little stale and it has that old lady smell to it, otherwise pretty normal. Are you sure there are ghosts here? Maybe she just has an over active imagination. I mean after all, she is always dressed like a gypsy and burning candles and stuff."

"They're here. Just be glad you don't have to deal with them. It's gonna be a long weekend. Please let's not fight about Claire right now," Grace pleaded as she pecked him on the cheek. Quince grabbed her and gave her a deep kiss on the mouth.

"That is how you kiss your guy," he told her, letting her go abruptly.

"Get a room," Ethan called from across the living room. He was looking at the photos on the table along the sloping stairwell wall behind the sofa. "There are no pictures of Claire growing up, just as a kid."

"They all stopped smiling by the time Claire had turned ten or so. They stopped taking pictures when they stopped smiling. There is one of her Dad before he died. Claire sneaked that shot when Henry wasn't looking," Grace explained.

"Morbid," Ethan stated, staring at the photo of a tired, beaten old man sitting on a rocky ledge, ocean waves splashing up at him. Ethan thought the man looked like he wanted to jump; but he kept that thought to himself.

"Here comes the hard part. Will you help me get her into the house?" Grace asked as she headed out onto the porch.

Vincent bounded down the stairs and headed outside to help her. Quince just stood watching Grace and Claire. Ethan was engrossed in the photos on the table.

"So much drama. You feel anything, Ethan?" Quince asked.

"Just cold. We should find the heater in this place," Ethan said even though it was the beginning of summer.

CHAPTER TWELVE

Claire stared out across the ocean not willing to turn and look at the house she had left so many years ago. She had closed her eyes as Grace drove down Peninsula Road. She didn't want to see it. She didn't want to be here at all. When Grace told her all the motels and hotels in the Harbor were booked, she wanted to go back home, to their safe, warm apartment. Grace refused to let her leave the Harbor in case her mother took a turn for the worse during the night. Claire had vowed she would never step foot in this house again, and yet here she was, thanks to of all people, her mother. Claire started to feel trapped again, like she always did in this house. It was like the house would not let her get away. She worried that the house might have done all of this just to lure her back. But for what purpose? What did they want from her? All those ghosts probably wanted her to take her aging mothers place. The thought sent chills down her spine.

"You ready?" Grace asked, taking her by the arm and turning her toward the house.

"No," Claire whispered, resisting the turn toward Templeton House, keeping her eyes on the sea shell covered driveway.

"We can't stand out here all day."

"Sure we can, we used to do it all the time."

"Yeah, but we were kids then and there wasn't a hurricane," Grace stated brushing the windswept hair out of Claire's face; the wind quickly blowing it back again. "Come on kiddo, we can do this together just like old times."

Claire turned all the way around, staring at the ground. She took a deep breath and then looked up at Templeton House for the first time in seven years. The house looked the same from the outside, bleak, lonely, weather beaten. Shutters were drooping or missing boards. Paint peeled off the shutters. Even still, the house looked formidable. It had stood the test of time, proof it still wasn't going down without a fight.

The inside of the house Claire knew would be different. Inside would be clean and polished. The floor would shine. Not a speck of dust would be found anywhere. Her mom would have kept up the inside of the house. Claire doubted if her mother had even left the house anymore. Food was always delivered by whichever new bag boy worked at Harbor Mart ever since her dad passed away. The boys at school used to tease the boy unlucky enough to have to work for the grocery because he had to deliver the weekly supplies to the house. She was always hated most by whoever that boy was at the time. It was worse on Raymond Dogg. Everyone already made fun of his name. When he worked for the grocery and had to deliver their packages, the ribbing got even worse.

Grace tugged on Claire's arm. Vincent took her other arm and they led her toward the house. Claire walked stiff legged; it was as if her legs were made of concrete. She knew she would be okay until she got through the door.

But the inside the house itself was a nightmare. Claire calculated that there must be at least a hundred or more spirits residing in her house. Do they know her mother is still alive? Would they pounce on her the moment she walked through the door? Would they recognize her after all these years? In a strange way, Claire wished her house was only haunted by one ghost. One ghost you could deal with, hundreds of ghosts were out of the question. Claire fought her thoughts as she lifted first one leg and then the other to climb the porch stairs.

Maybe I'm just crazy. The ghosts probably left when her mother was taken from the house. Maybe her mother tried to take her life because all the ghosts were already gone leaving her lonely without them. Maybe this was all a dream and she would wake up in her apartment and go to work as always. She longed to wake up and be safe in New York. They stopped short in front of the door. Claire braced herself against the door jamb refusing to go inside.

"It's okay, Claire, we're here to help you," Grace told her. "You see Ethan and Quince? They're fine. You will be fine too. Nothing would be crazy enough to hurt you while we're here with you. You know we won't let them hurt you."

Claire pleaded with Grace using her best puppy dog eyes.

"You are my best friend Grace. I beg you, please don't make me do this."

But she knew she had to go inside. The wind was too strong, even if the air was warm from the summer storm, to make the porch a safe place to seek shelter. She took another deep breath, lifted her right leg and stepped across the threshold.

Instantly voices cried out to her as ghosts assaulted her from all sides. Claire thought she herself had screamed, but she couldn't hear over the hundreds of angry and sad voices that came at her all at once. Bombarded from all sides she couldn't seem to catch her breath. She felt extreme pain and anguish choking her as the spirits crowded around her, taking up all the space and air she needed to breathe. Slowly the room seemed to fade.

CHAPTER THIRTEEN

Grace and Vincent grabbed Claire before she hit the floor. Everything had been fine until she had stepped across the threshold of the house. Before her foot hit the floor, Claire began screaming and did not stop until she passed out.

"I warned you," Grace told Quince, who finally came to assist them. "Take her upstairs please."

"Are you sure she will be alright up there?" Quince asked.

"We can only hope. That was the worst I've ever seen. Now that she's inside the house, hopefully she will be able to handle it. Just in case, we'll keep an eye on her. What other choice do we have?" Grace asked looking at the storm brewing outside. Vincent and Quince carried Claire upstairs. Ethan dropped down onto the sofa, a stunned look on his face.

"That was crazy. She's crazy," Ethan stared straight ahead, still shocked.

"Don't you ever say that again. You don't know what she saw or felt. Consider yourself lucky," Grace tried to get control of her outrage. Ethan was a friend and a part of their crew. She could not tolerate anyone inside their own circle bashing Claire right now. She needed them, all of them on her side. It would kill Claire if she had heard those cruel words coming out of Ethan's mouth.

"If that is how you feel, then stay down here," Grace said as she mounted the stairs.

"By myself...?" Ethan cried out, "Not on your life, sister."

"I thought you said she was crazy?" Grace raced up the stairs trying to leave Ethan behind, alone.

"Yeah, but I'm not stupid," Ethan bolted up the stairs behind her.

CHAPTER FOURTEEN

Claire came around and sat bolt upright in her mother's bed. The crew surrounded the bed staring at her. Her skin began to crawl when she saw the ghost of a German sailor standing behind them. Claire was sure no one else could see him. Even more disturbing was the spirit of a little boy, pushing his way past Grace to get closer to her. Claire closed her eyes for a moment and tried to figure out how to react. She did not want to scream or jump and scare the crap out of everyone else. She trembled with fear and could not breathe.

"She's cold," Grace said, reaching for a throw blanket at the foot of the bed.

Claire felt weak and wasn't sure how long she could put on a brave front. What had just happened? She was certain the others did not see the ghosts downstairs or hear their cries, they did not feel them crushing in against them. But she was sure they had heard her, and she was sure she had screamed. They did not seem to notice the ghosts around them now, either. Claire tried not to panic.

"You okay kiddo? You gave us quite a fright." Vincent said.

A hand brushed Claire's hair from her face. The boy ghost, she thought. She jumped. Her eyes opened wide just in time to see Vincent draw his hand away. She breathed a sigh of relief.

"Yes," repeated Ethan softly, "Quite a fright." Grace smacked Ethan in the arm.

"You're okay, honey, we're all here for you," Grace said, reaching through the ghost boy's stomach to hold Claire's trembling hand in her own.

Claire watched as the boy inched closer to her, unaffected by Graces arm reaching through him. She pulled back. Grace must have thought she was pulling away from her.

"It's okay, Claire. Relax," Grace told her. Claire trembled from head to toe. She forced a breath and tried to pretend that her best friend did not have her arm reaching through a dead boy who was staring up at her.

"I need to go get the boys settled in your room. Will you be alright until I get back?" Grace patted Claire's hand.

34

Claire was in a panic. She grabbed Grace's hand.

"Don't leave me!" she begged her friend.

"I'll only be gone a few minutes. Quince can stay here and keep you company. Nothing can happen with this big lug watching over you."

"Please," Claire hated to contradict her friend, but she doubted Quince would do much except run from the room screaming if he could see what she saw.

"Why don't you two go and make up the other room? We'll be along shortly," Grace told Vincent and Ethan.

"Coming to the house was a mistake, but we have nowhere else to go. Perhaps we should have hunkered down in the waiting room at the hospital. Anything would have been better than this."

"I feel so stupid," Claire said more to herself than to her friends.

"Don't." Grace stressed.

"These guys have never been through this with me. It was a mistake to come here."

"I know. But I can't see us all sleeping in the car, can you?"

"Yes, the car. That would be a much better idea," Claire smiled for the first time since entering the house. "Or all of you can stay in the house and I'll stay in the car."

"You can't spend the weekend in the car."

"You guys can't see the ghosts. They will leave you alone. Even my mother had never been harmed- until now. But can't you see, I am not safe here.

"No car. It's just two short days and we are out of here. Most of the time we'll probably be at the hospital anyway." Grace stated, patting Claire's hand.

For the first time, Claire allowed herself to look around the room. They had brought her to her mother's room. Why would they bring her in here of all places? Then she realized that the rest of them were probably just as scared of being in her mother's room as she was. Her own room down the hall would offer them some sort of comfort while they stayed in a strange and formidable house.

"Guess my mom is no Martha Stewart," Claire said as she noticed her mother had removed all the family photos and wall decorations and replaced them all with wooden or silver crosses. A rosary hung across the corner of the dresser mirror. A large wooden cross hung on the closet door and sure enough, Claire looked up to see a giant wooden cross hanging over the head of the bed.

"Yeah, she did a little redecorating," Grace tried to ignore the crosses and concentrate on Claire. "How are you feeling? You okay."

"Yeah, a little fuzzy I guess," Claire stated and tried to sit up.

"Slowly," Quince held her back. "You don't want to faint again."

"See anything else besides crosses everywhere?" Grace in-quired carefully.

The shadow figures that bombarded her downstairs were gone, but besides the sailor and the little boy there were a few on lookers hiding in the dark corners of the room watching, waiting.

"No, nothing," Claire lied. She could not tell her dearest friend that they were being watched by not one, but five ghosts. A haggard old woman, whom Claire hated the most, was standing near the closet, glaring at them, she always had a knife in her hand. There were two other shadows she did not recognize, barely formed figures hiding in the shadows the room afforded them.

"Well, that's a good thing, isn't it," Grace said. Claire's bangle bracelets jingled as Grace let go of her hand. The sudden unexpected noise made Claire jump almost clean out of her skin, but she forced herself to remain in control.

"Yeah, good thing."

CHAPTER FIFTEEN

Ethan looked wildly at Vincent who just shrugged his shoulders and walked out. Ethan followed slowly behind him, not eager to leave the safety he felt being near the others. At least if Claire could see the ghosts, he would know where they were, if they were there at all. The idea of ghosts all around him in every room that he couldn't see scared the crap out of him. For all he knew he could be standing inside of one right now. The idea gave him chills. He rubbed his arms for warmth.

Vincent was halfway down the stairs before Ethan realized he was unable to move . Fear of being alone in the house overpowered his fear of moving, so he dashed down the steps to catch up with Vincent.

"What in bloody hell was that? Did you see her face when she screamed?" Ethan inquired.

"No, I was a little busy catching her, remember?"

"Yeah, well, you should've seen her face. It twisted. It was really messed up." Ethan hit the bottom of the stairs one step behind Vincent.

"What do you mean twisted? Like contorted?" Vincent asked.

"Yeah, that's the word I was looking for: contorted. It was really creepy," Ethan grabbed two bags of luggage and followed Vincent back up the stairs. "What do you think it was?" he asked, banging the luggage against the wall and the stair rail as he climbed the steps.

"I'm sure I don't want to know."

"Do you think she saw anything? Really?" Ethan inquired softly, taking a quick look around the living room below him.

"Are you saying she was faking it?" Vincent asked, astonished by the suggestion.

"Well, no. I... Heck, I don't know. You ever seen her act like that before?"

"Never, but I also have never seen her here, or ever heard her talk about here. Like Grace said, if Claire saw something, we should all be thankful that we didn't. I mean, she is used to seeing it and look what happened to her," Vincent hit the top step and headed for Claire's mother's room.

Ethan followed closer behind than before, glancing every-where as he followed. He wanted his sweater out of his bag and wondered if anyone was going to find the heater in this damn place. He wasn't about to mention it in case they elected him to do the job. The idea of wandering around this old house alone did not appeal to him. Vincent stopped at the mother's bedroom door and Ethan ran into him.

"Uh, where do you want this stuff?" Vincent asked, shoving Ethan off of him.

"Leave Claire's stuff here. Oh and mine, too. You guys can stay in Claire's room across the hall," Grace offered. She did not even glance at Quince when she gave room assignments. The boys were sure they had seen Quince's face turn a slight shade of green.

CHAPTER SIXTEEN

"Why am I here? Why do I even try?" Quince said out loud as he, Vincent and Ethan headed off for Claire's old bedroom. "I'm never going to separate these two no matter what I do. It's a lost cause."

While he felt better venting to the boys, he couldn't give up hope that Grace and he could be together, with Claire on the outside of their lives, like normal people. He held onto that hope while he festered over being shunned off with the boys, as if he had no relevance in her life at all.

"So, do we sleep head to toe or what?" Vincent asked as he opened the door and saw the double bed in Claire's room and wishing it was a king.

"I call the middle," Ethan shouted as he bounced onto the bed.

"The middle?" Vincent shook his head, "No one ever wants to be in the middle of a pile of men. Not even if no one else knows about it."

"Ethan would." Quince winked at Ethan.

"You can make fun of me all you want. At least the ghosts will get you two first," Ethan said.

"Two days." Vincent muttered under his breath.

"Just two days! Did you guys see that fridge? There's no food and crap its cold in here," Ethan added. He jumped up and rummaged through his luggage for his sweater.

"It was a mistake coming here," Quince said.

"You're just mad because your squeeze is gonna be sleeping with her squeeze all weekend instead of with you." Vincent teased.

Quince threw a pillow at Vincent, hitting him in the head.

"Sore loser," Vincent said. He tossed the pillow back at Quince.

"What do you suppose she saw down there?" Ethan asked.

"Don't know. Whatever it was I still have goose bumps on top of my goose bumps from it," Vincent said. He seemed unhappy to be back on the subject again.

"Do you think they might be up here? I mean, with us, right now?" Ethan asked as he sat down on the bed, rubbing his arms to warm himself in his sweater. All three took a cautious look around. Then gave each other a silent look, not wanting to discount any ghosts that might be there even if they were unseen by them.

"And what about Claire? Did you see anything down there?" Quince asked, still angry at being tossed aside by Grace.

"I didn't see anything," Vincent said.

"I didn't see anything either, but I did see Claire. Man she wigged out."

"Give it a rest Ethan," Vincent said and then gave Ethan a quick warning glance.

"I'm just saying. Nobody saw anything, and yet she squealed like she was attacked by the hounds of hell. And now she's all quiet and calm upstairs. Maybe it was an act, you know, for us, to maybe feel sorry for her or something," Ethan said.

"Maybe," Vincent added," Claire always leans on Grace, and us too sometimes, but she has never sought out attention like this. If anything, she hides from things and people. We have to trust that this is the same Claire we know and love. She may be seeing things that only she can see. That would suck. Who would trust you if they couldn't see it, too? Grace trusts her. That should be all we need to know."

"Doesn't it bother you that if she is right then there are hundreds of ghosts trapped in this house and they are all around us?" Ethan asked.

"Yes. Yes it does. We can dwell on that or try to ignore what we don't see as long as we go unharmed. Someone gets hurt and its ass kicking time."

"Amen." Quince added. He watched his friends unsure what either of them thought they would do if they were able to see the alleged ghosts. He for one did not believe in them, but it didn't stop him from being on his guard. That said, he still had no idea what he would do if things heated up. How does one fought ghosts anyway? They could do cool things like walk through walls and appear out of nowhere.

"I say we get through the night and head straight to the hospital at first light. Then we stay there until they throw us out. There is heat and food there, even if the food comes from a vending machine. I for one can live off of stale cake and soda pop."

"I second that," Quince said.

"Yeah, as much as I hate hospitals, I have to agree with you, Ethan," Vincent added.

None of them seemed to be aware of the darkening shadows in the room as faces started to appear out of the walls. The ghosts came to watch these strangers who had moved into their house.

CHAPTER SEVENTEEN

Hunger overrode their fear of the house. The boys searched the kitchen for food. Vincent looked under the cabinets for pots and pans. Quince searched the pantry bringing out two cans of green beans and carrots. Ethan stuck his head in the refrigerator looking for anything good to eat. The old woman didn't have a lot of leftovers.

"You'd think there would be cakes and cookies," Ethan said, putting a piece of cooked chicken and a slab of mystery meat on the table.

"Why? Just because she was an old lady you think she baked a lot?" Vincent asked, pulling out a huge pot and a frying pan.

"Well, yeah," Ethan said.

"There was no one here to bake for," Quince chimed in, setting the canned vegetables on the table. Vincent stared at the slim pickings on the table. There were five of them. They would have to improvise.

"Ethan, check the freezer for something for tomorrow. Quince, was there any rice or noodles in the pantry?" Vincent asked.

"Rice and spaghetti," Quince answered heading for the pan-try again.

"Grab the rice. We can make soup out of all this," Vincent said as he washed his hands and started to pull the chicken off the bones.

"Is it cold in here or is it just me?" Ethan asked, rubbing his arms for warmth. He was glad to have his sweater on, but it seemed to do little to keep him warm.

"Yeah, come to think of it, for summer, it is awfully cold in here," Quince said.

"You know you're right. It's colder than it was when we first came in," Vincent noted.

The boys never saw the old woman with the knife as she entered the kitchen heading toward them with her knife drawn.

CHAPTER EIGHTEEN

"I have to get out of here," Claire told Grace when the boys left the room.

"I know being here is not the best option, but it will have to do for now."

"No, you don't understand. I need to get out of here. Now."

Grace stared at Claire for a minute. Claire could be so stub-born sometimes.

"Why?" she asked hoping to get a clue as to how to calm her down.

"You know why. This place is infested with ghosts. I thought I could do this, but I can't."

"Can you at least give it a chance? It's just for two days. Surely with our help you can hang in there for that long."

"There is a little boy ghost sitting on the bed with us. Your arm is reaching through his belly right now."

Grace pulled her arm away and wiped it off as if she could wipe the ghost away. "You're kidding, right?"

"Not kidding. Did you even feel him at all?"

"No."

"Really? That's just crazy."

"Okay," Grace said standing up abruptly. "Now I have to get out of here, too."

"Front porch," they both said in unison as they jumped up and ran for the stairs.

As Claire started down the stairs a ghost stepped in front of her, blocking her path. She stopped suddenly and stepped aside. The ghost moved with her. She took a deep breath and held onto the stair rail.

"You first," she told Grace.

Grace looked down the stairs and then back at Claire, unsure if she might be walking through another ghost.

"No way. You can see them. You go first."

"Go, now!"

They both dashed down the stairs. Grace oblivious to the ghosts she was running through. Claire held her breath as if that would help. She felt

42

the ghost's crowd around her. They knew. They knew she was fleeing the house. They were going to try and stop her. Panic took over as she almost ran Grace over at the bottom of the steps.

"Slow down."

"Can't. Gotta go," Claire said as she pushed passed Grace. Now she was completely surrounded by ghosts. They crowded in closer to her. They reached out to stop her. She felt their cold hands pull at her arms. She had never felt the ghosts before. She could see them and she could hear them, although she never understood what they said, but she had never felt them touch her before. She cringed as she lunged for the door handle. The feel of their cold hands on her skin sent chills to her very soul. Does this mean they could actually stop me from leaving? This idea scared her even more. She pulled at the door, but it wouldn't open. There were too many ghosts in the way. How was that even possible? They had no substance. She jerked at the door several times, but it didn't budge.

"Move," Grace pushed Claire out of the way and pulled the door open. Claire tried to run out the door but the ghosts blocked her path. Grace seemed to be in a panic herself. She shoved Claire out the door. That worked. Once Claire passed the threshold of the door the ghost were unable to stop her. They cried out to her but she ignored them. Grace slammed the door as if she too could hear the ghosts crying out.

"What the hell was that all about?" Grace asked, taking a seat beside Claire on the porch swing, wiping her arms in case she might have ghost residue on her skin.

"I could feel their cold dead hands on me."

"That's new."

"Yes, it is." Claire rocked the swing trying to remove the memory of all those hands from her mind and her body.

"Wow, what do we do now?" Grace asked.

"I'm not sure.

CHAPTER NINETEEN

Claire and Grace sat on the porch swing in silence. Neither knew what to say at this point. Everyone had moved into their respective rooms for now. To Ethan's delight, the boys decided to put something together from the kitchen for them all to eat. Claire refused to go inside the house to help them cook. Grace wasn't too keen on going inside herself right now. She stayed on the porch with Claire.

Claire stared out toward the ocean. She loved the sea and wished she could love this old house as well. Her family owned the number one prime beach property on the harbor. Too bad no one wanted it. She missed the beach. The rhythm of the waves crashing to the shore used to lull her to sleep at night. The sea mist and sand that most people found annoying about the beach was the part Claire liked the most. She loved burying her feet in the sand up to her ankles while the sea mist sprayed her face. But the one thing she never missed was this house. She kept her eyes toward the beach to keep from looking at it.

Ghosts peeked out of every available window, standing in layered rows, vying for the best view of Claire and Grace. The small boy peeked out the window next to them. The sailor was there, too, and many, many others. They waited and they watched. Claire worried about the boys alone in the house, but she felt sure all ghosts were present and accounted for. It was her they wanted.

"They all speak at once. They are all eager to be heard. I can't separate them like my mother can. Mom would talk to them all the time. I don't want to be like mom. I don't want to hear. Maybe that is why I don't listen so well to people. I have learned to block things out."

Claire staring out toward the ocean. There was movement in the sea grass, she was sure of it. She hugged herself tighter. What if one of the ghosts had escaped the house? They had never been able to do this before. She remembered the feel of their cold hands on her skin. She figured she could no longer think in those terms. She searched the sea grass and sand hills for a clue to whether the movement was human or ghost. Someone was out there, that she was certain. But who would be lurking in the sea grass this late at night before after a storm?

She felt silly for asking such a stupid question. What better time to walk the peninsula than on a night like this, the warm wind blowing her hair and her clothes, the moon peeking out behind the clouds. Being on the beach was powerful on nights like this.

"I'm sure Quince won't be happy about our temporary living arrangements. I'm sure he thought he and I would be staying together for once," Grace rambled on.

There it was again. The grass moved. Someone was walking around out there. She was sure of it. She wished Grace wasn't there so she could dart out into the grass and investigate. Grace would think it silly to go off in the dark chasing shadows. But Claire didn't fear anything outside of the house. She only feared the house itself and its occupants, the non-living kind. Real people on a beach she could handle. She watched the grass as Grace rambled on about Quince.

"So then he stabbed me and killed me," Grace sighed.

"Ah," Claire offered as she saw a head pop out above the sea grass and Claire identified it as human. She thought she even noticed the gait of this particular human. A stirring in her stomach drew her toward the person in the sea grass. She thought she knew who it was.

"I realize you have a lot on your plate right now, but you could at least listen once in a while," Grace snapped.

"What?" Claire pulled her attention back to her angry friend.

"Do you ever listen to what I say?" Grace asked.

"I listen to everything you tell me..." Claire let her attention drift back to the sea grass.

"That's it. What the hell?" Grace stood up to leave.

"Where're you going?" Claire asked.

"Surprised you noticed I was leaving," Grace said. "I'm going to check on the boys. I don't know about you, but I'm starving." Claire was surprised that Grace would want to go back inside the house, but then she remembered that Grace didn't see or feel anything. It made it easier to forgive and to forget.

"Okay," Claire continued to watch the sea grass. Once she heard the screen door shut she vaulted off the porch and out onto the beach. At first, she moved quietly wanting to surprise him. Then she tired of searching for him and called out into the dark night.

"Julian! Is that you? Julian?" Mists of sea salt sprayed her face lightly. She licked her lips. The smell of the sea and the taste of the salt brought back old memories of sneaking out to meet Julian on the beach at night.

"Julian, it's me, Claire. Julian!" she called again and again. The movement was gone. She had taken too long. He was gone now. "Damn it Grace!"

Claire sat down in the sand, the warm wind whipping through her hair.

She was upset at herself for being so angry with her best friend. She was upset over her mother injuring herself and blaming her for it, and even more for having to come back to this God forsaken house. And now she had missed Julian as well.

Memories of her and Julian sitting here in the sand, talking for hours, flooded her mind. She could see his face; feel the weight of his hand on hers. She could even smell him. If he was here tonight then he knew she was back. Why didn't he come up to the house. The old Julian would have met her at the hospital. But this new Julian, the one who hadn't answered all the letters she had written to him over the years, he hadn't come.

"Julian, damn it, Julian!" she called into the wind. She needed to feel the security and comfort of his arms. She wanted him to hold her tight and tell her everything would be alright and that he would be here for her, just like the old times. Claire wept into her hands screaming his name between her tears. She had never felt so alone.

CHAPTER TWENTY

Grace entered the kitchen to find the boys huddled around a huge crab pot cooking on the stove. Crabs? There was no way Mother Templeton had fresh crabs in the house, she never went outside.

"So what's for dinner?" she asked.

"Soup," Vincent said. His grin went from ear to ear. The look on Grace's face took his grin away.

"What, you don't like soup? Who doesn't like soup?"

The boys all laughed. Grace shook her head. She didn't have the heart to tell him he was cooking soup in a crab pot. To him it was just a really big pot.

"I love soup," she reassured him.

"Good, because that's all we have," Vincent said.

"Okay then. How long?" she inquired.

"About ten minutes, maybe," Vincent called as he turned back to the pot. Ethan was rummaging through the cabinets.

"What on earth are you looking for?" she asked.

"Bowls," Ethan told her, "Big bowls. I'm starving."

Grace walked over to the cabinet Ethan had not come to yet and withdrew five large soup bowls. Then she walked to the drawer by the sink and pulled out five large soup spoons.

"That's what I'm talking about!" Ethan cheered. "Now if somebody could find that damned heater." He rubbed his arms briskly.

Quince walked up behind Grace and wrapped his arms around her waist. Grace snuggled into them, happy to have someone who gave back instead of sucking the life out of her like Claire did sometimes. Grace had never felt that way before, but all of a sudden the feeling overwhelmed her. Let Claire sit on her stupid porch. Grace preferred to be inside with the boys. She snuggled deeper into the warmth of Quince's arms. He buried his nose into her hair, smelling her. She suddenly felt that everything was right with the world. To heck with going back to the city, perhaps she and Quince could talk Claire into letting them stay here.

47

CHAPTER TWENTY ONE

Taking his usual coffee break on the peninsula, Deputy Raymond Dogg pulled his police cruiser into the turn out and put it into park. He reached across for his lunch sack and poured himself a steaming hot cup of coffee. Another hurricane off the Florida coast still threatened to come north. While the rain had stopped for now the wind buffeted the cruiser occasionally. The sky was still filled with clouds. It was a beautiful sight. This was something he felt he would never tire of seeing.

Many of his high school friends left the Harbor in search of better things. For Raymond Dogg, this was his better thing. He loved the Harbor and beach life. This place called to his soul. He looked across the choppy waves as he sipped his thermos cup of coffee. He breathed in deeply, enjoying the coffee and cinnamon scent. It soothed him.

As he glanced down the beach toward the Templeton House, he saw movement in the sea grass behind the house. He shifted for a better view. The Chief had told him that Claire Templeton had come home today and would be staying at the house. He could see lights on in the kitchen and upstairs bedrooms. The movement in the grass made him worry that some of the restless summer visitors might have come out to spy on Claire, or maybe even scare her.

"Harbor Two to base," He called it in.

"Base. Go ahead, Dogg," Deputy Mac Charleston answered. "Mac, there is movement behind the Templeton House. I'm going to check it out. Might be someone playing a prank on Ms. Templeton."

"Yeah, and it might be some hot chick bathing nude on the beach," Mac responded.

"Don't you ever get your head out of the gutter?"

"Never if I can help it," young Mac responded.

"No girl in her right mind would be out tonight even in a swim suit," Dogg called back.

"Unless she was a swimsuit model shooting pics for a magazine," Mac sounded hopeful.

"Well I'll go check it out and let you know," Dogg shook his head. Mac was a hopeless case; lifeguard turned police officer just like himself, but

Mac was never going to change.

Dogg got out of the SUV, removed his pistol from its holster and crept out onto the peninsula. He planned to walk down to the house via the beach and come up behind whoever was wandering around out there. It would be dark any minute now, and he would have good cover to hide in. Beach sand filled his police issue black patents and he wished he had the sense to leave them in the cruiser. The discomfort of the sand in his shoes distracted him. He tried to focus on the movement on the beach.

When he came up behind the house he could hear whimpering. Someone was hurt. He searched all around, with his eyes and his ears. He listened for the direction of the sound. He found the whimpering ahead of him and to the left. He stealthily moved toward the crying sound. As he cleared a bunch of sea grass he saw a woman dressed in gypsy garb, sitting in the sand. She was sobbing. She appeared to be uninjured. He looked around to see if someone might have assaulted her. There was no one else around.

"Excuse me, Ma'am, are you alright?" he asked pointing his pistol toward the ground beside him.

The woman looked up immediately. Dogg was sure she would realize he was a police officer, but he identified himself anyway.

"Police Officer Raymond Dogg, Ma'am. Do you need assistance?"

"Dogg? Ray? Is that you?" the woman said as she brushed her hand across her face to wipe away her tears. Raymond struggled to recognize the woman through her windblown hair. She looked amazing even in this wind. Before his mind could register who she was, she spoke.

"It's me. Claire. Of the House Templeton..." she waved her hand back behind her.

"Claire? I...sorry to bother you. I saw movement down here and I was afraid some locals had come out to welcome you home, if you know what I mean," he faltered.

"Yeah, I know exactly what you mean. I saw someone, too. That's why I came out here. But I guess whoever it was, is gone now," Claire sniffed, wiping the tears from her face. He pretended not to notice.

"Sorry about your mother. I was the one..." Dogg started to say when he realized he had forgotten his police training. He was saying too much and not listening enough.

"Yes, Ray?" she looked up, waiting for him to finish his sentence.

"I was wondering how you were taking it. I know your relationship with your mother has been strained," he covered. He didn't know if she knew how her mother was found, or that he was the one that discovered her mother last night.

"Yeah, I'll be alright, but it's hard. I can't figure out how I'm supposed to feel. I hate being back at this house. Not sure how long I have to stay, or even if I can," Claire added.

Dogg noticed she was shivering in the warm wind. He wondered if she was cold or if it was from the shock of everything. He thought he should get her back to the house to warm her up, but he was in no hurry to go back in there again. Glancing back at the house he noticed the living room lights were on and he thought he saw movement in the house as well.

"My friends came with me. Grace and three colleagues," Claire explained. He felt better knowing that she had people with her.

"We tried to get a motel, but everything within a hundred miles is booked up," Claire started to get up. Raymond took off his jacket, offered it to her and took a seat beside her in the sand instead. Perhaps she will want to talk a little, away from her friends. It was windy, but he didn't mind.

"Grace, no kidding," Dogg said. He pulled a hanky from his pocket and handed it to her. She wiped the tears from her face.

"She and I left the Harbor together. Took a flat in New York," she said, grabbing her brightly colored skirt up in one hand to prevent it from blowing about, "We design stuff like this for the rich folks in Manhattan."

"No kidding," Dogg wondered why this was the only thing coming out of his mouth. He seemed unable to speak around her, just like in his high school days. He fancied Claire, but Claire was Julian's girl. She never had eyes for anyone else.

"All that way just to be back here," she said.

"I believe in everything for a reason," Dogg answered realizing she might misunderstand his meaning and think he wished ill on her mother. "I meant maybe your Mom will recover quickly, and you two can work things out."

"That would be nice," Claire smiled and snuggled into his jacket, pulling it tight around her neck. "Police Officer? I would have thought you would have made deputy by now."

"I did. It just doesn't help you control an unknown situation when you cry out 'Deputy Dogg'," he blushed.

"I could see how that could be a problem," Claire smiled again, her eyes still filled with tears. He wanted to wrap his arms around her and protect her. She always had that quality about her. She always seemed frail and in need of strong arms. That must have been why she had chosen Julian. He was a jock, tall with big strong arms. When she was with Julian, away from this house, she smiled. Raymond loved that smile. It could carry him away.

"You okay?" she asked.

"Me? Oh, yeah. Um, I just have shoes full of sand. Do you mind?" He asked as he grabbed his right shoe.

"No, go ahead. That must have sucked walking over here in those," Claire said.

"Yes, yes it did," he dumped sand from both his shoes. He tied them together by their laces and tossed them on the sand next to him. "I think I will go back in my bare feet. It will be easier." His socks were full of sand too, so he took them off and turned them inside out, shaking a mountain of sand out of them.

Claire smiled again. He could see the pain behind her eyes, but he also saw a light in them. And for once it was for him. His heart leapt, and he took a deep breath to get himself under control. It was just a smile, nothing more. Yet it warmed his insides and made his stomach cramp all at the same time.

A banging sound came from the house followed by voices.

"Dinner is served, Claire. Dinner..." everyone in the house seemed to be on the porch shouting at once.

"I'd better go," she said. Raymond rose and offered her a hand up. She was light, like air. He tried to concentrate. The wind changed direction, and he caught a whiff of her sweet perfume.

"Let me walk you back to the house," he offered, and immediately regretted it. He wasn't sure he could stand much longer, let alone walk. She was like a siren, she captivated all his senses. He had never been this close to her before. He had no idea how difficult it would be to actually be near her.

"Good, then you can meet everyone," Claire smiled up at him as they walked back toward the house.

Meet everyone. He hoped his delight at being with Claire did not show on his face. He was sure the others would see in his eyes what she couldn't. To her he was just Raymond Dogg from high school. He wondered if she was dating or married to one of the men that had come from the city with her. As they approached the house and he saw the three young men standing on the porch, he was sure one of them must be with her. He thought it might be the tall one until Grace wrapped her arms around that one and kissed him on the cheek. Dogg swallowed hard. He needed to be a professional in front of these people, but when it came to Claire, he wasn't sure he could pull it off.

CHAPTER TWENTY TWO

"Well if it isn't the Dogg!" Grace said, as she stepped down the porch stairs to greet the police officer escorting Claire back from the beach. "What trouble has she gotten into now, Officer?"

"No trouble at all," he seemed to blush. "I just saw some movement on the beach and came to check it out."

"It's Deputy now," Claire said, blushing.

"Deputy Dogg?" Quince asked, surprised.

"Yeah," Dogg blushed too.

"Sorry to hear that, dude," Quince said as he shook his head.

Grace hugged Raymond and she felt him stiffen in her arms. She was always the friendly type and he was always a little standoffish. Grace thought she might have been too forward for him. She let go and stepped back.

Claire was wrapped up in Raymond's police jacket. She was trembling, but smiling. That was something Grace hadn't seen for a while; a real smile on Claire's face. She always was good with the men, wasn't she. Claire got Julian on the first try. Everyone else wanting to date her, but they were terrified of her house, so instead they made fun of her, but not Julian. He never cared how the others felt about Templeton House or its occupants. He was gaga over Claire. He even fought his own mother every day over his relationship with her, but he would not let her go no matter what. Grace was surprised that this had never bothered her before. Today it really pissed her off. She tried to shake it off. Claire was her best friend. She loved her.

"Well, Claire," Grace said, "Give the nice officer back his jacket so he can get back to work."

Raymond helped Claire out of his jacket. He removed his shoes from his shoulder, and put the jacket on. Then he grabbed his shoes again, his socks still stuffed tightly inside and swung them back over his shoulder.

"Sand," Raymond said and blushed again.

"Say no more," Grace replied, understanding the beach sand and shoes issue.

Grace watched as Raymond said good-bye to Claire. He seemed at a loss for words and stumbled all over himself for a simple good night. And he blushed, a lot. The sad part Grace though was that Claire was oblivious to him. Sure she smiled and was polite, but you could tell she just didn't get it. Grace's temper raised another notch.

Raymond walked off down the beach back toward the cul-de-sac where he must have left his cruiser. Claire stood watching him, Grace was sure it was only to avoid coming in the house.

"The food is done. Can you come inside?" Grace asked impolitely.

"I'll try," Claire whispered.

"Good, let's eat then, we are all starving," Grace said hoping Claire caught on that she was delaying everyone's meal. This whole new attitude toward Claire was beyond what Grace could understand. She was always so patient with her. Nothing about Claire ever bothered her before. What is up with me today? She shrugged it off to lack of sleep and stress, but she now that she felt this way if things would ever go back to the way they were again.

CHAPTER TWENTY THREE

Everyone sat in the dining room off the kitchen. The soup pot dominated the center of the table along with a half- loaf of bread. The boys dug in quickly ignoring the two girls. Claire seemed to be shut down, as if ignoring the entire house and her group of friends. Grace sat back in her chair staring at Claire, her nostrils flaring from time to time. Quince found all of this amusing. Maybe he would get Grace away from Claire after all. There seemed to be a growing tension between them he had never seen before.

The house was interesting to him as well. He had been told it was supposedly built by pirates. That added a level of charm to the house. Not everyone got to spend the night in a pirate's hideout. At least not everyone he knew. He could feel a coldness about the house, but still it did not feel eerie. He didn't feel any type of presence around him at all.

Claire, on the other hand, supposedly could. Quince watched her as she slowly scooped soup into her bowl. On any other day, Grace would have made sure that Claire got the first bowl. Heck, Grace would have scooped it herself. Heaven forbid that dear Claire help herself. She fumbled with the ladle. Quince wondered if it was because of the newness of helping herself for a change or her fears that made her awkward at a normal task like scooping soup into a bowl.

"I don't get it?" Ethan said through a mouthful of bread.

"Don't get what?" Quince answered.

"All this ghost stuff," Ethan said shoveling another spoon of hot soup into his mouth.

"What do you mean," Claire asked. Something finally brought her out of her trance-like state.

"I haven't seen or heard anything unusual since we got here," Ethan grabbed another piece of bread and spread butter onto it.

"You mean you can't see the sailor standing in the corner behind you? Or how about the small boy who sits next to me on the floor watching my every move? Or maybe that pirate standing right behind you waiting to slit your bloody throat..." Claire yelled.

"Claire! That's enough." Grace snapped at her friend, Quince was certain, for the very first time in their lives.

"Enough what? Enough talk? Enough anger at people who can't see so they assume there is nothing there? Enough of this house and everything in it? This is my life every day here. It never stops for me!" Claire snapped back as she rose to her feet and slammed her spoon down on the table. "I am sick and tired of people thinking I'm crazy; especially when they are supposed to be my friends!"

Claire fled the room. Unseen by the others, the little boy ghost ran out of the room chasing after her. Quince heard some muttering from the living room. He thought he heard her say 'get out of my way' but he hoped that wasn't true. Then he heard the screen door slam. Claire was back on her porch. He wondered if she would spend the entire weekend out there. It was windy and could rain again at any moment. Part of him worried about her being out in the weather. Another part of him was glad because maybe then he and Grace could hook up, even if it was for just one night, alone without Claire in the way.

"I was just saying," Ethan pouted.

"Oh shut up, Ethan," Grace snapped. Scratch any idea of having a fun evening alone with her. She's in a rare mood.

"Anyone see a pirate standing over my shoulder?" Ethan asked, afraid to turn around.

"No!" the others yelled in unison. The pirate ghost behind Ethan grinned.

"What if we had a séance?" Vincent piped in.

"Séance?" Quince almost choking on his soup.

"Yeah, you know, have someone from outside of the house come in and talk to the spirits. Then we would know if they were here or not," Vincent stated.

"A psychic would say there were ghosts here whether there actually are or not. It's a scam to make money," Quince said, breaking his bread in half and dunking it into his soup.

"Not all psychics are scam artists," Grace snapped at him. "There is a psychic in town we all used to go see as kids. She predicted Claire and I would leave and become famous designers someday."

"Sure she did," Quince snapped back.

"What is that supposed to mean?" Grace glared at him.

"Anyone who lived here could have predicted that the two of you would leave. And oh, big surprise, that the you would try to become fashion designers since you made clothes for the tourist trade every summer. It's a scam. I could have predicted that, and I didn't even live here," Quince stood his ground. He wasn't going to let her foul mood rule his thoughts and feelings. If he was sleeping alone, he sure as hell was going to speak his mind.

"True," Ethan slurped more soup off his spoon.

"This psychic, do you think she's still in town?" Vincent asked, not giving up his idea.

"I'm sure she is. I'll look into it tomorrow. We pass her house on the way to the hospital," Grace straightened up in her chair and started to eat her soup with vigor. She was at her best when she had a plan. Quince could almost see the wheels in her mind turning as she planned the séance in her head.

"You're kidding right?" Quince looked at her in disbelief.

"Why not? What could it hurt?" Grace stared at him.

"For starters, we should investigate that idea. What could it hurt? If it sets off the ghosts that are supposedly around here, I for one don't want to be around for that," Quince glared back at Grace. "For another, do psychics clear houses? Didn't you say something about everyone who rallied against this house in the past suffered great losses? Is there anyone here willing to die to 'attempt' to clear this house?" Quince's old journalist traits kicked up in him. He had to know the facts before they did something this stupid.

"I didn't realize you were such a candy ass," Grace tried to stare him down.

"I'm just a realist, Sweetheart," he said, as Ethan slurped his soup again. Quince was glad for the distraction. Grace was getting all bent out of shape. He had never seen her like this, and he didn't care much for it, either.

"We'll contact Madame Zimmerman tomorrow and see what she has to say. Then we can go from there," Grace went back to eating her soup.

"Okay, but I have a few questions of my own," Quince added.

"Madame Zimmerman?" Ethan snickered.

"It might be a good idea to talk to her. You know, check it out. See what she says," Vincent looked around the room curiously. "If there is something here, it might need, and want, to be put to rest."

That was about all Quince could stand of this nonsense. If there truly were something in this house, these idiots had no idea what they were playing with. And if there wasn't, you can bet little Madame Zimmerman would want a pretty penny to clear it from the house and take all the credit. On the other hand, the séance could be all Claire needed to let go of whatever she was hanging onto from the past.

They ate the rest of their meal in silence. Ethan kept looking over his shoulder for the pirate he could not see; the pirate that wanted to slit his throat and watch his soup run down his neck.

CHAPTER TWENTY FOUR

Quince grabbed Grace around her waist from behind while she pulled the heavy spread off Claire's mother's bed. He breathed in deeply. She knew he loved the smell of her. She smiled at him, but squirmed away.

"Let me take these things down to Claire," Grace said pulling a pillow from the bed, "Then we can fool around a little."

"You mean I can stay here tonight?" He asked eager as a school boy.

"Maybe," Grace smiled, "If Claire decides to sleep on the porch."

Quince pouted.

"I'm ninety-nine percent sure she will sleep outside. Claire would almost choose death over being in this house," Grace assured him. "Be right back," Grace winked as she swaggered out the door with her load.

"Want some help?" Quince asked.

"I can manage. Why don't you check in on the boys?"

Grace headed down the stairs. She was going to actually get to spend the night with Quince, alone. The thought excited her in places she never knew existed before tonight. Normally she would forbid Quince from staying in Elizabeth's room with her on the odd chance, no matter how slim, that Claire might come back in the house during the night. Her mind seemed to be clearer right now. She could see her life outside of Claire's. She could think about herself and her own needs for once. It felt odd, but it also felt invigorating. Grace practically bounced down the stairs and out the door onto the porch.

Claire sat on the porch swing as usual. Nothing Claire did was out of the ordinary. She played everything so safe. She never ventured on a chance since they left the Harbor. Grace remembered how fearless Claire used to be. How she and Julian would challenge each other. How she loved winning and losing to him. The new Claire was sad and scared all the time. Once she had even told Grace she was afraid the ghosts from Templeton House would follow her to the city if they knew where she was.

Grace saw her friend in a new light now. She felt bad for her, but not responsible to save her anymore. Claire had some lessons to learn. Grace was sorry it had to be now of all times. She was sure Claire needed her now more than ever. She just didn't seem to have anything more to give, at least not to Claire.

"I brought you some blankets and a pillow. Thought you might be planning on staying out here tonight," Grace said, fearful that her friend might decide to sleep inside instead. It was getting cold, the wind was kicking up, and it was raining again. The porch blocked some of the wind, but it howled as it whipped around the porch. That howl bothered her, but she remembered how much Claire loved to hear it. The howl was natural. It was not a ghost.

"Thanks," Claire said. She seemed even more withdrawn than ever before. Part of Grace wanted to hug her and reassure her things would be okay, another part of her longed to be upstairs with Quince.

Grace placed the pile of blankets and a pillow on the swing next to Claire.

"Okay, well, I'm going to call it a night. I'm beat. We have a big day tomorrow," Grace said hoping Claire wouldn't beg her to stay out here with her.

"Yeah, tomorrow..." Claire was lost in her own world again. Grace didn't even try to get her attention.

"Well, good night," Grace called as she opened the screen door to the house. Claire never even looked up from her trancelike stare at the ocean.

Grace dashed up the stairs before Claire could change her mind.

CHAPTER TWENTY FIVE

"Everything all right in here," Quince asked, checking on Vincent and Ethan.

"Yeah," said Vincent from the chair across the room.

"If you want to call it that," Ethan piped in from the middle of the bed.

"What do you mean?" Quince asked Ethan.

"Well, the three of us in this tiny bed in a haunted house is not my idea of a good time if you know what I mean. I mean, normally it would be a great place to be, but here..." Ethan shrugged.

"Yeah, I know what you mean. Cheer up mate, looks like I'll be staying with Grace tonight in the master suite," Quince bragged.

"You're kidding, right?" Vincent shook his head.

"Nope, if Claire decides to sleep on the porch, Grace has agreed to let me stay with her," Quince smiled.

"Yeah, because she's scared of this house, too, and doesn't want to be alone," Ethan said.

"I don't really care what the reason. I finally get Grace to myself for once. Who knows how long it will last, but I am making good use of the opportunity," Quince leaned against the door jam.

"Go get her bro," Vincent said, dropping his right shoe on the floor beside the chair.

"I dunno," Quince teased, "Can I leave you two ladies alone for one night?"

"Don't look at me," Ethan sat up acting offended. "I can keep my hands to myself, but old Vince here, he gets a little randy during the night if you know what I mean.

"Shut up, Ethan," Vincent tossed a shoe across the room, hitting Ethan in the head. "Go to bed, Quince. We got it covered. Ethan has me to help keep the ghosts at bay, if he doesn't keep me up all night crying for his mommy."

Ethan had no come back. He was busy rubbing his head.

Quince heard Grace bounding up the stairs. He hoped that was good news.

"Okay girls, wish me luck," Quince said as he slid out the door.

"Yeah, you'll need it," he heard Vincent called after him.

Quince met Grace in the hall at the top of the stairs. She was smiling. That must be good. She pushed him up against the mother's bedroom door. The door knob jabbed him in the back, sending pain down his spine. He didn't care. He grabbed her tightly against him. She kissed him hard on the mouth. It sucked his breath away. Meanwhile her hands grabbed at his clothes.

"Down girl," he said as he reached behind him to grab the door knob, "Wait until we get into the room."

"I want you right here, right now," Grace breathed in his ear.

"Wow, I dig you, but the boys are right across the hall," Quince said motioning toward the boys door.

"So what," Grace breathed as she kissed his neck and nibbled on his ear, "let them watch."

"I'm sure they wouldn't mind, but I would," Quince was blown away by her comment. Normally, he was not allowed to kiss her in public, and if he slapped her bottom in front of people, he would pay for that offense for days. Now she wanted an audience?

The door finally clicked, and Quince nearly fell over as it opened. Grace pushed him inside and ripped at the buttons of his shirt. This was more like it. It was private and his goody- two-shoes girlfriend was acting like a sex craved maniac. Could life get better than this?

Quince fell against the bed. Grace pushed him back and started to undo his zipper. He pulled her shirt over her head, exposing her lacy bra. The site of her white skin against the black bra made him melt. He had waited so long for this night, had wanted it to be slow and special, not all fast and frantic like this. He fell back on the bed too excited to care.

The old woman with the knife walked through the wall and stood at the end of the bed. She watched as the two of them ripped at each other's clothing. The wind howled through the window frame.

CHAPTER TWENTY SIX

Morning couldn't come fast enough for Claire. She must have grown some since she left home because the porch swing that used to fit her like a glove suddenly seemed too small. The hard wood beneath made her wiggle around in search of a comfortable position. She had to wiggle her legs out the sides of the swing to get room to straighten out. Despite the steady rain and howling wind she loved so much, she didn't get any sleep all night. She wished she had decided to stay inside. Indeed, she probably would have gone inside if she hadn't heard Grace and Quince going at it like a couple of rabbits all night long. She wondered where they got their stamina. As soon as she thought they were done and she could sleep without all the huffing and puffing, Grace would cry out in passion, or the old bed springs would start squeaking all over again. Claire blushed at the thought of it.

Claire hadn't been with anyone since Julian. Actually, she realized, this was the first time she had even thought about it since she left. Why hadn't Julian come with them? Why hadn't he ever called or came after her? She left him a note before she left and sent him letters every month. He never answered her letters. He never called.

On the beach last night she was sure it was Julian she had seen. She would have gone by his house to see him herself except his mother always hated her. The woman could look right through her with eyes of steel that wanted to stab at her.

Her bones ached as she pulled her legs out of the side rails and raised herself up in the swing. She scanned the beach as she twisted her stiff neck into motion again. There was no one out there. She glanced across the porch and toward the house. She needed to know if it was okay to go inside yet. She could really use a cup of coffee, and she needed to pee.

The faces staring at her from the window told her it was not yet okay to go inside. Even though they were behind the window glass, Claire could feel them press around her, making it hard to breathe. She wondered how much longer until the sun rose. Then she wondered why that even made a difference to a ghost. All her life she always felt safer in the house during the day. The ghost energy seemed to dissipate during that time. Was there some unwritten rule that ghosts had to leave you alone in the day time? Do ghosts slept during the day. She was sure she had seen some ghosts during the daytime, but they never harmed her then. It was always at night when their presence in the house was strongest. That was when they would attack her.

The bed upstairs started to squeak again and Claire could hear Grace panting. She rolled her eyes and shook her head.

"Give it a rest," she said to no one.

Claire thought about last night, chasing after Julian, and meeting Raymond Dogg instead. That was not how she would have planned the evening. She would have preferred to meet Julian instead. She knew Raymond had a crush on her in school, but she only had eyes for Julian. She hoped that Raymond wouldn't try to make a pass at her now that she was back and alone. She was determined to find Julian and find out what had happened to him. They didn't even have a fight. They went to the graduation beach party, and she never saw him again. Her heart ached as she thought that Julian could have been like the other boys in town. That maybe he had run off with one of her classmates for a wild fling in the sand dunes. Then maybe he decided to stay with her or was too embarrassed to come back to Claire because of what he had done. Or maybe it was his stupid mother. She didn't care what the reason was anymore. So much time had passed since then. She would accept him back with open arms if he would just stop hiding from her.

The wind kicked up howling as it blew around the porch. The porch overhang prevented the wind from throwing the rain in onto her. She pulled the bed spread around her shoulders and snuggled deep into the blanket. She really had to pee. She glanced quickly at the house windows. The ghosts were still piled up at every window. They watched her intensely. What the hell do they want from me? Her friends were not attacked when they had entered the house. Why was it that the boys and Grace could be in the house without being accosted, but she couldn't? Why did they want her dead and not the others? Claire was filled with questions and she had no answers.

She looked back toward the shore, tears filling her eyes. She longed for the warmth and safety of their New York apartment. She longed for work that satisfied her as well as kept her mind occupied. She longed for the warmth of Julian's arms. She scanned the beach again for movement although she was certain no one in their right mind would be out in the rain.

It was getting easier to see now that the sun was starting to rise over the horizon. She scanned the beach grass and saw movement. Someone was running away from the house toward town. Claire dropped the bed cover and bounded down the stairs. Whoever it was wasn't going to get away this time. Oblivious to the rain and wind, Claire raced out toward the beach.

Once she cleared the beach grass she saw a small woman racing down the shore ahead of her. She was dressed in jeans and a rain coat. She had a massive umbrella. The umbrella was being buffeted by the wind.

"Stop!" Claire called after her. "Wait, I need to speak to you!"

The woman slowed and turned. Then she slowly walked back toward Claire like a kid being scolded by her mother, slow and skittish. Claire wanted to call out to her, but was afraid of scaring her away. She waited impatiently for the woman to come near enough not to have to yell over the wind and the surf.

"Hello," she said, as the woman came close enough to hear her. "I'm Claire Templeton."

"I know who you are. I'm Madeline Zimmerman. Don't you remember me?"

"The psychic?" Claire asked, looking closer at the woman.

"Yes, you could call me that," the woman blushed.

"What are you doing here? Were you spying on me?" Claire asked, surprised at the identity of her visitor. The rain pelted her and the wind whipped at her hair, but she didn't care. She was going to get to the bottom of this.

"No. And yes. I came to see if you were alright. I heard about your mother. I knew you were back. Something just drew me out here." The woman tried to explain.

"Drew you out here? In the rain? What could possibly bring you out in this?" Claire asked, shocked.

"I had this strong feeling that something was wrong, that you needed me. I tried to ignore it, but it wouldn't go away," The woman went on.

"Most people would come to the door. Knock." Claire said, cautious of the woman's intentions.

"I felt foolish. Didn't want to bother you if you didn't need me," The woman called over the crashing surf.

"You were always so bold when I was a kid. What happened to you? You seem so weak, scared." Claire said, watching the woman shiver, not just from the rain.

"It's this house. We have a history. I've been here before. Your father invited me out to try and clear the house for you. He said you could see the ghosts your mother saw. He was afraid you would get tied to the house just like your mom, and never leave. He didn't want that kind of life for you."

"My father? He called you?" Claire was shocked. She reeled from meeting this woman on the beach. She felt faint. She tried to concentrate.

"Yes, your father, before he passed away. He feared for your life and his own. He wanted to take you away from here, but your mother refused to leave. The house took him. I am sure of it, to keep you here as well." The woman blushed. "I'm sorry, I didn't mean to..."

"The house? What do you mean the house took him?" Claire cried out over the heavy surf and pouring rain.

"He came to me, after he died. It was during a séance I was doing for someone else. He told me the house had taken him. That he tried to protect you, but he couldn't. He knew that you had to get out of there. I was relieved when I heard you had left after the graduation party. I was afraid you would never leave, that the house would take you, too. To be honest I often wondered if the stories of your leaving for New York were false and that you were still in the house, trapped, like your mother, or worse...like your father." The woman shivered.

"Come up to the porch. It blocks some of the wind and rain." Claire told her. The fear on the woman's face was evident. "You'll be okay, it's safe there," Claire assured her.

The older woman hesitated, than followed Claire to the porch. She stopped at the bottom of the steps and stared at the windows of the house, the rain pelting her umbrella.

"What do you see?" Claire asked, no longer having to yell over the surf.

"Fear, I see fear and desperation. There is so much anger in there," the woman slowly climbed the stairs and joined Claire on the swing.

"You don't see them?"

"No, I don't see ghosts. I feel them."

"It's okay, the porch is safe," Claire gave the woman's hand a little squeeze to reassure her.

"Tell me about the last time you were here."

"It was just before your father passed away. He said he never saw anything in the house. He listened to your mother speak to the ghosts, but thought she was a little crazy. But he didn't care, he loved her very much. Then, once you saw them, he knew it was true. There were ghosts here. He had no reason not to believe you. You were his world. When he saw how upset they made you, he knew you did not make them up."

"When did you come here? I never saw you," Claire asked. She could feel rage growing inside of her. This woman knew the truth about her father's death and never told her.

"It was late at night. You were asleep. Your mother was asleep. He sneaked me inside. It was so terrible, the cries of anguish and desperation, the fear, the anger. I was pawed at and attacked from so many sides at once. I nearly passed out," she went on

Claire could relate to that.

"They want something. Every one of them wants something. There is an awful need in there. It's overwhelming." The woman continued as she stared at the windows.

Claire could relate to that, too.

"You said my father believed that the house took him?" Claire asked.

"Like I said, he came to me when I was reading for someone else. He said the house took him away. It was not natural causes. I had nothing to go on and no proof, so I kept it to myself and I kept myself away from here. I knew the house would try to take me, too, just to keep me silent. Your father told me that your mother would not leave the house. I knew that she would not believe me." The woman was shivering, Claire knew that it wasn't all due to the wind and her soaked clothing.

"Do you think the house would try to take you now?" Claire asked.

"I don't know. I've never been back here since. I don't know if the spirits know that I know. Or if they even care." The woman looked hesitant.

Dark clouds still filled the sky and the wind showed no signs of letting up anytime soon. The rain was relentless. Claire really needed to go inside and use the bathroom. She could see some of the ghosts fade away from the window. The little boy and the old woman with the knife were still there, each in their own window, but faded.

"Would you come inside with me?" Claire asked.

"I would rather not," the older woman answered.

"I have to pee, really badly and I could use a towel," Claire scrunched her face.

"Ah," the older woman shook her head, "me too. The cold rain has a way of doing that to you," Madam Zimmerman blushed.

"We can look out for one another," Claire offered.

"Okay, but I am subject to leaving without notice," the older woman said.

"Me too!" Claire let her know. Me too!

CHAPTER TWENTY SEVEN

The bed squeaks slowed, then stopped. Grace brushed her sweaty hair out of her face and caught her breath while she turned her head to listen better.

"You hear that?" she asked.

"Yeah," Quince lied, "I think so." They had been going at it all night, and he needed a break. A noise sounded like a good reason to stop. "Want me to go check it out?"

"No. Stay put," Grace glanced out the window and saw Claire and an older woman walking up the beach in the rain, toward the house. "Who the hell is that?" Grace yelled as she climbed off of Quince.

Relieved to be free for a while, Quince jumped up and looked out the window with her. Indeed, there was an older woman walking up from the beach with Claire. When they got to the house, Quince lost sight of them as they stepped under the porch roof. Weird, he thought, but then everything had been weird since they had gotten here.

"Get dressed. Let's go see what this is all about," Grace slipped on her robe and headed down the hall to the bathroom. He heard her washing up. He threw on his pants and headed down the hall to join her. Just as he got to the bathroom door, it opened.

"Hurry up," Grace barked. "We have to get downstairs."

"Sure thing, babe," Quince looked at Grace as if she were a stranger, barking orders, sex all night, guarding something, but what? It made no sense to him. He went in the bathroom and locked the door, glad to be on the inside alone, and not with Grace. What is that? He thought he must be going crazy. He loved Grace. And the sex last night was incredible, even mind boggling. But this morning she was like the house Nazi.

After washing up, he met her in the hallway. Grace had dressed quickly and was on her way downstairs when he opened the bathroom door.

"Let's go!" she called after him.

"Okay, okay," he said, growing impatient with her. They headed down the stairs in time to see Claire and the old woman coming inside the house. Grace stopped on the stairs and watched, holding Quince back with one hand.

"It's her," Grace said, as she sat down on the step, using the banister to hide.

"Her who?" Quince asked as she grabbed him and pulled him down with her.

"Madame Zimmerman," Grace whispered.

"The psychic?" Quince whispered back in disbelief.

"Yes. Shh!" she hushed him.

They watched as the two came inside the house slowly. They looked around and then at each other and giggled. They said something in relieved voices. Then they headed for the stairs.

Grace jumped up, pulling Quince along with her, scaring the two women as they almost ran headlong into them. They screamed bloody murder, than they laughed when they saw it was just Grace and Quince.

"You scared the crap out of me!" Claire cried out. "Let me past before I pee my pants." Claire pushed past them with the older woman right behind her, visibly shaken. Both women went into the upstairs bathroom together.

"They are going to the bathroom- together?" She looked at Quince in disbelief.

"Strength in numbers, I guess," Quince answered, as con-fused as she was.

Vincent and Ethan came out into the hallway.

"We heard screaming!" Ethan said, holding a shoe as if it was a bat.

"It was just Claire. We scared her by accident," Grace told them. "She's with the psychic."

"Really?" Vincent asked. "Interesting."

"They're in the bathroom," Quince told them.

"Together?" Ethan asked.

"Yup," Quince said.

"No kidding," Ethan shook his head.

The two women came out of the bathroom giggling. It seemed a nervous giggle to Quince.

"Everything okay?" Quince asked them.

"Better now," Claire put her hand to her belly.

"Yes, much better," the older woman agreed.

"Shall we get some breakfast?" Claire asked everyone. "I'm starved."

Quince was surprised to see Claire seem so much in control this morning and Grace so much out of it. It was quite a switch. He headed down the stairs, the rest of them following closely behind.

CHAPTER TWENTY EIGHT

Claire and Grace started getting pans ready while Quince got the last of the eggs from the fridge, and Vincent found some potatoes in the back of the pantry that Quince had missed the night before. The potatoes were a little soft, but he was sure they were still good. Ethan sat at the breakfast table with the psychic.

"I don't know why," the psychic said, "But I just had an urge to be here. Like I was needed or something."

"No kidding," Ethan shook his head and made eyes at Vin-cent.

"Isn't that something," Vincent said, making eyes back at Ethan.

"Well," Quince said, seeming not as surprised as the others to see the older woman. "It's kind of funny that you should come along today."

"Why is that?" the psychic asked.

"Because we were thinking of having a séance," Vincent piped in before Quince could be rude.

"A séance?" Both Claire and the psychic asked at the same time.

"Yes," Grace jumped in, "Vincent thinks a psychic could somehow clear the house."

"Really?" asked a surprised Claire.

"Yeah," Grace said, "He thinks it could help."

"Who?" asked Claire.

"You know, the ghosts," Grace answered. "If you ask me I think we should all get the hell out of here as soon as we can and forget about messing with the ghosts."

"That must be why I felt so strongly that I needed to be here," the psychic said.

"Of course," said Quince sarcastically. Grace slapped him across his arm.

Ethan watched his friends and the psychic as if from a distance. He was amazed that the psychic had come to them instead of them going to her. They thought about her and there she was, sitting in the kitchen, about to have breakfast with them. Then there was Claire, who seemed somehow calmer than last night. And Grace, he just shook his head to himself. She went from being mother hen to bossy bitch. She ordered Quince around like he was a slave. And all that sex. Vincent seemed to be the only one who acted the same.

While he didn't believe in the whole ghost and psychic thing, he had to give it some credit since she had shown up all on her own. That scared him a little though. If the whole ghost thing was true, then a dead pirate really had stood behind him during dinner last night. And if that were true, he looked around carefully, than another dead pirate or ghost could be hovering over him right now. The thought made him shiver.

"You're okay, honey," the psychic told him.

That freaked him out more than ever. Could she read his mind?

"Will you have a séance for us?" Vincent asked.

"I would rather not do that here," she said.

"Can you do it somewhere else?" Ethan asked, surprised.

"Yes. But this is the ideal place to do it," she answered, completely confusing him.

"Yes. I can do this at my place. Will it have the same effect as here? Probably not," the psychic said, "But it will make me feel better."

"Ah," Vincent shook his head, "I get that."

Ethan watched Quince smirk in the corner.

"Maybe we should do this somewhere else," Grace chimed in. "It might make us all feel safer."

"Yes, but it will not be as beneficial," the psychic told them.

Ethan thought somewhere else would be good too. He could deal with that. He was suddenly afraid of the house and what might be in it.

"So you'll do it here?" asked Quince curiously.

"Yes," the older woman answered.

"Tonight?" Quince pushed the issue. Grace frowned.

"Sure. I could do it tonight. But I need everyone to be here. And I will need to bring a friend along. He keeps me safe while I am in a trance. He will bring me out of it if I get into trouble," the psychic told them.

"Trouble?" Ethan asked, "What kind of trouble?"

"Just if a spirit gets out of control or tries to harm me," she told him.

"They can do that?" Ethan asked frightened.

"That probably won't happen," she tried to assure him.

"Here it probably will," Ethan frowned at the thought. "Can we just skip the whole thing and go home now?"

"No!" Quince and Vincent said at the same time.

"So it's settled then. Séance here tonight." Quince closed the deal.

No one seemed too happy about the idea, especially the psychic.

CHAPTER TWENTY NINE

The trip to the hospital was made in silence. Grace was glad for the respite. She had enough on her mind right now without having to deal with the usual chit chat. Claire was as needy as ever. Grace could not understand why she had wasted so much of her life wrapped up in Claire's needs. She had given up so much of her own life as it was.

Last night with Quince was unbelievable. She was driven by a need to consume him that she had never allowed herself to experience before. Of course, like with Claire, Grace became totally involved in pleasing Quince. She seemed to be an all or nothing kind of girl. She would have to work on that.

Was the whole psychic thing as predictable as Quince thought it was? Quince had made certain predictions himself after the psychic left the house. He predicted that she would indeed 'feel a strange presence', that someone was trying to reach out to her but she couldn't quite get a fix on them, then suddenly she would become completely aware of trapped and troubled souls crying out to her.

If they were real, there was the chance that the ghosts could become agitated. Grace wondered if everyone would be in jeopardy then.

Now they were headed to the hospital. Claire had new in-formation about her father from the psychic. She had been pissed off all morning. Will Claire confront her mother with the psychic's story? It would take away a lot of the guilt Claire felt most of her life. Elizabeth made sure to remind her daily how her father was gone and it was all her fault. Claire must feel relieved, yet angry over this new information. But Grace suddenly wasn't sure she could trust the psychic.

She glanced in the rear view mirror. Ethan sat between Vin-cent and Quince. He seemed lost in thought like the others. But he also seemed scared for the first time.

Claire and Grace never talked about the Harbor or growing up. They lived in the present. Everyone knew them for who they were, not how they became who they were. In the city, no one questioned the lack of extended family. Holidays alone were normal for many city dwellers. Claire and Grace always had each other, so no one ever pushed for more information about their families.

Perhaps it was because they themselves had been so superficial with everyone. Even the girls knew very little about the boys lives before New York. Oddly enough, none of them asked any questions about where they grew up or what their families were like. The common thread in their lives seemed to be that everyone was glad to be out of their own neck of the woods and eager to live in the here and now.

Grace felt a sadness seep inside of her. For the first time she felt alone and lonely. And she felt vulnerable. She wasn't used to feeling like this. Usually she was the one in control. She was the strong one. She made the plans while others had no idea what they wanted to do. Simple things like where we should have lunch brought on a distant look in everyone's eyes as they tried to launch their brains to make a plan. Not Grace. If she felt like soup today, she wanted to go to the Soup Buffet on West 105th Street. If she needed a meaty burger and greasy fries, any of the major chains would do. She knew how she felt all the time. She knew what would make her feel better or worse, and she always opted for better.

The others never knew where they wanted to eat. They never knew where they wanted to go. They were like cattle, they simply followed the herd, especially Claire. She had to be led everywhere in life. If she needed food, Grace picked the place. If she needed to pay her bills, Grace took care of it. Claire did little for herself save her designing. That she could do very well. Claire could design amazing clothes. Take what she was wearing to the hospital. It was a Claire Templeton original: a bright purple vest-like blouse with a flowing multicolored, multi-layered skirt underneath, jeweled flat leather sandals on her dainty manicured feet. Her hand bag was oversized and filled with all kinds of crap. Bracelets dangled from her wrists. The waist band of her skirt jingled with every move. In her clothing she was loud and proud.

Grace wondered what Claire would have been like if she hadn't grown up in Templeton House. She had the potential to be bold. Templeton house sucked away all signs of life from her. And her mother was the chief sucker. If her mother was awake by now, there was no telling what she would blame Claire for this time. The woman took no responsibility for her own life or mistakes.

Elizabeth Templeton had grown up in that house. When her husband joined her, he joined her life. Indeed, she never left the house. Groceries were brought to the house by bag boys. Even while Henry was in the house, the groceries were delivered. That was odd, but so was everything about Templeton House.

Was the house due for a grocery delivery today? Did they already know Claire's mother was in the hospital? Grace would take bets that the bag boys were hoping that Elizabeth never returned.

If her mother passed on, Grace was sure Claire would sell the house. She could not imagine her friend wanting to live there. Attempts in the past to burn the house down only resulted in burns on the people who tried to burn it down. It withstood the hurricane winds that beat on it each year. Short of taking each and every board off by hand, Grace knew of no way to defeat the house.

Taking it apart by hand would be a chore in itself. The house was built by pirates. Each heavy plank was stolen from a ship and was attached by wooden pegs driven through the boards. You could probably break the windows. Other than that, there wasn't much you could do to take that house down.

Selling the house would be impossible. Not even ghost hunters who enjoy haunted houses had been interested in the Templeton House. The house seemed evil more than haunted. The normal cult that would be drawn to a haunted house avoided this one. No scientists ever came to study it. No kids dared each other to enter or even to ring the doorbell. People just stayed away. There would be no selling it. That would tie Claire to the house forever. She would be ultimately responsible for it until she died. What a terrible thought. Grace really hoped Mrs. Templeton would pull through, for Claire's sake.

Of course she could always give it to Quince and me. We could take care of it. Where did that come from? Grace brushed the thought away.

CHAPTER THIRTY

They entered the hospital like a gang. Everyone walked side-by-side taking up the entire width of the expansive hospital hallway. All their faces were stern. Nurses moved against the wall as they passed through. When they entered the elevator, a mother and her child inside pushed themselves up against the back wall of the elevator in fear. There was no idle chit chat among them. No smile or admittance of fear or concern. Just glum, grumpy faces staring dead ahead.

As they exited the elevator, the mother grabbed her child by the arm and pulled her over to the selection panel and quickly shut the elevator door, despite an old man in the wheel chair asking her to wait.

They walked to the ICU waiting room and joined another family already waiting there. They huddled in one corner of the room, giving space to the other family that was clearly distraught. They all sat down and stared at one another.

"You want me to go in with you?" Grace asked when Claire didn't budge from her chair.

"If you don't mind," Claire said. She wasn't sure what was going on with Grace today and had been afraid to ask her friend the favor. But she knew she did not want to enter that room again, alone.

"The Chief said only one person could go in at a time," Ethan stated.

"Yeah, well the Chief of Police isn't here right now, is he?" Grace snapped.

Ethan stared at Vincent and Quince as if to ask for help, but neither spoke up, so Ethan stared at his feet instead.

The two girls walked slowly towards the ICU, pressed the button and were admitted after a short wait. Claire used that time to try and get herself under control. Visions of her mother sitting up in the hospital bed, still tethered at her wrists, growling at her, made her skin crawl and her stomach ache. She longed to go back to New York.

In front of her mother's door she hesitated. Grace tugged lightly on her arm and pulled Claire into the room. Her mother was still hooked up to a variety of machinery. A heart monitor beeped annoyingly. Claire was glad it was beeping for her mother's sake, but would like to have ripped it out of the wall. An IV ran into her mother's arm. A urine bag hung from the end of the bed. The whole hospital thing was more than she could stand, and that awful hospital smell. She so wanted to flee.

Grace stood beside the bed in silence. Usually she would be full of 'it will be okay's' and 'you can do its.' Today she just looked at Claire's mother in silence. Claire couldn't read her friend's thoughts or feelings today. Normally they could finish each other's sentences, not unlike twins. Today they were like strangers. Claire struggled to keep in control while her knees knocked. And now she had developed an eye twitch.

"She is doing so much better today," the ICU nurse announced as she strolled in the room with a fresh IV bag. "The doctor is on rounds and would like to see you this morning. I'll let him know you're here," she told Grace. Grace pointed toward Claire. "Oh, I'm sorry," the nurse fumbled disconnecting the old IV bag. Her face reddened.

"Is everything okay?" Claire asked, wondering if anyone else had been subjected to an episode like she had last night.

"The doctor will explain everything when he gets here," the nurse placed the new IV bag on the hook and quickly left the room.

Grace glanced at Claire and raised her brows. Claire shook her head. She didn't know what to do now, either. They both stared down at her mother, obviously still in a coma, bandages wrapped around her wrists up to her elbows. Her arms were still tied off to the bedsides. Claire assumed this was for her own safety when, and if, she ever woke up. Claire was thankful for those straps.

The nurse popped back into the room. "The doctor would like to see you in the hall, Ms. Templeton," she said, then quickly went on her way.

"Goody," Claire said without thinking. Then she took a deep breath and walked out into the hall to face the doctor. Was he afraid to enter her mother's room as well? Grace followed slowly behind her. The doctor was too young, about her age. Unbelievable, what had she accomplished in her life by now? A few designs on runways in the New York market only. Here was a man her age tending to patients in the ICU.

"Ms. Templeton," he extended his hand to her. "I'm Dr. Kilmer, your mother's physician," he said, leading Claire away from her mother's door. "We like to speak to relatives of our coma patients away from their rooms. There is still so much we don't know about what coma patients do and don't hear."

"I see," Claire responded stiffly. She prepared herself for the worse, and she realized that anything he had to say was going to be the worst thing she had heard so far, no matter what he said. She had never had to speak to a physician before, let alone in an ICU.

"Ah, well, your mother came through surgery okay. We had to repair some tissue damage and mend some tendons as best we could. A lot of the damage will take time, lots of time, to heal properly. She will most likely require care eating, dressing, using the bathroom, those kinds of things. Her hands will pretty much be useless for several months, maybe even years. We'll put her on physical therapy to rebuild the use of her hands as quickly as possible, but it is really up to the patient after that. And at her age, well we just don't know."

"I see," Claire repeated without realizing it. All she could think about was months, or years, in that house spoon-feeding her depressed and angry mother while being attacked each night by ghosts. The room started to slip away from her again. She leaned against the wall for support.

"Our biggest obstacle right now is that she never came around after the surgery. Everything went well. There really is no reason for her not to have awakened after a reasonable amount of time," the doctor seemed to be avoiding the real issue.

"Go on," Claire said.

"It appears as if whatever drove your mother to do this to herself is keeping her from coming around," the young surgeon stated bluntly.

Claire remembered the psychic's words this morning: "Your father said the house took him." She tried to shake the thought.

"Whatever bothered her enough to want to hurt herself is still a strong enough stressor for her not to want to wake up. Something has her very upset. Something she still doesn't want to face just yet," the doctor went on.

It was easy to see what was bothering her mother, but it had never bothered her before. It was that blasted house. Perhaps she found out about Dad? Claire shivered again. Her mind wanted to snap into a million pieces. She longed to be in a hospital bed of her own, hooked up with machines, oblivious to the world around her.

"What can we do," Grace asked.

"There isn't much we can do for her. Other patients have responded to the voice of their family members. Others appear to go deeper into a coma," the doctor turned a light shade of red, "Since I do not know you or your family I can't really recommend which is best for her. I understand you have had a strained relationship for many years. It could go either way."

Claire stared at the doctor, but could not speak.

"I understand there was an incident last night...," the doctor said.

Claire had hoped to forget that incident altogether. She was still terrified to see her mother this morning and had no plans of being left alone with her at any time in the near future.

"I...," Claire didn't know what to say. If she told the truth, she could be locked up in the loony bin. If she didn't tell them what happened, they would think she had tried to harm her mother. Claire tried to find a middle ground.

"She sat up and spoke to me," Claire paused, knowing they would not believe her. "She said it was my fault that she was here."

Grace took a step back and stared at Claire in shock. Claire was sure she could not believe that Claire had hidden this from her. She had no intention of telling anyone, but she didn't want to be accused of hurting her mother again either.

"I see," stated Dr. Kilmer. "That was most likely a stress re-action. You had quite a shock finding out that your mother had tried to take her own life. Given your stained relationship and your tired state from driving in from the city, you probably imagined what you expected her to say. It's a perfectly normal stress response. An anxiety attack if you will," Dr. Kilmer said as if he had just diagnosed a cold or fever. "Did we check the video from the room last night?" he asked the nurse. Claire's heart skipped a beat. A camera? She was excited that there would be video proof of what occurred the night before.

"Yes doctor, the video feed seems to be down right now. There was just snow. No audio at all either. A tech call has been placed to have it repaired as soon as possible."

Claire's heart sank.

"We would like you to speak to your mother. The nurse and I will be there to keep an eye on her monitors and see how she responds. If she responds badly we can stop and try again at a later time," the doctor suggested as he lead them back toward the room. Claire's bracelets jingled on their own as she trembled, not wanting to enter the room again. Having witnesses in the room was great, but it didn't calm her fear of a repeat of last night. Her mother had acted like she was possessed.

The small group entered her mother's room, followed closely by the ICU nurse. Everyone gathered around Elizabeth's bed and seemed to stare at Claire. She had no idea what to say to her mother, and she was afraid to get within striking distance in case her mom broke free of her restraints.

"It's okay," the doctor said as if he had read her mind. "Just say whatever comes to mind."

All the things that Claire wanted to say were inappropriate for this situation. With the new information about her father and the house, she wanted to scream at her mother for blaming her, her own daughter, for killing her father. And now she blamed Claire for her own suicide attempt as well.

The doctor stiffened and seemed to grow impatient. He motioned to the nurse with his eyes. The nurse raised her eyebrows in response. Claire didn't think they knew she had seen this.

"Momma," Claire fumbled. "Momma, we're here, Grace and me. We are here for you," she said stiffly.

The doctor watched the monitors closely. Claire half hoped it went poorly, so he would remove her from the room and tell her not to return.

The monitors beeped unchanged. She wondered if that was a good sign or a bad one.

"Momma, we're gonna stay as long as you need us," Claire saw Grace step away from the bedside, a wild look in her eyes. Grace recovered quickly when she saw Claire watching her. Grace understood that the incident last night was not a stress reaction on Claire's part.

"It's okay, Mom. We can help, whatever is wrong, we can help you," Thinking that the doctor and nurse expected it, Claire stepped awkwardly forward and gave her mother's bandage wrapped hand a light squeeze. She stepped back immediately as a buzzer went off sending a shrill siren echoing off the walls.

Claire watched her mother in horror, expecting her to sit up again and start accusing her. She stepped back quickly, bumping into Grace, who had already backed up against the window sill herself.

The nurse was at Elizabeth's side grabbing wires and reset-ting buttons on the monitor. The doctor lifted Elizabeth's eyelids and checked her pupils for response.

"It's okay. You just knocked off this little guy right here," the nurse said, re-clipping the oxygen monitor to Elizabeth's finger.

Claire felt the heat rush in her face and knew she was blushing.

"Happens all the time," the nurse reassured her.

"I think that's enough for today," the doctor said, taking a deep breath. He seemed relieved to be able to leave the room. He led Claire and Grace back out into the hallway. "We'll limit visits to once or twice a day with nurses' supervision for right now. You are welcome to stay, but there is no need. Jennifer will call you if there are any changes. You both look like you could use some rest." Then he was gone.

Claire stood in the hall staring at the large tiles on the floor. Her body trembled. She needed air.

Grace looked just as shaken.

"Why didn't you tell me about last night?" she whispered.

"I didn't want you to have to live with that too. I was hoping it was just a bad dream. Or like the doctor said, a hallucination."

"You still should have told me."

Grace was right, but she had been so terrified of the whole situation, she didn't want Grace to remember it forever as well.

CHAPTER THIRTY ONE

When the boys were told they were all free to leave the hospital, Grace could see the joy in their faces. None of them knew what to do since they expected to be at the hospital all day. Everyone seemed thrilled to be leaving, but on one wanted to go back to that house and no one wanted to admit to it.

"So, what do we do now?" Ethan asked, looking lost.

"We go to Murphy's and get a milkshake," Grace took control of the lost crowd. Claire smiled. Ethan perked up at the thought of food. Quince grabbed her waist tighter as if in thanks for the suggestion of anywhere other than the house.

It was a short drive from the hospital to the boardwalk, but Grace took a quick detour.

"I thought we were going to Murphy's," Claire asked, sitting upright in the passenger seat of the rental car.

"We are, but I am not paying twenty dollars to park just to get something to eat. Its tourist season sweetie and we are not tourists!" Grace smiled as she pulled into a parking slot in front of City Hall. She grabbed the registration and insurance cards from the glove box.

"Good thinking," Claire said. Grace knew Claire wouldn't think of a parking permit. Neither of her parents ever owned a car, and she had never gotten her license to drive. Anywhere they wanted to go was close enough to walk or bike. Grace's parents did own a car, and every year her father would bitch about having to get his parking permit before they were all gone.

"Come on," Grace said to Claire, not letting her sit in the car while she took care of everything. The boys must have thought she was talking to them as well, because they all followed her into City Hall.

"Is there a problem?" Chief Harris asked as the entire crew entered the building.

"No Chief," Grace stated, "we are here for a parking permit."

"Uh...," the Chief scratched his cheek in thought.

"Is there a problem Chief?" Grace straightened, making her-self taller.

"Well, yes and no, see..." the Chief started.

"We are residents, Chief. If not Claire and I, then her mother is, and we are here on her behalf," Grace demanded.

"I understand. Residency is not the problem girls, it's the timing. I'm afraid you are a little too late. All the permits have already been issued for this year, and since Elizabeth Templeton never requests a permit, one was never issued to her." The Chief fumbled through his drawer. He pulled out a parking permit pad. "Of course, I am the only one who knows Elizabeth wasn't issued a permit," he said reaching for Grace's registration card. He filled in the information for the car and wrote E. Templeton diagonally across the entire permit. "Display this in the windshield, driver's side at all times when parking. I suggest you keep the doors locked as these are well sought after on the Harbor."

"Are you suggesting someone might steal it?" Grace asked, remembering her parents keeping their car windows up even in the heat of the day.

"Yes, Ms. Noble, I am suggesting just that," the Chief stated as he handed her the resident parking permit. "Not to mention that this particular parking permit will raise quite a stir in town. I am sure you know what I mean."

Grace knew exactly what he meant. He could not issue a permit to either of the girls as they owned no property in town. Therefore, the permit was issued to Elizabeth Templeton. Everyone knew that Elizabeth neither owned a vehicle, nor drove a car in her life. If Elizabeth in the hospital didn't create a stir in town, and the girl's return didn't raise a fuss, the parking permit was sure to get the residents going.

"I know what you mean Chief," Grace winked. "Anything else we should know?" Grace asked.

"I'll keep you updated as need arises," he smiled. Grace laughed to relieve the tension building in the boys, but she knew things could and would get ugly soon. The poor boys had no idea what they had gotten themselves into.

CHAPTER THIRTY TWO

Ethan watched Grace place the resident parking permit in the driver's side window as they pulled into a parking space at the boardwalk. Due to the weather, finding a parking place was easy today. Ethan was thankful to be getting out of the hospital and the house for a while. He wanted to get out and stretch his legs. He hated being in the back seat and really hated being in the middle all the time. He longed for the city bus back home.

Claire got out and breathed in the salt air. He didn't get the whole breathing in sea air thing. He just thought it stunk like dead fish or something. He breathed as little as possible as he followed behind the others, half walking, half running, toward the boardwalk. The rain felt cold.

He noticed the shops along the sidewalk displayed surf boards, large hand bags and sun tanning lotions. All the beach items seemed silly in this rain and wind.

"Hey, that looks like your style, Claire," Vincent said, surprised as they passed a cottage selling beach attire.

"It sure is," Grace said, almost as surprised. "Well, I'll be. She only paid you to use that outfit for one season, and she's been selling it all these years."

Claire didn't say anything, but he thought he saw a slight smile cross her face. They all stared briefly, and then took off running for the cover of the boardwalk shops.

Ethan was happy when they turned the corner onto the boardwalk. The building seemed to block some of the rain that pelted them. Grace led them into Murphy Malts, all the way to a booth in the back. There was a long counter that ran along the right side of the shop. Stools lined the counter. Every seat at the counter was full probably because the rain kept most people off the beach. Oversized booths lined the wall on the left. Grace led them to a booth at the back. It was large enough to hold all five of them comfortably. The seats were old and cracked, but still comfortable. The backs of the seats were extremely tall, which allowed for semi privacy while eating your meal. A fan overhead stirred the cool air which made them all shiver. He wondered why no one had turned them off today.

Grace ordered waters all around before the waitress left the table.

"Can we kill the fan?" Grace asked her. The waitress nodded that it was okay.

"Quince?" Grace asked and pointed toward the fan. He looked at her as if she were crazy. "Just hop up on the bench and turn it off," she told him. After a brief look around the room, he jumped up onto the bench seat and awkwardly turned off the fan. The girls looked briefly at the menu.

"Murphy Burger with cheese" they said at the same time, "and Murphy's Mega Fries." The girls giggled. Apparently this was an old haunt of theirs. Ethan cringed at the word haunt. He was glad to be out of that creepy house. He glanced back at the menu for something vegetarian. He wasn't a vegan, but he preferred not to eat meat all the time. He found a Caesar's salad and settled on that, but then he realized he was practically starving, so he added a chicken sandwich anyway. Vincent ordered a Reuben with mega fries.

Quince held hands with Grace under the table as if no one knew. They stared at each other with that stupid lovers' gaze. He hoped that tonight would not be a repeat of last night. All that banging kept him awake all night; he had been afraid he would miss hearing a ghost over all the racket they had made. Could ghosts kill you or did they just scare you to death? He wasn't sure he wanted to find out.

The waitress brought several glasses and a pitcher of water. She took their orders as Grace excused herself to go to the ladies room. Claire, of course, joined her. The men each ordered hot coffee.

"What are you so happy about?" Vincent asked him as the waitress left the table.

"Glad to be out of that God forsaken house," Ethan said. A grin stretched from ear to ear.

"...and the hospital!" Quince added. "How did we get so lucky? Now if it would just quit raining."

"It looks like there aren't many places to eat around here either. It's this or the Dairy Whippe," Ethan said.

"Takes a gay boy to notice the Dairy Whippe," Quince teased him.

"Speaking of gay boys, you two gonna let us sleep tonight or what?" Vincent piped in.

"You, how about me? I didn't get any sleep either," Quince added.

"Yeah, but at least you were enjoying all that bouncing around. We weren't," Vincent said.

"It wasn't all fun and games, guys," Quince pouted.

"Yeah, right," Ethan said, still looking at the menu, not sure about the chicken sandwich he ordered. Perhaps he should have ordered the Mega Burger instead.

"It wasn't." Quince bent down and spoke softly. "She was like a maniac.

Someone I never knew. None of it was enough for her."

"Now who's gay?" Ethan asked.

"No, really. She never wanted to come up for air. I was dying up there," Quince whispered.

"Wow," said Vincent, stunned. "You serious? Like she's too much for you? And you're really going to admit to that?"

"No man, like I think that house got into her somehow," Quince said, sitting up a little.

"Into her like what?" Ethan asked. He was afraid of the answer.

"I don't know, but that was not Grace I was screwing last night. She is not like that. Ever. And she is always in control, but not bossy. Now, wow! She is out of control." Quince straightened his napkin as the girls came back to the table.

"Okay, you can stop talking about all the bikinis now," Grace ordered as she returned to the table.

"It's not the bikinis we're discussing," Ethan said. Quince kicked him.

"It's what's in them," Vincent said, covering Ethan's comment.

Ethan thought about what Quince had said about something getting into Grace. He had no idea something in the house could get inside any of them. Was this spirit or whatever inside of her now. She looked normal. She acted normal, well almost. She seemed on edge, but then they all did. The others chatted back and forth while waiting for their meals. Ethan sat silently watching Grace for signs of possession. She was in her element, he thought. This place was a blast from her past. She seemed to notice he was staring at her.

"Is there a problem Ethan?" she asked.

"No. Just ah..." he stumbled for words. This time Vincent kicked him under the table. That seemed to satisfy Grace and she went back to holding hands with Quince under the table.

The waitress brought a huge tray of food, followed by a tall, crooked man. He looked painfully bent somehow. He set a stack of napkins down on the table.

"I know how messy you girls can get," he said in a gruff voice that sounded older than he must have been. The girls giggled.

"You know it, Mr. Murphy!" Grace said.

Claire sat up straight in her seat. The waitress handed out their food while the old man stood by.

"You back cause of your Momma?" the old Man spoke.

"Yes sir," Claire fiddled with her napkin and fries.

"Thought so. Didn't expect you to come back here though," he stated as he stared at the girls.

"Well, a girl's gotta eat," Grace said, stuffing fries in her face.

The old man made a growling noise. "Need anything ask," he grumbled as he turned and headed back behind the counter.

Ethan found it hard to tell locals from tourists. Everyone was clad in bright colors and smothered in tanning lotion despite the rain. The smell of coconuts overwhelmed even the burgers, but it was pleasant. He smiled as he took a big bite into his Chicken sandwich. He was hungrier than he thought. The salad would have to wait.

Two ladies in clear rain coats over sundresses came through the door and made a bee-line for their table. The angry look on their faces made him think they might have taken the girls' table by mistake. He feared being thrown out of his seat to eat on the floor, or worse yet, to have to get a to-go bag. He wasn't eager to return to that house. He wanted to stay right where he was, even if it was chilly.

"Will you look at what the cat dragged in," The tall one said.

Grace choked on her burger as she looked up. "Speaking of cats! If it isn't Wendy Meyers and her little minion Ruth Ann."

"Is your Momma here?" Ruth Ann asked Claire, looking around the restaurant for her.

"I'm sure you know my mother is in the hospital," Claire said.

"That's funny, because that rental car outside has your mother's beach pass in the window," Wendy said.

"It belongs to us while we're here," Grace stated as she glared at the girl.

"So which hospital is dear old mum in anyway?" Wendy asked with such an attitude even Ethan wanted to smack her.

"St. Anthony's," Claire said.

"Oh, I thought perhaps she was in the loony bin." Wendy twirled her blond curls as she spoke.

Grace started to get up, but Quince had a hold of her hands under the table. She tugged hard against him, but he wouldn't let her go.

"If you know what's good for you, you'll shut your big trap and leave," Grace said, still trying to break free from Quince.

"I see Grace is still fighting your battles for you Claire. Some things never change," Wendy said.

Cat fight, Ethan thought. This could be good for entertainment. Then he reminded himself that these were his friends he was talking about.

"You'd better move along before I break your face. Oh and where exactly is your mother, Wendy? At Gale Presley's house doing her husband while she's at work again?" Grace said. Wendy turned pale.

"Guess we better go warn the rest of the town to lock up their sons since Claire and Gracie are back in town," Wendy whirled around and headed for the door.

Grace Quince yanked a hand almost free. Claire just sat there. This was not the Claire Ethan knew. She was loud and proud. Bold. Ethan was sure Claire would have spoken her mind if she were back in the city.

"We'll be sure to alert the Chief that someone besides Elizabeth Templeton is using her beach pass," Ruth Ann said, as she turned and strolled out behind Wendy.

"Oh yeah, and we'll make sure we tell Julian you're back in town, Claire!" Wendy said from the door. She and Ruth Ann giggled as they open the door and left. Grace closed her eyes and slid back down onto the bench. She took a deep breath and stared at her Murphy's Burger. Claire stared blankly at her food as well. Grace shoved a French fry in her mouth and chewed loudly. Everyone else ate in silence.

CHAPTER THIRTY THREE

Madeline Zimmerman entered her house and began rummaging through her papers. She was looking for a recent report on multiple spirit hauntings and séances she had saved. The article dealt with the danger of handling too many spirits at one time. In multiple hauntings, the more dominant spirits tended to take over during a séance. Madeline's fear was that there were too many dominant spirits within Templeton House.

"Where the fuck have you been all night?" Herbert Varden said. Madeline cringed. She could smell the booze on him from across the room, and it wasn't even noon yet.

"Not here," she stated, surprised at her own boldness.

"No shit. Out where?" he slurred his words as he spoke.

"You mean with whom, don't you?"

"Yeah, I mean with whom?" he said.

"No one, I was at the beach on a job."

"You never go on a job without me. Besides, I went by the shop and you weren't there," Herbert said, bumping into her. She hated to be around him when he was drunk. She pushed him back and kept looking for the article.

"I was scoping out a job, okay?" she said tired of being grilled by a drunk.

"Really, and just who would this job be for? That slick bastard Jemison from Jersey? I heard his wife had to go back to the city yesterday. I know he has the hots for you."

"Not Jemison. It was Claire," she said, realizing he had no idea who she was talking about. "Claire Templeton."

That seemed to get his attention. He quit questioning her and took a seat in the corner of the room watching her carefully. It was obvious he wasn't sure if she was lying or not. He always thought she was lying when he was drinking, which was pretty much all the time anymore. And he always thought she was sleeping around on him. She longed for the old Herbert back. The guy she knew before he started to drink.

"Why?" he snapped after a minute or two. She wasn't surprised at how long it took for his brain to work when he was drunk. It made her head hurt.

"Her mother is in the hospital, remember. Claire is back in the house," she said, as she looked through the papers on the top of her file cabinet. It had to be there. The article had fascinated and terrified her all at the same time. It made her think of the Templeton House and all of its many ghosts. She knew there were more ghosts there than even she was aware of. The number of hauntings was mind boggling. The article discussed some trauma that could bind all those spirits to a house. Madeline figured it had to be the pirates murdering them all. But was that enough to hold them there? Something in that house was keeping them from leaving, something dangerous.

"So..." he continued.

"So, she is thinking about trying to clear the house while she is here," she stated. She caught sight of him out of the corner of her eye. He almost fell out of his chair.

"And she wants you to do it?"

"Yes," she was agitated now. "She wants me to do it. Regardless of what you think, some people have faith in me."

"I have faith in you-," he started, but she cut him off.

"No you don't. You never believe in anything I do anymore. Oh, you enjoy the money it brings in, sure enough, but you never really believe," she vented.

"Sure I do. It is just that some of this stuff is so whacked out and boring."

"How do you do it?" she turned to face him.

"Do what?" he asked, dumbfounded.

"Help me with all of this if you don't believe? Most psychic's helpers truly believe in them. You just come along to make sure I'm not out screwing somebody instead of working," she snapped.

"That's not true," he said while he his face blushed red. "I do what you tell me to do," he tried to say, but it came out all jumbled.

Madeline looked at Herbert and thought about the upcoming job. She relied on him to keep her safe while she was in a trance. He used to make her feel safe. Then he started drinking. Now, with the biggest job of her life on the line, she actually feared that Herbert wasn't the man she needed to do the job. If he didn't believe in what she did, or her ability to do the job, he could actually get her hurt or killed. She needed someone she could rely on. She needed someone she could trust. Right now she had no trust in Herbert other than that he would still be drunk tonight.

She needed to call someone who could help her. She had no idea how she was going to break this to Herbert, but she couldn't worry about that right now. She grabbed her purse and headed for the door. She needed to contact someone, but Herbert would never understand. She needed to make this call away from her house.

"Where the hell do you think you're going?" Herbert yelled as he slid off the chair to follow her.

"I need to get some candles and supplies," she called over her shoulder.

"When we gonna do this thing?" he asked, scratching his belly as he stood in the door watching her leave.

"Tomorrow. Maybe the next day," she lied again. She had never lied to him before and she didn't like it, but she had to think of herself first this time.

Madeline slid behind the seat of her yellow VW bug and drove away. She drove to the market and parked on the side of the building that blocked the rain and wind. It was mid-morning, and the rain showed no sign of stopping. She put the car in park and let the heater run. Rain drops dripped down the windshield, catching up to one another as they made their way to the bottom of the windshield, making crazy patterns on the glass.

Out of her purse she pulled a business card book. She fumbled through it while searching for her cell phone inside her purse with her free hand. She knew the phone was in there, she just couldn't feel it. She searched the other side on the bottom. Just as she found her cell phone, she also found the card she had been looking for. After taking a much needed deep breath, she dialed the number. Her stomach knotted at the thought of making this call, but she needed him.

"Paranormal Research Institute, Jennifer speaking. How may I help you?" a research assistant answered the phone.

"Robert Chambers please," she said, the knot growing tighter in her abdomen.

"May I ask who is calling?"

"Madeline. Madeline Zimmerman."

"Please hold and I'll see if he is available," the girl stated politely. A voice came over the phone line explaining the services offered by the Institute.

While she listened, she checked the polish on her nails. She wished her abilities worked in such a way as to give her notice of upcoming events in her life. It would have some been nice if she could have had her nails and hair done. She looked in the rear view mirror with disgust at all the gray roots. She had really let herself go over the past few years.

"Robert Chambers. How can I help you?" a deep voice answered the phone. Madeline melted at the sound of that voice; it was hypnotic.

"Mr. Chambers. I know you're very busy. Thank you for taking the time to speak to me. You probably don't remember me, but I attended one of your seminars a year ago on 'The Science of the Paranormal and Multiple Hauntings," she said. She hated that she always got so nervous in new situations.

"Yes, Ms. Zimmerman, I remember you," he stated.

"Oh. Good, well, I have a situation you might be interested in-," she started to explain.

"Does it involve the Templeton House?" he asked, catching her off guard.

"As a matter of fact, it does."

"Good, I was wondering how long it would take for you to invite me in on this one," he stated. "I thought perhaps you were keeping it all to yourself."

"Well, it just became a situation for me this morning," she stumbled over her words. She had no idea he was that interested in Templeton House.

"Yes, but you were aware of the house and its potential for quite some time," he added.

"Yes, but to tell you the truth, I have tried to steer clear of it myself," she told him.

"You disappoint me. You seemed fascinated by it when I spoke with you last."

"Fascinated, yes," she said, that knot in her stomach was just about to double her over now. "But that old house scares me," she took a chance and told him the truth.

"I bet. It is a formidable opponent."

"You could say that."

"When are you going to invite me down to view this magnificent specimen?"

"Well, that is why I've called. I have been asked to do a séance in the house. Tonight actually," she hesitated.

"So soon?"

"Yes. The woman I told you about is in the hospital. She at-tempted suicide. She's in a coma actually. The daughter has returned home and is staying in the house right now," she started to explain the urgency.

"From what you've told me, that could be very dangerous for the daughter."

"Yes. And she came back with friends. There are about five of them living in the house right now."

"Are they there now?" He seemed concerned.

"They're all at the hospital visiting the mother this morning. I just left them about an hour ago," she told him.

"They should be alerted to the danger of staying in that house."

"They know, but there is nowhere else for them to go right now. Her friends don't seem to believe in any of this stuff. So they are not worried about staying there, yet."

"Do you need help getting them to understand?"

"Well," she hesitated. She really needed him to come with her on this reading. But she knew he was busy and scheduled things well in advance. "Yes." she said.

"Give me the address. I'll have my assistant Google it, and be there in a few hours," he stated, surprising Madeline.

"Uh, great," she looked in her address book for the street address to Templeton House.

"I would like to bring a team with me if you don't mind," he added.

"Uh, well, I'm not sure how they'll feel about that. They seem skittish. Don't get me wrong, the more the merrier for me," Madeline was afraid she had just gotten Claire into something she wasn't ready for. And she was sure Chambers wouldn't agree to come if he couldn't bring his team along.

"How about if I come with you and meet with Claire. I can have my team on standby near the house?" he added quickly. Voices could be heard behind him making lists of items to pack. Madeline's stomach churned.

"Well, like I said, there is no housing down here. All the hotels are booked through the summer. That's why Claire and her friends have to stay at the house. Perhaps you could just meet with me tonight, and we could plan something big for the off season," Madeline tried to keep the meeting informal.

"You and I both know that if you plan to do what you have in mind, there'll be no waiting for later. Things will escalate there. People could get hurt," he pled his case. His deep hypnotic voice drew her in.

"I guess you're right," she nearly whispered.

"Guess, Madeline? Or know?"

"Know," she conceded. This thing was about to get huge. She didn't think she was ready for huge. But it was better to have experienced help at her side in this than her drunken life partner.

"Great. We'll be there in a few short hours. We'll bring the RV we have outfitted for this type of event. You and I can meet with Claire and then we can contact the team to bring the RV over to the house."

"Okay," she gave him the address to the house. She hung up wondering what she was going to do now. There was no way she could go back to the house without Herbert following along when she left that night. Once he learned that she had enlisted outside help, he would be offended and he would be drunk by the time they arrived at the house. She couldn't deal with him right now. But she wasn't sure she could deal with Robert Chambers, either. Listening to him speak at a seminar was one thing. He had been so charming. He was quite another one-on-one. Forceful and bossy.

At best, she had expected some advice from him. She never dreamed he would want to be involved. Or that he would so successfully take over the situation. She was thankful for the help, but overwhelmed by the idea of a team involvement. The most she had ever done with anyone else before was a reading in front of a news reporter doing a piece for the summer edition of the local paper. She wasn't sure she was in Mr. Chambers' league. Suddenly she was embarrassed to do a séance in front of him. Unfortunately, it was too late to change things now. The wheels were in motion. Now she had to do was get Claire and Grace to accept it.

CHAPTER THIRTY FOUR

Robert Chambers stepped out of the huge RV parked at the Harbor Mart. He was even more stunning than she had remembered. She absently fixed her hair as she climbed out of the VW bug to greet him. She hoped her hair didn't smell like hair dye. While she waited for Chambers and his team to arrive she had stopped by the beauty shop and gotten a quick cut and color and had her nails done. Then she went shopping for a new outfit. Even so, she felt that the wind and the rain ruined any improvement she had made with her hair.

"Madeline, how good to see you," he said giving her a warm hug.

"We have to clear the RV with the store owner. There is no RV parking here, but I think you might be able to convince him," Claire told Chambers, leading him toward the store. Chambers had a way of convincing almost anyone into almost anything. Several people stepped out of the RV and ran into the store ahead of them.

Madeline informed old man Jones, the owner of the Harbor Mart, that the RV was going to park temporarily in the lot until they called for it. She did not mention where they would be calling from or why.

Mr. Jones said it was okay as long as the RV was gone by closing time. He wasn't going to have people parking overnight in his lot.

"Let one person and you have to let them all," he told her. "Pretty soon it's an RV park out there." Mr. Jones was set against the RV, but Chambers worked his magic and Jones gave his approval.

Madeline trembled in Chambers presence. She hoped it wasn't noticeable. Add to that the fact that Templeton House literally scared the crap out of her, and she was sure she would not be able to pull off this séance. Driving the VW bug out to the house just before dark, Madeline regretted stopping to speak to Claire this morning. She felt she should have just kept running away. The whole situation embarrassed the hell out of her now.

"Once you make the introduction, let me do the talking," Mr. Chambers said.

Madeline could not believe how forceful he was. It partly put her off and partly excited her. When she had met him over a year ago, he seemed interesting, friendly. The man that sat in her passenger seat now seemed driven. It made her uncomfortable, and she dreaded the idea of introducing him to Claire. She was afraid Claire would refuse to let Chambers inside the house. More so, she wondered how Claire's friends would react. Perhaps they would just cancel the whole thing.

As they drove down Peninsula Road, Mr. Chambers started to cluck. The ticking of his tongue against the roof of his mouth made her uncomfortable. It was embarrassing.

"That must be the house," Chambers cried out as soon as Templeton House came into view. His shout made Madeline jump. "Impressive, impressive," he clucked some more. My God, what have I gotten myself into? She had a sinking feeling her awful night ahead of her had just gotten worse.

She regretted the whole idea, but by that time, she had al-ready reached the house. Claire sat on the porch with Grace and some of her other guests. Madeline could not remember everyone's names except for the charming one, Ethan. She had enjoyed watching Ethan react to the house at breakfast. She could tell he was a non-believer. But depending on how tonight went, who knows what he would believe tomorrow.

CHAPTER THIRTY FIVE

Ethan perked up when he saw the VW bug pull into the driveway. There were two people in the car as expected, the psychic and her helper. It looked like this thing was going to happen after all. Ethan was starting to become very frightened by this house. He wondered how much of his fear was just group hysteria? If everyone else believed it was haunted, perhaps he would start to believe it too, whether it was true or not. He longed for the safety of the city and his usual routine.

Madam Zimmerman stepped out of her VW bug and pulled a huge bag out of the back seat of her car. The man with her stepped out from the passenger side. He was talking to someone on his cell phone. He and Madeline made a mad dash for the porch to get out of the rain.

"I would like you to meet my assistant, Robert Chambers," Madeline seemed to be uncomfortable introducing the man to Claire.

"Nice to meet you," Claire stood and shook the man's hand. She seemed to sum Chambers up in a hand shake.

"Ms. Templeton. I have heard a lot about your house," the man shook Claire's hand roughly. He was clearly excited about being here.

"Not all good I'm sure," Claire took her hand back.

"All good, it's all good. Madeline brought me in on this case because she knows your house is special. What is needed here is beyond the realm of a mere reading. There are things going on here that are more complicated than a normal haunting."

Claire looked shocked to hear him talk about her house like this. He spoke as if he knew the house, but Ethan was pretty sure this was the first time he had ever been here.

"So, you don't usually assist Madeline?" Claire asked, con-fused.

"No. I'm Robert Chambers from the Paranormal Research Institute. Madeline and I met at a seminar on multiple hauntings about a year ago. She told me about your house then. I have been eager to see it ever since."

"I see," Claire seemed taken aback by this.

Grace jumped up from the swing and took control of the situation.

"Pleasure to meet you Mr. Chambers. What exactly do you plan to do today?" Grace got right up in Mr. Chambers personal space. Mr. Chambers did not back up. Instead he leaned in toward Grace. He seemed like a man that enjoyed a challenge.

"To be honest, I have a team of people in town that are eager to come and investigate your house. Multiple hauntings can be dangerous Ms...?"

"Noble. Grace Noble. I am Claire's best friend since child-hood."

"Ms. Noble- Grace- if I may," Mr. Chambers asked. Grace nodded. The man's face lit up. "Grace, multiple hauntings can be very dangerous for the simple fact that you are not dealing with one entity. Like in real life, the more people involved in a situation, the more difficult it can become. Usually a dominant spirit will surface and take control of a séance. Madeline tells me that there may be several dominant spirits in this house. That can be very tricky as the spirits compete for control of the Medium. It can be very dangerous for Ms. Zimmerman if this happens."

Vincent sat in silence taking in what the others were saying. This was all his idea. Ethan expected him to pipe in any time now, but he sat in the wicker chair and just listened and watched.

"Well, if it's that dangerous, perhaps we should cancel the reading for today and get back to you at a later date, when we can all be better prepared."

"Oh, we are prepared, Grace. Like I said, I have a team waiting for the go ahead in town right now. My team has several years of experience dealing with these sorts of things. We are prepared for any situation that might arise. We won't allow any harm to come to our Madeline, I assure you." The man flashed a huge smile at Grace. Ethan could tell he had a charisma about him and was probably used to getting his own way. The problem with that was Grace could usually see through people like him.

"Well, I am not sure that we need a team of experts swarming the house right now, Mr. Chambers. Claire's mother is in the hospital in a coma and things are very difficult," Grace said, dismissing the man and his experts.

"I understand. Perhaps we could take a walk through the house for starters. Then if you feel better about it, I could call in my associates." Mr. Chambers batted puppy dog eyes at her.

"I think not," Grace told him.

"No wait," Claire spoke up, "He came all this way. The least we can do is let him have a look around." Ethan suspected that Claire wanted an expert's opinion about her house. And she seemed to have hope in her eyes. Perhaps she believed he could clear her house.

"Okay then," Grace took a step toward the door. "Let's take a walk." Things were finally starting to get interesting around here instead of just creepy. He thought he just might enjoy this after all.

CHAPTER THIRTY SIX

Quince came down the stairs as a herd of people walked in through the front door. Grace led the way with Madeline Zimmerman and a man that must be her helper following her. Behind them was Ethan, Vincent and Claire pulled up the rear.

"So, we're going through with this after all," Quince stated as he came down the stairs.

"We're discussing it," Grace said. "This is Mr. Chambers. He is from the Institute of Paranormal something or the other," she brushed her hand in the air as if to dismiss him and his institute. Quince smiled. He loved watching Grace when she was on, and right now she was really in her realm.

"Paranormal Research Institute," the man corrected her as he swept across the room and shook Quince's hand. "Robert Chambers at your service. And you are?"

"Quince Johnson, Photographer. You mind if I get some shots of you checking out the house?" Quince asked as he headed toward the stairs again. "I have a camera in my bag upstairs."

"No, not at all, in fact, I was telling your Grace here that I have a team, some associates, in town who would love to come out and have a look at the house as well."

"That would really be up to Claire and Grace. I'm just along for the ride," Quince said, not wanting to interfere with whatever decision the girls had already made. If the man was asking Quince, then he had already asked them and been shot down. Quince was not about to step on their toes. Grace winked at him. Quince rushed up the stairs and grabbed his camera bag. He bounded down the stairs as fast as he could, pulling his camera out of the bag and wrapping the strap around his wrist. He was glad to finally have something to do that he enjoyed.

Madeline seemed to be taking a back seat to this Chamber's guy. Quince thought that was weird since she was the one who was supposed to be doing the séance, and this man was supposed to be her assistant. Something wasn't quite right. Quince was sure Grace would get to the bottom of it all. He took a few shots of Madeline who seemed very nervous.

By the time he had gotten back downstairs, the group had moved on to the dining room. Mr. Chambers walked slowly around the room. He tilted his head as if listening to something the rest of them could not hear.

"Yes, there is a strong presence here. Anger. Fear," Mr. Chambers made a weird clucking sound with his mouth as he walked around the room. Quince watched Grace as she seemed to size him up.

"There are so many spirits here, some very strong ones, some not so strong. Perhaps even more that haven't shown themselves yet. Tell me about the mother, the owner of the house."

"She grew up in this house, married, had me, lost her husband," Claire threw out at him.

"Yes, the husband. Madeline, didn't you say you thought the house had taken him," Chambers said absently. Then embarrassed, he restated his question. "I'm sorry Ms. Templeton. I am just trying to get a feel for the house. No disrespect intended. Madeline seemed to give the impression that your father thought the house had taken him. I believe she discussed this with you earlier today."

"Yes she did," Claire said, not offering any comfort to Mr. Chambers for his poor choice of words.

"And what do you think of that possibility?"

"She just learned today that her father may have been killed by this house or something in it, while her mother lies in a hospital bed in a coma. How can you ask her something like that?" Grace had become agitated.

"I am just trying to get a feel for the house and what Ms. Templeton-Claire, feels about it. That is all," Chambers stood his ground.

"I think it sucks. I already hate this house. It is just one more reason I should not be here," Claire said.

"But your mother doesn't agree with you. Does she know of this?" he asked Madeline.

"No. I have never told her about it, and I'm sure Claire hasn't had a chance to tell her either," Madeline said.

"I see. And how do you think your mother would react to this information if she were told?" Chambers asked Claire.

"I think she would have a meltdown. She has blamed me for killing my father my whole life. Hearing that her beloved house was responsible... I'm sure she would not believe it."

Quince knew Chambers was pumping them for information, and he was getting a lot of it. It would be easy for him to tell them things they would believe just based on what he had heard so far. The guy was sharp. Quince was afraid he might be able to pull the wool over their eyes.

"Enough of this, Mr. Chambers, I thought you were here to tell us what is going on, not for us to tell you," Quince redirected him, snapping off a few more shots.

"Yes, of course," Mr. Chambers continued on to the kitchen. He stopped near the island. He looked left and then right. "There is a woman angry woman. With a clever or a large knife," Chambers tilted his head again as if listening to something.

"She is angry about something, at someone. I'm not quite sure what," Chambers acted like he was trying to tune in some kind of ghost radar.

"Yes the woman with the knife," Claire added. Quince cringed. He wished she would just shut up and make the man work for it instead of spoon feeding him information. Quince longed to be in control of this walk through.

"Enough," Grace said, as if she could read his mind. "Mr. Chambers, we would like to hear your impressions without input from the rest of us. We already have our own ideas about the house. We want to hear your expert opinion," Grace said.

"Oh course, this woman with the knife, she is angry; perhaps at her husband. But there is more. She is angry with Claire, and her mother. Oh yes, she is a dominant spirit this one," he clucked some more. "She is one of the spirits that would be most likely to come through in a séance. She could be a key to the others. But I am not real sure. Something is...off," he rambled.

Madeline also seemed to be listening to whatever Chambers had tapped into, but didn't look too eager to hear it. She seemed to be closed off to the house for someone who was about to open it up to the spirit world. Quince could sense that she was truly afraid of this house and what was in it. Madeline had lived in this town her whole life. She had most likely heard a lot of stories, and believed most of them. Quince didn't put much stock in the psychic thing, but he thought he understood people. Madeline believed there were spirits here. She was afraid of them. She would tell Claire what she wanted to hear and think she was telling her the truth.

Mr. Chambers, on the other hand, was smooth, a real charlatan. He would feel out what he believed the others wanted to hear, than he would feed it back to them as if it were the truth. Quince snapped more photos as he followed them around the house.

CHAPTER THIRTY SEVEN

Quince snapped loads of photographs as the group continued their walk through the house. Grace refused to let Claire speak to Mr. Chambers until he was done with his assessment. She believed in Claire. And Claire believed the house was haunted. But she didn't want Claire feeding this Chambers guy any more information. She didn't trust him. She didn't want Claire to give him valuable information. If he really was an expert at this sort of thing, he should be telling them things, hopefully things they didn't already know, like how to get rid of all these ghosts.

Grace kept mental notes of his observations. So far the man had said nothing that they didn't already know. There were supposedly multiple spirits in the house. Some of them were angry. They were trapped somehow, all the obvious stuff. Grace heard nothing that made her believe this man knew anything more about this house or its occupants then they already knew. She enjoyed watching him put on his act though. He was captivating, a real showman.

As the man wandered throughout the house, Grace warmed up to the idea of meeting his team. She didn't feel threatened by Mr. Chambers and thought it would be an interesting evening to watch these people put on their act. They could all use the distraction and the more people in the house the better.

"Mr. Chambers, why don't you call your team in and let us see what they can come up with," Grace said. If anyone disagreed, she was ready to argue the point. No one said a word. Quince gave her a curious look, but seemed to agree with her. If nothing else, she knew he would enjoy photographing them at work.

"Great. Let me give them a call so we can get this thing started," Chambers directed Madeline to the porch where he called his team and gave them directions to the house. Quince sidled up beside her and whispered in her ear.

"So, we're going to do this?"

"Let's just say it is going to be a long night, and we might as well have some entertainment while we are stuck here," she informed him.

"I agree."

"We should keep Claire away from his team though. Make them come up with their own conclusions," Grace told him.

"He got way too much information out of her already."

"Yeah, and who knows what he already pumped out of Madeline before he got here," Grace said.

"Is it just me or does she seem even more nervous than this morning?"

"Something is up there. Not sure what, though. It could be this Chambers guy is too strong of a personality for her. She is used to being in control. Her boyfriend usually accompanies her at readings. I wonder what happened to him?"

"Maybe they broke up," Quince offered.

"Maybe," Grace watched as Chambers hung up his phone and seemed to be giving Madeline instructions of some sort. Madeline looked very uncomfortable. Grace thought perhaps she should be feeling the same way, but Mr. Chambers just amused her. She didn't feel threatened by him in any way. She hoped she was right.

It didn't take long for the team to arrive. Grace joined the others as they watched the huge forty foot RV pull into the driveway. It didn't stop until it was almost on top of the front porch, parking too close for Grace's comfort. Chambers seemed to sense her unease.

"They just need to hook up to shore power for the equipment. We can run longer jumper cords if you prefer," he tried to reassure her.

"This'll be fine," she said, picking her battles carefully. This was not worth arguing over. She would save her objections for more serious offenses. Grace joined Claire on the porch swing in part to watch the show and in part to keep Claire away from the so called team of experts.

"You okay with this?" Grace asked.

"Sure. If you think it's okay," Claire answered.

"For now, when it gets not to be, I'll toss them out. Okay?"

"Okay," Claire's words were barely audible. Grace patted her leg and watched in amusement as the four young men and a young woman bounded out of the massive RV. Two of them carried equipment, eager to get to work. The others just ran onto the porch to get out of the rain. The two with the equipment headed straight for Chambers. He pointed toward the house, and they seemed to hang on his every word. He noticed Grace and Claire watching him as he gave instructions to his assistants. As she suspected, the man knew how to put on a show.

"This is Bonnie Stevens and Michael Barton," he said walking them across the porch to introduce them to everyone. Vincent shook Bonnies' hand a little longer than usual. She was taller than the rest, with long blond hair. She was wearing cargo pants with wires, tape and pens sticking out of every pocket. Michael looked like a test book geek right down to the plastic glasses, short hair, dressed in tee-shirt and cargo pants like the rest of Chambers crew. Quince just nodded at them from his wicker rocker. Ethan sat on the porch rail and took it all in.

"Do you mind if we go inside and start setting things up?" Chambers asked.

"Go right ahead. Quince will go with you. I think he is enjoying himself with his camera," Grace said. After they went inside, she turned to Vincent. "So, Vincent, was this what you had in mind?" Grace inquired as Chambers took his assistants inside the house to get set up.

"Nope," he said, "Way bigger."

The rest of the team came over and introduced themselves. A short, round kind of a guy with long, dirty blonde hair stepped forward first.

"Hi, I'm Chuck. I run the RV crew. Basically we sit out there and record everything that happens inside. This is Marty. He's my right hand man. He specializes in heat and motion, EMF's and stuff like that," Chuck introduced the blond-haired guy that looked like a surfer, Grace guessed he was about twenty- five too. "This here's Jim. We call him Jimbo. He's our all- around dude. New to the crew, so he gets to be our gofer right now," Chuck said, introducing a slim man that still had a bad case of acne. Everyone was introducing themselves as Chambers stepped outside the door.

"We powered up yet Chuck? Daylight's a wasting," Chambers said. The RV crew scrambled to grab wires and bags out of the side boxes on the RV. Then they rushed inside the house.

"Yup, this is going to be real interesting," Vincent said. Grace couldn't agree more.

CHAPTER THIRTY EIGHT

Madeline watched as Chambers put his students to work setting up their equipment in the dining room. Several cameras were set up to record the séance from various angles.

"This camera is used to detect changes in temperature. Usually if there is a spirit present, the temperature will drop in one area. This camera will pick up that change," Bonnie told them as she set a camera up in the corner of the room. Chambers and Michael set cameras up across from one another.

"These cameras are designed with night vision. They will record everything that goes on during the séance," Chambers explained. "We use more than one camera to see if phenomena are repeated on both cameras, not just one."

Sensors were attached to the table to measure vibrations. "In the old days the table would rise during a séance. We use this to measure movement of the table. Heat and motion detectors will be set up around the room as well."

Since Madeline's phone call to him, Chambers had success-fully taken over her séance. She felt like an outsider at her own gig. Robert told her she was to do the séance as she had planned. He and his team would film and monitor the situation. Her growing fear was that he and his crew would continue to film and monitor the séance whether she was in trouble or not, wanting to capture the drama of the situation and not be concerned for her life. She didn't feel a great sense of comfort from their presence.

They were not a talkative bunch other than their description of various pieces of equipment. It appeared the short, round one, with the dirty blonde hair, was Chuck. He ran the RV crew and didn't spend much time inside the house. Jim was part of his crew. Jim ran the wires into the house. Marty on the other hand, was constantly checking and rechecking his meters and monitors. Marty climbed up onto the dining room table and hung a camera from the chandelier. He checked via walkie- talkie with Chuck in the RV to make sure they got a clear view of all the gadgets placed on the table, as well as every seat at the table.

"Don't worry this camera won't have wires to interfere with your séance. It uses batteries and has its own disc to record."

Madeline was thankful for that. The place was already a maze of wires run across the floor. She set her bag on the dining room table and started to unload her own gear. It was getting late. It would be dark soon. She wanted to get this over with and get out of this house. She wished she could sit out on the front porch with the others and just let Chambers do all the work. Quince brushed past her to get a better shot of Marty adjusting the camera over the table.

"Sorry," he said when he bumped into her.

"Not a problem," she said. She was glad Quince was inside the house with them.

Chambers, on the other hand, she was growing less fond of by the minute. If he could do this thing without her, she thought, he would have seen to it that she was out on the porch with the others. He was a control freak. She regretted contacting him. Then she thought of the alternative. If she had brought Herbert to this house, he probably would have still been hung over from last night. Or worse yet, he could still be drunk. He wouldn't have been sharp. He would have been argumentative and an embarrassment. Madeline just shook her head. She never had it easy. Things never went the way she wanted them to go. She decided she would have to separate Herbert from her professional life. She needed someone she could trust. And she didn't plan on calling on Mr. Chambers again anytime soon either. This was her job, her deal. Even if this particular job scared the crap out of her, it was still her show. Chambers was taking that away from her.

At each corner of the table Madeline placed thick candles. She added her well-worn Bible to the objects placed on the table. Then she pulled out the chair she had chosen for herself, and she thought of the order she wanted for the others to sit. She placed Claire close to her so she could feel Claire's reactions to what she said. She put Grace on the other side of her, so she could get a feel for her reactions as well. She knew that Quince was a skeptic so she needed him to be as far away from the three of them as possible, so she decided to seat Vincent and Ethan on either side of the girls. She wished there were more people for the séance, but then thought about all the extra people that were mingling around in the background. This would have to do. There already was too much going on.

"You almost ready?" She asked Chambers.

"We just have to finish running the wires out to the RV," Chambers said. He seemed to be settling in, realizing he needed her more than she needed him.

"I'll get the others prepared," Madeline told him and headed for the porch. Everyone on the porch sat in silence, watching what was going on at the RV. Wires were being run inside through the screen door while other cords were plugged directly into the RV itself. There was a lot of check and double-check talk from the boys as they set up the RV. Bonnie was the only girl on their team. She came outside from time to time to check on the progress in the RV.

"We are just about ready," Madeline announced. Quince joined her on the porch. He shot a few wide angle photos and then joined the others. As expected, everyone started to fidget. She wasn't sure how many of them had been through this sort of thing before, but she was sure the answer was none. Truth be told, this would be her first time dealing with multiple entities and it scared the crap out of her, too.

"Since this is probably new to most of you, let me give you a run down on what is about to happen," Madeline stated finally in control of the situation. She told them that they would start off with a prayer which raised a few eyebrows. Most people assumed that psychics were non-believers. Then she announced their seating order before they got inside. She wanted to handle any arguments over seating before she got to the table. She needed the group to be cohesive; negative thoughts and feelings were not welcome during a reading.

"Quince, is there a problem?" she inquired.

"Nope. I'm sure you have your reasons," he answered. He seemed to be enjoying himself, snapping away with his camera.

"Good. I need everyone to focus on good thoughts and keep the negative thoughts out of your mind. Even if you don't believe, at least open yourself to the possibility that this will work. I need all of the positive energy we can create," Madeline informed them. "Any questions?"

Ethan raised his hand as if he were in school.

"Yes, Ethan," she asked.

"Can I use the little boys' room before we get started?" He asked timidly.

"Yes. Good idea. We should all use this time to prepare ourselves. We'll get started in about ten minutes."

While everyone took care of potty breaks and got a drink of water, Madeline made sure that Chambers was ready to go.

"We're having technical difficulties with our main camera feed. Chuck is working the bugs out, and we should be ready any minute," Chambers told her. Chambers was sure that Chuck was on top of it and would be ready to go when she was. Madeline decided to use this time to go to the bathroom herself.

After she took care of her business, she stood at the sink and washed her hands. She stared at herself in the mirror. She looked old despite her new hair color, too old to be doing this sort of thing anymore. She thought about just doing readings from her home from now on. Read for the summer tourists and leave the real stuff to younger people like Bonnie and Michael. She took a moment to compose herself before heading downstairs. She touched the wall and spoke to the house.

"What do you have in store for me today?" Her life as medium had been so mundane. Only the fact that this house scared the crap out of her caused her hesitation. This was how she thought all séances were going to be when she was younger, exciting and terrifying all at the same time. Most were dull and she had to make up some drama or the other for the sake of the paying customer. That was part of the reason Herbert had taken to drinking. He was bored to tears.

Before she removed her hand from the wall, she felt an electric shock run through the wall into her hand and up her arm. She got a severe pain in her chest and thought she was about to have a heart attack. It felt like the air was being forced out of her throat, like she was being choked. She couldn't breathe.

"Dear God, not now," she said out loud. Not before she could get this séance out of the way. She wanted answers as much as Claire did. She wanted to help the house find some peace. Most of all, she wanted to get out of this house before she died. She did not want to die here and become part of the ghostly menagerie that was Templeton House. She jerked her hand away from the wall. The pain slowly subsided.

She straightened her top and said a little prayer of her own. She prayed that she be given the guidance of the Divine One and to reveal what He saw fit. She asked the angels Michael and Gabriel for the protection of all those involved.

"Let's get this thing started shall we," She said to the house as she left the bathroom and headed for the stairs.

"Thank you," Madeline heard a very faint whisper all around her.

"Henry, is that you?" she called out. There was no answer. Chills ran down her spine as she raced down the stairs to join the others.

CHAPTER THIRTY NINE

Chambers gave Madeline the thumbs up to start. She called Claire and her friends into the house. Everyone assembled around the dining room table. The candles had been lit and the lights were turned off. A meter was placed on the table to detect EVP's:, electronic voice phenomena, and an EMF that would detect the electromagnetic field in the room. To record all of the activity at the table, a camera had been placed on the chandelier looking directly down onto the table. Madeline sat down last after being sure that everyone was seated in order. Chambers had wanted to wire her for sound, but she had argued against it. Instead, a microphone sat in front of her on the table.

"Place your hand on the hand of the person next to you. Just touch each other, don't hold or grab. The idea is to let energy flow from one person to another," Madeline told everyone in a slow soothing voice. She took a deep breath.

"Father, we pray for your guidance so that we do your will today and not our own. We pray that you protect everyone at the table and around the house. Father, we pray for peace for the Templeton House and for the entities that have not yet moved on. We pray for the release of their tortured souls," Madeline felt Claire twitch as she spoke. The poor girl was trembling already, and they hadn't even gotten started yet. "We ask the Angels Michael and Gabriel to watch over us. Please prevent any evil from entering this room and from doing harm to anyone inside or outside of this house."

A silent prayer was added at the end, so that the others didn't hear. Madeline prayed that Chambers knew what he was doing and that he would be there for her if she needed him. She found herself wishing again that Herbert were here and sober.

Her voice deepened as she settled in to the séance. "We call to the House Templeton, with your many secrets, with your many souls. We ask that one of you come forward and speak with us. We wish you peace and no harm." Madeline spoke with a soft, deep, soothing voice. She could feel Claire's hand tremble in her own. Madeline gave her hand a tiny squeeze to let her know she was okay.

"Any spirit is welcome. We would like to speak to you. We are here to help you," Madeline went on for several minutes. Nothing happened. There was no spirit bombardment that she had feared. No assault by a dominant spirit. Not even a minor spirit seemed to be interested in coming forward tonight. The whole evening was a bomb. Madeline's stomach churned. 'I'm a failure,' she thought. Herbert is right, I can only do card tricks for tourist. When it comes to the real deal, I am a fraud, a fake. I suck.

Madeline caught herself and tried to push all the negative thoughts from her mind. She continued to call upon the spirits. She spoke in her soft, soothing voice even though her insides were wreaking havoc. She started to shake on her own. She needed to focus.

All the calling she did had not enlisted a single spirit from the house. There was the woman with the knife. She knew she could call on her and had expected her to come straight away, but Madeline wasn't sure she could control the old woman. Claire had mentioned a little boy and a sailor to Ethan. He had told her while the others made breakfast this morning about the incident at dinner last night. Madeline thought she could handle a child. Probably even the sailor.

"There is a young one among you, a small boy. Can you hear me? Will you come and speak to us? Claire would like you to come and speak with us," Claire's hand was shaking visibly now. She was sure the vibrations were being picked up on Chambers' meters. She hoped he would realize that it was from fear and not some psychic response.

"Everyone take a deep breath. Hold it. Now release it slowly. Think about the boy. Call to the boy," Madeline instructed the others. Minutes went by and nothing. Then there was a cry that sounded far off. It sounded like a small child, but the boy would not come forward. Madeline tried the sailor. Many minutes past and still the sailor did not come forward either. Madeline started to doubt herself again. Maybe I had only thought I heard a small child cry out. Could they have been wrong about this house? Was this a case of group hysteria? Was the house really void of all spirits? Her self-doubts returned in force. She had bombed. There would be no séance tonight. She decided to call it off, regroup and plan a better attempt when Mr. Chambers and his crew would not be around. Perhaps all his machinery was keeping the ghosts at bay.

Madeline looked forward to stopping. Her nerves were shot. Claire shook so hard the table vibrated. Grace seemed to twitch now too. We could all use some Valium.

"We thank the spirits of the House Templeton for allowing us to come before you. We are here for you if you wish to speak to us at a later date. We mean you no harm and ask that you harm no one in this house," Madeline started her closing prayer.

"Father, we thank you for this opportunity to help these lost souls.

Please watch over those living souls that will remain in the house. Please watch over Elizabeth Templeton and help bring her safely back to us."

Chambers stirred from behind his camera.

"What are you doing?" He yelled. "You can't stop. We don't have anything yet."

Madeline could not believe that he would interfere. She continued closing the séance against his will.

"This is preposterous," Chambers came around to her side of the table to speak in her ear.

"You will keep going until we have something. I don't care if it takes all night. We are not stopping now. Do you hear me?" he was so close to her ear that she felt his lips move.

"No one is coming forward. There is no point in going any further today. Perhaps your cameras have scared the spirits away. Maybe if you turned them off," Madeline whispered back at him.

"Turn them off? Are you out of your mind? Move over. Grab another chair," Chambers said as he pushed her out of her seat, onto the floor, and grabbed Grace and Claire's hands.

"Look here, there will be none of that," Quince jumped up.

"Sit down and shut up. Concentrate," Chambers snarled at him. "I call on the spirits of Templeton House. I call upon the woman with the knife. Come and speak to us. We mean you no harm. Come forward," Chambers went into his soft, soothing voice in an instant. Madeline was amazed that his change in personality could happen so quickly. This man was dangerous, and she vowed never to work with him again.

"To the woman with the knife, we call you. We know you are angry. Tell us what you are angry about."

The rain outside started to pelt the dining room windows. Lightning flashed and thunder shook the house.

Madeline wanted to flee the room, but she could not abandon these people to Chambers' sideshow. He was here because of her. To help the others remain calm, Madeline joined the circle between Ethan and Quince. The boys both seemed relieved that she was still with them.

"Tell us what you are angry about," Chambers called to the old woman.

Calling the woman with the knife was a bad idea. Madeline had avoided it because she knew the old woman was out of control, and that meant she probably couldn't be controlled. Not even the mighty Chambers was a match for her. Madeline was sure of it. If the woman was real, and Madeline believed she was, then Chambers was a bigger fool than she thought.

The temperature of the room dropped a few degrees as the lightning and thunder show continued outside. Madeline wasn't sure if the others had noticed the temperature change. There almost seemed to be a light breeze in the room. The temperature continued to drop a few more degrees. A loud crash occurred behind her. One of the pictures that hung from the wall was flung to the floor at her feet. The glass in the frame shattered, spraying tiny shards of glass into her ankle. Thunder rumbled through the house as if to applaud the chaos.

For a moment, Madeline thought that Michael or Bonnie had thrown the picture to the floor. But she had no idea how they had changed the temperature of the room. Then she realized she did not know what all the equipment they had brought with them was used for. They could have brought in some device that could drop the temperature in the room without anyone knowing. Madeline listened for a hum, or vibration such a machine might make. She heard none.

"Bring your knife for safety if you need it. Come and speak to us," Chambers called out to the old woman. Lightning flashed again, the thunder clapped almost immediately. The storm was directly over the house. "That's about enough," Quince called out. "We don't need any knives being brought-."

"Shut up, you fool. She will come if she feels safe. Her knife makes her feel powerful. It makes her feel strong," Chambers hissed as another picture flew off the wall, more glass shattered across the floor. The temperature dropped again. Madeline shivered. She felt Ethan shiver next to her. This was getting out of hand. She needed to stop this now before someone got hurt.

CHAPTER FORTY

Claire jumped as yet another picture flew off the wall and stuck her in the back of the head before it fell to the floor. She could hear the glass from the picture frame shatter. Part of her wondered if Chambers and his crew had caused this to happen. The chill in the air told her something else was at work here.

"I think we have had enough," Madeline cried from across the table. Claire could hear Madeline push her chair back. She was going to leave the circle. As quick as Madeline rose, she was slammed back down into her chair.

"Sit down you filthy whore," Chambers voice changed slightly, becoming more feminine. "No one said you could leave," he hissed like the old woman. Every cell in Claire's body turned cold the instant she heard the voice. Every muscle in her body tensed. She tried to pull her hand away from Chambers. She wanted to break the circle and end this before something terrible happened. She broke her hand free from his grasp, but he latched onto her wrist and squeezed hard.

"Where do you think you are going you little bitch," Chambers hissed again. His face looked up toward the ceiling, but his words were directed at her. Lightning made a double flash and the house shook on its very foundation.

"I..." Claire looked around the darkened room for support. Chambers had a death grip on Grace as well. Ethan held onto Claire's other hand with a death grip of his own. Quince and Vincent watched the walls for flying debris. Madeline sat awkwardly as if some unseen force were pushing her down into her chair.

"Shut up, you stupid bitch. If you weren't such a candy ass, you could have helped some of these poor wretched souls living in this house a long time ago. They have cried out to you since you were a child. Did you ever listen to them even once? No!" Chambers squeezed her wrist so hard now she thought the bones would snap.

"I..." was all she could get out before a picture came off the wall behind her and struck her on her head again. She tried to grab her head where the pain stung, but neither Chambers nor Ethan would release her. "I am going to kill you, you little slut. I saw you look at my husband. He is mine. He will always be mine. I see the looks you give him. I know," Chambers hissed.

"Father, we pray that you end this séance right now," Madeline called from across the table. "Father, we enlist your aid. We call upon you to send this spirit back to where she came from. Release her and let her be at peace," Madeline's voice trembled.

"You! You couldn't get rid of me before. I'll be damned if you will get rid of me now. It is too late," Chambers hissed at Madeline.

"Release her spirit, Father. Let her soul rest in peace."

"I will kill you all. This is my house. You have invaded my home," Chambers snarled as his body began to tremble. He shook so hard the table moved under them.

"This is my house," the old woman's voice was clear now as she bellowed out those words to be heard above the thunder. Chambers was just a vessel for her anger. The Bible on the table flew and hit Madeline hard in the face. Madeline broke the circle and grabbed her nose as blood ran down her face.

"Holy crap! I'm out of here!" Claire heard Michael say as he fled from his place behind his camera and left the room. The dining room door slammed hard behind him.

"I will call for help," Madeline said, as she was released from whatever had held her down as soon as the boys broke free of the circle. She rushed for the door. The door wouldn't budge. She rushed over to the doorway to the kitchen. She felt the breeze as the door slammed shut in her face. There was another flash of lightning. The house shook as the thunder rolled. Rain poured down outside the window.

"No one is leaving this room tonight. No one is leaving this house. You're all going to join me!" The woman's voice cried out filling the whole room as if it echoed from the very walls themselves.

Chambers hand cut into Claire's wrist. Vincent was on his feet heading for Chambers. Quince took the short cut and bounded onto the table top and grabbed Chambers hand, trying to pull Grace free. A candle fell over and the microphone was knocked aside. Vincent reached for Chambers hand that was holding Claire's wrist in a death grip. Chambers was too strong for the both of them.

"Help me," a faint version of Chambers own voice leaked out. He was struggling against the spirit; he was trying to regain control.

"Ignore him. He is mine now."

"Plea...se- help me," Chambers cried out again. Quince started to shake Chambers hard. When that didn't work he slapped the man hard across the face. Quince raised his hand to slap Chambers again when he went airborne. He was slammed against the wall.

CHAPTER FORTY ONE

Outside in the RV, Chuck watched the monitor in horror. He didn't like what he was seeing. He could not believe things had gotten so out of control in there. The psychic bled from her nose profusely. She banged on the kitchen door and kicked at it, pulling on the door knob to no avail. The tall guy they called Quince was hitting Chambers in the face repeatedly. Pictures had flown off the wall. Michael had fled the room. Chuck had no idea where he went, or if he even made it out of the house. He hadn't come to the RV yet if he had gotten out.

The storm was out of control as well. Chuck had already switched the RV over to generator power; every feed from the house power was dead.

"I know Chambers has a strict policy, but I think perhaps you had better call for the police," Chuck called over his shoulder to Marty who was watching his own monitor in horror. "You with me, dude?"

"Uh, yeah. Right," Marty reached for his cell phone and dialed 911.

"Now you all die," Chambers hissed in the woman's voice on Chucks screen.

The monitor feed went dead.

"Oh crap. Not now," Chuck yelled. He beat on the monitor. That didn't help. Then he checked the wires. The screen was still dead.

"We'd better get in there," he cried out, abandoning his screen and heading for the RV door. "How is that call coming?"

"I don't know if it's a joke or anything, but I am speaking to a Deputy Dogg! Isn't that a cartoon character?"

"It must be interference from the house. Hang up and come on." Chuck called as he bounded out of the RV. Jim sat staring at Marty. He couldn't seem to move. Marty slapped him hard.

"Let's go, dude! The ghost busters are needed inside," Marty called to his co-worker.

Jim stood and followed slowly behind Marty. He seemed to be in a trance of some sort. He moved like a robot. Marty knew he would be useless to them. Chambers and the others needed him. He bounded out the door after Chuck. He couldn't let Chuck take all the credit for busting this ghosts' ass. Marty picked up speed and made it up the porch stairs before the heavier Chuck. He reached for the door handle, but it wouldn't turn. Inside, Michael beat on the glass with a vase. The glass didn't break. The lightning flashed, lighting up the front door window. They both jumped back as if struck by lightning themselves.

"Gnarly dude," Marty said to Chuck. "This is some wicked mojo here." Marty grabbed a chair and struck the window beside the door. The chair bounced back at him. Chuck ran off the porch and back toward the RV.

"Where you going man? I kind of need some help here," Marty called after him. He couldn't hear what Chuck hollered back at him, but he heard the RV possum belly hatch open and he heard tools. Tools would be good. He he tossed the chair back at the window. The chair crashed to the floor and broke into pieces at his feet. The window remained in tack.

CHAPTER FORTY TWO

The hurricane seemed to have reached the harbor again. The hospital took the force of the winds in stride, but the rain and wind worked against the windows in the ward rooms. The alarm for room 318 went off at the nurses' station as the power flickered off. A few seconds later a generator somewhere deep in the belly of the hospital clicked on as vital power was returned.

The three nurses on duty were filling out charts and preparing to make another series of endless rounds. All three hit the floor running when the alarm went off in Elizabeth Templeton's room. Overhead they heard the code being announced on the intercom. The doctor on call would be alerted.

As the nurses entered the room, they found her writhing in the bed. She jumped and twitched all over. The first nurse rushed to her side and tried to hold her steady. As frail as Elizabeth was the nurse was afraid she might break her bones restraining her. She checked the monitors. Elizabeth's heart was beating rapidly. Her blood pressure was 190/175 and rising. Her lips were turning blue.

"She's not getting any air." The other nurse was already checking the oxygen system.

"The oxygen is working; it must be her," the second nurse called out as the doctor burst into the room and started giving orders.

"And call her daughter," he yelled at one of the nurses behind him.

CHAPTER FORTY THREE

The phone started ringing in the living room as Quince picked himself up off the dining room floor. Claire cried out in pain as Chambers squeezed her wrist even harder than before. Grace's eyes were wide with fear, but she didn't move. Madeline kept beating on the kitchen door, trying to get out.

"Try the window!" Claire yelled at Madeline. Even the window wouldn't budge.

Vincent still tried to break Chambers hold on Claire's wrist. Ethan sat dumbstruck, his head shaking from disbelief.

"Forget that. Madeline, get over here, now!" Claire ordered.

"Father, we ask you to take this spirit back to where it came. Release her grip on Grace and on me, Father, we beg you," Claire shouted out. She tried following the example of Made-line's earlier prayer. This seemed to snap Madeline out of flight mode and bring her back to the fight. Madeline went back to her chair beside Ethan. She grabbed Ethan's reluctant hand. He looked toward Claire as she grabbed his other hand.

"Repeat what I say," Madeline told her.

"Father, we pray that you bring peace to this spirit. We pray that you release her from this house," Madeline started and Claire followed.

Chambers entire body shook, slamming Claire's hand down into the table over and over again. The pain was incredible, but she feared this was nothing compared to what could be happening to her right now. There was so much commotion and the phone just kept on ringing. Claire thought the whole world had gone insane. She tried to concentrate.

"Father, we pray that you release this spirit's hold on this house. We pray that you release the doors and stop this rage at once," Madeline said, and Claire repeated.

"Fuck off," called the old woman's voice from Chambers throat, the voice echoing from the walls again.

Claire stared at Chambers in disbelief as a mist appeared from behind him. The mist soon became a human form. At first, she thought it was Quince. Then she noticed the clothing was from another time. The hair long, stringy. She was certain this form was that of a pirate. The pirate stepped up behind Chambers and started to choke him.

"You can't stop me now," cried the old woman's voice through a choke hold.

"Aye, but I will," called another, deeper voice.

Madeline continued her chant, but Claire was unable to speak. She just stared at the pirate. She wasn't sure if he was friend or foe, but she did not get good vibes from his presence. While the pirate was fighting the woman, Claire sensed that he was a stronger spirit and had no good intentions toward the living. Her skin crawled as she watched the spirit pirate squeeze Chamber's throat.

"Not going," the woman's voice broke up through the choke hold.

"Aye, but you are. We have let you wander around far too long 'm afraid. If you don't want to become dust, I suggest you stop carrying on w' des folk," the pirate told her.

"No." she cried out.

"Aye," he insisted. The walls became movie screens as scenes played out with pirates yanking people off their boats and bringing them to this house by their hair. She saw blood strewn on the dining room walls and floors. She heard screams and wailing. Other pirates stepped out of the walls all around them.

"Follow me," Madeline cried out to Claire.

"But the pirates...," Claire called back, confused as to who to help first. The images of pirates kept playing on the walls around her.

"Pirates? What the hell are you talking about?" Madeline yelled above the constant ringing of the phone and Quince and Vincent's attempts to bust the doors down.

"For starters, the one that is choking Chambers," Claire called back to her.

Madeline shook her head and continued her chant. The pirate continued to squeeze the air out of Chambers throat. Chambers released Grace and Claire, than grabbed his chest instead of his throat. He shook violently.

Grace fled to Quince and Vincent's sides. She rubbed her hand where Chambers had been squeezing it.

"Can't you do something?" Grace cried out to Bonnie who was still filming the event.

"I just record. I have no psychic skills," she called to Grace from behind the camera tripod.

"No, but you have human ones," Grace called back to her in disbelief.

"I am forbidden to leave my post no matter what happens, it's company policy," Bonnie called back to Grace.

"Even while your own boss may be dying?" Grace could not believe what she was hearing.

"Let him go!" Claire demanded of the pirate. Her voice deepened, and her eyes almost glowed in the dark. "Release him, both of you! I command it!"

"No!" the woman's voice slowly turned back to Chambers own.

The pirate stopped choking Chambers and stepped back into the mist. Chambers shook for a second or two, his hand still on his heart. His face was turning blue. Quince grabbed the door handle and ripped the door open. He practically fell on his ass as the door opened with ease. Vincent raced to the telephone.

"Hello!" he shouted too loudly as the house suddenly quieted down.

"This is the ICU. Can I speak to Claire Templeton please? This is an emergency," the nurse told him.

"She is a little tied up in an emergency of her own at the moment,"

"Well, her mother is suffering a heart attack and she needs her to get here as soon as possible."

"Honey, we are having a heart attack of our own right now and could really use an ambulance on the double," Vincent told her as sirens blared from the end of the road. "Wow, that was quick," he said, in disbelief, as two police cruisers pulled to a stop beside the RV. Michael opened the door, and Marty and Chuck fell to the floor.

Inside the dining room, Chambers slumped over the table. A terrible odor of feces permeated the room as his bowels let go.

CHAPTER FORTY FOUR

Deputy Dogg stormed the house with his partner Craig Henderson. They each grabbed an arm of the boys that had fallen to the floor. The house was like an ice box.

"I thought you were a cartoon," Marty said in disbelief.

"Yeah, I get that a lot," Dogg said, as he stood the boy up. He tried to make sense of the scene around him. The lights were off. Candles burned on the dining room table. Claire and Grace were in the dining room. A man he had never seen before was slumped over the dining room table.

"What is going on here?" he asked as Henderson turned on the living room lights. The glare of the lights blinded everyone for a second or two.

"Thanks for the cops, lady, but I think we need an ambulance too," Vincent spoke into the phone.

"What?" the nurse asked confused. More sirens wailed in the background as an ambulance pulled into the driveway behind the house.

"Wow, can I have a Ferrari too?" he asked the dumbfounded nurse. She hung up on him.

"I guess not." He placed the phone back into its cradle.

The paramedics rushed through the door and looked con-fused as to at where to begin. Deputy Dogg was standing beside a man slumped over the dining room table. He was checking for a pulse. The paramedics joined him. They took over working on the man, leaving Dogg free to question Claire.

"What the hell happened here?" he asked, surveying the damage. Someone had turned on the dining room lights as well. Broken pictures littered the floor. A torn Bible lay on the floor across the room. Claire trembled uncontrollably. There was a severe bruise on her left wrist which she continuously rubbed.

"Are you okay?" the Deputy stepped close in front of her and whispered so the others would not hear.

"Yes, I think so," she whispered back. Claire glanced at Madeline who had returned from upstairs. There was blood all down the front of her shirt. She had managed to wash the blood off her face and held a paper towel to her nose.

"Are you alright?" Dogg asked Madeline.

"I am now," she nodded even though she shivered from the cold.

The boy named Ethan sat at the table seemingly unable to move. There were so many people who needed to be debriefed or helped. He and Craig couldn't handle this on their own. Dogg needed to step outside and call for back up. This mess was bigger than either of them.

"I have to take care of something. Will you be alright?" he asked Claire checking her wrist.

"Yes, I think so," she repeated. He was afraid she was also in shock.

"Shut that thing off," Dogg called to the woman behind a camera on a tripod. She reached over and turned off the camera. Grace stepped around Madeline and punched the woman behind the camera in the face. Cheers went up all around the room.

Deputy Dogg shook his head and stepped around the paramedics who now had the slumped man on the floor and were performing CPR. He stepped up to Quince and Vincent at the dining room door.

"You guys okay?"

"Getting better," Quince beamed at Grace.

In the living room some guy rambled on about cartoon characters, and Dogg wanted to die. He was in no rush to run off Chief Harris, but he sure couldn't wait to stop being a deputy.

Outside, the driveway was crowded. There was a huge RV pulled up almost onto the porch. Madeline's VW Bug, the rental sedan, two cop cars and an ambulance. Dogg was sure there had never been this many vehicles in this driveway before. He stepped over to his own car and started to call for back up. Then he thought about all the locals and summer residents that kept police scanners of their own. Instead he opted for his cell phone. He dialed Chief Harris' cell number.

"Dogg! What in the hell is going on out there?"

"It's a real mess, Chief."

"I know. I heard the call go out on the radio earlier. I'm pulling onto Peninsula Road right now. What am I walking into?"

"It appears as if there was some kind of a séance going on. There's an RV and some guy I've never seen before. I think he is DOA. Possible heart attack, but I am not sure. There are a bunch of strangers in the house. And cameras, gear."

"Cameras? Gear?"

"Probably came with the RV. Wires are run into the house," Dogg told him as he walked toward the RV. He glanced inside and called out for anyone to come out. There was no response so he climbed inside. Banks of monitors blinked on counters that lined both sides of the RV. A cell phone lay on the floor. He turned to check out the monitors.

"Yeah, there are monitors in here. I can see the dining room," Dogg told Chief Harris. He saw the flash of lights as Harris pulled into the driveway. "Meet me in the RV," he told Harris and then hung up the cell phone.

Harris came up the stairs and surveyed the RV. He made his way around the abandoned chairs to view the monitor Dogg was watching. Inside the house Grace and Claire were huddled around Madeline, all of them trembled. Dogg wondered if it was as much from the event as the chill in the house. The boys that came with Claire sat talking near the girls. They all watched the paramedics working on the man on the floor.

"If this was taped, we need to confiscate them immediately before they conveniently disappear," he told Dogg.

Dogg found the tape banks and pulled the video tapes. He looked around and found a large baggy that must have held some gear that was in use. He put the tapes in the bag and fol-lowed Harris out of the RV. The girl Grace had punched in the face sat on the porch steps holding a paper towel to her bleeding nose. When she saw Chief Harris, she stood up and talked around the paper towel.

"I want to press charges," the girl told the Chief. "Against him, too," she pointed at the Deputy. "He didn't do anything when that girl hit me."

Dogg started to explain, but the Chief held his hand up to silence him.

"We'll get back to you in a few moments, miss," he stepped around her and surveyed the porch. Wicker chairs lay on their sides, cushions were strewn about. He looked at Dogg who scrunched his shoulders. They both walked into the living room. The Chief shook off the cold and approached the boys that must have come with the RV.

"What is your name, son?" he asked the round one.

"Chuck. Chuck Warner, sir," Chuck stood up.

"Who owns the RV outside?" the Chief asked.

"Ah, the institute," Chuck told him. Seeing the blank look on the Chiefs' face he added, "Oh, and Mr. Chambers." Chuck turned and pointed to the man on the dining room floor. Paramedics were putting the man on a stretcher.

"I want the keys to the RV, and no one is to go inside of it until I say so."

"The um, keys are inside the ignition. We keep them there so we don't lose them."

And for quick getaways, Harris thought.

"Who is the girl outside?" he asked.

"That's Bonnie Stevens. She's with us," Chuck stated.

"Okay. I want you all to stay here until one of my deputies has an opportunity to question you."

The boys all nodded, and Chuck sat back down.

The Chief led the way to the dining room. Deputy Henderson was still in there assisting the paramedics.

"What's the verdict?" he asked quietly.

"DOA," his deputy told him as the paramedics covered the man's face with a sheet.

Who is he?" the Chief asked.

"One Robert Chambers, head of the Paranormal Research Institute. He was supposed to be here to investigate paranormal activity in the house. I've been busy giving Davis and Thompson a hand," the deputy stated pointing toward the paramedics, "...so that's all I know so far."

"Okay. Find out more about him and his people," the Chief instructed his deputy.

"It hasn't even been 24 hours," Harris turned and whispered to Dogg, referring to how long Claire had been back in town. Dogg shook his head in agreement. The Chief turned back toward the motley crew behind the dining room table. Harris wasn't even sure where to begin.

"Madeline, are you alright? You're bleeding," Chief Harris approached her first.

"Yes, I think the bleeding has stopped now."

"What happened to you?"

"I guess you could say I was Bible belted," Madeline's answer seemed to break the tension in the room.

Dogg had seen the Bible on the floor. He was going to have to take that into evidence.

"And you, Claire?" Harris asked.

"Better now, Chief," she said as she rubbed her wrist.

"Grace?"

"I'm okay too," she said. Nods from the others said that they were okay as well. Except for the one they called Ethan. He stared off into nowhere.

"Who's bright idea was this?" asked Harris. Everyone pointed at Vincent. "I see. Now, someone care to tell me what the hell happened here?"

CHAPTER FORTY FIVE

Everyone had been taken to the hospital for a once over. Chambers' crew was released first along with Vincent and Quince. Claire refused treatment until she had seen her mother. Chief Harris told her she couldn't see her mother until she have been cleared by a physician. She was alright. Her wrist was sprained. The doctor taped it up and gave her an ice pack. Grace's hand was fractured; it was taped up and iced down. Her other hand was bandaged as well from punching Bonnie. Both girls had finally been released to go check on Claire's mother.

Harris had already called upstairs and knew that her mother was back in her coma. She had been unable to breath earlier and suffered a heart attack. Just like the guy at the house. Only he had died. Harris wasn't one to believe in such things, but he tried to keep an open mind.

That house was dangerous. He told his deputy to seal the house once he had finished photographing it and the Institute people got all their equipment out of the dining room. Chuck had seemed to take control so Harris went to him as their leader. Bonnie still whined about pressing charges until Vincent and Quince said something about suing her for not assisting them in an emergency in which her own boss had died. She countered with some crap about policy, but shut up when Grace gave her the evil eye. Harris looked the other way as if he hadn't seen a thing.

Dogg had gotten anything of use out of the RV with help from Chuck. They had the video tapes, sound bites, and records from various sensors Harris had no idea how to read. He confiscated them anyway in case he needed them and to keep them from appearing on You-tube any time soon.

Ethan Parks was in shock and was still in the emergency room under observation. The doctor thought Ethan could be released later today.

Harris called Herbert despite Madeline begging him not too. Harris knew Herbert liked to drink. And he expected that since Herbert wasn't at the house during the séance, he must have been left out of this deal. He wanted to make sure that Herbert understood there would be no handling of the situation, if Herbert understood his meaning. Herbert agreed that he did, and he seemed genuinely concerned for Madeline. Harris let him see her. The surprised Madeline was greeted by a hug and concern instead of a drunken brawl, at least for now. Harris was afraid of what might happen when she was released to go home. He would keep an eye on that situation as best he could.

Dogg arrived at the hospital, and Harris sent him upstairs to check on Claire and Grace. He also released Vincent and Quince to go upstairs to the ICU waiting room with him.

Now all Chief Harris wanted was a good cup of coffee and a nap. Since a nap was out of the question, he opted for the coffee. He would be up for several more hours sorting this mess out before he could return home and sleep.

The girls and their friends could not be allowed to go back to that house. Harris made several inquiries to find them a place to stay in town. He was waiting for a call back from Marsha Stance. She owned a little cottage outside of town. When she moved to Florida to enjoy the balmy winters, she had boarded up her cottage home. The town folk thought she would rent the house out during the summers, but she was dead set against strangers living in her home. The house stayed vacant. He only hoped she would agree to let them use the house for a short while until the situation resolved itself. His dilemma was in whether to tell her who he planned to stay in the house. Marsha felt towards the Templeton's like most of the other people in town. Once she found out who it was for, she would change her mind for sure. If he didn't tell her who would be staying there, he knew she would hear from her neighbors in a few short hours. That would be awkward. He decided he needed to be upfront with her.

Chambers and his institute were from out of state. Harris called his friend at the FBI to see if he had to get them involved. He was sure he did, and he was right. In a way he felt that was a good thing because they had access to people and equipment he did not. The tapes taken from the house would need to be analyzed by people who knew what they were looking at. The sensor tapes would make no sense to him or any of his people, so he needed the FBI's expert assistance on this case.

Harris also felt he was too close to the case to be objective. This was a small town. He knew everyone except for Chambers' team and the crew of boys that had come up with Claire and Grace. He felt he could not step back far enough to see what might be staring him right in the face. Besides, he was going to have his hands full with the townspeople right now. Everyone in town must know something happened at the Templeton House tonight. The house stood alone on the peninsula and there was more traffic out there tonight then had ever been to that house before. Dogg had been smart to use the cell phone to call him, but Harris was afraid it was too little and too late. When he crossed off the peninsula and came into town toward the hospital, the streets and pier were lined with folks checking out all the excitement at the house. Harris had called a few more of his deputies in to handle crowd control. Problem was, in such a small town, he was running out of officers and still needed a full crew for the morning shift. With the summer season just getting started, Harris knew he would need to put on a few more deputies to handle this situation.

Dogg and Henderson would have to be assigned to this case to assist the FBI. Clearing up this mess would take weeks by itself. Dogg was his best man. Indeed, he had Dogg in mind to take his place if, and when, he ever decided to retire. He didn't plan to leave the force anytime soon, but made sure that Dogg could step into his shoes at any time. In fact, Dogg was on the night shift to take his place at the end of the day. He felt he could trust him and tonight proved him right. Dogg could think on his feet.

Harris put out a few calls to people he knew were interested in the next available deputy positions. It was a small town. He didn't need to go look up their names or numbers from their applications. He placed the calls.

CHAPTER FORTY SIX

Elizabeth had fallen back into her coma. Her monitors beeped consistently. A nurse hovered over her checking tubes and lines nervously.

"Okay, everything looks good. Call me if you need me," the nurse said as she fled the room. News about the event at the house had spread quickly throughout the town. People were already afraid of them, as if they were the cause of Chamber's death.

Grace and Claire stared at the haggard old woman in the bed. Neither seemed to want to talk about what had happened at the house. They were too shaken. After a few minutes, Grace decided that they had to have a plan. She broached the subject.

"I know we aren't supposed to talk in front of your mom. Can we take a walk?" She tugged at Claire's arm lightly with her bandaged hand.

"Yeah."

The two girls walked out of the room. Two chairs were set by the window for doctors and visitors to sit. The girls made their way toward those chairs. They walked slowly, not in a rush to be anywhere. Claire stared at the huge tiles in the hallway as she walked.

"I don't want to go back to that house," Grace said.

"Me neither."

"We can go get our stuff and maybe stay here today. The boys will probably feel better that way. Then we should head back before dark tonight."

"I guess so. I don't know what to do about my mother. She isn't getting any better. The heart attack could have been worse." Claire stared at the tiles on the floor as she walked.

"I know. Maybe Chief Harris can find a place for you to stay while you're here. The boys and I can go back to work. Charlie will understand if you don't come back with us," Grace watched Claire for a reaction. She knew Claire couldn't be left alone, but she and the boys had to return to work. They couldn't all be gone at the same time.

"Maybe," Grace knew Claire would hate the idea of staying with someone in town. It was bad enough to be here in her own house. Staying with the prying eyes of the town folk would not appeal to her. Yet, she was sure she would not stay at that house alone.

She wasn't sure how they were going to get their things out of the house without incident. They would have to wait until day break for sure. But even then she was afraid of how the house might react after the terrible tragedy. Chambers' death could just be the fuel the spirits in the house needed to set them off.

The door to the waiting room buzzed. The girls turned to see Deputy Dogg burst in. He stopped by the nurses' station for a brief second before he headed toward them. Grace allowed a small smile to cross her face to let him know she was glad to see him, even if it meant he might be angry with her.

"Ladies, mind if I join you?" he asked, as he fell into step with them.

"Not at all," Claire grinned. She, too, seemed happy to have Dogg along.

The girls each grabbed a seat at the end of the hallway while Dogg leaned against the wide window frame to face them. Lightning still flickered off in the distance, and the rain still pelted the windows, but for the most part the storm was moving on.

"Your mother seems to be back in her coma."

"Yes." Claire seemed to force a small smile.

"Have you given any thought as to what you are going to do now?"

"I think the boys and I should head home tonight. We need to find Claire a place she can stay other than that house."

"Yeah, about the house, right now it's a crime scene. I can take you back there to get your things, but I doubt the Chief will allow anyone to stay there."

"I can stay here," Claire looked back over her shoulder to-ward the ICU.

"Not sure they allow that, either. Harris is working on finding a vacant house or someplace you can get a room for a few days. There isn't much available in town right now."

"Anything would be better than that house," Claire added. Grace agreed.

"I hate to ask, but I kind of need to know what happened out there last night," Dogg straightened up and pulled a small notebook out of his breast pocket.

"Madeline came by the house yesterday morning. Apparently the boys had talked about having a séance. We thought we might be able to clear the house while her mom was in the hospital. It seemed like a good idea at the time," Grace lied. It never seemed like a good idea. A séance was just their way of doing something besides going crazy in that house.

Dogg just stared at her. He made no comment and no notes in his pad.

"Anyway, Madeline brought this other guy with her. He had some equipment. We thought maybe he was an expert, and could save us all if things got out of hand," Claire added.

"That was my fault. I figured he couldn't hurt anything, and it would be amusing," Grace blushed. "If I had any idea it would have-"

"Don't blame yourself. From what I have heard about this Chambers guy, he was a pretty forceful fellow. And his equipment is impressive."

"Anyway, Madeline started the séance, but it didn't seem to be working. She tried to stop it," Claire said.

"That was when everything got crazy. Chambers threw Madeline out of her seat. He called the ghost of that crazy old woman, and things went to hell in a hurry," Grace said. "Claire and I tried to get away from him, but he wouldn't let go," she told him as she raised her bandaged hand. "Claire got her hand free, but he latched onto her wrist. Quince even tried to stop him." She rubbed her bandage absently.

"We tried to tell him not to call that woman. He wouldn't listen. The old woman took over Chamber's body and started yelling about killing us all. That was when the first pirate came out," Claire told him. Grace stared at her in disbelief. This was all news to her. She had not seen any pirates.

"The first pirate attacked Chambers. He kept telling the old woman to shut up, but she wouldn't listen, so he started to choke her out."

"I never saw any pirates."

"Didn't you at least hear him?" Claire asked, dumbfounded.

"No. I only heard the old woman's voice. I never heard any pirates."

"Didn't you hear the pirate tell the old woman to quit?"

"No. I thought she was talking to Chambers. He kept begging for help." She noticed Dogg's ears perk up at this information. He scribbled something in his notebook.

"He begged for help?"

"Yes. The old woman was out of control, so strong. He tried to get free of her. But she hung on. Then he started to choke like she was forcing the air out of him or something," Grace added.

"That was the pirate. He started to strangle Chambers. I think to shut the old woman up."

"So this pirate killed Chambers?" Dogg pried.

"I don't think so," Claire got quiet for a moment. She stared at her wrapped wrist. Then she looked Dogg right in the face and pushed on. "I believe the pirate ghost let go of her before Chambers had his heart attack. I think he couldn't take all that had happened to him. It was too much for him."

Grace looked at her like she had been in a different room and watched a different scene. She had no idea a ghost could strangle someone. A heart attack she could understand. Someone could be scared to death. But Chambers didn't seem like the type to shy away from a ghost.

"Why do you think the ghost stopped?" Dogg asked.

Claire stared at her bandaged hand not wanting to say anymore.

"Claire jumped in and tried to stop the old woman. Madeline had been struck in the face with the Bible and was bleeding all over herself. Quince tried shaking Chambers, but it wasn't working." Grace told Dogg. He made some notations in his pad.

"So how did it finally stop?"

"It was Claire," Grace said. "She commanded the ghost to let go of Chambers and it did. It was no surprise that she left. Claire scared the crap out of me, too!"

Claire stared at Grace. "I remember taking over the séance, repeating what Madeline had said before. But the ghosts didn't respond. Even when Madeline helped me, there was no change. Then something happened. I became enraged, lost control. I remember screaming at the ghosts. Then they stopped. I believe that was when Chambers had his heart attack." Claire shivered when she stopped speaking. Dogg stared at her as if he had never seen her before. It must have made her nervous because she picked on a loose string on her ace bandage, avoiding his gaze.

"Then you showed up and saved the day," Grace added to break the tension. "Our hero," She grinned. "How did you know we needed you?" Grace asked as she realized Vincent had been on the phone with the hospital and there was no way the hospital could have called for help that fast.

"It's kind of embarrassing," He said. "Perhaps you can see the humor in it. Marty called me from the RV. I forgot and answered the phone 'Deputy Dogg' like an idiot. He told Chuck that he was talking to a cartoon. Chuck thought it was the ghosts playing tricks on them, so he told him to hang up." Dogg blushed.

"Wait. If he hung up, how did you know where to go?" Grace asked.

"Uh," Dogg fumbled, "Templeton House is the only place that is supposed to have ghosts that I am aware of around here. And all the locals know about my name. Even the summer crowd has grown used to it. If the person on the phone didn't know, then it had to be someone new. You and your friends are the only new people on the Harbor that I am aware of. I just figured if the guy didn't know my name, he must be with you."

"Oh," Grace wasn't sure she believed his explanation. Her group had met Dogg the night before. Quince even commented on the name. The blush on Dogg's face made her drop the questioning. She understood how people felt about Templeton House. She didn't need to beat that out of Dogg.

"So what happens now?" Claire asked.

"The house is sealed off again. I'm sure I can get Chief Harris to allow me to cut the tape long enough to get your stuff out of there. But right now it's a crime scene. A man is dead. Until we get an autopsy, we have to rule it suspicious."

"Oh crap, does that mean we all have to stick around?" Grace asked. She could barely wait until evening to head home. The thought of having to stay here terrified her.

"I don't think so. They are rushing the autopsy. Harris insisted. I think he expects you to be leaving this evening. Claire, he probably expects you to stick around because of your mom. Ethan should be released in a few hours. He is pretty whacked out by the whole situation. Did anything in particular happen to him?"

"No. But he was scared to death." Grace thought of Chambers and blushed at her poor choice of words. "I don't think he believed in any of this stuff. This weekend has been a real eye opener for him. He doesn't even watch horror shows. He is more of a chick flick kind of a guy."

"I got that. He should be okay. He might need counseling, but he should be able to leave with the rest of you. Be easy on him. No kidding around at his expense. He really is shook up."

"We're good at taking care of people, Dogg," Grace told him. She would make sure no one messed with Ethan. After tonight she doubted that anyone would be cracking jokes at anyone else's expense for a long time.

"Okay, that's enough for now. I am going to go out and question ..." Dogg consulted his pad for their names. "Vincent and Quince. They are out in the waiting room right now."

"Do you mind if we join you?" Claire asked. She seemed eager to leave the ICU ward.

"I would prefer to speak to them alone. Maybe you should check on your mom. That way we can all go down and check on Ethan together when I'm done." Grace could see he hated to deny Claire anything, but she understood him wanting to hear what the boys had to say without them around. Indeed, she wondered what they would have to say herself. She was sorry she had gotten them into this in the first place.

CHAPTER FORTY SEVEN

C hief Harris looked in on Madeline. Her injuries were minor. She had suffered a broken nose. There would be some bruising in the morning. The nurse was writing up her orders so she could be released.

"That's good news," Chief Harris said to both her and Herbert.

"Yeah, it could have been much worse," Madeline said, thinking of poor Robert Chambers. Things could not possibly have gone more wrong last night. Then Madeline realized she was wrong about that. Things could have been much worse. They all could have died in that house if it hadn't been for Claire. Madeline envied Claire's ability to control the ghost of that crazy old woman.

"Perhaps we should limit the séances for a while. And maybe next time you could give me a heads up first," Harris told her.

"There won't be any more séances for a while," Herbert said. The Chief raised his eyebrow. "It could have been her, you know, that got killed out there."

"He's right, Chief. I'm done with this for a while. Last night was insane. I'm thinking of opening a baked goods shop instead. You know donuts and cakes. There are a lot of birthdays during the summer. And people like Danish for breakfast year round. Besides, Danish doesn't throw Bibles at you."

Harris was relieved to hear this. He didn't want Claire to get a bug up her butt about trying to clear the house again. The Harbor would become crazed for readings now that this incident happened at Templeton House. They would want any excuse to pump Madeline for tidbits of information they could take back to their friends about what had happened last night.

"We could use a good bakery on the Harbor." Harris smiled.

"She didn't say anything about it being good. Have you ever tried her cooking?" Herbert joked. Madeline slapped his arm.

"I bet it'll be great," the Chief said, not wanting Madeline to change her mind.

The nurse came in with Madeline's marching orders. Harris took that moment to excuse himself. He slipped across to the other side of the ER and looked in on Ethan. A psych aide sat with him to observe him and determine if he could be released.

"How's he doing?" Harris asked as he entered the room.

"He's doing better," the nurse said with her mouth, but her eyes said something different. She obviously didn't want to say anything in front of Ethan.

"Ethan, would you mind if I stole your pretty nurse for just a minute?" he asked. Ethan looked straight through Harris. He did not respond at all. Harris signaled the nurse who joined him out in the hallway.

"How is he really?" Harris asked, in a near whisper.

"He has not responded to me since I've been in there. He has no response to pain, cold or heat. He just stares straight ahead of him."

"That can't be good."

"Considering all that supposedly happened in that house tonight it is hard to believe they all are not like this. I've called for Dr. Ponce to evaluate him. His friends want him released so he can go home, but I'm not comfortable with that right now. He needs to respond to pain and to be talking first. And what he says has to make sense. Right now he is locked up in his brain somewhere."

"How do we help him?"

"Find a way to make him feel safe. I'm not sure he even knows he's out of that house yet. What the hell happened out there?"

"We're still trying to get to the bottom of that."

CHAPTER FORTY EIGHT

At day break Deputy Dogg drove Claire and her friends out to the house to collect their things. Behind them in a second squad car, Deputy Henderson had the team from the Institute with him. A third cruiser brought Madeline and Herbert to collect the VW Bug and her gear.

Dogg had no idea where everyone was going to go, but he knew that they had to get everyone out of that house. Ethan was still being held at the hospital. The doctors weren't sure if he could be released today. He had yet to respond to anyone or anything.

The house looked normal as Dogg pulled around to the back. He was afraid the townsfolk might have come out and tried to burn the place down during the night, or at least spray paint the walls outside, maybe vandalize the RV. It looked like no one had shown up. That was a good thing, but it also told Dogg something about the mentality of the people in town. They were petrified of this house, too scared to even react like normal people. It was going to be a long summer.

Everyone disembarked from the cruisers. Dogg cut the police tape on the door and opened the house. Madeline entered the house behind him. She seemed very eager to leave suddenly. Herbert came behind her. He hesitated at the door, than rushed in after her. Dogg could see Chuck giving orders to his team outside as wires were disconnected from the RV. Chief Harris had given Dogg the keys to the RV. He handed them to Chuck as he crossed the yard. Dogg heard the RV fire up outside. It appeared that Chuck was in a hurry to leave as well.

Madeline went into the dining room ahead of Dogg. She grabbed her bag and started to stuff the candles inside the bag. She searched for her Bible on the floor, but it was gone. Before Dogg reached the dining room, Madeline was already on her way out the front door. Herbert left a step behind her.

Chuck brought his team in the house and they started to dismantle their equipment; everyone except Bonnie, who was ordered to stay in the RV for her own safety. Each of them worked quickly and in silence. They rarely made eye contact with anyone.

Grace had her own crew upstairs packing up their luggage. Dogg walked out onto the porch to discover that Claire was still in the driveway looking out toward the sea grass. The rain had finally stopped. He scanned the grass to see what she was looking at. He decided he had better go and get her or she might not come inside.

"Hey, you okay?"

"What? Yeah. Fine. You?"

"See something?" He pointed toward the sea grass.

"No," she spoke almost too quickly.

"Why don't you come in the house? I'll help you pack," he said as he reached for her hand. She snatched her arm away from him and frowned.

"I think I'll be staying for a while," she shocked him.

"Why?" he asked unable to believe she would want to stay in that house ever again.

"Chief Harris said he had no leads on a place for me to stay, and I can't leave just yet. I can spend most of my time at the hospital. There would be little time I would need to actually stay in the house. I can do this."

The Deputy wondered who he was talking to because the Claire Templeton he knew would not enter this house with friends. How was she going to stay at the house by herself? And better yet- why? He searched the beach grass in the direction she had been looking but didn't see anything. Claire saw his gaze searching the sea grass. She grabbed his arm and turned him toward the house.

"We should get inside and help the others. They might not want to be in the house alone," she told him. Who was this woman and why did she suddenly want to stay? He let her lead him toward the house, but his radar stayed tuned in to the sea grass. When he reached the porch, he turned back for another look. He didn't see anything of interest. If there were people in the grass watching the house, Claire needn't worry. Apparently the house could take care of itself.

Claire pulled him inside the house and closed the door.

CHAPTER FORTY NINE

laire hoped Dogg did not see what she had seen in the sea grass outside. This time she was sure she had seen Julian out there watching from the sand dunes. She had caught a glimpse of him as they pulled in. He seemed to flee down the beach, but she recognized his gait. It had to be him this time. She was sure of it.

After all these years, she could not leave without finding out why Julian had abandoned her and their great escape. He had to have a good reason. If he had cheated on her at their graduation party, she was willing to forgive him. Perhaps he didn't come up to the house because he married whomever he had run off with that night. Maybe they had kids. Claire didn't care. She wanted Julian now more than ever. With Grace likely to move in with Quince and leave her alone, she felt she would deal with whatever she had to just to be with Julian again. She even tossed around ideas of sneaking around with him if he was married. That totally was not her way, but for Julian she would do anything.

The idea of staying in this house was insane. If she couldn't do it with her friends here, how did she plan on doing it alone? And what would the house be like now that it had taken another life. It was all too much for her to think about right now. She would do this Grace style, one step at a time. Right now her job was to keep Dogg from finding out what she had been looking at and explaining to the others how she intended to stay in this house alone when she wasn't quite sure herself.

She decided not to tell them.

Vincent and Quince came down the stairs with their bags. Vincent carried Ethan's bag, and Quince carried Grace's.

"Grace is packing for you, Claire, she's right behind me," Quince said as he headed out the door toward the cruiser. Grace came down right behind him. She seemed eager to leave the house too.

"I can take that," Claire said reaching for her bag.

"Don't be silly, I have it," Grace said as she hustled out the door. Dogg gave Claire a strange look when she didn't insist on leaving her luggage in the house, but he looked relieved. Grace went out and put Claire's bag in the police cruiser. Everyone else's gear went in the sedan.

"Do you need me to stick around?" Henderson asked.

"Yeah, not sure what might happen here after last night," Dogg told him. "I have to wait for Chuck and his team," Dogg said. He motioned toward the team behind him dismantling the cameras and other gear.

"I think I'll sit on the porch if you don't mind," Claire told him as she headed out the door after Grace. She left Dogg to watch over the Chambers team.

Out on the porch, she searched the sea grass again. She was certain that Julian had left already, but wanted to make sure he hadn't come back. No one would understand her need to stay for him, especially if he was married.

Claire decided to keep a low profile and go back to the hospital with everyone else. Once her friends headed back to the city, she would tackle the Chief about staying in her own home. She was sure he would fight her on this. If worse came to worse, she would sneak back to the house on her own and watch for Julian from the porch swing. She didn't even need to go back in the house at all.

Chuck did a final walk around and told Dogg he could secure the house. The RV was packed up and ready to go. Everyone said their regrets and good-byes. Chuck told Dogg that the board of directors would be meeting Monday morning to decide the fate of the Institute. He was afraid they might all be out of jobs. He had a doctor's thesis hanging on his work at the Institute and hoped to be able to finish it before they dismantled the place. He wanted to meet with the board and suggest a few good people to take over for Chambers. Since Chambers owned the Institute, everything hinged on the provisions he had written in his will.

Dogg had Henderson move his squad car, so the RV could pull around the loop and leave. Everyone waved at Chuck and his team as they left. Dogg seemed a little bit relieved to see them go. After he resealed the police tape on the front door, he rounded everyone up and they left Templeton House as well.

At the hospital Ethan was being released as long as he agreed to see a therapist in the city as soon as he got home. After a short rest he came around and would not stop talking about what had happened at the house. Chief Harris told Grace he had debriefed Ethan, and they were all free to go. Everyone seemed relieved to be getting out of Butcher Harbor; everyone except for Claire, who stayed at the hospital by her mother's side, at least for now.

CHAPTER FIFTY

Deputy Dogg carried Claire's bags into the hospital and led her upstairs to her mother's room in the ICU. He placed her bag in the corner. She took the chair by her mother's window and stared out at the town, not looking at her mom.

"You okay?"

"Yeah."

"Crazy night." He tried to draw her out.

"Yes, it was."

Dogg called Chief Harris on his cell phone.

"Any word yet on a place for Claire to stay?" He asked the Chief. "I see. Keep me informed. She's in her mother's room for now."

"No luck?" Claire asked almost pleased.

"It's a no go on the places Chief Harris was checking on. We'll keep looking though," Dogg told her. He would love for her to camp out at his place, but felt it improper to suggest the idea to her. He would if it meant she had to go back and stay at that house.

"What is the ruling on my returning to the house?"

"That's out of the question. It's a crime scene right now. Until we finish our investigation, no one can enter without a police officer. If you need anything from the house, let me know and I can take you back there, anytime. Don't hesitate to ask me." He hoped she did not ask to return right now. They all needed a break from that house.

"Will you be alright if I step out for a minute?"

"Sure," she told him. As he reached the door, she added "Hey, Dogg, Thanks, for everything. You have been a real trooper. No pun intended." Her small smile made him feel warm all over. He blushed as he headed for the nurse's station.

"Hey, Dogg," the heavy set nurse said as he approached the desk.

"Hey, Nancy, I was wondering if you can tell me anything about Elizabeth Templeton's condition?"

"Despite her heart attack and loss of air earlier she seems to be back to her original state- a coma. The doctor is not sure yet how the loss of oxygen and the heart attack will affect her once she wakes up. If she wakes up."

"What are her chances?"

"I really shouldn't say, but my guess is she is running out of time to wake up successfully. Based on tonight's events, I wouldn't think she'd have all of her wits about her if she does wake up."

"Thanks. Has anyone shared that with Claire?"

"To be quite honest, Ray, she kind of weird's everyone out. She's not the grieving daughter type. She's hard to read."

"There is a lot between her and her mom that has to be worked out, if they get the chance. Thanks."

"Anytime Deputy," she blushed. The nurse enjoyed the view as Dogg walked back toward Elizabeth's room.

Claire still sat by the window. She watched her mother with a blank expression. It made him sad to know that she and her mother had such a strained relationship. Raymond loved his mother very much. His family meant everything to him.

"Your Mom is still in the coma. She still may come out of this. It might take some time," he lied to her. The lie made Dogg feel sick to his stomach. He never lied before now, but he couldn't bear to make her feel any worse.

"Thanks. I know things are bleak right now. Every hour is a strike against her."

"Miracles happen sometimes."

"My miracle would be waking up to find out I lived in Iowa, on a farm, with both my loving parents at my side." Her statement didn't surprise him.

"Yeah."

Dogg stood at the end of Elizabeth's bed not sure what to do. He wanted to pull up a chair and keep Claire company, but he knew that was beyond his call of duty. The gesture could put her off and that was the last thing that he wanted to do.

"I better get back to work. Henderson is writing up the police report. Who knows what he is likely to report. I better help him out." he said, but he still hesitated.

Claire gave him her small smile again. Her eyes never lit up when she smiled at him like he wished they would. Her eyes lit up for Julian. Dogg wished one day he would see that same light when she smiled at him. But for now he would take any smile directed at him. He said his good-byes and left her as she stared blankly at her mother.

CHAPTER FIFTY ONE

Claire waited until evening to leave the hospital and sneak back to the house. She left her bags there, and walked back to the house along the beach side of the peninsula, away from the road. The last thing she needed was to be seen by anyone, especially Dogg or Harris. Her plan was to catch Julian from the beach, where he couldn't run away, unless he ran into her.

The events at the house played out in her mind. First there was the chilled air. Chuck said they had no equipment that could make the temperature drop. According to him the Institute was an upstanding research facility that only recorded events. They did not create them. Then there were the pirates. No one else seemed to have seen them, not even Madeline. That surprised her. And she worried about Ethan. He chattered non-stop, on his way to the sedan, about the events of last night. She hoped he could pull himself together. She loved Ethan and the rest of her friends, and didn't want anything to happen to them. She was sorry she had gotten them involved in all this in the first place.

As she came off the beach front, toward the house, she saw motion ahead of her. She ducked into the sea grass and watched carefully as a man walked away from the house toward her. The man was tall with long blond hair like a surfer.

"Well hello stranger," she said, as she popped out of the tall grass in front of him. He nearly fell over with fright. "Oh, I'm sorry," Claire said. She felt bad for startling him.

"Claire? Is it really you?"

"In the flesh," she told him.

"I heard about what happened earlier. I was afraid, well, you know," Julian blushed.

"I know. There was just one fatality tonight; a research director from some paranormal institute. He didn't respect the house and what it is capable of. The house doesn't like that."

"Yeah, I remember."

"How have you been?"

"I'm okay. How about you?"

"Okay. Can you sit with me for a while?" she asked him.

"Sure," he said. They found their old spot in the beach grass and sat down.

"I have missed you, dearly," she said.

"I've missed you, too." He sifted beach sand through his fingers while he looked out at the ocean, and not at her.

"Are you with someone?"

"No." he said.

"What happened?" she asked.

"I'd really rather not talk about it right now. Let's just deal with the here and now."

"Okay." It really wasn't, but she didn't seem to have a choice. She was glad just to have him sitting here talking to her.

"How's your mom?"

"She's in a coma," she told him.

"How do you feel about that?"

"I'm sorry she isn't doing well, but I'm still so angry with her. I don't know how to feel right now."

"Sorry to hear that," he finally looked at her. He seemed sad and was so quiet. This wasn't the Julian she knew and loved. The old Julian was playful and happy. She longed for that Julian. She hoped that they could get back the feelings they used to have for one another. She remembered Grace's words again, take things one step at a time.

"How is your Mom?" she asked.

"Same old same old."

"She probably isn't too happy that I'm back on the harbor."

"You could say that," he said, still sifting the sand through his fingertips.

"Sorry."

"Not your fault."

"This house is like a curse. It has ruined all of our lives," she started to cry.

"Don't."

"You staying here in the house?" he asked her, as if to change the subject.

"Not really. I'm not supposed to be at the house right now. But I don't want to stay at the hospital either. I think I'll just stay here on the porch like always. Mix that up with visits to Mom. I almost hate it there as much as I do here."

"Aren't you afraid of the house?"

"Yes and no. Something happened last night during the séance. It was like I had all this rage and it exploded at the spirits in the house. Grace says they went away because I commanded it. I didn't think so. I was just scared shitless. But I did feel stronger somehow towards the end."

"Wow. This is new."

"Yes, it is."

The sun set as they talked. The rhythmic waves, still high from the hurricane that had blown through, crashed on the shore and washed their way toward them, then ran back into the sea as if the sea itself was afraid of Templeton house as well.

CHAPTER FIFTY TWO

Julian left just before midnight. Claire reluctantly headed for the house. The porch window to the dining room had never locked properly. Mother would never have thought to fixed it. She could enter the house through that window. She trembled as she remembered the last time she entered the house at night. This would not be good, but it was worth getting to see Julian again. As she slid the window open, she took a deep breath and prayed that the spirits wouldn't kill her.

Claire slid one foot over the window sill and straddled the jam. She pulled her other foot into the house as she came face to face with the German sailor. Then another ghost was suddenly at her left side. Another appeared to her right. Ghosts started to close in around her. She couldn't breathe. They surrounded her on all sides and all spoke to her at once. Even though they took up no physical space Claire felt crowded. Her muscles contracted as she shrunk herself inward against the assault. She was so terrified she was afraid she might actually pee her pants. She could feel their desperation and sorrow. It choked her. This time instead of screaming, she started to sing "The itsy bitsy spider climbed up the water spout," as loud as she could, to drown them out. Careful not to turn on any lights that could be seen from town she bounded up the stairs and headed to her old bedroom. It was hard to see in the dark, but she used to sneak around the house at night when she was a kid; she knew every step by heart. When she reached the bedroom, she slammed the door behind her. The ghosts floated in through the closed door, the floor and the walls.

"Damn," she cursed, as she tried to ignore their anguished cries, "forgot about that."

She went to her old nightstand and pulled a lighter out of the drawer. Alongside the lighter she felt and found a small candle. The lighter wouldn't light. Claire had to flick it again. She put the flame onto the wick, but the candle wouldn't light.

"Shit."

She wiped the wick between two fingers to remove any dust or debris. On the second try the candle lit, and she headed for her dresser. There were so many ghosts in her room that she had to walk through them as she

140

moved about. The air chilled her to the bone as she passed through them. She tried not to think about it. Their sadness seeped into her veins making her want to cry out as well.

Her clothes were still in the dresser. That meant her mother had taken her stuff, and put it back after she left. This just made her even angrier. There was an old sweater and t-shirt in the drawer. In the bottom drawer she found a pair of gray gym pants. To hell with fashion, she thought; tonight she needed to be comfortable and warm. She blew the candle out and let her eyes adjust to the darkness that surrounded her as thick as the ghosts themselves. The ghosts were still filling the room even in the dark. Their voices filled the air. She kept singing to drown them out.

"And the itsy, bitsy spider climbed up the spout again." With the candle and lighter in hand, she had trouble grabbing the comforter from the bed, but she wrangled it and managed to grab a pillow by its corner. She shoved the clothes inside the pillow case with the pillow and fled the room. The ghosts reached for her, pawing her. Their touch was like icicles that raked against her skin. She pushed the feeling from her mind and concentrated on the song.

Going by memory, she dashed down the stairs and headed into the dining room. She continued to sing the song, trying to ignore their voices, talking over one another. This was like being in a meeting hall when everyone's feathers were ruffled at once. Her skin felt as if she had goose bumps on top of her goose bumps. She shook uncontrollably but refused to let it show.

The window was just a few feet away. She pushed on. When she reached it, she threw her blanket and pillow out onto the porch. Then she dove out the window on top of them. As she flew through the air, the ghost reached for her, grabbing at her ankles, but they were unable to get a hold of her. The impact with the porch was softened by the down comforter and her pillow case full of clothes. She made it! It occurred to her that she should close the window, but her fear of being pulled back inside overrode her need to close the window. They are not coming out of there. Of course, they were doing a lot of things that they had never done before.

In the dark, Claire stripped out of her gypsy attire and put on her sweat pants and tee shirt. The sweat pants were a little short and snug. Luckily, she had always liked her t-shirts big when she was younger. Now, seven years older, the t-shirt still fit her. Next she pulled her bracelets and her necklace off. She tossed them in her purse and pulled the sweater over her head. Once she had changed, she made up a bed under the porch swing. The first night at the house taught her that she had out-grown the swing. Sleeping under the swing, with it so close above her head, made her feel safer somehow, like being in the bottom bunk of a set of bunk beds.

Now that she was out of the house, she could reflect on what had just happened to her. She could feel the anguish and despair slowly dissolving in her veins. Warmth was coming back to her as she snuggled deeper into the comforter. She had expected worse from the house. Not that what she had just endured was a picnic in any way, but she just expected it to be more difficult after Chambers death and the séance. The biggest surprise of all was that the old woman with the knife had not been present. That baffled her. She expected a full on assault from that woman. And the little boy was not anywhere around either. She was confused and concerned. Things kept changing. It was easier when things stayed the same; she knew what to expect then.

The swing moved slowly in the light breeze lulling her to sleep.

CHAPTER FIFTY THREE

Dogg pulled his cruiser into the Shady Lady Restaurant. It had been a long night, and he looked forward to some home cooked food and conversation that did not involve the Templeton House.

The sun would be up soon, and he would be off patrol. He was looking forward to a good day's rest. The night had been full of townsfolk complaining about Templeton House and the freaks that lived there. He wondered how they were going to be able to keep this incident from escalating into a full blown mob, complete with torches, going after Claire and her mother and their house.

The regular crowd was in the restaurant eating breakfast be-fore heading out on their fishing boats, or taking tourist on day trips out to sea. His mother wasn't in the dining room, which meant she was in the kitchen cooking. He walked around the counter and poured himself a cup of coffee. After pouring coffee for a couple at a table near him as well he took a seat at the end of the counter in his usual spot. This was where his mother came and went from the kitchen. It allowed him to talk to her while she worked.

"Well, if it isn't my favorite son," Lila said, as she stepped out of the kitchen, wiping her hands on her apron. Dogg was Lila's only son, but she liked to call him her favorite, it was a game they played and it made her happy. He loved to make his mother happy. With his father now passed away, Dogg was all she had left.

Lila wiped her hands on the apron she almost never took off. It seemed like she lived in it for the past thirty some odd years that Dogg could remember. Her short black hair curled all over her head. Her eyes were huge black orbs that seemed to see inside your soul. Dogg got his height from his father. Lila was barely five feet tall and thin as a rail, but she was scrappy and didn't take shit from anyone.

"Hey Ma, how's your day going?"

"Better than yours from what I hear," she said. "Are you alright?"

"Yeah, just another day on the job."

"God hates liars, Raymond."

"I know, Ma. It just isn't as bad as it must sound."

"The talk is everywhere, and it's ugly. They practically want to lynch Elizabeth and her daughter. I'm worried about you. I don't think the Butcher Harbor Police Department is up to this level of policing."

"We have Federal back up now."

"Won't they take over your case?"

"Not likely. They'll probably assist us with the technical stuff, but there's no big criminal element here, no conspiracy. They'll tire easily of this small town and its tiny situation."

"I don't think you can call this situation tiny. They say a man died out there last night," she whispered.

"I know Ma, I was there remember?" he whispered back. "You know I can't talk to you about work stuff," he told her in his normal voice.

"You don't have to say anything. I heard it all from him." Lila motioned toward the man sitting in the booth by the front window. Two other men sat with him, and had been watching Dogg ever since he walked in the door. He knew what they had on their minds and he didn't care for it. Rory Lynch liked to stir things up and this was just the sort of thing he liked to stir.

"I've got your breakfast on, you want anything else?"

"Just fix me some biscuits and coffee to go. That's all I need today. I'm real busy."

"You're not leaving here until you eat something substantial." She ignored his plea for food to go, and went back into the kitchen.

"Ought to run that city tramp and her mother out of town, far as I see it," Rory spoke too loudly to his friends. Dogg knew when he was being baited.

"Settle down, Rory," Dogg called with his back still to the man.

"Shame the damn police department is so chicken shit they can't handle a frail old lady and her freaking kid," Rory snickered to his friends. The other men laughed, but didn't jump into the conversation. These men were Rory's boat crew. He led and they followed.

"Police Department's doing just fine. As for the frail old lady, have some respect for your elders, Rory."

"Gonna kill the tourist trade this year. Folks already pulling out," Rory sniffed, as he watched yet another rental car, loaded down with gear, drive down Main Street. Dogg knew he was right. He had seen several people leave already, and heard of a few more packing up today. Dogg knew that even a small loss of revenue would hurt this tiny beach town.

"We'll be fine. We always are," he lied. It seemed he was doing this a lot lately.

"We don't always have witches having ceremonies and getting themselves kilt either," Rory said, as he slammed his coffee cup down. His action had the desired effect; everyone was paying attention to him now.

"There are no witches. It was just a normal reading. No big deal," Dogg regretted his words as soon as they left his mouth.

"You call a dead man no big deal?" Rory snapped. "Ain't nothing ordinary 'bout that house, or them people. Even their own runt left soon as she could. Now she's back'n all hells broke loose. People gonna get hurt again. It's already started."

Dogg knew part of what Rory said was true. Claire was back and trouble had already started. Just stirring up the townsfolk could incite a riot on any long, hot night this summer. Graduation was just a week away. Folks would get antsy from the growing heat, and boredom, and look for a fight. Who better to take all that pent up energy out on than a frail Elizabeth and her daughter? This was the one aspect of small towns Dogg didn't like.

"We gonna have to take care of this one ourselves, Deputy?" Rory challenged him.

"I think Harris and the boys have it under control."

"Maybe them FBI folks could wrap this one up for you."

Dogg ignored his comment. From the kitchen came the great smell of bacon, hash browns, and eggs making his stomach growl. His mother burst through the door with a hot plate and headed for him. He took a deep breath, inhaling the good scent of fresh cooked breakfast. He dove into the hot food, hoping to end his conversation with Rory. His mother refilled the salt and pepper shakers. He knew she did this just so she could watch him eat. Even though he was all grown up now she still had the mother need to be sure he ate all his food.

"A few boys are already talking, Dogg." Rory continued his rant.

"You better not be one of them. I don't think you want to be locked up in a cell if a mob does get started. You'd miss all the fun," Dogg was getting too close to the case to be objective. He was losing his temper and wanted to walk across the restaurant and knock Rory's lights out. His mother shot him a stern look, and then flashed him a bright smile. Her smile calmed him and he went back to eating.

"That ain't gonna happen. I'll be the first one to get my gun, Deputy," Rory warned him.

"Yup. That's why you'd be locked up in jail, while your bud-dies wander around wondering what to do next. Townsfolk haven't solved the Templeton problem after all these years. They aren't about to solve it tonight."

"We'll see about that, Dogg," Rory emphasized the word Dogg as he and his table mates got up, threw a few bills on the table and walked slowly toward the door, staring Dogg down as they left. Dogg regretted letting Rory get to him. He made a point to deal with Rory again later, when he was calmer. Maybe Rory would get drunk again tonight, like most nights, and Dogg could throw him in jail long enough for things to cool off a bit.

He really wished all this had happened during the off season.

"You going to be alright?" his mother asked, as she refilled his coffee cup.

"Yeah," he lied, for the third time today. For some reason, Claire Templeton had him all turned around.

"I'm worried Ray. I hear things. And that young girl...what was she thinking? A séance... with outsiders? A death? All while her mother, God help her, is in the hospital. Shouldn't she be with her mother and not at that house stirring things up?"

"That young girl is just trying to survive in a crazy world she never asked for, Ma. She's not like Elizabeth. All she wants is out. That's why she left in the first place."

"Yeah, but people don't like that either. She wants to be away from here as if we're the bad guys." His mom poured more coffee then placed the coffee pot back on the warmer.

"It's not us she wants to escape. It's that house, and every-thing about it. Also the looks and whispers she gets behind her back all the time. Claire needs our support right now Ma, not our condemnation." He looked at his plate and not his mother. He never raised his voice to his mother before and this felt like it, even though his voice was even and calm. He didn't like it, but he felt the need to stand up for Claire.

"People get what they give."

"People should be a little nicer and give the poor girl a chance."

"Wake up, Raymond. You know that will never happen. Not in this town. Not after everything that has happened."

Dogg knew she was right. He was glad she didn't know how close he was to the situation. How close he wanted to be to the situation. He wanted to take Claire in his arms and protect her from all harm. Somehow he didn't think his mother would ever understand that.

CHAPTER FIFTY FOUR

Her mother chased her through the house. She ran into the kitchen to get away from her. The ghost of her father came out of the kitchen wall. He caught her and held her there while her mother charged her with a knife that looked just like the old woman's. Ethan sat in the corner of the kitchen island, crying. Grace tried to soothe him. Claire cried out to her for help, but Grace was too busy tending to Ethan and was unable to help her.

Her mother raised the knife and stabbed her just below her ribcage. Blood ran down her top, onto the floor, where it puddled up. She fought against her father, but could not break free of his hold while her mother stabbed her again.

Suddenly she was staring up at the bottom of the porch swing. A hand shook her. Her heart raced. Confused, the breath knocked out of her from shear panic, she was rigid, unable to move.

"Hey, it's just me," Dogg said. He knelt beside her, still in his uniform.

"What the...?" Claire tried to wrap her brain around the fact that she was awake and okay. She felt her side for blood or a stab wound. There was none. Relief finally started to sink in. Her knight in shining armor had come to her rescue. Then she remembered she was not supposed to be at the house; it was a crime scene. She realized that it was more likely that her knight was about to arrest her.

"I was afraid I might find you here," he told her, as he brushed the hair out of her face. She was wrapped up in her comforter and could not seem to escape. Dogg helped her get free and stand up. She tried to shake the sleep off.

"What are you doing here?" she asked, as she took a seat on the porch swing.

"I could ask you the same thing." He gave her a disappointed look.

"I...see..." she didn't know what to say to him. "Well, I really hate hospitals and I couldn't get to sleep. So, I came back here." Would he find that excuse as lame as it sounded to her?

"Back to a house that you probably hate more than hospitals?" He gave her a stern look that reminded her of how her father looked at her after she ate all the cookies in the cookie jar, and then tried to say she didn't.

"Is that coffee?" she asked, taking a huge sniff of air.

"Yes. And biscuits."

"For me?" she was surprised to see Dogg, and even more surprised that he had brought food.

"Since you aren't supposed to be in the house," he motioned toward the open window, "I thought you might need something to eat."

"I needed a blanket." She blushed. "I didn't touch anything downstairs," she hoped that would suffice and my finger prints are already all over the house".

"You know if Chief Harris gets wind of this we'll both be in hot water."

"So, I can stay?"

"Yes. As long as you stay out of the house," he closed the window as he spoke. "But I still don't understand why you would want to."

"As sad as it may sound, it is home," she said around her biscuit. Until she had smelled the coffee, she had no idea how hungry she was. "Man, I am starving. Thanks," she smiled at him as she chewed.

"You can have the other biscuit, too. Mom made sure I had a full plate of food before I was allowed to leave the restaurant." He took a seat beside her on the swing.

"I knew this was your Mom's. I love the cinnamon in the coffee. I forgot how good it was."

"I'm addicted to it myself. She credits my good health to all these years drinking her coffee."

Claire smiled. It must be nice to have a family that takes care of you.

"What is your plan? You going to sleep on the porch the entire time you're here?"

"Works for me. I spent most of my life on this porch. It's my safety zone."

"Ah," he pushed the swing gently with his foot while Claire ate her second biscuit and sipped her coffee. The sun was up and a cool breeze blew across the porch. The sea was still a little rough, but it was calming down some.

"By the way, nice duds," Dogg said, referring to her sweat pants and t-shirt.

"You like it?" she asked.

"Not really. The whole gypsy thing kind of suits you better. Drab does not become you."

"Thanks a lot."

"Just being honest."

"Well, this is it for now." My bags are at the hospital. I'll have to change later."

"Speaking of hospitals, do you want a ride over there this morning?"

"Nah, I have to take care of a few things."

"Care to share?" he asked, as he continued to rock the swing.

"Nothing interesting."

"Don't touch anything in the house. The FBI will be here later today to run through it. They won't release the house until they see it, and photograph it."

"I kind of expected that."

"News about the séance and Chamber's death have spread quickly around town. Old man Rory was mouthing off about it at the restaurant this morning. It'll be hard to settle him down. After being cooped up during the storm, people are restless and need something to talk about. He'll stir the pot until it boils over. You know how he is."

"All too well."

"I've got to get home and grab some shut eye. I go on day shift tomorrow until this whole séance thing is cleared up. Stay out of the house, and don't be here when the FBI shows up."

"Am I in trouble?"

"No. It's just standard procedure."

There isn't anything standard about what happens at Templeton House. It was bad enough when what happened out here was her own business; now the whole town was involved. She wondered how she was going to deal with them this time-all alone. All of her old defenses went up like jail house doors slamming shut. She could hear them echo.

CHAPTER FIFTY FIVE

Claire stored her blankets inside the chest on the porch when Dogg left. It was used to store outdoor seat cushions during storms. Her mother never came outside anymore, so there were no cushions to store. Spider webs grew along the inside walls of the chest. Claire brushed them away before placing her blankets inside. It would have been better to take them inside the house, but Dogg had been adamant about her staying out of the house. She would never have thought she would ever need a cop to tell her that. Besides, with the blankets out here she had no reason to go back in there.

Claire could have gotten a ride to the hospital with Dogg, but she wanted to stretch her legs. Besides, she might run into Julian again. That would be a good thing. Talking to him last night had been just like old times. Nothing seemed to have changed, except that Julian would not talk about why he had stayed behind. He said he had not married anyone, and was not dating so there was hope. Even though the house upset her, she was bubbling with excitement over meeting him again. Once she had spent a responsible amount of time at the hospital, she would return here again tonight and look for him.

The walk to the hospital did nothing to help her wake up. The talk with Julian lasted almost until morning. Then she had had the nightmare about her mother with a knife. Dogg had come by with coffee and biscuits. Now all she wanted to do was to lie down in a nice comfy bed and go to sleep for a very long time. She would have to settle for a hospital chair when she got there. That idea did not appeal to her.

Butcher Harbor was a very small town, but today it seemed to grow larger in front of her. Each step beat her down, and made her want to just lie down in the sand and sleep right where she was. Claire pushed herself onward toward town. When she crossed Peninsula Road and got onto Main Street, she became aware of people watching her. She put her head down to avoid meeting their gaze, and trudged on toward the hospital. She knew they were talking about her. She could feel their hurtful words bombarding her just like the ghosts.

In front of the florist, she almost ran head-long into Julian's mother,

Caroline Laws. Claire managed to sidestepped her at the last minute. Caroline would not like the fact that she had returned to Butcher Harbor and would absolutely hate it if she found out Claire was seeing her son again, even if they were just talking.

"You smell that? Something dead and rotten," Caroline said to the woman beside her.

Claire wished she had taken that ride to the hospital after all.

CHAPTER FIFTY SIX

Chief Harris arrived back at the hospital in the afternoon. He needed to make sure Claire was alright. None of the people he had tried were able to help him find her a place to stay. The hospital had agreed to let her stay there with her mother for now. He knew she was terrified of the house, so at least she would not go back there.

When he entered Elizabeth's hospital room, he found Claire curled up in a chair, sound asleep. The nurse was exchanging Elizabeth's IV bag.

"Has she been in that chair all night?" Harris asked. She looked uncomfortable, and he knew she wouldn't get much rest there. He was glad to see she had spent the night at the hospital, and not back at that house.

"I couldn't tell you. I just came on," the nurse told him.

"Can she sleep in the other bed?"

"It's against hospital policy."

"Can't you make an exception under the circumstances?"

"Nope. I don't have the authority to do that. I can check and see if we have one of those chairs that folds out into a bed. If they aren't all being used," she told him as she finished hanging the bag.

"That would be great. And can we get a blanket too? It's kind of cold in here," the Chief asked as the nurse left the room.

The cold hospital air reminded him of how cold it had been when he had entered Templeton House the night before. He expected to see icicles hanging off everyone's noses. Chuck said his crew had no way to make the air cold inside the house. He explained equipment like that would make too much noise and be noticeable to everyone, not that they would have considered using it. The tapes from the RV showed the temperature in the house dropped at least thirty degrees by the end of the séance, leaving the temperature in the house a cool 42 degrees by the time he showed up.

The FBI agents had already arrived and were entrenched in his office, going over video tapes and sensor readings. Harris had stayed for the first viewing, but grew tired of the constant replaying of the tapes. They were looking for signs of foul play from the living. Harris was sure they wouldn't find any. He wasn't one to believe in ghosts, but he had grown up in Butcher Harbor and had heard all the stories about that house. He believed there was something evil there, something not of the living world.

The nurse brought in a warmed blanket and handed it to the Chief. He unfolded it and placed it gently over Claire. She snuggled into it. He felt sorry for her. Here she had left her world of high fashion where she was making a name for herself in the world and came back here to ghosts, séances and townspeople who could have lived their whole lives without seeing her again.

Caroline Laws was one of them. He reminded himself to stop by and speak to her before he went home tonight. He didn't need Caroline starting a lynch mob of her own. She had never wanted Claire to date Julian and after all that had happened, he was sure she would be the first one in line to start trouble.

CHAPTER FIFTY SEVEN

Claire awoke to find herself wrapped in a hospital blanket. There was no one in the room but her mother, but she thought a nurse must have brought it while she was sleeping. She glanced at the clock over the door and realized she had slept most of the day away. Soon she would be able to leave the hospital and head back to the beach. She hoped that Julian hadn't been there looking for her and left already.

A heavy set nurse came into the room. Her name was Nancy. She checked her mother's IV bag, her pulse and the wires attached to the many machines that monitored her mother's condition.

"Someone ordered you a lunch tray. It will be here shortly," the nurse told her.

"Thanks," Claire said as she stood to stretch.

"You can use the shower if you like," the nurse motioned toward the bathroom by the door.

"That would be nice," Claire said. She hadn't bathed since she had gotten into town. All she had allowed herself was a quick wipe down with a wash rag at the house. She didn't want to spend any more time in there then she had to.

"There are some towels on the rack. I will see that more are left for you tomorrow."

"Thanks."

Claire stripped off her sweats and t-shirt in the bathroom. She wanted to get to the house as soon as she could so she showered quickly. There was no shampoo in the shower so she used the bath soap to wash out her hair. The bath soap would make her hair dull and lifeless, but at least it would be clean. She took the hair brush from her purse and brushed her tangled hair as best she could. She set the brush down on the sink and got dressed.

By the time she had dressed and gone back to her chair, she found her lunch was waiting for her. The bland chicken sandwich and bowl of fruit salad were eaten quickly. The tiny juice just made her thirsty. She considered filling her cup with ice water from the pitcher by her mother's bedside table, but after the last episode with the ice water and her mother she decided against it. She settled for tap water from the bathroom sink.

It made her nervous to be in her mother's room, but she knew she would have to get used to it. No one would understand if she stayed away from the hospital altogether. They would understand even less if they knew she was spending time back at her house, a house that was haunted and where a man had just passed away.

CHAPTER FIFTY EIGHT

Agents from the FBI still camped out in Chief Harris' office. Harris had taken up residence at Dogg's desk. He had given Dogg the night off so he would be ready for the day shift tomorrow. Harris was very pleased with one of his new deputies, and was considering replacing Dogg on night shift with him. Then he could keep Dogg on day shift with him full time as an investigator. There was an investigators seminar coming up. Harris leafed through the brochure while he contemplated sending Dogg to it.

"The natives are restless again," a deputy told him.

"Who is it this time?" he asked, over the brochure.

"Caroline Laws wants to speak to the FBI agents."

"Great. I'll take it." He threw the brochure down on the desk and reached for the phone, looking questioningly at the deputy.

"Line two."

Harris prepared himself for the call, and pressed line two.

"Caroline. How are you?" he said in his most pleasant voice.

"Not well, Chief. That little witch is walking around town like she owns the place. She almost ran me off the sidewalk into oncoming traffic this morning."

"I'm sure you are mistaken, Caroline. Claire was at the hospital all night. I saw her there myself."

"Oh, so it was my imagination that the dirty little tramp al-most knocked me down in front of the Florist?"

"Perhaps you have mistaken someone else for her. That's all I'm saying."

"You think I have nothing better to do with my time then call you and make false accusations?"

"I'm just saying she was at the hospital all night Caroline."

"I see. Well, I have witnesses that saw her practically plow me down."

"Even if she was out on the street, that still is not a crime in this town."

"So we can just walk around town knocking people over whenever we want?"

"Say it was her...What would you like me to do? Arrest her for not paying attention while walking. The poor girl has a lot on her mind right now."

"Yeah, and we all have to suffer for it as usual. She is bad news Chief. If I were you I would get her on the next bus back to the big city where she belongs."

"Well, we can't do that as long as her mother is still in the hospital, now can we?"

"If you don't do something about that girl, I will."

"Is that a threat?"

"It's a promise."

"We have enough vigilante wannabes in town right now Caroline. You're not helping the situation any."

"From what I see, neither are you. That family is going to get away with murder again on your watch, Chief."

"The FBI is here to determine the cause of death at the house, Caroline. They are in charge of the investigation. No locals will be deciding what happened out at that house the other night."

"Good, then I want to speak to an agent."

"I'm sorry, Caroline. I did not realize that you were at the house the other night, and are a witness to what occurred."

"I... Well... Look here, Chief Harris. Your little tricks aren't going to work on me. That girl has a past, and these agents need to know about it."

"The agents are well aware of the Templeton's and their past. It is all part of the investigation."

"I promise you if something isn't done about that house and this family, you won't be the Chief for very longer."

"Thank you for taking the time to call. I have to get back to work now," he told her as he hung up the phone. He knew from the past that he could go around-and-around with her all day long and get nowhere. Caroline Laws was an unhappy woman who liked to blame the world for all her misery. Unfortunately, she had the ear of most of the people in town. He knew he would have to deal with her soon enough. Between her and Rory Lynch he was going to have his hands full.

The FBI agents cracked the door to his office and motioned for him to come inside. He entered his office and took the seat closest to the door. The Agent in Charge, Clifford Moss, who sat behind his desk, reached across and handed him a brief.

"They expect the autopsy report to come back as a heart at-tack. No foul play suspected," he let Harris look over the report they intended to file before he continued. "The video shows no foul play that we can find. Apparently, the beating he took in the face from one Quince Johnson was not sufficient to cause his heart attack or his death. Under the circumstances, no charges will be pressed against Mr. Johnson. It looks like an unfortunate incident without criminal intent."

He was relieved to hear this. Perhaps the whole thing would just blow over now.

"Mr. Chambers, on the other hand, seems to have been involved in some possible fraud cases, so we'll be taking a good look at his Institute and his people. Seems he created some spirit activity to get his Institute off the ground. Two more incidents occurred after that, before he appears to get involved in legitimate investigations. No charges were ever brought against him, but there was suspicion and reports were made. We are going to go up there next and check them out."

"I see. So you're done here?"

"Not yet. We still have agents checking out the house. We expect to get a clean report. None of the tapes suggest foul play from anyone at the house. There has been nothing on the tapes to suggest Chambers tampered with anything at the house. But there was a lot going on there. He could have placed those people in jeopardy if he created any of those antics that went on out there. Given his history, we have to consider the possibility; the locked doors, the temperature drop, pictures flying off the walls. It could have all been staged by his people."

"You think he might have created all that?" Harris pointed to the video monitor in the corner still looping over the incident.

"I can't really say until I hear from my agents at the house."

"Even if he did create the scene, the man is dead; you won't be able to prosecute him."

"No, but we can shut down the Institute. Prevent his people from scamming others."

"What would have been the point in scamming the Temple-ton's? They have no money. No assets other than the house. What could he possibly have gained?"

"Mr. Chambers could have been after the house itself. His Institute could have wanted to use the house to entertain tourists and promote his business," Special Agent Lafferty said from his seat by the video player.

"Have you been out to the house, SA Lafferty?"

"No, I have not. I have been deciphering these tapes all day."

"I see. Well, nothing about Templeton House screams bed and breakfast. The shingles are gray and ugly. The interior is bleak. And as far as interest by tourists, even the summer visitors steer clear of that house. No one even plays pranks out there or paints graffiti' all over it like people do with alleged haunted houses. No one goes out there."

"What are you saying, Chief Harris?"

"That no one in their right mind would pay to stay in that house."

"That might be true now. But a little bit of restoration goes a long way. And Mr. Chambers seems to have a great PR team at his disposal. You would be surprised what people would pay to see. And if Chambers did rig the house, he could rig it for tourists as well. Meanwhile he drums up business for his Institute. It all makes sense," Lafferty insisted.

Not if you knew that house, Harris thought. This was no run of the mill haunted house. There were things going on out there that not even he could explain. The townspeople had tried to remove that house for centuries and gotten nowhere. People disappeared there. Entire families fled in the middle of the night, leaving everything they owned behind. The ones that didn't get out may have become ghosts themselves. Harris didn't think the FBI had a good understanding about the past history of Templeton House. As far as he was concerned, it was not the past, but the future of the house he was interested in.

CHAPTER FIFTY NINE

The three-man FBI team lead by Special Agent Trevor Morris entered the house after checking the grounds. There were no signs of tampering on the exterior of the house and the agents looked forward to getting inside where something exciting might be found. Morris cut the yellow police tape, and the agents entered the house carrying black bags full of instruments and cameras.

Trevor motioned for SA Clark and Masters to spread out. Their first job was to clear the house, then investigate the dining room. Masters and Clark headed upstairs, guns drawn. Morris handled the downstairs search himself.

Masters and Clark cleared the mother's bedroom. They noted the giant cross over the bed and the crosses throughout the room. Each of them hung upside down.

"Maybe some kind of cult or demon worshipers," Masters told Clark.

"It could be. Did you see the girl in the video? She was wearing gypsy garb," Clark called back as he swept the room. He opened the closet door and checked under the bed. There was no one present. Nothing was out of the ordinary except for the upside down crosses.

"Clear," Clark called out loud as he moved to join Masters in the hall. The closet door behind him swung open. Both he and Masters trained their guns on the door and yelled 'Freeze' simultaneously. Clark back tracked to the door and threw it wide open with his left hand, his right hand pointing the gun into the closet. He moved the clothing on hangers to the side. He searched the closet ceiling and the floor. There was no one there. He and Masters had a good laugh and walked out of the mother's room into the hall after securing the closet door, again.

Masters moved inside the daughter's room. This time Clark stayed in the hall, his gun trained on the opposite side of the room. Masters found more upside down crosses. He cleared the room, taking extra precautions with the closet door. He wasn't going to make the same mistake Clark had just made. Once the closet door was secured, he turned to leave the room. There was a loud cracking sound. He spun around, leading with his gun. Clark entered the room and backed up to Masters.

"What the hell was that?" he asked, as he waved his gun from side to side.

"Hell if I know," Masters scanned the room not sure where to look. There was no one under the bed. The closet was cleared and secured. Then he saw it. The mirror over the dresser was cracked from the left side bottom to the right side top. The crack ran right up under a photograph of an old man. Morris moved toward the mirror. Clark covered the door.

"This wasn't cracked before," he said.

"Nope."

Masters looked behind the mirror for wires or anything that could have been triggered to make the mirror break. He didn't find anything. He felt around the mirror itself and still didn't find anything unusual.

"How's it going up there?" Trevor called from downstairs, startling both of them.

"Almost finished," Clark called downstairs.

Morris continued to look over the mirror. We are seasoned agents, grown men, trained investigators with years of experience chasing all sorts of bad men and woman, yet here we are shaking in our shoes over a cracked mirror and an opened closet door. This house was getting to him, but he couldn't explain why. It was his job to find out the whys and he was determined to do it.

Once he cleared the mirror and took a few snaps shots of it, he and Clark reentered the hall and walked down to the bathroom. The door was open. Clark swept the room with his gun before entering. He threw back the shower curtain. The shower was empty. He called 'clear.' He turned to leave the room. He passed the mirror over the sink. Motion in the mirror caught his eye. Clark froze and stared into the mirror as a hazy bearded man reached out toward him from the tub. He turned swiftly pointing his gun in the direction of the man, ready to fire. There was nothing there. He turned and looked in the mirror, but the image was gone.

"What is it?" Masters asked Clark.

"Nothing," Clark pushed past Masters, eager to get out of the bathroom.

The two men checked the attic door. It worked. They pulled it down, and Masters went up to check out the interior. He stuck his head up above the floor and glanced quickly around the attic. There didn't seem to be anyone there. He moved up the steps and walked down the sides of the room searching for wires or gadgets that could have been used during the séance. Either Chamber's from the Institute or the Templeton's could have been playing a prank on everyone else. If they found that Ms. Templeton, or any of her guests, had created a hoax, then Chamber's death would be considered a homicide. As he crossed the room to clear the other side, a ruckus occurred behind him. He turned and was smacked hard. A big black crow bounced off his face. He swatted the bird off of him with his gun.

The bird circled around the room then flew out a broken corner of the attic window.

"What the hell," Clark called as he stuck his head up into the attic.

"Just a damned black bird. Bitch hit me right in my face." Masters rubbed his nose.

"If everything is clear up here, then let's get down stairs." Clark said. Masters agreed.

Downstairs they found Morris working the dining room.

"Everything okay up there?"

"Yeah," Masters said. His nose and face were still red where the bird had struck him. There were scratches across his cheek from the bird's claws or beak, he wasn't sure which.

"What the hell happened to you?" Morris asked.

"It was just a black bird in the attic, I must have scared it."

"Shit. Need some ice?"

"Nah, let's just finish this and get the hell out of here."

"Okay. I searched the walls. No wires or signs of chemicals that could have caused the pictures to fall. No wires anywhere in the room. Of course we don't know what the Institute people took with them. I can't believe the Chief let them dismantle their equipment and take it with them. It would have been good to take a look at that," Morris said.

"Yeah, small town police, not always the brightest bulbs in the box," Clark said.

The men continued to photograph the room and search for devices. Gradually the temperature of the room started to fall. Clark became aware of it first. He searched for the source of the temperature change. He couldn't find anything.

"You on to something?" Morris asked him.

"It's getting cold in here. You feel it?" Clark asked as he continued to search.

"Yeah, now that you mention it," Morris said, as he joined the search. Masters took more photographs of the room.

"Damned if I know," Morris said after searching the room. He went out and checked the living room and kitchen. They were cooling down too, just not as fast as the dining room.

"Masters, check the temperature upstairs. See if these phenomena are occurring up there as well," Morris told him. "Clark, get a reading on the temperature."

Clark searched through his bag and brought out a device that measured the temperature and the time and printed it out on a tiny slip of paper. He walked around the room with it, reading out the changes. "Dining room: fifty-five degrees. Living room: sixty-four." He walked into the kitchen around the island reading his device. "Kitchen sixty-two." He walked back into the dining room. "Dining room: fifty-one and dropping."

Masters climbed the stairs with caution. He didn't really want to go up there again, at least not by himself. As he breached the upstairs landing the temperature was cooling down, but it wasn't as cold as it was downstairs. He checked each bedroom, careful to close each door, as he cleared the rooms. The rooms were warmer, but there was a chill in the air that wasn't there before. Masters shut the bathroom door as a bearded man reached for him. Unaware of the bearded man, he turned and bounded down the stairs.

"The source must be down here. The bedrooms are warmer, but cooling down."

"I can't find a source anywhere. There is no air conditioning in the house. No fan on anywhere. No vent forcing cold air. I have to tell you I'm stumped," Trevor told them.

"Dining room: forty-six degrees and falling," Clark called out. "This seems to be the epic-center of this activity."

Masters was not one to believe in ghosts, but he was starting to get concerned. This house gave him the creeps. He preferred to chase real men with guns over unseen entities and freaky phenomena. If he wanted to be a ghost buster, he thought to himself, he would have joined something like Chambers' group.

The upstairs doors all slammed at once.

"I thought you cleared upstairs," Trevor snapped at Masters.

"I closed every door. Every one of them," the men headed for the stairs when all the doors downstairs slammed closed.

"What the hell?" Trevor called out.

Masters headed for the dining room door while Clark took the kitchen. Morris covered the men. Masters feared the dining room door would not open, just like on the video of the night before. Then he became afraid the back door might not open as well, and they could become trapped inside the house. He started to freak out as the door handle to the dining room gave way, and he opened the door. Clark's door opened as well. The door from the dining room to the kitchen was also closed. Clark walked through the kitchen and opened the door. When Masters saw Clark at the open door he headed for the front door. It opened as well.

"What the hell are you doing?" Trevor asked him.

"Just making sure there is an escape route." Masters said, as he grabbed a small table and lodged it between the door and the jam.

"Sissy boy. Want me to tell the guys back at the station that you made an 'escape route' for crying out loud. Man up," Trevor told him. Masters was embarrassed, but he refused to remove the table from the door jam.

"Better safe than sorry."

"What was that?" Trevor asked.

"I said I was sorry," Masters lied.

The men cleared the rest of the house without incident. They took photographs and readings from each room. The temperature started to rise to normal range. They recorded the changes. On the way out they resealed the police tape. During the ride back to the police station, they rode in silence until they cleared the peninsula.

"What are we going to put in our report?" Masters asked.

"Everything that happened," Trevor said. He seemed shocked that Masters would ask such a question.

"The bird?" Masters asked.

"And the temperature change, and the slamming doors. All of it," Trevor stated.

"People will think we're crazy. I for one would like to get promoted in the future," Masters said.

"People won't trust you if you don't report the truth. What if something is discovered later that is found to have created those incidents? You want to have egg on your face when it is discovered that you covered it up thinking it was what? A ghost? Give me a break. There's a logical explanation for everything in that house. We just need a special team of experts and some more time to find out what it is," Trevor told him.

Clark sat in the back seat thinking about the man he saw in the tub. He wasn't putting that into any report.

CHAPTER SIXTY

Claire watched as the FBI agents left the house. She had sat a ways down the peninsula watching for them to leave for an hour or more. While she waited, she did not see Julian come or go. Perhaps he had seen the FBI agents as well and stayed away.

Once the FBI sedan pulled off Peninsula Road, she walked back to the house. She knew that she could not go inside. That was okay with her. When she reached the house she sat on the porch swing and watched the ocean waves and steel gray sky. The second of two hurricanes had just hit the Florida coast and was due to hit the Harbor any day now. These were the kind of days Claire used to love at the beach. Now it just made her sad.

While at the hospital she raided the vending machine and loaded her purse with candy bars and snack crackers. The soda machine provided her with a can of diet pop, a bottle of apple juice and a bottle of water. Now she did not need to enter the house again and run the risk of being arrested or assaulted. Surely Dogg and Harris would not arrest her for sitting on her own porch. To stay at the house she would have to lay low. She still wore her sweats to avoid standing out in a crowd in her gypsy attire. She loved all the bright colors and soft layers, but today she was going incognito.

Claire opened her purse and took out the bottle of water. She took a small drink to make it last, than put it back in her bag. The water bottle fell against her bracelets, making a soothing chiming sound. She pulled them all together and jingled them in her fingers. She loved the way they sounded. It reminded her of the pieces of glass that washed up on shore. Each colored piece of glass was worn down by the constant motion of the sea. When they clanged together they made a soft glass chime sound that was so soothing to her. The bracelets let her take a bit of that sound with her everywhere she went.

"It's amazing. That sounds like nights at the beach," Julian said, as he took a seat next to her on the swing. His sudden appearance startled her. The swing lowered just a bit from his weight.

"Yes, it does," she smiled, happy to see him.

"Still not going inside I see."

"I have a great excuse," she pointed toward the police tape on the back door.

"I've been thinking about what you were telling me last night."

"Which thing would that be?" she asked. Last night they had talked about a lot of things.

"About the ghosts, they bombarded you when you returned. Do you think it might be because they miss your mother and they were happy to see you?" He must have seen the dumbfounded look on her face. He tried to explain better. "Like Sandy, when we would come home from school, she would attack us. Not because she meant us harm, but because she was so happy to see us. Her intention was not to scratch us and knock us down, even though that was the result. Her reaction was one of delight and affection. Dogs hate being left alone. Maybe ghosts do, too."

Sandy was Julian's golden retriever. On rare occasions, when Claire went home with Julian after school, they would be met by an overzealous dog, happy they were home. Claire had suffered many bruises and scratches from that dog. It seemed unreal to compare these ghosts to Sandy.

"So they attacked me because they were happy to see me. Seems strange, but when you put it in those terms, it is hard not to consider the possibility, I guess," Claire played absently with her bracelets.

"What if you were to talk to them? Soothe them in some way, the way petting Sandy calmed her down."

"There was no calming her down. She was wound up for at least a half an hour or more."

"Okay, so say you got a chair. Sat outside the open door," Claire motioned toward the police tape, "Okay, how about the window? And just talk to them, softly."

"And what do you suppose I say to them? Hey honey, I'm home?"

"How about hello. They know you, but they don't know the real you."

"You mean tell them my hopes and fears?"

"Well, probably not your fears. They might use that against you."

"Like they need any help there."

"You should give it a go. I'm game if you are. I can sit here and watch you. If you need help, I'm right here," he raised his eyebrows in a 'what do you say' fashion. She never could refuse him anything, but there was always a first time for everything. Claire considered exchanging the horrid idea with a quick romp through the sea grass and surf with Julian hot on her heels. That idea sounded better, just like old times.

"Oh, alright," she said. His puppy dog eyes had won her over.

Claire got up and placed a wicker chair about three feet in front of the dining room window. Then she slid the window pane open too slowly; the window stuck open about four inches up from the bottom sill.

"Think that will be enough?" she asked Julian.

"Nope. I think you should open it all the way up. Let me help you."

Julian went over and grabbed the window pane, and they both tugged hard. The window flew open with ease, almost breaking the glass from the force.

"Try that," Julian said, taking his seat back on the swing.

Claire sat down in a wicker chair that wasn't broken. She had no idea what to say or do.

"You feel ridicules," he stated.

"Is it that obvious?"

"Go with that," he encouraged her. His high school psychology course seemed to coming in handy.

Claire took a deep breath and then sat up straight in the chair.

"Here goes..." She shifted in her seat. "Hello everyone, you know me, I'm Claire Templeton. This is my house. I guess it is yours, too. I feel really stupid talking to you like this, but I don't know what else to do."

"Good, keep that up."

"I would like to be able to come inside my house, your house, our house, I guess. I would like to be able to sleep in my own bed. Shower in my own bathroom without total fear or being watched. Oh, and to make a meal in the kitchen without freaking out. That would be nice."

"Tell them what you would make."

"Salads. I love salads. Chopping vegetables. Carrots. Celery. Oh, and apples. I love crispy apples in my salads. I also love chopping vegetables for soup. I'm not a big seafood fan despite growing up on the peninsula. Tuna is okay. And fish sticks smothered in ketchup. I love those, too."

Claire looked around at the clap boards that covered the house, at the storm shutters, at her feet. She had no idea how to do this, or if it was even going to work.

"Now tell them why you don't cook in the kitchen."

"Well, I don't cook there because they attack me."

"Not me. Tell them that."

"I don't cook here because you attack me. Every time I try to walk through that door it's like you come after me. It overwhelms me..."

"And..."

"And I run away. There. I said it. You attack me and I run away. I shut you out."

"Good. Now tell them how you would like it if you had to live here with them."

Claire gave him a crazed look. There was no living with them. It was them or her. She could not do both.

"Tell them."

"I guess they do their thing and I do mine."

"Not good enough. Why do you think they got along so well with your mother?"

"Because she loved them. She was here for them."

"Okay. What can you do to be there for them more?"

"Are you insane? Have you seen what that has done to my mother? She's in a coma for crying out loud."

"Today, but all the other days she was not. Forget about the coma," he saw her face scrunch up, "for the moment. Concentrate on what she did when it worked."

Claire had no idea what her mother did. She had never seen her mother talk to the ghosts although many times she had entered the room and found her mother talking to herself. If she was folding towels she would say "I am folding these towels now and will put them away. I like the smell of clean towels." When she questioned her mother about it, she said she just liked to hear the sound of conversation in the big empty house. They had no radio or TV for a very long time. Except for the ghosts, the house was very quiet.

"If you let me go about my own business, I guess I could include you in my day. Tell you what I am doing or why." Claire hated this idea. She didn't want any part of this, but she could not let Julian down. He seemed so sure this would work. He made her feel like it just might.

"Good, now if you would just stop and listen to them. They might actually tell you what it is they want from you."

Now she was certain he had gone insane while she had been away.

CHAPTER SIXTY ONE

"There have been a number of disappearances associated with that house over the years," AIC Moss told Chief Harris from behind his own desk. "Based on the report from my boys," he pointed toward SA Morris, Masters and Clark, "there seems to be something going on out at that house even now."

Harris was not surprised, but he felt his heart sink. Having the FBI in town was not as exciting as he thought it might be. They took over his office. They took over the case. He was left out of the loop unless they needed more information or assistance from him. He felt like an outsider in his own precinct.

Moss handed Harris the report filed by SA Morris and his team. Harris leafed through it. It was full of FBI jargon and matter-of-fact reporting.

"Some doors slammed and a mirror broke," Harris tried to sound bored.

"And the temperature changed, just like during the séance," Moss pointed out.

"A bird?" Harris questioned. Masters face blushed making the bird scratches stand out even more. "Birds do occupy most of the attics in Butcher Harbor. Should we investigate them as well?"

"I don't think that will be necessary," Moss snapped.

"Doors slam all over the Harbor as well. A stray wind or breeze blows doors shut all the time. We are all used to that," Harris explained.

"There was no breeze," Masters said under his breath.

"What SA Masters?"

"I said there was no breeze, sir. The house was still. The doors were closed when they slammed shut."

"A house may seem still, and yet doors will slam. It happens all the time," Harris continued.

"The doors were shut at the time. And what about the temperature change? I suppose that is some beach phenomena we are not aware of?"

"No. That one's got me stumped too. Perhaps it was a draft of some sort. Probably causes the doors to slam by a sudden change in temperature. I'm sure it can be explained." Harris remembered the bitter cold when he entered the house the night of the séance. That was no draft.

"What about the mirror in the daughter's room?" Moss asked.

"Perhaps your men got a little carried away and broke it during their investigation, and want to cover it up," Harris regretted the words as soon as they were out of his mouth.

"Speaking of covering up, Chief Harris, can you explain why you let the Institute take all of their equipment out of the dining room? And I understand the house guests removed their luggage as well. There could have been something of importance in one, or all, of those items. You clearly did not secure the CS." Morris grilled Harris.

"CS?"

"In layman's terms, the crime scene," Morris stated.

"Well, we are a small town here. I'm afraid we have very few crime scenes, I mean CS's here. I let people go home, that's all," Harris played the dumb small town Chief to his benefit.

"Some might say it was a cover up," Morris added.

"Yeah, well, we are not all as highly trained as you, Special Agent Morris, or we would be working for the FBI, too," Harris could not believe he let the man bait him so easily.

"That's enough. If my man says the mirror cracked on its own, then that is what happened. If Harris did not properly secure the scene, it was due to inexperience in this type of situation, not a cover up. Are we all clear?" Moss demanded.

"Clear," everyone said at once.

"Was there anything else that happened out there?" Harris asked. "Perhaps something that's not in the report."

Everyone said no, but Harris was sure he saw a slight crimson shade appear on SA Clark's face as he spoke.

"So, where do we go from here?" Harris asked.

"We go back to headquarters and file our report. Then the powers that be, and the prosecutors, decide if we send out a team of paranormal experts to explain what is and isn't happening in that house, and to investigate the previous disappearances for foul play or not," Moss said, as he stood and started to fill his brief case with reports.

"Just who do you suppose is behind any suspected foul play?" Harris asked.

"It could be someone who lives in the house. Could be someone from town," Moss said, putting his lap top in his brief case.

"Which someone from the house would that be? Do you mean the woman in the ICU in a coma or her frightened daughter?"

"You would be surprised what people can do when they want, or need to Chief Harris," Moss stared down at him.

The others stood and collected their gear as well. Harris, who remained seated, observed the FBI pull out of his office. He wanted to be sure they only took what belonged to them. Once they had all their gear packed and said their good-byes, Harris followed them all out of his office. He shut his office door behind him officially reclaim it as his own.

CHAPTER SIXTY TWO

Dogg sat at his mother's restaurant counter in his usual spot. For dinner his mother served him a huge plate of pot roast with a side of coleslaw and a large, warm, buttered bun. To his mother's delight he devoured the food she had placed in front of him.

The restaurant door opened and Chief Harris walked over to take a seat next to Dogg.

"Thought I might find you here," Harris said while Dogg tried to clear his mouthful of food.

"Where else?"

"Change in plans. The FBI cleared out today. No more investigation at this time," Harris said. Dogg raised his brows and wiped his mouth with a napkin. "Yeah, they're gone. According to AIC Moss, they will file the report, and let us know if they will be sending a team of paranormal investigators in to solve all the strange disappearances at the house over the years. I guess they think it is somebody in town or a Templeton doing all this stuff."

"You mean Claire? Did she sneak back from New York during the night and force her mother to attempt suicide? Or kill Chambers with her bare hands?" Dogg was astonished.

"It's the FBI. Everybody's a suspect."

"What did they find at the house?"

"Apparently all the crosses in the house were upside down. That makes them think Claire and her mother are running some sort of cult out there. Or that they are Satan worshipers, a lot of slamming doors. The temperature dropped again while they were out there. It appears to center around the dining room. Oh, and they broke a mirror in Claire's bedroom."

"The FBI?"

"They said it just cracked. Who knows? The mirror is broken, and we will never know how it got that way. They wouldn't admit to breaking it if they did."

"Care for a plate?" Dogg's mother asked as she wiped the counter in front of Harris.

"I would love some, Lila," Harris said rubbing his hands together. He needed to have dinner at home with Becky, but the smell of hot roasted beef in warm gravy coming from Dogg's dinner plate made him realize how hungry he was.

"I'll leave you two to talk," Lila said, as she turned and went into the kitchen.

"So what do we do now?" Dogg asked.

"Go back to normal. I need you back on night shift. I can handle things during the day, but at night the natives are going to get restless. I need someone I can count on to keep things under control here." As Chief Harris spoke, Rory Lynch sauntered through the door with his boat crew. The group took their usual seat by the front window. Rory liked to see and be seen.

"Speaking of the devil," Dogg watched Rory take his seat and call the waitress.

"Yeah, that would be one of them," Harris said. "We've been fielding calls all day long asking that Claire be removed from town. The house plowed under. They have all but asked for Elizabeth to be unplugged. We might need to station a guard on her door for a few days. These nice folks could be stirred into a mob by the likes of Rory in no time. We are going to have our hands full with all this. Graduation is this weekend too. We'll be spread thin."

Dogg looked over the usual crowd of people he had grown up with his entire life. It was hard to believe that these simple folk could be rallied into a mob. But he was well trained; and he knew it could happen in an instant. The fatality during the séance was just the sort of thing that could trigger it.

"How are things out at the Witches' Temple, Chief?" Rory called from across the room.

"Things are under control, Rory," Chief Harris turned to face the loud mouth.

"Yeah, and how about that witch and her demon daughter? They under control, too?"

"Elizabeth is still in a coma. Claire is at the hospital with her mother. The house is sealed. All their friends have returned to New York. All the FBI men have gone home," Harris said. Lila came out of the kitchen and served him a huge plate of pot roast. Harris turned around and took a deep breath, inhaling the wonderful scent. He loved Lila's cooking more than Becky's; even Becky would agree with him. He already knew the pot roast would melt in his mouth.

"Someone should pull that old witch's plug," Rory said more to the crowd then to Harris and Dogg.

"That someone will spend a lot of time behind bars," Harris called back over his shoulder.

"And burn that house down while they're at it," Rory egged the crowd on, ignoring Harris. The Chief could hear people start to agree with him.

"Shut up, Rory, and leave these good folks to enjoy their meals," Lila said referring to all the diners. "All this commotion isn't good for digestion."

"Go back into your kitchen, Lila, and mind your own business," Rory said.

Dogg clenched his fork and took a deep breath.

"I'll take care of this," Harris said as he grabbed Dogg's arm. Harris stood and walked slow and steady across the room. He used that time to gather his thoughts. Once he was at the table, he grabbed Rory's hand and held it tight using his body to shield his action from the crowd. The shock on Rory's face was what Harris had hoped for.

"You're either going to shut your mouth and let these folks eat in peace. Right now!" Harris spoke softly in Rory's ear. "Or you and me are going to have problems, you got me? And if you and me have problems, then you, me, and the fishing commission are going to have problems. You see where I'm going with this Rory?"

"Yeah. Sure, Chief. I got you," Rory agreed to eat his meal without comments. Harris returned to the counter and finished his meal with Dogg. Despite quieting Rory, the Chief knew he was too late. Harris could already hear bits and pieces of hushed conversations from around the room, each of them centered around Elizabeth and her house. One particular man worried Harris, as he was the father of one of his newest deputies. Harris longed for Elizabeth to recover, to return to her house where she would stay out of site and out of mind. And he longed for Claire to return to the safety of New York City soon.

A cell phone rang, and both Dogg and Harris reached for theirs. It was the Chief's cell phone that was ringing.

"Harris."

"Chief, we just got the autopsy report faxed in. You said you wanted to know as soon as it arrived."

"Read it to me, Mac."

"Robert Mason Chambers, 54 year old male Caucasian."

"Just the give me the cause of death, Mac."

"Oh yeah, cause of death...heart attack."

"Any cause for the heart attack?"

"Plaque."

"Thanks, Mac. Put the report on my desk. I'll get to it as soon as I get in."

"Chambers?" Dogg asked the Chief.

"Yeah. Died from a heart attack due to plaque build- up in his arteries."

"That why they ruled out foul play?"

"Yup. The Templeton House is no longer a crime scene. Guess I'll take a drive out there and remove the police tape before I go home."

"I can take care of that for you," Dogg said a little too quickly. "You know I take my coffee breaks out on Peninsula Road. I can take it down while I'm out there."

Harris thought Dogg sounded a little too eager to take care of this chore himself, but he trusted his Deputy.

"Okay, tonight then. There's no rush anyway. I don't want Claire in that house, especially not alone. There is no telling what will happen after the séance and Chamber's death. Besides, I worked it out with the hospital. They are putting in one of those chairs that unfolds into a bed in her mother's room. She's better off there. She slept in a chair all last night. I saw her there this morning. It must have been uncomfortable for her."

"I bet." Dogg looked confused for just a moment.

"We'll put a guard on the room tomorrow if things heat up. Meanwhile, check in at the hospital during the night just in case."

"Sounds like a plan."

"Gotta have a plan," Harris looked over his shoulder at the humbled Rory. He wondered how long his little talk would calm the man down. If he knew Rory, it wouldn't last for long. He had to step up his game. All deputies had to be put on high alert. It was no longer a matter of simple crowd control at a crime scene; it was mob prevention at the hospital and Templeton House. Harris couldn't remember the last time the town had to deal with a mob. He was thinking it was fifty or so years ago and the mob was led by his predecessor, the town's own Chief of Police.

CHAPTER SIXTY THREE

Raymond was relieved when Chief Harris agreed to let him open up Templeton House. He knew that Claire had been to the hospital; Harris said he had seen her there. But Dogg also knew she would be determined to return to that house. He decided to go out to the house first and see what she was up to.

The sun was just about to set when Dogg stopped the cruiser before reaching the house. He didn't want the sound of the tires on the shell and stone road to give him away. He stepped out of the cruiser and headed for the sea grass. This time he had left his shoes in the car.

As he approached the house, he saw Claire sitting in a wicker chair and looking at the dining room window. She was talking to someone. Dogg hunched down lower and crept closer to the porch. The dining room window was open. Damn. She must have gone back inside the house again. He would have to explain to her that it was illegal to enter through the door or the window. Not that it would matter since he was here to remove the police tape anyway. But still, she had to have respect for the law. He crept up close to the porch. He could hear her soft voice, but he couldn't see or hear anyone talking back to her.

"Dogg? Is that you?" Claire asked startled.

"How did you know it was me?" he asked, still crouched below the porch.

"You smell like your mother's coffee."

Damn cinnamon. He would have to remember that in the future. It might tip off his presence in a bad situation.

"I will have to stop drinking cinnamon coffee then," he said as he stood up from beside the porch and joined her.

"Don't you dare. I love that smell and I love that you smell that way. It's sweet."

"Sweet is not necessarily the thought a deputy wants to con-vey. Tough. Rugged. Terrifying. Those work for me. Sweet? Not so good," he said as he took a seat on the empty swing and gave a slight push with the tip of his foot.

"You spying on me?"

"I came out to remove the tape off the door. The house is no longer a crime scene."

"Yippee!"

"Don't get all excited. The Chief doesn't want you in there. Especially alone."

"But I'm not alone. You're here."

"Now. What about later? He wants you to stay clear. I will allow you to sleep on the porch if you must. But I prefer you stay at the hospital. We have a lot of angry town folk who just might be overcome with enough fear to want to take this house out and you with it."

"Do you know how hard it is sleep at the hospital?"

"Harris said you did just fine there last night."

"And how did he know that?" Claire blushed. She knew Dogg knew she had stayed at the house last night.

"Apparently he saw you there this morning, asleep in a chair."

"Cool. So he doesn't suspect that I came here?"

"I don't believe so."

"And you didn't tell him?"

"No. I didn't tell him. But I should have. I have never with-held information from the Chief." Dogg was beginning to get concerned about his lack of honestly lately. Claire seemed to make him do things he had never done before. That scared him a little.

"Well, I appreciate it."

"I still don't understand why you want to be here. And who the hell were you talking to?"

"The house. Ju...I thought it might help to talk to them. See what they want. Maybe they won't bombard me anymore and I can actually live inside the house for a change."

"You think that'll work?"

"Only one way to find out, Deputy. Care to remove that tape?"

"Depends? You gonna leave if it gets bad in there?"

"You bet."

"Okay. Let's open her up and see what happens."

CHAPTER SIXTY FOUR

The house seemed quiet when Dogg removed the police tape and opened the door. Claire stepped over the threshold, and nothing came at her. Indeed she couldn't see anything or anyone. She listened to the house, but did not hear the noise of a hundred ghosts. She was relieved, but refused to let her guard down.

"How you doing?" Dogg asked as he scanned the walls. He looked confused. Everything looked the same as always. She wondered what he was seeing that concerned him.

"So far so good. I don't see or hear anything."

"Is that normal?"

"No. I usually can't get through the door."

"Maybe the séance worked, cleared the house."

"You almost say that like you believe in the ghosts and the séance."

"Well, I know you believe." Dogg blushed.

"So you say what I want to hear? Is that how it works, Dogg?"

The Deputy got quiet. He seemed to be considering the question and how to answer it best.

"Be honest Raymond."

"Okay, I don't believe in all this stuff. I think it is bunk, especially the whole séance thing. I do believe in energy and that some negative energy might pool up in certain places like this house. I believe that negative energy can be discharged- or cleared."

Claire stared at Raymond as if for the first time. She was glad he was being honest about how he felt.

"Honesty. That's good. Well, I do believe in ghosts as I have seen and heard them. They could be trapped energy. I like that idea. I believe the house can be cleared. There are just so many ghosts here. I think it would take someone bigger and badder than me to do the job."

"I'm not so sure about that. Look what happened to Chambers. He was supposed to be a big expert in the field."

"But the house still managed to take his life."

"Autopsy report shows no foul play. The man had a heart attack from eating too many French fries."

"The autopsy has no way to measure paranormal influences."

"True. But Grace said that you stopped the séance. She said it was like you commanded it and it happened. Maybe you are stronger than Chambers and you just don't know it."

"If that were true, I'd be sleeping in my own bed and not under the porch swing or at the hospital."

Claire could not consider taking on the entire house at once. Julian had told her to take things one ghost at a time. She wasn't even sure she was strong enough to do that. Raymond did not believe, so he wouldn't be able to help her take on this task. She needed an expert. Tomorrow she would contact Madeline and see if she knew of someone else who could help her clear the house.

"Okay, so now what?" Dogg asked.

"Mind if we check out the upstairs?"

"After you..." Dogg bowed and swept his arm to his right. Claire laughed as she walked past him toward the stairs.

"Bad dog!"

"Oh, like I've never heard that one before."

"Sorry, it just came out."

Upstairs felt calm, too. Claire could not believe that the sun had just set and yet she was not being bombarded by ghosts.

"I'm baffled. I don't hear or see anyone. It's almost like they are gone. But not gone."

"What does that mean- not gone?"

"I can still feel them. Like something that gets under your skin. But I can't see them. And there are no voices. Usually there are hundreds of voices all at once."

"Now there are none?"

"None," Claire was blown away. She opened her mother's door and looked around. Again, Dogg got a strange, confused look on his face. Claire took a closer look at the room. Every-thing seemed in order. Again she wondered what he was seeing that she wasn't.

"Something wrong?"

"No."

"Honesty, Dogg." She didn't believe him and pushed for the truth.

"Okay, okay. Chief Harris told me the FBI reported that all the crosses in the house were upside down."

Now Claire looked confused. All the crosses in the house were upright. In fact, she had never seen the crosses any other way since she came back. She wondered how the ghosts could have known that the men in the house were FBI, or at the very least were checking up on things inside the house. Why had they messed with those men?

"What else?"

"Well, the mirror in your room is broken. The Chief gave me the impression he thought the FBI had broken it and blamed it on the alleged ghosts."

"Alleged ghosts?" Claire couldn't help laughing. "How about alleged energy sources?"

"Okay. I deserve that."

The two of them left her mother's bedroom and stepped across the hall into her room. All the crosses were upright there as well. They moved across the room to the dresser. Claire snatched the photograph of her father and tucked it in the waistband of her sweatpants.

"My mother took that from me before I left."

They stood in front of the mirror and stared at it for a minute.

"Was it supposed to be a big crack?" Claire asked, taking a closer look to see if maybe there was a hairline fracture.

"No. It was supposed to be across the entire mirror, bottom to top." The mirror was intact. They looked at each other, raised their eyebrows and went back to staring at the mirror. Neither of them could detect a crack anywhere.

"What do you think it means?" Dogg asked Claire.

"That the house didn't like the men from the FBI either."

CHAPTER SIXTY FIVE

Dogg left the house after about an hour. He said he didn't like leaving her there all alone, and he reminded her that Chief Harris preferred she stay at the hospital for a while. She insisted that she would be okay and wouldn't spend much time in the house alone. When Dogg left, Claire sat on the porch swing uncertain about entering the house when no one was there to protect her if she got into trouble.

After a while of just sitting on the porch she got antsy. She needed to use the restroom and wanted a cooked meal. She stared at the screen door to the porch. They had left the inside door open. There were no ghosts in the door or the windows.

It could be a trick to get me to come inside. Perhaps the ghosts had decided they would convince her to come inside knowing she would be alone. She pushed the porch swing with her foot and considered the idea.

I can do this. She decided to leave the front door open for a quick exit. First she would run upstairs and use the bathroom. Then she would take it one step at a time from there. Claire stood up, smoothed her sweat pants and ran her fingers through her hair. At the screen door, she stopped and took a deep breath.

"I am coming inside to use the bathroom," she told the house as she stepped over the threshold, one foot still outside the door. Nothing happened. She brought her other foot through the door. Again, nothing happened. Then she bolted up the stairs before they changed their minds.

She left the bathroom door open for her benefit, not theirs; again, she wanted to have a quick exit. They let her pee in peace. She washed her hands and face and moved slowly toward the stairs. As she passed her bedroom door she considered rechecking the mirror but decided against it. She didn't want to get on the subject of ghosts and hauntings. All she wanted to do right now was raid the refrigerator and get back on the porch.

In the kitchen, all was quiet as well. She turned on the light and made her way to the fridge. There was next to nothing in there. Dogg had promised her a ride to the store when he got off his shift in the morning. He explained that after Chamber's death, Old Man Jones used the opportunity to say he would never deliver groceries to this house again. Claire knew that her mother wouldn't be too pleased about that. It was just one more thing to blame on her.

The refrigerator was bare. There were a few eggs, ketchup, mayonnaise, mustard, strawberry jam, some butter and a small jar of olives. Claire checked the pantry. There were a few boxes of scalloped potatoes that looked really old, on the shelf and some canned vegetables still left after the boys cooked soup. She moved the boxes of potatoes and found some peanut butter. She searched through the pantry for some bread but didn't find any.

She settled for the eggs and found a pen and paper to make a list of things she would need to get from the grocery store tomorrow. Under the counter she found the pan her mother always used and got the eggs from the refrigerator. As she cooked the eggs, she used her peripheral vision to watch for any movement in the room. It scared her to have her back to the room while she was tending to the pan, but she was hungry. Her ears were tuned in to the slightest change in sound around the room and the house. She heard nothing out of the usual. It was all so unsettling. While she was afraid of the occupants in the house, she found that she was even more afraid of not knowing where they were or what they were up to.

When the eggs were done, Claire turned toward the island to put them on her plate. Sitting calmly on an island stool was the little boy she had seen in the house for so many years. She almost dropped the eggs, but instead managed to set the pan on the island counter before it could crash to the floor. Trembling, she took a deep breath and tried to calm herself. The boy cracked a tiny smile.

"Well, hello there," she tried to make it sound like she was not terrified out of her mind and that her skin was not crawling with goose bumps. "I'd offer you some eggs, but I imagine that you don't eat much these days."

The boy spoke, but all she heard was noise. Her blank stare caused him to speak again.

"...never liked eggs..." she pieced out of what she heard him say.

"Oh, so you don't like eggs. What did you like?" she tried to stop her hands from trembling as she placed the eggs on her plate.

"...mother...fried chicken...best." She could only make out every other word of what he said. Then she remembered Julian telling her to be still and listen. Maybe she wasn't getting every-thing the boy said because the words weren't making it past the fear sensor in her brain.

"You liked your mom's fried chicken?" she asked as she leaned against the kitchen sink to keep from fainting with fear, plate in her hands. She took a bite of eggs.

"Yes. She makes the best chicken," he said. This time she heard every word, or at least she thought she did.

"My mom makes good fried chicken, too," she tried to make conversation with the ghost of a dead boy.

"When will she be coming home?"

"Who?" She asked, confused if he was talking about his mother or hers.

"Your mother."

"Well, she is very sick right now. She is in the hospital. It may be a while.."

"I need her to come home. I miss her."

"She takes care of you?

"Yes. She makes the others behave. It is scary now she's gone."

Claire thought that in some way it must be like losing his mother all over again.

"Where is your mother?"

"I don't know. I keep looking for her, but..."

"When did you see her last?"

"I came in from playing, and they were all gone."

"Gone? Did something happen to them?"

"I don't know. Mom had been crying for days. Something bad happened and she stopped talking to me. She would call me, but when I came she acted like she didn't see me. Then one day they were gone. Everyone." He wiped a tear from his eye.

"Who was everyone?"

"My mom and dad. And Bessy, that's my sister."

"I see." Claire didn't know what else to say.

"But there were all these new people in the house. They were everywhere, talking, always talking to no one in particular, never to each other. Like they didn't know or care that the others were here."

"I've met a few of them myself."

"They don't like each other."

"Why not?" she asked setting her plate in the sink.

"I don't know."

Claire realized she was asking a lot from a little boy.

"I'm Claire Templeton. What's your name?"

"I know who you are. My name is Jeremiah Smith," he perked up when she asked.

"Jeremiah. I like that. How old are you Jeremiah?"

"Seven," he said proudly, then added, "and a half."

"Wow, seven and a half. So you are not a baby anymore," she hoped to gain his confidence.

"Nope."

"Cool. Well, Jeremiah, what do you think happened to make your mother sad?"

"She lost something she wanted very badly and she couldn't find it."

"Do you know what it was?"

"No. She kept calling me, but didn't answer me when I talked to her," he paused, "But I never stopped trying. I knew she was sad, but I didn't want her to forget about me."

"Why would she do that?"

"Because she was so sad. She wouldn't even talk to Dad or to Bessy either. That made my dad sad. None of them would talk to me."

"Jeremiah, would you like it if I could help you find your mom and dad?"

"Would I!"

"Let me look around and see what I can find. Maybe I can find out what made your mommy sad. Then maybe I can find out where they went."

A door slammed upstairs. Claire tried to ignore it, but the little boy didn't.

"Oh no, they are mad," he said turning toward the door.

"Why?"

"They don't like it when your mother talks to me. They must not like me talking to you either."

"I see. Well, they will just have to get used to it. I like talking to you, Jeremiah. I think I can help you find your family."

Another door slammed upstairs. The hairs on the back of Claire's neck started to stand up. Her goose bumps were back.

"I should go now," he said, as he dashed toward the kitchen door.

"Wait!" she called back to him, but he was gone. Claire looked around the room for other guests, but found none. The slamming doors seemed to stop for the moment. She took this opportunity to run back onto the safety of her porch. The whole conversation with Jeremiah was interesting, but it also gave her the creeps. Even when she reached the safety of her porch swing, she could not stop the tremors that ran throughout her body.

CHAPTER SIXTY SIX

The small group met at sunset on the Wayward, the fishing vessel that belonged to Rory Lynch. Rory made sure there was plenty of beer on board tonight to soothe his guests. Sam Sharp was a short, squat man, dressed in coveralls, and a dirty t-shirt. He had been fishing for several years with Rory on his boat. Tonight he sat on the port side of the fishing boat staring at his feet. He seemed uncomfortable about the meeting. Willy Bradford, another of Rory's crew, dressed the same as Sam and Rory sat on the starboard side of the boat. Willy always wore a hat to hide his bald spot. He looked around nervously. His skin, like Rory's, was tanned to the look of leather from years in the sun and at sea.

They were joined tonight by Caroline Laws' husband Jeremy. He was taller than the rest and dressed in khakis and a sport shirt. Unlike the others, his skin was fair. Jeremy was a councilman and spent most of his days behind a desk. It was his wife's idea that he come to this meeting despite his arguments that it wouldn't be good for his career. Caroline assured him it wouldn't be good for his marriage if he didn't come.

Standing next to Jeremy was Nathan Parks. He owned the dry goods store on Main Street. Tonight he was dressed in jeans and a sport shirt. He wore too much cologne which didn't mix well with the fishy scent of the wharf; the combination of that and the rocking of the boat at dock were making Jeremy sick to his stomach.

Sitting in a seat across from Rory was Black Jack Johnson. They called him Black Jack all his life for his desire to play Black Jack and his skill at the game. He made his living off of bored husbands during the summer months. He made enough money that he never had to work during the winter. He used the slow winter months to keep his game sharp playing the local talent. Tonight he had given up a game to come here to the secret meeting on board Rory's boat.

"You all know our relatives have had a go at that house," Rory spoke softly. "Now it's our turn. We have to do something before any more of ours gets hurt. But we have to go about it smart like. Chief Harris thinks he can scare me by threaten my living. I know people at city hall too," he motioned toward Jeremy.

"I can only do so much..." Jeremy started to fidget. He didn't want to get in too deep with this group.

"If we do this right, we won't have to worry about who we know, everyone will be involved. You can't say that everybody you have spoken to today is not outraged by that little snot and her mother, and all that voodoo witchcraft stuff going on out at that house."

"Do you see how Claire dresses now? She looks like a tramp in all those layers and bracelets," Nathan Parks threw in, reaching for another beer.

"God knows what she has gotten into since she left the Harbor. She brought a herd of people with her. All men," Sam Sharp brought up.

"Her and Grace and all those men out there at that house doing who knows what," Willy added, searching the dock for eavesdroppers.

"We have to devise ourselves a plan. Everyone has to be in this to the end. And that house torn down has to be the end. Anyone not agree'n with that best leave now," Rory said regaining control of the group of men. Jeremy shifted in his place but did not leave.

"I'm in," said Nathan Parks. "My granddaddy almost died trying to burn that place down. I owe him."

"I'm in too," Willy Bradford offered. His granddaddy ran from Templeton House after Nathan's granddaddy caught on fire. It was something Bradford never brought up, but always had to live down. Jeremy had heard the stories over the years.

"Me, too," said Sam, eager to be in on anything. His grand-daddy was one of the previous mob leaders with Rory's granddaddy and father. Sam opened another beer.

"Jeremy?" Rory cocked his head toward Jeremy who seemed present, but not a participant. Rory stared at Jeremy's unopened beer.

"I'm not sure this is a good idea. Others have tried to take that house down too many times since it went up. No one has succeeded yet. What will make this time any different?" Jeremy asked.

"Because we are gonna make a plan, and we are gonna stick to it. Because, sissy boy, we are going to bring everyone in on it. And because we know what we're up against," Rory spoke out of the side of his mouth.

"What about the Chief?" Jeremy questioned.

"My granddaddy brought the old Chief under his fold. Made'em think he was leading' the whole damn thing himself," Rory grinned.

"Okay, but how do you expect to bring Chief Harris under your wing? He seems to be pretty partial to Claire. Always has. And now I hear Raymond Dogg is holding her hand nights too. How are you going to turn them against her?" Jeremy wanted all the hard questions answered before he agreed to go any farther with this harebrained scheme of Rory's. The others in the group were followers. Anything Rory said to do they would do. But Jeremy had a mind of his own, and a career he had spent his entire life cultivating. He couldn't throw that all away unless they had a foolproof plan. Right now, he saw the Chief and his deputies as quite a monkey wrench in the works.

"We'll turn them against her," Rory said.

"How are we going to do that?"

"Maybe we'll leave that part up to you; that way you'll be sure it gets done right. Use your boy. You never wanted him anywhere near that witch's daughter anyways."

"Leave my son out of this," Jeremy snapped.

"If everyone is not involved, then this ain't gonna work. Everyone including your boy," Rory said. He was used to getting his way and apparently didn't care much to be challenged.

Jeremy loved his wife and son, but he didn't think he had it in him to be involved in a mob against the Templeton's and their house. His mind drifted and he imagined the mob successful in their endeavor. It would look bad if he hadn't been a part of that. Where would his career be then? He remembered Willy's granddad. Jason Bradford hung his head in shame ever since that day he turned tail and ran. Willy still hangs his head today because Jason was a coward.

"Okay. I'm in," Jeremy conceded.

"You gonna open that beer or just hold on to it?" Rory challenged Jeremy.

Jeremy opened the now warm beer and took a swig. The warm beer added to the smells of Nathans' cologne and the harbor made Jeremy want to hurl. But he refused to seem weak in front of this bunch.

"Okay then, Jeremy will work on the Chief and his deputies. That's good since he works in the same building and all. Nathan, stir up your customers. I know they got to be talking by now. And Black Jack, get them husbands riled up. You know they are all restless with all this lazing around the beach. They need something to do. Let's give it to them," Rory ordered. "Me and the boys here will take care of the fisherman. Hell, we'll attack by land and sea if we have to," Rory passed out another round of beers and popped the top on his own. He seemed quite pleased with the way things were turning out.

"Now, how about that witch in the hospital? What're we gonna do about her?" Rory asked.

CHAPTER SIXTY SEVEN

Raymond Dogg finished his rounds then stopped off at home to change. He didn't want to be seen in the Harbor Mart with Claire while he was still in uniform. He got into his red convertible Mustang and headed for the peninsula. He wasn't sure how much trouble he would get into helping Claire stay at that house, but he couldn't leave her out there on her own. He was sure she wasn't going to stay put at the hospital like Harris wanted her too. She could be as stubborn as Harris was some-times.

When Dogg pulled around the driveway, he noticed Claire's blankets bundled under the porch swing. She must still be sleeping on the porch. He wondered how good of a nights' sleep she could possibly get there.

He grabbed the doggy bag he brought with him from the restaurant after he ate breakfast with his mom. He was sure his mother would start wondering why he suddenly needed to take food home with him after every meal, since he always ate at the restaurant with her, but she never brought it up.

The cop in him made him survey his surroundings before he stepped onto the porch. No one seemed to be lurking in the sea grass or on the beach. No one seemed to be hanging around the house. Claire was still sleeping. He stomped on the stairs to wake her up. She jumped up and hit her head on the swing.

"Sorry. Just meant for you to wake up, not knock yourself out," he told her.

"Shit, Ray!" she yelled at him, rubbing her forehead.

She climbed out of her blankets and ruffled her hair.

"Wow, don't you look sexy in the same sweat pants and tee shirt from yesterday," Dogg was surprised to see she had not showered or changed her clothes.

"One step at a time. I actually cooked food and ate in there last night."

"Well, today is step two because you aren't going anywhere with me until you shower and change your clothes. I have a reputation to keep around here and it doesn't include driving around with bimbos. I save that for my night job."

"Ha ha. Is that food I smell," she said, eyeing the white bag he held in his hand.

"It could be. Why don't you shower and come find out."

"I'd much rather eat and then shower."

"Ah," Dogg made a sniffing noise and curled up his nose. "No. You had better hurry before it gets cold."

Claire pouted, but he did not give in. After a moment she dashed in the house and up the stairs. He could hear the shower water running. He used this opportunity to check out the house. The crosses were still in the upright position. The dining room was as comfortable in temperature as the rest of the downstairs. He didn't venture up the stairs because he didn't think Claire would appreciate him snooping around. The shower water cut off, and he stepped back out onto the back porch and took up a seat on the swing. He expected Claire to sit on the swing as well. She always did. He wanted to be close to her.

"You're losing it Dogg," he said out loud to no one.

Claire bounded down the stairs, drying her hair with a towel. It looked like she was wearing the same gray sweats and tee shirt she had on when she went upstairs.

"Claire, did you forget something?"

"What?" she asked looking behind her.

"Aren't those the same clothes you had on when you went upstairs?"

"No silly. This is a different pair of high school gym clothes."

"Prove it."

"What?"

"Prove it. Come here and let me smell them."

Claire stopped drying her hair, as she stood on the back porch staring at Dogg as if he had lost him mind.

"You want to smell my clothes? Is there anything about you I should know?"

"Now."

Claire walked over to Dogg and practically climbed in his lap. She grabbed her tee shirt and stuck it up in his face. He choked at the musty smell in the cotton.

"Yuck!"

"What do you expect? It has only been in my drawer for seven years. Look- moth holes," she said turning around to show him a small series of holes missing from her tee shirt. "All my clothes are at the hospital. Okay. I will run a load of clothes before we go to the store. You are taking me to the store, right?"

"Do I have to? You stink!"

"Fine, I'll stay here in my stinky clothes and starve to death, if the ghosts don't get me first." He could see by the look on her face she was sorry she had said that. He knew how set she was on staying at the house. Reminding him of the danger she was in was not a good way to stay here.

"Speaking of ghosts," he said handing her the bag of food. She started to sit down next to him on the swing. "Over there stinky," he told her, pushing the swing up on an awkward angle so she couldn't sit down next to him. He pointed to one of the wicker chairs by the window.

"Gees. You must deal with stinky people all the time in your line of work. Drunks. Hookers."

"Exactly. At work."

"So what, are you at play now?" she teased him. "You come to play with little Claire Templeton. Sorry, my mother isn't home, or I'd invite you in." She batted her eyes.

"Eat your breakfast," he told her as he tossed two biscuits her way. She licked her lips as he held up the coffee.

"Stay there. I'll bring it to you." He took her the coffee then made a scene about rushing back to the swing. The seat flew back so far he almost fell off. It rocked awkwardly for a moment then stopped.

"Well, that was graceful," she said. They both laughed.

"Stop changing the subject. How did it go last night? What did you do?"

"Well, I cooked some eggs. Chatted with a few ghosts and killed a few psychics." His face dropped. He could not believe she had just said that.

"Just kidding, Dogg. It's something Grace does to make sure I'm listening to her. I was just checking to see if you were actually paying attention."

"Don't do that again."

"I'm sorry."

He sipped his coffee while she ate her breakfast. Looking at her dingy clothes and tousled hair he wondered what he was going to do with her. They would eat her alive downtown if they saw her right now.

"Maybe we should stop by the hospital so you can change before I take you shopping."

"Don't be silly. Didn't you say you would give me a ride back to the hospital after groceries?"

"Yes. I did."

"Okay. I'll change after groceries."

Dogg felt a knot in the pit of his stomach. He had just gotten her to notice that he even lived and breathed and he didn't want to lose her attention. But he didn't want her to make a spectacle of herself either.

"I can take you to change and then take you back after the groceries. You'll have your clothes back, bright, colorful Claire."

"Dogg, it's silly to run back and forth. This'll do for now. You've seen some of the things these ladies wear to the store, haven't you?"

"Yes, but they aren't Claire Templeton."

"What is that supposed to mean? It's okay for them, but not for me?"

"I meant you are better than them. You have style, class."

"Then it should show no matter what I am wearing," she pouted.

Dogg sat in silence watching the waves as she ate. He was afraid to say anything else. Suddenly he understood why his Dad got quiet and stared off into nowhere when he and his mom were arguing. It wasn't something he had shared with a woman before. He didn't like it much. Yet at the same time, in an odd sort of way, it felt like they had been together for a long time. That feeling he liked.

When Claire finished eating she threw away the trash, going in the house with no apparent problem. Then she came back to the back porch.

"Ready."

Dogg didn't want to say a word. He simply pointed to her unkempt hair. Claire held her head still and looked up at her hair with her eyes.

"Oh. Crap. My brush is at the hospital in the bathroom."

"I have a comb in my car."

"Okay. Let's go then."

Claire sat in the passenger seat of the car. She ran her hand across the dash.

"Damn nice car, Dogg."

"It's a 1969-"

"Shelby GT 500 convertible!" she finished for him.

"You know about clothes and cars?"

"I just know about this car. It is one of my favorites. We've used it in a few photo shoots. When I get big enough to be able to afford to park a car in New York City, I want to get one of these. Can you spin wheels out of the driveway?"

"Need I remind you that I am the law out here. You want me to spin out? What kind of example would I be setting?" he asked as he gunned the car and spun out of the driveway. They both laughed as Dogg raced down Peninsula Road.

Out on the ocean Rory Lynch was heading out to deeper water to fish. The red car racing down the peninsula caught his attention. He watched as Deputy Raymond Dogg spun out of the Templeton driveway in his Mustang. Rory watched to see if there was an emergency. He noticed Dogg and Claire Templeton laughing as they drove. There was no emergency.

"Look at that," he called over to Willy who was leaning over the starboard side of the boat. Willy looked up at the peninsula and saw a red car racing down the road.

"Deputy Dogg and that little Templeton slut!" Rory called to Willy. Sam also looked up and watched the car race down the road.

"We better get movin' on this thing before she puts a spell on the whole damn town," Rory said as he spit over the side of the boat.

CHAPTER SIXTY EIGHT

The trip to the store was exciting, a fast ride in a fast car. Life seemed to be moving in slow motion lately. Claire found herself wishing that the trip to the store had taken a little longer. Dogg pulled up to the market and parked. They both got out laughing and enjoying their morning.

Inside the store Claire was at a loss. Grace had taken care of her for so long, all she had to do was come along and pick out the extra things that she wanted. Luckily, she had made a list of items that she knew she had to have. The list was in her purse. As she pushed the shopping cart down the aisles, she searched for the blasted list, but could not find it.

"Damn."

"What's wrong?" Dogg asked.

"I forgot my list. I know I put it in here."

"You can stop looking."

"Why?" she asked thinking maybe he had found her list or maybe made a list of his own.

"You'll never find the shopping list until you get home. It's a proven fact. Not until after you have forgotten the one thing you needed most."

"Is that some kind of shopping list conspiracy?"

"No. Just an observation," he said, reaching for a jar of peanut butter. Claire nodded that she needed that. Then she searched her brain for everything else she had written down.

"Stick to the essentials, then we can go back and get the extras," Dogg told her. That was a good plan, except Claire had no idea what the essentials were. She knew she needed milk and eggs, some bread. But she wondered if there was some unwritten list of essentials all other people in the world knew except for her. She could not bear to ask Dogg what those essentials might be. She would sooner starve first. Instead she quietly walked down the aisles loading the cart with the things she thought she needed. She started with jelly to go with her peanut butter.

"You need some coffee? You know, in case I can't come by some morning," Dogg asked without thinking. He blushed.

"Do you plan on deserting me so soon?"

"Just thinking you might want coffee and ..." Dogg started to say.

"It's okay. I know you have other things to do besides babysit me," she smiled. This was fun, shopping, spending time with Dogg. He watched out for her, but he didn't hold her hand like Grace and the others did. He expected things from her, like to know how to shop. While shopping for the first time made her feel stupid, she hid that from him because he expected that she already knew what she was doing. She did her best not to change that expectation as it gave her a strange sensation of power and strength.

At the end of the third aisle, Dogg walked over and browsed the meat counter at the back of the store. Claire wondered if that meant she had her essentials, but she hadn't picked up milk or bread yet. She started down the next aisle wishing she had that silly list.

"Speak of the devil..." she heard, as she turned her cart into the next aisle. Two women with carts facing in opposite directions had stopped to chat with one another about halfway down the aisle. Claire recognized them but could not remember their names. They were friends of Caroline Laws. They continued to whisper as she walked down the aisle wishing she had joined Dogg at the meat counter.

"And Julian..." she heard them say as she tried to concentrate on the boxes of noodles on the shelves. She picked out a jar of sauce she knew Grace had bought for them. As slow as she tried to go, she caught up to them in no time. Both women shut up as she got closer. One woman moved her cart to the side so Claire could get past.

"Well, hello Claire," the first lady spoke.

"Welcome back to the Harbor," the second one said, trying not to laugh.

"Thank you," Claire said, pushing her cart past them as fast as she could without appearing to be rude. As soon as she passed, she thought she heard giggles and snorts behind her back. She walked out of the aisle and around the corner, hoping they would head in the opposite direction. Claire's chest ached and then she realized that she had hardly taken a breath since she had passed the ladies carts. She took a deep breath, but it did little to stop the slight tremor she felt in her body.

Down the next aisle was clear. She took another deep breath and tried to regain that awesome feeling she had when she walked into the store. She looked over the items on the shelf, canned vegetables and soup, canned meat, she heard the women in the next aisle still sharing a laugh at her expense. Claire grabbed a few cans of green beans, peas and carrots, and rushed down the aisle to get farther away from these ladies and closer to Dogg. She doubted they would have acted that way if he had been by her side, at least not in front of him.

At the back of the aisle as she prepared to join Dogg and the safety of his company. He brought some chicken and pork chops over and placed them in her cart.

"Go ahead," he motioned for her to continue down the next aisle. "I'll get you some hamburger. How about some hot dogs? Quick to fix," he said as he walked away. Claire felt abandoned. She wanted to chase after him like a child anxious for its mother. The thought made her feel silly, but the feeling was real, and it was strong.

"That would be great," she called after him, but he was al-ready at the meat counter.

Claire turned down the next aisle afraid of what she might find there. It was empty, and she was glad to avoid any more encounters without Dogg by her side. She shopped slowly afraid to turn down the next aisle and find more gossip at her expense. Claire looked over the toilet paper and didn't see the brand Grace usually bought. She struggled with prices and advertising slogans all touting the softest tissue and the most economical package, yet the prices were so different for all of them. She settled on a brand she was sure she had seen on television.

A cart turned down the corner ahead of her, and Claire held her breath. As the woman followed the cart around the corner she stopped, a shocked look on her face. The woman gave Claire a fake smile as she jerked her cart around and headed for the next aisle. Claire wasn't sure which was more insulting, cackling laughter or blatant avoidance. She felt like she must have large oozing scabs all over her body. The idea of it made her feel dirty, and she longed for a hot, soapy shower.

"You should see her hair," Claire heard chuckling coming from the next aisle over. She couldn't bare turning the corner and facing the woman and whoever she was talking to. A tear ran down her face before she realized she was crying. She brushed it away and tried to stand up straight. She ran her fin-gers through her hair. How good would you look if you had to shower in the presence of ghosts? She had to remember shampoo.

Unable to face the women around the corner, Claire turned her cart around and headed toward the back aisle and Dogg. Before she could stop, Dogg turned around and walked right into her cart.

"Oh, I am so sorry," she said.

"Accidents happen. You don't have to cry about it," he said pointing to another escaped tear drop.

"Dust or something in my eye," she said as she wiped her face with the back of her hand.

Dogg nodded like he believed her, but his eyes seemed to search around the store as he placed the hamburger and hot dogs in the cart. Claire smiled as if to say everything was okay, but inside she wanted to die.

"Can we go now?"

"Do you have everything?"

"I still need bread and milk, but I think that's all."

"Sure, we'll grab them on the way out," he pointed toward the last aisle. This time he went with her, and she was grateful. They got to the last aisle, and Dogg grabbed two cartons of milk.

"Regular or unleaded," he asked confusing her, "Just kidding. You want whole or fat free?" Claire had no idea. She opted for a third choice she knew Grace bought.

"Two percent," she said pointing to another jug in the cooler. Dogg put the other two back and grabbed the blue capped jug.

The end of the aisle had bread and buns and Claire was glad to almost be done shopping. Dogg tossed a package of cheese into the cart, and she was glad he had thought about that because she hadn't. She grabbed the largest, cheapest loaf of bread she could find and rushed to the checkout.

"You got everything?" Dogg asked with a concerned look on his face.

"Yeah, this will do for now," she told him. He nodded and let her get in line at the checkout. He helped her unload the groceries onto the checkout counter.

"Hello, Raymond," the cashier said eyeing Claire, but not acknowledging her.

"Hey," Dogg answered without looking up. He continued to unload the cart.

"Hello, Sherry," Claire said, in a snotty tone of voice, making sure she knew Claire was there.

"How are you, Claire?"

"As well as can be expected," she said, giving the cashier the evil eye. Dogg looked up in time to witness her display of bad behavior. He gave her a shocked hurtful look she had never seen before. She hadn't meant to be so mean; she was just tired of all the snide remarks and laughter at her expense. Dogg frowned and finished helping her unload the cart. She paid for the groceries as the bag boy loaded the last bag into her cart.

"You need help out?" he asked.

Claire could see the relief in his eyes when Dogg told him they could handle the groceries by themselves. This boy probably would have been forced to deliver these very packages to her house if Mr. Jones hadn't insisted there would be no more deliveries to her home. She blushed as she followed Dogg out of the store. The cart was full, and she hoped these groceries would last until she could go back to the city. She didn't think she could handle another visit to the grocery store. It was then that she realized she had forgotten the shampoo, but right now all she wanted to do was get as far away from this store and the other shoppers as she possibly could.

Back at the house, Dogg helped Claire unpack the groceries and put them away. Then he took her to the hospital. There was little conversation. Claire was too upset to speak and too embarrassed by her actions in front of the Deputy. He must have been embarrassed by her as well because he barely spoke to her the entire time.

"You'll be okay if I go on ahead? I have some errands to run, and I've got to get some sleep," he stopped the car at the front door to the hospital.

"This is fine," Claire said as she got out, "Thanks for every-thing, Raymond, really," she said almost as an apology for her bad behavior.

"Just doing my job," Dogg said as he sped off. Claire's face burned as she turned beet red. She was glad he wasn't there to see it. All this time she thought he was helping her out to be nice. She had no idea he was just following orders, doing his job. The safety and security she felt with Dogg crumbled at her feet, leaving her feeling naked in this public place. A man walked past her and stared at her as if she were some sort of an alien. She wished she were invisible as she turned and took the dreaded walk into the hospital. She was tired. Sleep at the house was sporadic at best. At least sleep would be something she could do during her obligated visits to the hospital.

CHAPTER SIXTY NINE

Chief Harris came by the hospital around noon. He found Claire asleep in the folded out chair he had asked for; she had a hospital blanket wrapped around her. In the hospital bed, her mother remained in a coma. Each day made it more likely that she would not come out of it, but the doctor seemed to think it was more her own will than a medical condition that kept her in that state, so things could change. Harris couldn't think of any reason Elizabeth would want to come out of her coma. The relationship with Claire was difficult at best. The house probably drove her to suicide. Her husband was gone. There wasn't much left for a tired old woman to live for.

Claire stirred, but did not wake up. Harris backed up and walked out of the room. He stopped by the nurse's station and slipped the nurse a twenty dollar bill.

"In case she needs something. I would suggest a bath," he said.

"She showered yesterday. We order a plate every meal for Elizabeth and give it to Claire," the nurse said passing the money back to the Chief.

"Keep it. Just in case," he told her. The nurse stuck the money in Elizabeth's chart.

The phone rang. "ICU," the nurse said excusing herself to answer it. "I'm sorry, hospital policy doesn't permit us to give out that information to anyone except family," the nurse told the caller, then hung up the phone. "They call day and night," she told him. "Want to know if the old woman has 'kicked the bucket' yet."

"Any other problems besides the calls?"

"No one can get in without being buzzed in. So the other nurses and I feel safe... you know, for the patient's sake," the nurse fumbled. Harris understood their fears. "We have gotten several of these." She handed him cards from the local florist.

"Wishing you not well. Get sick soon. Die bitch." Harris read the cards as he flipped through them. "Why would the florists send flowers with cards like these?"

"Patricia just hands the cards to her customers. They write what they want and seal it in the little envelopes. We open the card and place it on the flowers so the family can see who has sent them. But these were too awful to put out."

"I didn't notice any flowers in her room," Harris said looking back toward Elizabeth's door.

"We've thrown them all away. They have sent black roses or worse, half dead flowers. None of them have been appropriate for the patient or her daughter," the nurse said going back to her charts.

"Give me the cards as they come in," he said as he left the nurses' station. Harris was sure Caroline Laws was behind this. She had never wanted her precious son going out with Claire. She must be very upset now that Claire was back in town. He would have to go and see her in person. His conversation on the phone didn't seem to do much good. If he could control Caroline, all of her friends would follow suit. She and Rory were the biggest threat to the Templeton's at this time. He felt he had handled Rory yesterday. Today he would tackle Caroline. This was something he wished he could send Dogg or one of his other deputies to do. But he knew how important it was to make sure Caroline was under control. This was something he would have to deal with himself.

The Chief left the hospital and drove through the housing side of town. Small cottage like houses sat on sandy front yards. Most of the houses were white. Occasionally there was a light pink, green or blue shade house. The bright colors were saved for the stores down town and on the boardwalk. Everywhere bicycles were propped up against porch railings. Bicycles were the number one means of travel in town. The locals had their own bikes. Tourist rented bikes or brought their own bikes with them.

Harris dreaded this conversation. Caroline could be so stubborn, and without her husband at home to tone her down, she would be difficult. Harris pulled up in front of her house, walked past the pile of bikes near her porch and knocked on the front door. After a few moments, Caroline answered.

"Well. Hello, Chief," she said through the partially opened door, her body well placed in the opening to keep him from seeing past her.

"I need to speak to you for a moment, Caroline."

"As you can see I have company. Perhaps you could come back later," she winked at him as if this were a social call.

"This is business, Mrs. Laws. Please step out onto the porch if you aren't going to invite me in."

"Oh, alright. I'll be right out," she disappeared behind the door. There was a burst of laughter then she came out on the front porch alone. Harris was sure he could see a few of the other women from town peeking through the sheers.

"Caroline, I need you to stop harassing Elizabeth Temple-ton."

"Chief, that would hardly be ladylike behavior to harass someone in a coma, now would it?"

"I know about the flowers. I can't stop the florist from sending them, but I can sure as hell make sure they are never received. You will just be throwing away your money."

"You can't be serious. Sending flowers to the ill is something that we do from time to time as part of the Welcome Wagon."

"This is how you cheer people up?" he asked fanning out the cards the nurse had given him at the hospital. Caroline looked at them as if she had never seen them before. She is good.

"How awful, who would do such a thing?"

"I am sure neither of us needs me to go down to the florist and investigate the purchases of these flowers. It could be embarrassing to a few of your lady friends. But if I have to, I will. This stops today."

"I assure you ..."

"Today!"

Caroline huffed and got quiet. He was sure he had stopped the awful flowers and their cards from being sent, but he was afraid of where the ladies' efforts would go now. The flowers were already being intercepted. The cards were never seen by the family. Now that he stopped the flowers from being sent, he wondered what Caroline and her friends would have up their sleeves next.

"Stay away from the Templeton's and their house."

"I assure you I haven't been near either one. In fact if you remember I called you because that little runt practically ran me off the sidewalk by the fl..." she stopped suddenly.

"By the florist. I remember." He stepped off the porch and walked back to his cruiser.

CHAPTER SEVENTY

Claire awoke at the hospital around one o'clock in the after-noon. After she folded up her chair and blankets, she grabbed her brush and tackled her hair. It was a mess from no shampoo, but she didn't have time to shower right now. If she hurried she thought she could make the library and check up on Jeremiah. If she knew his story, then she might be able to help him leave the house. The idea of handling even one ghost at a time scared the crap out of her, yet it was the easiest solution.

With her hair fixed as best she could, she grabbed her hand bag and left the hospital. She felt bad because she hadn't said a word to her mother while she was there, but she didn't know what to say to her anyway. There wasn't anything nice she could think to say right now. It drove her insane every time she thought about Madeline's story about her father saying that the house had taken him.

At the library, the librarian helped Claire find the books of old newspaper articles.

"You have to read through them in here." She led Claire into a side room with glass windows. "There is a copy machine for anything you want to keep a record of," the thin librarian told her. She looked hesitant to leave Claire alone with the books.

"Thanks," Claire dug in. The librarian stood over her shoul-der making her nervous.

"You have to be careful with those pages. They are very old." the librarian stood behind her with her hand prepared to snatch the old articles from Claire's unworthy fingers at any moment.

"Can I check out?" an impatient mother, with two small children clinging to a stack of books, called from the door. The librarian snorted and followed the mother to the check out. Claire took a deep breath then went back to the beginning to search in private.

The time period for Jeremiah was a problem. She had forgotten to ask him the date he last remembered seeing his family. She took a guess and opened a book. After about an hour and about twenty books she hadn't found anything on the boy. She started to close the book when she saw a photograph of the German sailor printed on the next page. He was there with photos of the twenty-three other sailors. Their ship had wrecked off shore and all were believed dead, including Volker Waldmunt. The year was 1941. Claire wondered if all of the sailors were in her house. She had only seen the one. She found some change in her purse and made a copy of the page. She dumped her change purse on the table to use for more photocopies when she needed them.

The next three books were duds. There was nothing about the house or its occupants. Then, in the fourth one, she found an article about a family of four that went missing. She thought that she had found Jeremiah's family, but it turned out the little boy's name was Frederick. The year was 1936. According to the article Frederick Whitman and his entire family were gone from the Templeton House and had never been seen again. The family had resided in the house for less than a year. There was no note and all of their belongings were still inside the house. No foul play was suspected and no one in town seemed to know anything about their disappearance. Claire photocopied that page. She was pretty sure she knew where they were. She just had no idea how or why.

The clock ticked by at three-thirty and Claire panicked. The library closed at four o'clock and she had so many more books to go through. She wanted to rush through the books but was afraid she would miss something important. The article on the Whitman family was very small. If she hadn't seen a photograph of the house she would have missed it entirely. Claire cursed herself for sleeping so long today. This was going to take so much longer than she had anticipated.

When she turned the page, she jumped when she found a sketch of the old woman with the knife, without her knife this time. Her husband's sketch was next to hers on the page. The story read that Mrs. Edith Coldburn had stabbed her husband, Charles, to death before she turned the knife on herself. There was no note, or any indication of what had caused her to do such a horrid thing. The Chief, at the time, believed it was a murder/suicide because Mr. Coldburn had been brutally stabbed 37 times in the chest and his face had been slashed in several places. Residents were shocked by the brutal actions of a woman so in love with her husband. Claire photocopied that page too.

Halfway through the next book she found a sketch of Jeremiah. She couldn't stop staring into those haunting eyes. A small article stated that Jeremiah had gone out to play on September 16th, 1929. He was never seen again. His mother was distraught and blamed herself for her son's disappearance. There was no comment from Jeremiah's father who was staying home from fishing to care for his grieving wife and daughter. Claire photocopied the page and looked over the next few weeks.

After two months had passed there was another article with the same sketch of Jeremiah. The article said that the heartbroken family had decided to sell the house and wanted to move away from Butcher Harbor. Claire photocopied that page as well. In the back of that newspaper was an ad for the house. There was no mention of Peninsula Road or any history of the house. The price for the house was half the price of other houses for sale at that time. She copied that page as well.

A few more pages back in the book, she found a story that the family abandoned the house when it would not sell. Claire could understand that. She was photocopying that page when the librarian came in.

"We need to put all these books away," the librarian said as she snatched books from the table and started to re-shelve them. Claire huddled over her photocopies as she scooped them up and flipped them over so the articles could not be seen. Then Claire helped the librarian put the rest of the books away. While they put the books back on the shelf, the librarian sneaked reproving glances at Claire.

"Did you find what you were looking for, dear?" the woman asked, taking the last stack of books from Claire.

"Yes. Thanks," Claire tried to avoid telling her any more. The librarian looked down her nose at Claire as if awaiting some explanation.

"Politics," Claire scrambled for a legitimate story. "I'm doing a research paper on old styles of politics and how they have evolved over the years to our current way of voting and campaigning," she hoped her lie wasn't as transparent as it seemed to her.

The librarian stared at Claire for a moment then walked over to shelve the books. Claire clutched the haphazard news articles to her chest, excused herself, and left the newsprint room. In the main library she saw people sitting around at tables whispering and snickering. She tried to tell herself that not everything was about her, but she caught words like Templeton, that house, and Julian Laws, so she knew for certain they knew exactly who she was, and that they were indeed talking about her. Claire tried to make herself as small as possible as she fled the library. She became conscious of her scruffy hair and smelly sweat pants. For the third time today she wished she were invisible.

Instead of going back to the hospital, Claire walked down to the boardwalk to find Madeline. She needed to ask her a few questions about Jeremiah. She hoped Madeline would come and help her clear the little boy from the house. Armed with her photocopies she scurried across the boardwalk from Sixth Street instead of Boardwalk Boulevard to avoid as many beach goers as possible. When she finally reached the store and tried to dash inside before she was seen, she was startled when the door would not budge. The door to the storefront was locked. The sign hung in the window said 'Closed for Renovations'.

"She's not here anymore," a voice came from behind her. "It had something to do with that house across the peninsula. Some guy died during a séance. I hear she plans to open it as a bakery." The woman offered as Claire turned around to face her. Claire was sure she did not recognize the forty something woman standing before her wrapped in a beach towel and holding her sandals in her hand. But as Claire had turned to face the woman, she saw the realization on the woman's face that meant she had noticed her. The woman stepped backward away from Claire as if her face were missing all its flesh.

"You're her," the lady said pointing across the Peninsula to-ward Templeton House.

"Yes," was all Claire could get out of her mouth before the beach towel clad woman fled down the boardwalk. Claire sighed as she slipped around the corner of the building before the fleeing woman attracted attention. Claire skulked down the side road toward Madeline's house.

After Claire turned down several side streets she came across Madeline's V.W. Parked in her driveway.

"She's not home," Herbert's gruff voice came from the side of the house. He leaned on his rake.

"Oh, will she be gone long?"

"Could be all day," Herbert glared at Claire.

"I could wait for a while," Claire said thinking of all her newspaper articles she could re-read to occupy her time.

"I don't think so." Claire thought she saw him bare his teeth like an angry dog. She stepped backwards away from him, tripped and fell. The news articles fell around her on the ground. She grabbed at the pages, collecting them as quickly as she could to prevent Herbert from seeing the subject of her research. Herbert made no move to help her. The screen door slammed on the porch as Madeline came down the stairs, and without a word, helped Claire gather her copies. Madeline picked up the copy of Mrs. Coldburn. She scanned the article, than looked Claire square in her face.

"I've been at the library finding out the stories about the ghosts in my house," Claire said standing up. Madeline grabbed the last page from the ground. Jeremiah's haunted eyes stared up from the page. Madeline stood and faced Claire.

"I thought maybe you could help me," Claire regretting her choice of words as soon as she spoke. "I meant assist me, teach me. Tell me how to get these people out of my house. One at a time this time," Claire fumbled for the magic words that would melt the shocked and terrified look on Madeline's face.

"Maddy is done with that medium crap. She is starting a bakery," Herbert said suddenly at Madeline's side.

"If you could just give me a few moments, I just have a few questions,"

Claire stared at the silent Madeline.

"No!" Herbert grabbed Madeline's arm and pulled her toward the house. Madeline handed Claire the photocopies as she let Herbert drag her away.

"Madeline, please, just a few moments. You don't have to come out to the house, we can talk here," Claire called as Madeline was dragged into the house. The screen door slammed behind her.

CHAPTER SEVENTY ONE

Julian was sitting on the beach in front of her house when Claire walked up with her haphazard photocopies sticking out of her arms in all directions. She dropped down beside Julian and took a deep, cleansing breath.

"Hard day?"

"You could say that."

"You look like shit."

"Yeah, I've been getting that all day."

"I can see why."

"Thanks, bunches."

"You know I will never lie to you, Claire."

"But you have no trouble withholding information."

"That's not lying."

"Yeah, but it's not being honest either."

"It's been a long time. Some things are better left unsaid."

"According to you, but I need to know these things. Clear the air."

"Washing your clothes might be a good start to clearing the air."

Claire burst out laughing. The stress of the day had been too much for her. She enjoyed being with Julian.

"What's all this?" He asked leafing through the pile of photocopies.

"Research. I went to the library and found some information about a few of my ghosts."

"You went out in public like that?"

"Yes." Claire's shoulders slumped.

"What am I going to do with you?"

Claire searched through the photocopies until she found Jeremiah's sketch.

"Look. The little boy I always told you about. He disappeared one day. His mother was distraught. He was never found. They tried to sell the house and couldn't get a buyer. Finally they just moved out. I think the house may have taken him, like my father."

"But you said he disappeared. Your dad died; you buried him."

"Yeah, but I still believe the house took Jeremiah. I don't think he ever made it outside to play. We already know he is here. I have seen him most of my life."

"Okay, now what?"

"I don't know. I tried to talk to Madeline about it, but..."

"You didn't? She's so upset right now and scared."

"I know, but so am I. We have to clear this house. She is the only one that knows how to do that."

"Yeah, but you can't ask her to help, Claire. You just can't."

"Then what do I do?"

"Show the little boy the paper. See how he reacts."

"Come with me."

Julian looked toward the house then back at Claire. She realized that Julian had never been inside her house before.

"Alright, but I'm out the door at the first sign of trouble."

"Fair enough," she said, scooping up the papers at her feet, shaking the sand from between the pages. They walked to the house and placed the photocopies on the dining room table.

"What else did you find?" Julian asked glancing through the pages.

"Here, the German sailor's name is Volker Waldmunt. Seems his whole boat and crew were lost at sea. I think he is the only one here, but I'm not sure. I don't know how he got here or why. And the old woman, her name is Edith Coldburn. She suddenly turned on her husband, stabbing him 37 times and then she killed herself. No one knows why. I know she was jealous, but I don't think there was ever any reason for her to be. The paper didn't even allude to another woman. I think it was the house. I think it turned her against him."

"Is her husband here, too?"

"Yeah, but he stays to himself, sulks."

"Maybe he doesn't understand what happened to them."

"Could be. You think maybe I could get to her by using him? Clear him and she will follow sort of thing."

"Possibly."

"Julian, I'm so glad you're here."

"Me, too. I have missed you so much." Claire went to hug him but he pulled away.

"So how do we find the little boy?"

"Don't know. I guess we just call for him. Jeremiah..." Claire called as she walked into the kitchen.

"You think he's in here?"

"I spoke to him in here last night. Perhaps he will come back here."

"Okay, so what do we do?"

"We call him. And maybe start cooking. He seems to just show up. I think he likes to watch people cook. Maybe it re-minds him of his mother."

"Okay."

"Jeremiah," Claire called as she found a sauce pan and put on some hot dogs. "I know where your mom and dad are." she called out.

Julian watched her as she grabbed two plates and some bread. Then she took ketchup, mustard and relish out of the fridge.

"Claire?" Julian called to her as she struggled with the foil under the ketchup lid.

"What?" she said turning to Julian as the foil lid finally pulled free. She stopped when she saw Jeremiah sitting in the chair at the island. "Jeremiah!"

"Yes, Miss."

"You came."

"Yes, Miss. You called me."

"Yes! Yes, I did." Claire was blown away by how simple it had been to call Jeremiah to them.

"You said you know where my Mom is." He fidgeted in the chair.

Claire glanced at Julian. She had no idea how to do this or where to start. Julian nodded at her and she took courage by his presence.

"Yes, Jeremiah. I have a story to read to you."

Claire read all the reports about Jeremiah and his family out loud to the boy. Then she showed him the sketch rendering of him.

"So where are they now? Can you take me to them?"

"Well, yes Jeremiah, but a lot of time has passed since your family left. A lot of time." Claire had no idea how to explain this to the boy. "Do you know how many people have come and gone since they left?"

"A lot."

"Exactly. Well Jeremiah, your parents have gone to heaven."

"You mean they are dead?"

The pictures on the walls started to vibrate. Claire looked at Julian. It was clear the trembling pictures scared him, but he urged her to continue.

"Yes Jeremiah, they are dead."

"All of them?" the boy asked. He started to cry. The sight of his tears broke Claire's heart. The pictures on the wall shook harder than before. She glanced down at her fingers as they rattled from the vibrations that were now shaking even the kitchen island.

"All of them," She told him. There was a slight drop in temperature as she spoke.

"Jeremiah, do you know how to get to where your parents are?"

"No," he wiped the back of his hand across his nose as he spoke.

"Me neither. But I know they are out there and they miss you terribly. Do you think you could go to them?"

"You want me to kill myself?"

"No, Sweetie," Claire was lost. She had no idea how to tell a ghost he was dead. "I think maybe you have been dead for a long while. That is why your mother couldn't find you. I think you were the thing she lost that broke her heart." The island visibly shook under her hands and the temperature dropped even more. Claire stared at Julian who said nothing, he just stared wide eyed and kept glancing toward the door.

"But how?"

"That I don't know. I think it had something to do with this house." She said as a picture near the door crashed to the floor.

"You mean it was them?"

"Yes, I think so." Claire had no idea who 'them' were, but it sounded good to her.

"Those rat bastards!"

Claire was shocked by the boy's words. The island trembled and the temperature continued to drop. Claire used the boy's anger at the house to her advantage.

"Cease this racket!" She yelled to the house. The vibrations picked up, and the temperature dropped even more. "Right now!"

Julian looked shocked as the shaking of the walls and the table slowed. The temperature warmed a bit.

"That's better," Claire took a deep breath, thankful the vibrations stopped, but uncertain for how long.

"Jeremiah, I think this house took you. And then your family left, thinking you were dead. Now, they too are gone. That means you are all gone. That means you should be able to find them."

"But how?"

Indeed, how? Claire looked to Julian for direction, but he just shrugged. A haze started near the ceiling. There was a faint voice off in the distance. The voice grew louder as the haze transformed into a figure.

"Jeremiah? Where are you? Jeremiah?" the haze figure called out.

"Here, mommy. I am here!" Jeremiah jumped up and stood on the chair, reaching up toward the haze. The haze figure reached down and grabbed Jeremiah and pulled him to her.

"Mommy!" The haze faded as they both disappeared. All the doors in the house slammed at once pulling Claire back into the moment. Julian and Claire both fled the room. They did not stop until they reached the beach. They both fell to the sand and laughed nervously.

"That was incredible!" Julian said as he gasped for breath.

"Yes, it was," Claire said. Was that real or just wishful thinking? She had controlled the house, and she had helped Jeremiah escape.

"One down, who knows how many hundreds more to go," she said staring at the evening sky above them. "This is going to take a while," she said.

"Yes, it is," Julian smiled. She hoped that meant he didn't mind if she stuck around a while longer.

CHAPTER SEVENTY TWO

Quince knocked hard on the door to Grace's apartment and then let himself in.

"Have you heard from her?" Quince asked Grace. Vince and Ethan sat around the dining room table with them.

"No, she doesn't answer the house phone. My guess is be-cause she is still not allowed to be in there. But she is never at the hospital when I call there, either. I keep leaving messages for her to call me."

"Take a look at this," Quince opened the large manila envelope in front of him. "Remember all those shots I took back at the house when Chamber's and his crew were there?"

"Yeah," Grace said, eyeing the envelope with interest.

"There are some interesting photos here. At first I thought they were mistakes in the prints. But I developed the negatives myself."

Everyone except for Ethan seemed interested in hearing what Quince had to say. Ethan cringed and slumped down in his seat. He couldn't seem to take any more of that house or that night.

Quince pulled the shots out of the envelope and spread them out on the dining room table in front of his friends. They each grabbed the photo closest to them and examined the picture. Grace stared at a photo of Chambers in the Templeton dining room. He had his arm raised and was pointing above the table. In the photograph, there was a discoloration there. Grace glanced closer at the photo. The discoloration seemed to be a faint face. She dropped the photo when she realized what she was probably looking at; Ethan and Vincent did the same.

"Ghosts!" Quince beamed. "See here," he said, grabbing Vincent's photo, "The old woman with the knife. And here," grabbing the photo in the middle of the table, "Pirates! It was just like she said. That house is full of them." Quince grinned like he had discovered gold or the cure for cancer.

"Great," Ethan pushed himself away from the table a little.

"It is great. We have proof. Maybe we can get some real help to clear that house now."

Ethan whispered under his breath, "Maybe Claire could finally sleep indoors."

"You forget one thing. If the house really is haunted, Claire is there now. Alone!" Vince said.

"My God!" Grace's face fell as she dashed for the phone. She dialed the hospital and was told Claire had left during the afternoon shift and had not returned yet.

"Does she usually come back before dark?" she asked the night nurse.

"We never see Elizabeth's daughter at night. I have heard she comes here and sleeps during the day."

"Thanks," Grace told the nurse and hung up the phone. "If she is sleeping at the hospital during the day, that means she is staying at that house during the night."

"Isn't that kind of backwards?" Quince asked.

"Something is keeping her at the house. Do you think the ghosts have gotten to her?" Vincent asked the group.

"More likely she had gotten to them. You saw her at the séance. She was amazing. With the right training she could clear that house all by herself," Quince said.

"It could take years to train her to do that," Ethan whispered.

"Yeah, but it could be done."

Grace grabbed the phone and called the house. The phone rang without answer. Grace wished Elizabeth would have in-vested in an answering machine.

"What are we going to do? We can't leave her there by her-self," Grace said, dropping the phone into its cradle.

"Tomorrow is Friday. After work we drive out to the house and show her these photos. Maybe we could get Madeline to help teach Claire what she needs to do. Surely if Madeline sees these photographs she will help us," Quince said.

"Good luck with that," Ethan said.

"We have to try," Quince said.

"I'll stay here and hold down the fort," Ethan told the group.

"Bad idea," Grace said. "While we are off at the house, these ghosts could find out you are here, alone," Grace said. Quince knew what she was up to; Ethan needed closure he could only get by going back to that house.

"Nah, you don't think..." Ethan chewed on the idea.

"Pack your bags tonight. We'll make a weekend of it." Quince told them all.

"During lunch tomorrow I have an errands to run." Vince told them.

CHAPTER SEVENTY THREE

Chief Harris stopped by the hospital room to check on Claire and her mother. He walked in to the room to find Elizabeth alone in her room. Harris walked back out to the nurses' station.

"Do you know where Claire Templeton went?"

"No, sir. We haven't seen her in days."

"Wait a minute. Hasn't she been staying here at night?"

"No, sir."

Harris walked back to Elizabeth's room and sat in the chair by the window. He felt betrayed. If Claire wasn't at the hospital, where was she? He didn't think she would dare to stay at that house. After all, she was afraid of it. But, if she was there, did Dogg know about it?

Harris walked over to the bedside table and reached for the phone to call his deputy. As he dialed the phone, Elizabeth's heart monitor skipped a beat then started to race a little. Then her heart settled back down to a steady beat. Harris glanced at Elizabeth and was startled. Her eyes were open.

"Elizabeth?" he said, placing the phone back in the cradle. He pushed the nurse call button as he moved over her for a closer look.

"Who are you?"

"It's me. Chief Harris."

"Oh. Are you dead, too?"

"No Elizabeth and neither are you."

The nurse rushed in and took stock of the situation. She moved to Elizabeth's side and started to check all of her wires and tubes.

"Hello. You are in St. Anthony's. You are safe here. Do you know your name?"

"Of course I know my name, damn it. What do you think I am? An imbecile."

"No Ma'am, just checking. Can you tell me your name?"

"Pudintaine."

"I see," the tired nurse humored the old woman. "And do you know where you live?"

"Down the lane."

212

"Of course. I'll call Dr. Kilmer and let him know you are back among the living," the nurse said as she hurried out of the room.

The nurse's comment made Harris cringe. That was a bad choice of words for this particular woman. He watched Elizabeth for a reaction, but there was none.

"How are you?" he asked.

"How should I be?" she asked, looking over the bandages on her arms that were strapped to the rails on both sides of the bed.

"Well, awake is a good thing, I would think."

"And how is that good? If I am in the hospital, then obviously I could use a little rest. Why are you still bothering me?"

"I was just going to call my deputy, and see where Claire is."

"Claire! How the hell would your deputy know where my Claire is? She is in New York City, making clothes for rich folks. Thinks she is better than everyone else now, too good to call or come home, even for a visit."

"No Ma'am. Claire is here, in Butcher Harbor. I think she may be at the house," he said before he realized that might be a bad idea.

"At my house? Why?"

"Well, all the hotels are booked for the summer. She has to stay somewhere," he stated, even though he thought that was a very bad idea, too. He said it calmly in the hope Elizabeth might agree with him and not become upset.

"Get her out of there."

"Calm down, Elizabeth. Claire needs a place to stay," he tried to soothe the old woman.

"That's bunk. She is meddling in my affairs, and I don't like it. She left. Let her stay in her own home."

"Let me call her and get her over here. I'm sure she will be happy to see you."

"I doubt that. Go away. I am tired and need to rest now. I am in the hospital for crying out loud! Have some respect." Elizabeth closed her eyes and appeared to go to sleep. Harris wasn't sure if she was really asleep or faking it to get rid of him. He reached for the phone once again and dialed Dogg's cell phone number.

"Dogg."

"Funny thing. I'm at the hospital in Elizabeth Templeton's room, and I'll give you one guess who isn't here."

"Elizabeth?"

"Good try, Raymond. Where is Claire Templeton?"

"Maybe she went downstairs to get something to eat."

"Is that code for go look for her while I race out to the beach house and get her, race her back to the hospital and have her pretend she was at the gift shop or some other place? Cut the crap, Dogg. Where is she?"

There was no response.

"Dogg? Do I need to look for a new deputy tomorrow?"

"No, Chief. She may very well be at the beach house."

"And how exactly would you know that?"

"I might have seen her there once or twice."

"I see. And you didn't think I needed to know this?"

"I didn't think you would be very happy about it, sir."

"You'd be right about that." Harris checked for signs that Elizabeth was listening. He did not see any change in her expression.

"Do you want me to go and get her?" Dogg asked.

"Yes. I would like that very much. And while you are out there, tell Claire her mother is awake."

The line went dead silent again.

"Did you hear me, Dogg?"

"Yes sir. Her mother is awake. I am sure she will be happy."

"Cut the crap, Dogg. I need to know I have a deputy I can trust. This conversation is not making me feel very confident right now."

"No, sir. I think Claire will be upset as hell to know that her mother is awake and I assume speaking."

"You assume right. Get Claire here. Now!" The Chief hung up the phone as the night attending burst into the room. He checked Elizabeth's eyes and felt her pulse despite the heart monitor.

"She was awake?"

"Yes."

"She spoke?"

"Yes, she did."

"Was she aware of who she was and where she was?"

Harris remembered her wise cracks to the nurse; typical Elizabeth Templeton. "Yes and yes."

"Good. I'll make a note in her chart and have the nurse contact me the next time she wakes up." The doctor left the room as quickly as he came in. Harris wished he could step out of the room and walk away, but he knew that Claire's and Elizabeth's reunion would be difficult. He thought he had better stick around. he had a bone to pick with Claire and his deputy.

CHAPTER SEVENTY FOUR

J ulian spotted the headlights first as the car turned onto Peninsula Road. Claire followed his gaze and watched as the car approached the house.

"Shit, that could be my mother," Julian said as he scrambled to his feet.

"What? No. It's probably Dogg. He brings me coffee and sits with me sometimes. But usually in the morning," Claire said, trying to get Julian to sit back down again.

"Dogg? No. Dogg can't see me here either. I can't have my mother find out I'm coming out here."

"What are you- twelve? She will get over it, just like she got over it before," Claire said, standing up and reaching for Julian. He backed down toward the beach.

"I have to go," he said, as he ran off into the night.

"Julian? Wait!" she called but he was gone.

His quick exit made Claire feel uncomfortable. What secret was he hiding that he wouldn't tell her? Why did he not want to be seen with her? It had never bothered him before. Why now? Claire felt dirty again and cursed her house and this town.

Dogg pulled the cruiser into the drive and parked by the back porch. He walked up the steps to ring the bell as Claire came up behind him.

"Hey, Dogg," she called. Dogg jumped half out of his skin.

"Claire! You scared the crap out of me."

"I was just talking to-."

"Chief Harris sent me to get you." He cut her off. "Your mother is awake."

Claire fell silent for a moment, frozen in place. No thought entered her head. No words came out her half open mouth.

"Did you hear what I said, Claire? Your mother is awake. We have to get back to the hospital. Quickly."

Claire stared blankly at Dogg. She knew who he was, and she heard what he was saying; she just had no idea what the words meant. It was as if he were speaking a foreign language. Just as she thought she might make out a word or two, she seemed to slip farther away from herself. Dogg stepped down the stairs and shook her.

"Damn it, Claire. This is no time to wig out on me. I need you to snap out of this. Your mother needs you to be there. Whether she likes it or not, is beside the point. Now let's go. Get your handbag and whatever else you need, and let's go."

"Go where?" she asked, finally catching onto what he was saying. Claire felt like she had been watching a movie that was suddenly unmuted.

"To the hospital. Are you with me, Claire?"

"Why? Is something wrong?" she asked, checking his arms and torso for wounds. Dogg grabbed her hands and stared into her face.

"Your mother is awake. We have to go. Now!"

"Mother? Oh. Oh, my mother. Are you sure?" Claire asked, as she ran past him toward the door.

"Yes, Chief Harris just called from the hospital. And did I mention how pissed he is that you are here and not there? And that I knew about that?"

Claire exited the house with her purse clutched to her chest. She ran past the deputy and opened the passenger door of the cruiser.

"Deputy?" she called to the stunned officer.

"Oh, right," he ran down the porch and climbed behind the wheel. Claire snapped her seat belt against her chest as if to remind Dogg to buckle up as he sped out of the driveway. Dogg buckled his seat belt as he drove down Peninsula Road. He realized that he might catch someone's attention, so he was careful not to race down the road. He drove the speed limit to the hospital.

"What the hell am I going to say to her?" Claire asked, as she stared out the windshield at the lights in town.

"Hello? How are you?"

"No shit, Sherlock. Then what? What do you say to someone who accuses you of killing your own father?"

Dogg stared at her for a second before turning his eyes back toward the road. "She said that?"

"Yes, as she rocked my dead father in her arms, she accused me of being the reason he died."

"Wow. I'm sorry."

"Why? It's not your fault."

"I know. I just don't know what else to say. That must have been awful."

"You might say that."

"This isn't going to be easy is it?"

"No," she said, looking out the passenger window toward the black rolling sea. She wished she could be out there on a boat, sailing off into the darkness. Anywhere would be better than here. But she knew she was going to have to face the inevitable. She just didn't know how.

"So the Chief is angry with you?" She said to change the subject.

"Yeah. I lied to him. I have never done that before."

"I'm sorry. You can tell him I made you do it."

"It won't matter. I am his right hand man. He counts on me. I don't think he will ever be able to trust me again."

"Trust is a hard thing to regain."

"Yes, it is."

CHAPTER SEVENTY FIVE

"As eager as I am to do this whole ghost busting thing, I am not eager to get you back into that house," Quince told Grace.

"And why not? The house never seemed to bother you when you were there."

"I don't know. You, like, became this stranger. Someone else. It wasn't until we got back here that I felt I had the real Grace Noble with me again."

"Yeah," Ethan agreed.

Grace did not understand what they were talking about. She had been herself the entire time she had been at the house, in control, taking care of things.

"It was a little creepy," Vincent added.

"What are you guys talking about?"

"I don't know. You changed somehow, became bossier, protective." Vincent said.

"I am always bossy," She stared at the boys trying to make sense of what they were saying.

"Not like that," Ethan said, looking away from her as he spoke.

"Like what? What are you guys talking about?"

"It's hard to explain. You became like this psycho person." Quince told her.

"I did not. You guys are crazy."

"Yeah, crazy. That was it," Vincent said, smiling as he spoke.

"You say I was crazy and that makes you happy?"

"It is comical when you look back on it. Yes."

"Thanks a lot!"

"No problem."

Grace got up from the table and paced around the room. She ran her hands across her face and into her hair.

"What the hell does that mean?"

"It means that house changed you, somehow," Vincent told her.

"Really?"

"Yes," they all said at once.

Grace considered this.

"I never noticed it when I was there. How will I know if it happens again?"

"We'll tell you," Quince offered.

"Yeah," Ethan said. "We'll be sure and let you know."

"Great. As if going back isn't going to suck enough, now I have to worry about acting strangely, too?"

"I would worry more about why." Ethan added under his breath.

"What does that mean, Ethan?" Grace raised her voice. She never had to raise her voice.

"It just means why you changed is probably more scary." He turned toward the others for support.

"What Ethan means is that being at that house probably made you feel uncomfortable, and therefore you acted differently." Vincent told her.

"Bloody hell. What I meant to say was that that freaking house got into you somehow and made you someone else. That is what I meant to say, and these two bastards are just too afraid to say it!"

Everyone stared at Ethan. He had never spoken so harshly before. Most everything he said was under his breath or in soft, kind words. The incident at the house had changed him, too. This was one more example. It made Grace realize that they were probably right. The house might well have changed her in some way. She didn't notice any change, but apparently they did. That scared her.

"What do we do about it?" She asked.

"We keep an eye on you and let you know as soon as we notice anything strange in your behavior." Vincent told her.

"If we see anything strange at all," Quince added to calm her. "If it affected her that way, how do we know we didn't all change somehow?"

"Grace was the only one I saw act differently." Ethan said. Vincent agreed.

The phone rang and startled all of them. Grace picked up the phone, took a deep breath and then answered it.

"I see. Yes. Have her call me when she gets there. Thank you." Grace turned pale as she hung up the phone. "Elizabeth Templeton just woke up."

"Well, at least we will know where Claire is tonight," Ethan said.

CHAPTER SEVENTY SIX

The short ride to the hospital seemed to take forever. Claire wished she could have stayed in the car for at least that long.

"Let's go. They're waiting, and we're both in trouble," Dogg said, as he dislodged her from the cruiser. He dragged her toward the hospital. Finally she got her feet under her, ripped her arm out of his grasp, and walked on her own.

"I can do this myself."

"You sure about that?" he asked as he walked faster.

"Yes."

When they arrived at the ICU, Chief Harris was waiting for them.

"She's asleep now, but she was awake a little while ago."

"How was she?"

"Same old Elizabeth."

"That's what I was afraid of." For Elizabeth to be like her old self was the last thing Claire needed right now. She had hoped the coma would have softened her mother a little. Claire walked toward her mother's room.

"Not so fast, young lady. You both have some explaining to do."

"It's my fault, Chief. I let her stay at the house. She slept on the porch."

"And that's supposed to make it alright, because she slept on the porch? She could have gotten hurt by crazed town folk like Lynch and his friends. Who knows what could have happened just by sleeping on the porch?

"No Chief, it was my fault. I refused to leave. The deputy just made sure I was safe while I was there."

"You two can cover for each other all you want. It doesn't change the fact that you lied to me, both of you."

Claire and Dogg stared at the floor. Neither of them seemed to know what to say.

"Quit that infernal racket. The sick and dying are trying to get a little rest!" Elizabeth bellowed from her room. Claire closed her eyes as if it would block out the sound, but it didn't help.

"Your mother awaits you," Harris said, as if to get even with her for disobeying him. He always seemed to get angrier at her than with anyone else in town. It was starting to piss her off. When she was a teen, on the rare occasions when she could hang out and get into trouble with the rest of the kids in town, it was always her he yelled at. It sucked when even the Chief of Police hated you. She pushed past him and stormed into her mother's room.

"Mother, back among the living I see," she knew it was a poor choice of words and that was why she had chosen them.

"Not dead yet girl. Sorry to disappoint you."

"Oh, you could never disappoint me, Mother." Not any more than you already have.

"What are you doing staying at my house?"

"It's our house, Mother and I had to stay somewhere. It's the middle of tourist season."

"You need to stay at your own house, in New York."

"Would if I could," Claire hated this.

"That's enough, Elizabeth. There is nowhere else for her to go right now." The Chief surprised her by defending her right to stay at the house.

"Well, I'm better now. Let me out of this bed, and let me go home. Then she can go back to her apartment and leave me be."

"And not a moment too soon!" Claire said

"That's not going to happen," Harris piped in. "Elizabeth, you're going to need someone to tend to you until your hands and wrist start working again."

"I'll hire someone."

"There is no one else besides Claire who will go inside that house."

"Then I'll take care of myself. I've done it all these years."

"You go home with Claire, and behave yourself, or we'll have to put you in a nursing home where they can take care of you for the length of your rehabilitation," Harris told her.

"You just want to keep her here."

"She is free to go whenever she pleases," He said. It pleased Claire to leave right now. But she knew she couldn't.

CHAPTER SEVENTY SEVEN

"What have you done to my people?" Her mother asked from the living room couch where she sat with her bandaged hands in her lap.

"Nothing, Mother."

"Some of them are missing."

"One is missing, and by the end of the day, two."

The idea that her mother could tell a ghost was missing from the house scared her. All the years in the house she knew her mother talked to the ghosts, but she had no idea she kept track of them. She had been home a whole ten minutes and already she knew someone was missing.

"Let's play a little game, mother. Which one is gone?"

"Jeremiah. He always comes and sits with me. He hasn't come."

That made Claire feel a little better. The boy not coming she could handle. Her mom just knowing he was gone she could not.

"Right, his mother came back for him."

"No, she didn't. You did something to him. She can't get in here."

"I told Jeremiah what happened. His mother came back and took him," Claire knew she would tire of this constant bickering soon. She longed for Julian to come and take her away from this place, even if it was just for an hour or two.

"What do you mean by 'two by the end of the day'?"

"That means I will be sending another one on his way to-night."

"Leave my people alone. They don't belong to you. Find your own friends to play with. Like that bossy little snot you used to play with all the time."

"Grace?"

"That one. How would you like it if I sent her away?"

"She'll be here in the morning. She has something very important to show me. More power to you if you think you can send her away." Claire regretted those words as soon as they came out of her mouth. What if her mother could make the house take Grace, too? She pushed the thought away.

"Good, you can go home with her then."

Claire closed her eyes and took a deep breath. "You know I cannot leave or else you have to go to a home. Who will watch over all your 'people' if you are in a home?"

"Don't you threaten me."

"Just stating a fact mother."

"You can stay here if you have to. Sleep on the porch like you always used to. Just leave my people alone. They belong to me."

"They don't belong to anyone. And they have a right to move on."

"To what? Who will know who they are if they move on Who will know about their lives?"

"That is not our problem."

"I don't have a problem with them. They are my friends. They keep me company which is more than I can say for you."

"What the hell is that supposed to mean?"

"You left me here all alone. You never even said good-bye."

"Yes I did. Right out there in the yard. I said good-bye to all of you after you stole my stuff."

"Stole your stuff? What are you talking about girl."

"All my clothes, Dad's photo."

"It is all in your room where you left it."

"No, where you left it. I had it all packed up to move out after Graduation."

"So why didn't you just take your stuff with you?"

"Because you took it away from me."

"You're crazy. I don't know what the hell you are talking about."

Claire's blood boiled. "I'm going to make a sandwich. Do you want one?"

"I'm not hungry. And I want my boy back."

"You'll have to talk to his real mother about that." Claire turned around and ran into a purple bruised foot. It was cold and clammy. She looked up the foot and the leg to see a young girl dangling from a rope attached to the top of the stair case. The girl swayed in the air from contact with Claire's face. Claire fell backwards screaming.

"Don't be ridicules," Elizabeth stated.

"There's a dead girl hanging from the stair rail!"

"That's just Cynthia. It seems you have been ignoring her. She just wants some attention."

"Ignoring her? I have never even seen her before," Claire stood up and brushed herself off. "And her foot just hit me in the face, like she was real or something."

"Cynthia is as real as you and me, dear."

"Gees," Claire moved to the left to avoid contact with Cynthia and stormed into the kitchen.

"I can do this. I can do this. I can –NOT do this," she told herself. Things were getting creepier by the day. She wasn't sure how much more she could stand.

In the kitchen Claire got the bread, ham and mayonnaise out. On her way over to the table she had to walk around several ghosts who just stared at her. The room was crowded and she was the only person in there. She placed a cutting board on the island and got a knife out of the drawer. She started to cut a tomato from the basket on the island, for her sandwich, when Edith Coldburn, the old woman with a knife, came at Claire with her knife drawn.

"I'm going to kill you, you stupid whore!"

Claire had had enough of this.

"Best to go find something else to kill right now, Edith, I'm a little busy at the moment. Mother's in the living room, maybe you could go kill her." Claire's speech was much calmer than she felt. She hoped Edith couldn't see the knife trembling in her own hands, or the terror in her eyes. She kept focused on the tomato.

"That whore. I know she and Charles are getting together at night. I'll kill you first and then go kill your filthy mother."

"Back off, Sister, or me and Mr. Coldburn will be having a wild time of it ourselves tonight. If you know what I mean." Claire waved her own knife at Edith. The ghost appeared con-fused. She raised her knife and came toward Claire. Claire snapped, raised her own knife and glared at the ghost.

"Bring it!"

Edith lowered her knife a bit, raised it again, and then fled the room. Claire set the knife down on the table and took a deep breath. Her entire body trembled with fear. This was going to be much harder than she expected. It was exhausting her.

She realized it wasn't going to be easy to get Edith to move on. The husband would be the key. If she could get him to leave, Edith would most likely follow him. But, she didn't think she was strong enough to handle the two of them just yet. They would have to wait until tomorrow. Tonight she had someone else in mind.

CHAPTER SEVENTY EIGHT

Caroline Laws sat at her desk in her real estate office typing up an ad for yet another house on the market. She had tried to talk the owners into renting the house, but like several other people on Butcher Harbor, they wanted out now. Ever since that stupid séance, and the death of that psychic the stupid Templeton girl brought in to her house, people were putting their houses up for sale and renters were breaking their leases left and right. Caroline made more money renting local houses to tourists than she did off the sale of an occasional house. She needed those rentals.

The door burst open and Caroline prepared herself to face yet another angry owner. She looked up to see who was fleeing the Harbor this time.

"Rory?" He was the last person she would expect to flee the Harbor. He was a fighter. In fact, he and her husband were making a plan to take that house down.

"She's out! Took her home today," he yelled as he slammed his fist down on her desk, knocking over a photo of her, Jeremy and Julian taken on their sail boat in the Harbor. Caroline set the photo upright.

"Claire!" Caroline said, thankful to be done with her.

"No, her mother. The Witch."

"Elizabeth? She's awake?"

"Yeah, and she's back in that house."

"Damn."

"We'll have to move our plans up a bit," he said as he took a seat. "Like this weekend. Saturday."

"But it's Graduation Day."

"All the better. Police'll be busy with all the party'n," Rory's eyes actually lit up when he spoke. "Let 'em all know- Saturday night."

Lynch left as quickly as he came. Finally she would be done with that house and those people. Maybe that would stop all these owners from putting their property up for sale. And maybe some of the canceled rentals would re-sign, but she was afraid it was already too late for this season.

Caroline grabbed the phone and placed her first call of many she would be making today. "We're on for Saturday."

CHAPTER SEVENTY NINE

lizabeth was tucked in her bed for the night. It was still early evening, but she tired easily. Claire took this opportunity to clear yet another ghost from the house. She went into the kitchen in the hope she would be able to get him to come there. The kitchen was farthest from her mother's room; there was less chance to wake her there.

"Volker Waldmunt," Claire called. She hoped she had pronounced his name right.

Nothing. She called him again. No ghost and not even a tremor from the house itself. She wondered if Jeremiah was a fluke. Before she gave up she decided to try the dining room.

"Volker Waldmunt," she called in a half whisper. She didn't want her mother to wake up in case she tried to stop her.

Finally the sailor stepped out of the wall and into the room.

He started to speak in German. She had no idea how to speak German and didn't have time for a crash course.

"Stop, Volker. I don't speak German. I can't understand you."

"Hel-lo" he said in broken English.

"Hello," Claire said, delighted, even if she was scared out of her mind, to get at least one word across. She had no idea how to make him understand her so she shoved the copy of the news print at him, her hand still on the page.

"You were shipwrecked. You and your shipmates perished at sea."

"No sea. Here. We perish here. Men came in storm. We thought safe. They break boat. We have to leave before water come in. They take everyone. Most kilt that night, many others days later. Here."

Claire had goose bumps on top of her goose bumps. "I'm sorry. Those men are gone now. You are safe and you can leave now. All of you."

"Not gone, still here. Some died from wounds when taking our boat during storm. Evil men that came. Some of them die here in this house."

"But they can't control you now," Claire said as the temperature dropped. Here we go again, she thought.

"Yes, they control everyone, even you."

"No, Volker, not even me. We control ourselves. You are already dead.

Do you understand that? There is nothing they can do to harm you now."

"Yes. They are evil men."

The pictures started to rattle just like before. Claire was afraid the doors would slam again. That would wake up her mother. She had to finish this before her mom came downstairs.

"You do know you are dead, right?"

"Yes. I watched many my friends die. I joined them next night."

"If you knew, then why did you stay?"

"Can't go. They won't let us go." The temperature dropped again. The table started to shake.

"Stop this!" She yelled at the house. It did not stop. "Right now!" Nothing changed.

"Volker, you are free to go. Take your shipmates and leave. I deem it so."

The room seemed to warp around her and the walls made a sound like rusty nails being ripped from old wood. She could see her breath.

"They are angry."

"I don't care, Volker. They are about to get even more angry, because I am not going to stop clearing this house. Take your friends. You are free to leave."

Sailors started to appear behind Volker. This scared Claire even more. She shook against the cold and trembled from the fear. The ripping sound got louder. Volker was speaking to her, but she couldn't hear him over all the noise. Claire counted the ghosts as they appeared. There were twenty-three of them.

"You can all leave now." She said. "All of you are free to leave!"

They all just stared at her and then they were gone. The room seemed to warp even more and the noise became unbearable. A fear grew inside of her that she might warp with it. Frost was growing on her eye lashes.

"Be still!" She yelled, but it didn't seem to change anything. "I said be still!" she commanded and the warping stopped, but the noise continued.

"We are done here!" she said, and stormed out of the room. She thought she could feel the temperature rise a little before she left. Her own temperature was rising as she became frustrated with the unruly house.

As she walked through the living room, pictures on the walls and glass on shelves rattled.

"Done!" she yelled, ignoring the rattle and walked over to the front door. The ghosts pulled away from her, parting in front of her as she fled to the safety of the porch.

The whole house could rattle itself to pieces for all she cared. There were now twenty-four souls released from the house. The tiny part of her that wasn't scared shitless was proud of her accomplishment.

Tomorrow she would tackle Edith Coldburn.

CHAPTER EIGHTY

It was late afternoon as Claire tried to regroup. Her mother had slept through all the noise while she cleared Volker and his friends. That in itself was a miracle. Claire took advantage of the opportunity to stay out of the house for a while. She saw movement down the beach and rushed down for a better view. Sure enough it was Julian.

"It worked," she yelled and ran toward him.

"What worked?"

"I cleared twenty-three more people from the house!"

"The sailor and his mates? Good girl. That's cause for a celebration."

"Take me to Murphy's for malt," she said, before she realized she had spoken.

Julian looked down the peninsula toward the boardwalk. Claire was afraid he was going to decline again. He never wanted to be seen with her anymore.

"Everyone is busy getting ready for graduation. It's the only exciting thing around here except for the Fourth of July. The malt shop will be empty."

He seemed to consider this.

"What about your mom?"

"She's a big girl. She can take care of herself long enough for us to have a bowl of ice cream."

"Okay. But we have to share one so she's not alone too long. Deal?"

"Deal."

They walked slowly down the beach, splashing in the water, but careful not to get too wet. The sea was rough from the last storm that passed through and the next one on its way. Dark clouds loomed off in the distance. Claire didn't care. She was with Julian and she was happy. She pulled the legs of her sweat pants up above her knees.

"Still wearing those sweats I see."

"Butcher Harbor doesn't exactly scream bright, gypsy style clothing. I stand out like a sore thumb."

"I bet not half as much as you do in those. People saw you when you first came here, bright, colorful. People talk."

"Yeah? And what are they saying?"

"I don't know. I'm just telling you from experience."

"I guess so, since you have the world's biggest gossiper for a mother."

"Leave my mother out of it."

"Okay, okay." She hadn't meant to upset him.

They walked leisurely up the stairs to the boardwalk. Julian didn't seem to be concerned about being seen with her for a change. She didn't know the reason for the change, but she wasn't about to question it either. She opened the door, and they walked into the cool shop. The chilled air reminded her of the house. She pushed the thought out of her mind. She stopped at the counter to place their order.

"We would like a small vanilla in a bowl. Oh, and two spoons," she said to Mr. Murphy. Irritated that there was no waitress around to take her order, he called to the back of the restaurant for some help up front. Claire and Julian took a seat at their favorite booth at the back of the ice cream shop.

"How does it feel to be free of that house for a few minutes?" he asked.

She wanted to tell him it was marvelous since he was here with her, but she didn't want to press her luck. She was out, in public, with Julian Laws, again. There was hope for the future, one with him in it. She didn't want to scare him away.

"It feels good. Calm. Quiet."

"You want me to shut up so you can have some more quiet?"

"Never."

The waitress came up and placed the ice cream in the center of the table. Then she handed two spoons to Claire and walked away.

"So much for customer service," he said. They laughed while she dug into the ice cream.

"How long do you think we can leave your mother alone?"

"At least this long," she pointed with her spoon at the ice cream. She smiled and licked the back of her spoon, enjoying the real vanilla bean flavor.

"What do you think she would do if she woke up and found you were gone?"

"Probably change the locks and throw a party with all her dead friends." Claire was sorry she had said it as soon as she spoke. She didn't mean to be so disrespectful of her mother. She just needed to vent. "I don't know. She would probably be glad at first, until she tried to pee or get something to eat. Then she would need me. Needing someone and missing someone are two totally different things."

"Yeah, I guess you're right. I'd rather be missed than need-ed."

"Me too."

Claire scooped the last bit of ice cream from the bowl.

"Ready to head back?"

"Not really," she said, not eager to end this moment.

"We can always come back on another day," he said.

With the promise of a future ice cream date, Claire paid for the check and they left the shop.

"Hey, I have something I need to take care of. Can I catch up with you later?" he asked.

Claire was so happy he had come with her, she didn't mind if he had to leave so soon. His promise of a future date had her spirits flying high.

"It's okay. I'll see you later."

"Yeah, later," he said.

She watched him walk around the corner of the store headed toward his home. She loved looking at him, even if it was from behind.

CHAPTER EIGHTY ONE

Claire returned from the malt shop alone. The walk up the beach was exhilarating. She felt good after seeing Julian and actually having ice cream with him in front of people. Even the impending storm could not dampen her spirits. Claire wrapped her sweater around her against the blowing wind; a wind she had paid no attention to with Julian by her side. Coming through the beach grass to the house she noticed a rental car in her driveway. The gang had come up to spend the weekend with her. Then she realized she was probably in trouble.

"You promised you would call- everyday, what happened to that?" Grace asked as she walked across the porch and down the steps to meet Claire in the yard. Grace looked at her like the others in town had looked at her, like she was dirty and unwanted.

"It's been crazy here. Mom. The house. I meant to call."

"Not good enough. I have been worried sick about you."

"I was okay. I had Julian and Dogg to protect me."

Graces face dropped. Claire stared at her confused. She had to change this line of questioning or she was going to lose her great mood.

"I've been clearing the house. The little boy, his name was Jeremiah. His mother came and got him. It was so awesome, Grace. You should have seen it. Julian was blown away."

"Julian Laws?"

"Of course."

"Julian has been here, in this house, with you?"

"Yes. Is that so hard to believe? He still loves me. I know he does. We can get past his mother, eventually."

"That's impossible, Claire."

"I know. His mom can be a bear, but she'll have to come around sooner or later. He will be with me again. I can promise you that."

"He said that?"

The boys had huddled around Grace looking as confused as Claire.

"What's your problem? You have Quince now. And I will have Julian. I'd think you would be happy for me."

"Did he say that!"

"Say what?"

"That the two of you would be together again?"

"No. He won't talk about it, but I see him every day. He'll come around. We just had ice cream at Murphy's."

"Oh my God, Claire, did anyone see you there?"

"You're just like him. What is wrong with the two of you? So what if someone saw us together. It's not the end of the world, you know."

"Claire, you couldn't have had ice cream with Julian Laws."

Grace was really pissing her off now. She was supposed to be her friend, but like everyone else, even she didn't want to see her and Julian together. She must know why he didn't come to New York. She knows who he's been seeing. Claire could not believe that her friend knew all this time and never told her. Her great mood just turned black as the sky behind her. She stormed past Grace toward the house.

"I'm going in. I'm sure Julian will be back later, and you'll just have to deal with it." She brushed Grace's shoulder roughly as she passed.

"That's impossible, Claire...Julian is dead."

Claire turned to face Grace. She could not believe her best friend would say such a terrible thing.

"Julian is dead. You killed him."

Claire started to tremble. She could not believe her ears.

"Why are you being so mean to me? What have I done to you to deserve this?"

"I'm not being mean, Claire. It's the truth," Grace said, than almost in a whisper, "I thought you knew."

"Knew what? A lie?"

"No lie. It's real, unlike Julian. Whoever has been coming to see you has been dead since graduation night seven years ago."

"You couldn't stand it if I was happy. Then I could take care of myself. You couldn't stand that, could you?"

Her body shook as she tried to catch her breath. The world seemed to spin out of control. Tears burned her eyes.

"At the party on the beach, you and Julian challenged each other to another of your surfing matches. There had been a summer storm a few days earlier. Remember? Graduation had to be held inside because of the wind and rain. Everyone tried to stop you, but you both ran head long into those huge waves. They were too much for you. A huge wave took you out and sent you tumbling. Julian saw you fall, and he lost con-trol of his own board trying to save you. He crashed and didn't come up. We got you, took you to shore. Julian's body washed up a few minutes later. He was dead, Claire. All these years, I thought you knew this."

"You're lying. He was here. Look," Claire ran into the house. Everyone followed behind her. "See," She pushed the news clippings around on the table. "We have been working on this, together. We already know who some of the ghosts are and are clearing them one- by- one. Sure it will take a life time, but Julian and I will have a lot of time."

"No, Claire. He's gone. There is no more time for him."

"Mr. Murphy saw us, together. We just had ice cream. He can tell you. You're wrong. He didn't die. He must have survived, and you just don't know it."

"No, Claire. My mom called me and told me about his funeral. He was buried behind the church in the Laws' family plot."

"You're wrong. Old man Murphy can tell you," Claire ran out of the house and across the porch. Her mind reeled with images of the graduation party. It was cold that night. She remembered the wind whipping at their faces. The fire had to be built in a sand pit so the wind wouldn't blow it out. Her breath hitched, jerking as she tried to breathe. This can't be true. She would show them that it was a lie.

She took off running down the beach toward the boardwalk. As she ran, scenes from graduation night kept running through her mind. They were drinking. It was their last night in this Godforsaken town. The next day they were all on a bus out of here. Julian teased her. Said there was no way anyone could surf a wave as big as the ones coming in. That's when she said that she could surf the wave better than he could. She dared him to try and beat her. It would be their last show down at Butcher Harbor before they left for good.

Tears streamed down her face as she ran headlong toward Murphy's shop. Her body trembled, and she stumbled in the sand. She fell to her knees.

"Claire, stop before you make a fool of yourself!" Grace called from down the beach. She was trying to catch up with her. Claire stood up, brushed the sand off her hands and ran, even faster than before. She stumbled up the wooden steps to the boardwalk. These were the same steps she and Julian had so leisurely walked up on their way to get ice cream just a short while ago. She hit the boardwalk at a run, pushing through people as she dashed into the malt shop with Grace right behind her.

"Mr. Murphy! Mr. Murphy?" She couldn't see him anywhere. She raced around the counter as Mr. Murphy came out of the kitchen.

"Claire? What's wrong, girl?"

Grace burst into the shop with their three friends behind her.

"Mr. Murphy, I'm sorry about all this. Claire's a little con-fused right now. I'll take her home," Grace reached for her, but Claire side-stepped her and moved over to the booth she and Julian had sat at. Their ice cream cup was still on the table, not picked up yet since they left.

"See, right here, we sat right here and ate ice cream. Julian and me, one bowl, two spoons! See. We shared an ice cream- together. Tell her, Mr.

Murphy. Tell her Julian was here with me just a few minutes ago."

The look on Mr. Murphy's face said it all. He and the seemingly stunned diners were all in on this together. It was a conspiracy. Why would they want her to believe something so terrible instead of the truth?

"You're wrong. All of you are wrong. I'll show you." Claire pushed past her friends on her way out the door.

CHAPTER EIGHTY TWO

"What in the hell is she talking about?" Mr. Murphy stood stunned, staring at Grace and her friends.

"Claire has it in her head that she and Julian Laws just ate ice cream in here, together."

"That dead boy?"

"It's a long story. She doesn't seem to remember that Julian died. She thinks he is still alive."

"That explains a lot. She was beaming when she came in here. Said she wanted an ice cream bowl with two spoons." Mr. Murphy walked over to the table and picked up the dirty bowl and spoons, he showed them to Grace. "She was rambling on to someone, but there was no one with her. I thought maybe she was waiting on someone and she was nervous, so she was thinking out loud or something. You say she thought-"

"Yeah, she thought she was having ice cream with Julian Laws."

"I didn't see any one with her."

"I have to go catch her," Grace said turning to leave. An arm reached out and grabbed her. It was Chief Harris.

"I'll go," he said. "I think I know where she's going and I better get to her before she gets there. Meet me back at the house."

"Let's get back to the house. We can wait for news there." Grace told the boys. They didn't seem happy about that idea. Mr. Murphy still stared at the empty cup and two spoons in his hand.

"Do you think?"

"With Claire, who knows?" Grace said as she slowly walked out the door. Everyone in the shop stared at them as if they carried a plague of some sort. Grace suddenly knew how Claire had felt all those years. She felt dead inside herself as she and the boys walked down the steps, off the boardwalk, and headed back toward that dreadful house.

"Did you see her run inside the house?" Ethan asked.

"What?" Quince asked scanning down the peninsula for Claire.

"Before, when we were there, did you see her run straight into that house? She didn't even hesitate."

Grace thought about that for a moment. Claire had run into the house without any hesitation. That was progress. She wondered how far the news of Julian's death would set her back.

CHAPTER EIGHTY THREE

The tears burned her eyes and blurred her vision as she ran. Her body trembled and her breaths were hard to take, hitching in her stomach and chest. She brushed the tears away and continued to run as fast as she could. She had to get to him before someone called him. There was a growing fear that Julian might be in on this, too. He had never been that cruel to her before. She couldn't think of what would make him so angry that he could play such a horrible trick on her now.

She took a short cut through Mrs. Castor's back yard, like she and Julian used to do when they were kids. The bushes had become overgrown and a branch snapped back and smacked her hard across the face as she ran. She ignored the pain. It was nothing compared to the pain growing inside her.

She cleared Mrs. Castor's yard and dashed across the street into Mr. Whipple's yard. She sneaked across the back of his property, careful to avoid his prize rosebushes as she went. She wanted to lie down and cry, just sob for hours, but she had to get to Julian before anyone else did. She had to see him. She pushed on.

She ran up the back porch stairs and banged on the door to the next house over. No one answered. She banged harder.

"Julian! You come out here right now. I mean it. Julian!" She kicked at the door and banged on the wood with her fist, careful not to break the glass.

"What in hell?" Caroline Laws asked as she opened the door.

"I need to speak to Julian, right now!"

"Is this some kind of sick joke?"

"I know he's here. I need to see him now. Julian!" Claire tried to push past Caroline, but she didn't budge.

"Take your sorry ass off my porch and go back to that hell-hole you call a home." Caroline spoke slowly, but loudly.

"Not until I see Julian."

"You sick, twisted little bitch!" Caroline started to close the door. Claire stuck her foot in between the door and the jam as Caroline tried to close it.

"I want to see Julian, Now!"

"My son is dead, no thanks to you."

"No, it's lies. All lies. I know he's here. I wrote to him, every week."

"Just a minute," Caroline said, as she forced Claire's foot out of the door and closed it. Then Claire heard the lock turn. She stood on the porch waiting for Caroline to go and get Julian. His mother knew she was beat. Claire had always gotten the upper hand when it came to Julian.

The door unlocked and Caroline was back with a stack of letters in her hand.

"You mean these?" Caroline threw them at Claire. They hit her in the chest as they cascaded to the porch stoop.

Claire scrambled to pick them up.

"I collected those letters over the years wondering why you would write letters to Julian. Are you really that sick that you would write letters to my dead son!"

"He's not dead. I know he's not." Claire said, as she grabbed the letters off the porch.

"You poor wretched child," Caroline said as she slammed the door and then locked it.

It can't be true. They were making it up. Grace said they buried Julian behind the church. She ran back the way she came, so she could cut over to the church and see for herself. Surely they wouldn't go so far as to place a head stone for a boy that wasn't dead just to pull a mean, evil joke on her.

She clutched the letters to her chest as she dashed across the yards she had just come through. Mrs. Castor's bush struck her in the face again, but she didn't care, she plunged forward into the street.

As she ran across the street she felt a sharp pain in her left side, and she was sailing through the air. She slid across some-thing hot beneath her, which she realized was a car when she hit the windshield, breaking the glass. Before she knew it, she was sliding quickly backward. There was another impact as she hit the ground. She stared at the tires underneath the car and the underside of the motor. The bumper was above her head. Someone was reaching for her. She couldn't quite make out who it was through her tears. Her left side hurt everywhere, her heart was broken.

"I think you've killed her, Chief," a voice said as her world faded to black.

CHAPTER EIGHTY FOUR

There was a beeping sound in the background. It annoyed her. She thought it must be her mother's monitor. She wanted it to stop, but she couldn't find it. She drifted back to sleep. The beeping continued. Then she remembered tumbling, forever tumbling in the roll of the waves. It was night, and cold. "Is this how I am going to die?" Here in the sea? Then her thoughts came to Julian. Surely he would save her. He was her brave Knight, her Prince. He would come and yank her out of these tumbling waves. The bottom made contact, tearing her skin on the rough sand. If she weren't holding her breath, she would have cried out. She had to find the top. Find air. She struggled as she was tumbled to the bottom again. Suddenly she was being pulled quickly. She was afraid a shark had taken hold of her and was dragging her out to sea.

Instead she was out of the water. She coughed and fought for air as she was dragged out of the sea by at least three sets of feet. Their foot prints washed away as quickly as they were made. Claire watched the wet sand, coughing up water all the while, as they pulled her onto the shore. People gathered all around her. She heard a siren off in the distance. Voices asked her how she was doing. She couldn't quite respond. A nod of the head was the best she could do while she tried to get the last of the water out of her lungs. It stung, and she seemed to need big gulps of air.

There was another commotion. People were shouting and running. Another body washed up on the beach. More people dragged the body to shore as the ambulance arrived on the beach. The new Chief of Police was there. Harris. He took charge. The body was loaded onto the ambulance. The siren wailed. Flashing lights faded. It was gone. Her world went black.

The beeping sound continued. She had to find it and shut it off before she lost her mind. What was that beeping noise anyway? Down dark halls she searched. There was a light up ahead. As she walked toward it, the beeping sound got louder. It was in there. She ran toward the light. As she burst into a room bathed in the light, the beeping sounded shrill in her ears. She suddenly found herself sitting up on a hospital gurney, tubes running in her arms and across her face. She tried to pull the tube off her face. Someone grabbed her arm before she could yank the tube from her nose.

"You need that," the voice said. It was that new Chief. Oh no, she thought. I am in trouble now. We were surfing, Julian and I, at night. There were no life guards. What was she thinking, Julian was the lifeguard. She glanced around the room in search of him. The curtains were drawn around her bed on both sides, and she couldn't see anything.

"Rest, you've had a rough night," he said as he gently pushed her back. She fought him to stay in an upright position. He gently pushed her back again. She tried to get away from him. All she knew was that she could not lie back down in that bed; terrible things would happen if she laid her head back down on that pillow. Her world would end. She would die, or worse, wish she had died.

"No, I can't. Julian. Where is Julian?"

"Julian is gone, Claire. He drowned seven years ago."

That was it. The reason she couldn't lay back down on the bed because she'd been lying down before. The curtain between the beds was pulled up too far. She could see the other gurney. Julian. Tubes ran in his arm. Someone was beating on his chest. Another squeezing a bag hooked to his mouth. His head was bruised, misshapen somehow. Wrong. A shrill beep filled the air. Then it was gone.

"Time of death...3:42 a.m.," a voice called out.

Claire lay back in the bed. The ceiling tiles loomed above her. She started to count the holes in the tile. There were too many of them and she knew it would take her forever, but she had plenty of time now.

"Claire?"

There was time enough to count every single one. When she was done here, she would go down the hall and count the rest of them. It could take her a lifetime. It would have to take at least that long. She couldn't bear the thought of doing anything else.

"Claire, look at me," the Chief had her head in his hands. He turned her face toward him. "Julian is gone, Claire. Seven years ago. You are in the hospital now. I just hit you with my cruiser. Remember? You were running. You came out of the bushes and ran into my car."

Yes, I was running. But to where? And why? She just stared at his face.

"You had gone to Caroline's house. You were coming back toward town," he said.

Terrible pain in her left side seemed to come out of no-where. Her left leg, hip and head hurt the worst. She reached for the sand scars on her face from tumbling in the ocean. There were none. She was confused. She tried to concentrate, but the world seemed so far away. Julian was gone. That was all that mattered. He was gone. It couldn't be true. He had to get up. He had to open his eyes. Tell her how stupid an idea it was to surf in a storm surge. They would laugh at themselves.

As if two worlds collided, her mind came back to her, and she

240

remembered leaving Caroline's house. A handful of her letters clutched to her chest. Sobbing. Coming out of the brush. Impact. Then she was on the road, staring at tires and the underbelly of a vehicle.

Now she saw that the Chief was older, and so was she. There was no one behind the curtain next to her. Julian was gone. Seven years ago!

The deep breath she tried to take brought terrible pain to her left side. She clutched her side and found it was taped. She let out the air she had managed to take in and took another, smaller breath this time.

"You hit me?"

"Yes."

Claire took a good look at his face. He had let go of hers and stepped back a little, but not far. Tears welled up in his eyes. He didn't seem to notice.

"Chief?"

"Your friends are here in the waiting room. But Claire, there is something I have to tell you..."

It felt like a Star Wars moment. She expected him to tell her he was her father, but that couldn't be true. She remembered his hand holding hers too long when he came to tell her about her mother. The times he seemed to hover a little too close for her comfort. His scolding her throughout her entire life if she acted out like the other kids. He never bothered the others much, but he sure got angry with her. Now she thought she knew why.

"Don't say it. You can't be my dad. My dad is dead."

"No. Claire I am not your dad. But... the night I became a deputy my wife had to be rushed to the hospital. She was hemorrhaging. I found out she couldn't have children. She had to have a hysterectomy. It broke my heart. I wanted to tell her my good news about being made a deputy. But she was hurt and could never have children. I was crushed. When she was out of surgery and rested, I went for a walk on the beach. I found myself on the peninsula. I ran into your mother there. She was weeping, too. She and your father had a terrible argument about moving out of that house. He didn't seem to like it there. He wanted a house in town. She was distraught and so was I. We found comfort in each other if you know what I mean. I went back to the hospital and she went back to Henry. It was a mistake. Several months later I found out she was pregnant. I demanded a paternity test. She refused. I let it go afraid it would destroy my marriage. Then after your father passed away, I went back and demanded the test again. Elizabeth handed me an envelope. She had the test done when you were born. See, even she thought you might have been my child." He stopped talking for just a moment.

Her world seemed to be slipping away again. How can this be true? Just like with the house, everything she knew about her world was a lie.

"I was not your father. Henry was. It broke my heart. All those years we could not have a child. I thought you were mine. I held on to that idea so tightly. I wanted desperately for it to be true."

"So you're not my dad?" Claire's head hurt even more. She closed her eyes and tried to regain some sanity. "Then why would you even tell me this?"

"When you came crashing into my windshield, I thought I had lost you again, just like the night of the graduation party when they dragged you out of the surf. Even though you aren't my child, I have always thought of you as my daughter. Save for your mother, no one else knows about what happened between us or how I have felt all these years. When I thought I had killed you with my car, it shattered my heart into a thousand pieces. I can't keep this secret to myself anymore. The truth will destroy my wife, but I can't go on hiding the fact that I think of you as my own. I couldn't bare it if anything happened to you." He brushed the tears out of his eyes.

Claire didn't know what to say. She stared at him, his tan face from all those years on the beat; his skin almost like leather. There were deep lines in his face. His tall, slim body seemed frail, but was extremely athletic from years of service. Then she saw it, the fear in his brilliant blue eyes.

"It's been a crazy day. Julian. The car crash. Now this...I... I don't know what to say."

"You don't have to say anything. I don't expect anything from you. After all, I'm not your father. I just needed you to know and I just needed to say it."

"I understand, I think. So does this mean you will be bossing me around whenever I get into trouble?"

"Always have."

"Yeah," She smiled as she remembered. "Yeah, you did. I thought you just hated me as much as everyone else in this town. Grace could get into trouble, or Julian or anyone else for that matter, but I was the only one who caught hell for it. Makes sense to me now."

"You don't have to tell anyone, but I do have to tell my wife. I have kept it from her for way too long. She deserves to know."

"You aren't getting off that easily, Dad" she said just to break the tension, putting her hand on his and patting it lightly. He grabbed her hand and gave it a squeeze. Then he took it away and sobbed into it for several minutes. "Hey, I was just joking. You seemed to need a smile."

"It's okay. I just knew you would never have to call me that since I wasn't your father. And it was all I ever wanted to hear."

That was a terrible thing you just did; she had made light of something that went too deep for him. What an awful thing to do.

"Chief, I'm sorry. I didn't mean to hurt you."

He wiped his hands across his face and tried to regroup. "It's okay. I just wanted to hear those words for so long." She let him cry.

Claire remembered how she felt the night her father passed away; the terrible pain and weight of it. Now Chief Harris stood in front of her with that same look on his face. Her father was dead, and her mother was gone to her, lost in a world she could not belong in. Julian was dead. Grace and Quince would probably move in together, or even worse, get married soon. There was no one left in her life anymore. She felt such a terrible sadness herself. She began to cry too.

"Is it okay if I call you Dad from now on?" she asked through her own tears.

"Really?" He seemed shocked.

"Really." He grabbed her and hugged her too tightly for her wrapped up ribs. A moan must have escaped her lips because he let go abruptly.

"Oh, I am so sorry."

"Just a little sore. You did hit me with an SUV, you know."

"Sorry. Grace told me what happened at Murphy's and at the house. I knew you were probably going to Caroline's. I just ran in to you sooner than I had expected. Literally."

"Well, please don't tell me I have to stay here over night. I have to get home to...Oh my God, my mom! She's still home alone!"

"Calm down. Raymond Dogg is with your mom right now. He'll stay with her until you get home. I pulled another deputy on duty for the night shift. Dogg will stay as long as we need him."

"Dogg knows about all this?" Harris nodded his head yes. "And my chasing after Julian?" Another head shake yes. "Great. As if I don't feel like a big enough of an ass in front of my friends, now Dogg knows, too."

"I'm sure he is more worried about you than about what you did."

"Like that helps."

CHAPTER EIGHTY FIVE

"What would you need to do?" Harris asked. They all sat on the porch. Claire was in her swing with Grace by her side. Grace was rocking the swing with her foot. The rocking hurt her side, but she didn't say anything. It was soothing to her friend who had always done so much for her. Ethan, Quince, and Vincent sat along the porch railing. Harris and Dogg sat in what was left of the wicker chairs. The smooth rhythm of the ocean seemed to soothe them all. The sea was starting to get rough again. Another storm was rolling in. The wind whipped around the porch, giving Claire a chill. In everyone's laps were the photographs Quince had taken at the séance.

"Well, I think if I was able to clear Edith Coldburn from the house, the others might move along, too. I don't know why, but I think she has a lot of control here."

"How will she get the others to leave?" Dogg asked. "I mean, can we get them all out tonight?"

"It's possible, but such an undertaking. We would do better to get Madeline over here or someone who knows what they're doing."

"But you have been doing it Claire, on your own. You said you cleared that little boy and all those sailors." Quince told her.

"Yeah, but I had no idea what I was doing. It just sort of happened."

"But you made it happen," he encouraged her.

"I guess. But the house gets more upset each time I clear someone. It could get really ugly. We might not be prepared for that. Chambers died letting Edith talk through him."

"Yes, but we aren't going to let her speak through anyone. No séance, just you doing what you did with the others," Harris said.

"That could be all the difference we need," Grace added. "What if it gets out of hand?"

"You stopped it before, you can do it again." Dogg told her.

"What you guys don't understand is that I have been doing this by the seat of my pants. I have no idea what I am doing- how- or even why it works."

"But it does work. That's all that matters," Quince said.

"Okay, When are we going to do this?"

"Tonight." Harris said a little too quickly for Claire.

"What? No. I need to think about this, plan it out."

"No plan. You didn't use a plan before; you said you were flying by the seat of your pants. That is exactly how you will do it this time," Harris said.

"Not happening. I'm not ready. I need more time."

"It has to be tonight," Dogg agreed with Harris. "The town is becoming a mob mentality. They will march on this house soon, maybe even tonight. If we can clear the house before they get here, we might be able to convince them that the house is safe now."

"A mob?" Grace questioned.

"Yes. It is already being planned. We've done all we can do to control it, but they'll get out of control soon enough," Dogg added.

"How in the hell do you plan to stop a mob once it gets started, deputy?" Grace asked, stopping the swing from rocking to await the answer. The sudden stop of the swing jolted Claire's side. She winced.

"We get their fearless leader to enter the house. Show him it's safe," Harris said.

"What do we do, say take me to your leader to a bunch of townspeople with torches?" Grace asked.

"We already know who their ring leaders are," Dogg said.

"Leaders?" Grace asked.

"Caroline Laws and Rory Lynch," Harris said.

"Great," Grace said, rocking the swing again. "Can't you just arrest them now and put an end to this?"

"We are actually safer with them out of jail. Without them, the crowd will act blindly. With them directing the crowd, there is some control. We just have to control them, without their knowing we're doing it," Dogg said like he was planning a picnic instead of a hostile takeover of a torch wielding mob. Claire could not believe her life had come to this.

"Why don't we just burn it down ourselves?" Ethan asked softly.

"No matter what we think of it, it is still Elizabeth's home. Without her consent, we couldn't burn down her house."

"She would never agree to that." Claire said. "Can't I make that decision for her? We could find her a nursing home somewhere. She's not safe here alone. Look at what she did to herself. What happens when I leave?"

"Not good enough. She could hire a nurse to come by or get a companion. She hasn't run out of options yet," Dogg said.

"But we have run out of time," Harris said. "It has to be now." He got to his feet and held out his hand to Claire.

"You mean right this minute?"

"Is as good a time as any," he said. He walked toward Claire, took her hand in his and pulled her off of the swing. Quince was at her side, eager to get this thing started. Grace stood and took her other hand. She knew when she was beat. They had no idea what they were in for.

CHAPTER EIGHTY SIX

Everyone gathered around the dining room table. Claire re-fused to sit where Chambers had sat during the séance, so she took Quince's seat at the other side of the table. Grace and Dogg sat at her sides. Next to Grace was Quince. Next to Dogg was Ethan, then Vincent. Harris took Chambers spot at the center of the table directly across from Claire.

"Do we hold hands?" Vincent asked.

"Not this time. We leave the lights on. No hand holding. We are merely here for support." Harris told him.

"Works for me," Ethan said. His eyes were wide with fear. Claire felt bad for him, but Grace insisted he had to work through this if he was to move on in his life. Vincent broke out a bottle of water and sprayed everyone with it.

"What the hell?" Harris said.

"Holy water! I got it in New York," he said, proud of him-self. Everyone stared at him as if he were insane.

"Okay," Claire took a deep breath. "Charles Coldburn, I need you to come out. I need to speak to you."

Everyone looked around the room watching for Charles. Nothing seemed to be happening.

"Charles, it is very important that I speak to you. I think I can help you."

There was no response.

"I know you're scared, Charles, but I promise, I can help you."

There was still nothing. They all stared at Claire. She hunched her shoulders to show she had no idea what to do next.

Claire tried another tactic. "Charles, I can bring peace to Edith. I can help her. She can stop being so angry. She can move on."

The room started to chill. Harris smiled. He nodded for Claire to continue.

"Please come out. Help me give Edith some peace."

A small man appeared in the corner. He was timid and seemed unhappy to be there.

"Charles? Is that you?" Claire asked. Everyone turned in the direction she was looking. It was clear none of them saw him, because they all turned around to stare at her again.

"Charles, do you know what happened to you?" Claire asked and the temperature dropped again.

He spoke, but Claire could not hear him.

"Charles I can't hear you. Can you speak to me?"

He came closer to the table. His mouth moved, but she still could not hear a sound.

"Please Charles, I can't hear you. Can you speak to me so I can hear you?"

"She will kill me if I tell on her," the man said, looking around the room nervously. Everyone turned to look at Ethan. Charles' words had come from Ethan's mouth. Ethan stared dead ahead.

"She already has killed you, Charles. You are dead now. She stabbed you thirty-seven times!" Claire told him, not sure why this was happening, but not wanting to stop. Ethan didn't appear to be in danger and Charles was not a major entity in Templeton House so Claire continued.

"Yes, she went crazy, started to accuse me of sleeping with the grocer's wife. Then it was the milk man's wife. Soon she accused me of sleeping with every woman in town," Ethan said. Everyone stared at Ethan except for Claire. She watched the ghost of Charles Coldburn.

"Were you having an affair?"

"Never, Edith was my world."

Grace squeezed Claire's hand.

"What would give her the idea that you were sleeping around on her?"

Grace squeezed her hand harder. Claire looked at her to see what was the matter.

"It was the house. Like with me," she looked at Quince and Vincent in turn. They seemed to agree with her.

"What are you talking about?"

"When I was here last I got very jealous of you," Grace's cheeks turned red. "When Dogg brought you back from the beach, I got really pissed off. Mad about him and about Julian. They all seemed to be drawn to you. And I was jealous of all the time I had spent taking care of you. Don't get me wrong. I loved taking care of you, but when I was here last, it drove me crazy. I could have killed you myself if I had stayed around here much longer."

Claire stared at her friend as if she was the one insane, yet the temperature continued to drop. She must be on the right track.

"I think it was the house. I think maybe it got to her and made her think he was sleeping around. Perhaps it made her jealous. Maybe she lost her mind too."

"That makes sense," Quince said. Claire looked at him with disbelief. She had no idea what they were talking about, but the temperature was dropping like a rock. Charles started to fade away.

"No, Charles, wait!" she called and he stopped fading away. "Charles, can you take Edith out of here? Can you move on?"

He just stared at her. Claire realized she had made a mistake. She had asked him a question instead of commanding it.

"Charles, take your wife and leave this house. You are both free to go."

The room started to warp and that sound of ripping nails from wood returned. Claire spoke over the noise.

"You can go, Charles. It is alright. I will protect you."

Charles just stood there.

"You can-" Claire was cut off by a hard slap in the face. Edith Coldburn had come out of the wall and headed straight for her.

"You little whore. I knew you were sneaking around with my husband. Told you I would catch you, and now I am going to kill you. And all your friends while I'm at it."

Frost grew on Claire's eyelashes. She watched her friends tremble. It had to be from the cold because she didn't think they saw or heard Edith Coldburn.

"Edith, wait! You're mistaken. Charles loves you, no one else." Claire pleaded. Everyone except for Ethan looked around the room for Edith, but she still seemed to be the only one who could see or hear her.

"I know you have been seeing each other. I know you want him for yourself, but he belongs to me."

Claire had no idea how to get Edith to listen to her and she seemed to be running out of time. The frost on her eyelids was getting thick, and she was freezing from the cold.

"You're right, Edith," Claire changed her tactics. "I have wanted Charles all my life, but he doesn't want me. He only loves you. He wouldn't have anything to do with me. He told me so."

"You're my world, Edith," Charles said through Ethan. The others seemed lost.

"See, he wants you, only you."

"Come away from here with me," Charles said.

"Come away? Where? This is my home. This is my house!"

"You are dead, Edith, you killed yourself after you killed Charles. Don't you remember?"

"He wanted me to leave. He wanted us to get away from here. Leave this town, this house. I am not leaving this house. It is mine. You just want us to leave so you can have it to your-self."

"No, Edith. I want you to go so you and Charles can be happy again."

"Leaving this house will not make me happy. It's mine. You're just like him. You want me to give up what is mine so you and he can sneak around behind my back."

Elizabeth was a broken record, and Claire had no idea how to get her off that train of thought. She was trembling and she knew her friends were too. It was so cold in here now, and she had to shout over the noise of wood ripping apart. This had to end, but she had no idea what to do.

Before she could figure it out, a figure stepped out of the wall in the corner behind Charles Coldburn. It was Volker Waldmunt. But it couldn't be, he was gone. She had cleared him from the house earlier today.

"Volker. What are you still doing here?"

"It's _ trick" he said. His words were breaking in and out. The house was trying to stop him from speaking, or at least keep her from understanding him. She seemed to catch every other word.

"What trick? Is there some trick I need to use?"

"NO! __ a trick___ house__ let __ go," he tried to tell her.

"A trick. The house is playing a trick? On who? On me?"

"Yes, won't let __ go. Even __ boy __ here. Not __ mother."

Chills ran down Claire's spine that had nothing to do with the cold. None of them had left the house. It was keeping them here and making her think that they had gone away. But why? And how?

"Claire? What is it? What's wrong?" Harris asked.

"The house. It's all a trick. They never left. Jeremiah, Volker. The others, they're all still here."

"How can that be?"

"I don't know. Volker how are they keeping you here? What is making you stay?"

"Book __ deaths. In __chest. _____. The answer __ in __ Book of deaths."

"Where? Where is the book?"

"In __ chest. Find __."

"Where? Where is the chest?"

Volker faded away as Edith slapped her face from across the room again.

"No, you don't, you filthy whore. You will die before you ever find that book."

"What is it, Claire? Tell us!" Harris shouted over the ripping noise.

"Something about a book, in a chest of some sort. He said the answer lies in the Book of Deaths."

"What is that?"

"I have no idea."

"We'll help you find it. But first can you get this noise and the cold to stop?" he yelled.

"Be still! Stop this infernal racket and bring the temperature back to normal."

There was no change. She shook her head and tried again. "I said be still. Quiet that noise! Take away the cold!"

Edith laughed, her voice echoing around the room; this sound the others seemed to hear.

"Edith, go away! I'll deal with you later." Claire said, as Charles started to fade out of view. Edith did not go with him. "Edith, I am warning you, if you do not go away right now, I will take Charles away from you!"

A thousand voices seemed to start speaking all at once. She couldn't understand Edith over all the other voices. Her head hurt badly from all the sobbing earlier, and the noise of all the voices made her head ache worse. On top of all that, she was frozen to the bone.

"I can't do this!" she yelled to Harris.

"Yes, you can. You have to. You don't have a choice," he yelled back at her.

What pictures were left on the walls fell to the floor. Ice seemed to form in the corners of the room and on the windows. The table and chairs shook as the floor beneath them seemed to be coming apart. Claire had no idea how to stop this and there was no one else who could.

CHAPTER EIGHTY SEVEN

Graduation should have been getting ready to commence. Lines of students should have been forming in the gymnasium, ready to walk outside onto the stage, and receive their diplomas. Eager parents should have been sitting in the chairs in front of the stage.

Instead, there was a sea of empty seats. No one had shown up for graduation. The wind was picking up and dark clouds gathered over the horizon.

All the people were in their homes and garages busy preparing for the big event. Wives brought towels and rags to their husbands who had fashioned sticks, out of shovel and rake handles. Children ran back and forth from the gas station, filling up jugs with gasoline and taking them back home to their waiting parents. Kyle Simmons, the gas station owner, gladly pumped gas into those cans without charging the children one dime. The police would have been alerted to the situation in town, except that the newest deputies that were on duty were loyal to Rory Lynch, and not to Robert Harris. Even the remaining tourists were busy preparing for the event. The mob was preparing to march on Templeton House.

CHAPTER EIGHTY EIGHT

There was a sound like nails being ripped from wood. The house seemed to be coming apart at the seams. It appeared to Claire as if everyone could hear the voices now. The noise was about to drive her insane. The windows had become completely covered with ice. Icicles dangled dangerously from the dining room chandelier. The frost on her eye lashes was thick.

"We have to get out of here, so we can regroup. Make a plan," Harris called over the noise. Claire couldn't agree more. Everyone fled into the living room, but the windows were covered with ice there as well. The house still seemed to be coming apart at the seams. And the voices could be heard in there as well.

Dogg ran to the door to go outside where it would be quiet, so they could talk, but the door was frozen shut. He and Harris tried to break the glass window panes, but nothing seemed to have an effect on them. Claire and Grace ran to the back door to see if they could get out there. That door was sealed shut with ice, too. The boys tried to light books on fire to melt the ice on the door, so they could get out of the house. Each time they tried to light the lighter it would blow out. Soon the lighter too became frozen and would not work. They were sealed in the house by the ice that was forming all over the windows and doors.

"What now?" Quince yelled.

"We find that damn book!" Harris hollered back.

"We don't even know what we are looking for or where to look for it," Vincent said.

"It is probably the center of activity," Dogg yelled.

"The FBI said the dining room was the epicenter. It has to be in there." Harris yelled.

"There aren't any books or chests in there, not even a cookbook," Claire told them, as she and Grace pulled book after book off the living room shelves looking for the Book of the Deaths.

"It must be hidden in there then."

Claire's mother came down the stairs yelling. "What in the hell do you think you are doing?"

"Elizabeth! We have to find the Book of Deaths. Do you know where it is?" Harris called to her.

"Where? I don't even know what it is. What are you talking about? Why have you upset my house?"

"Can you calm it down? Can you make it stop?" Harris asked her.

"Of course I can. Quiet down now. I need to think," she yelled. The ice continued to form. The voices kept talking, and the walls continued to sound as if they were being ripped apart. "I don't understand."

Claire understood. The house was in control now. She and her mother would have no influence over it anymore. Their only hope was to find that book.

"Keep looking," Claire told Grace, who was still looking through the book shelf in the living room. Everyone else followed Claire into the dining room. They searched shelves and drawers. Harris climbed under the table and searched under the table top.

"What are you doing?" Dogg asked him.

"Looking for a hidden compartment," he said.

"Of course," yelled Quince, as he started to beat on the walls around the room. Vincent and Dogg stomped the floorboards. Claire checked the cabinet for a false door or opening. There was none. She turned back to see what the others were up to.

"Dad?" Clare said.

"Yes," Harris yelled.

"Dad, what are you doing here?"

The ghost of her father stood in the dining room. He pointed toward the floor under the table.

"It's my Dad. He's pointing under the table."

"Got it!" yelled Harris. He crawled out from under the table and shoved the table out of the way. "Give me a hand," he yelled to Vincent. They pulled the rug up and discovered a trap door that was hidden under the table all these years. Quince threw chairs out of the way and joined them. Vincent and Harris tried to pull the trap door open, but it wouldn't budge.

"It's not ice. Must just be stuck," Harris called over all the voices and ripping sound. As soon as he said that, ice started to form over the trap door.

"Everybody grab hold before it seals itself shut!" Harris yelled. They all huddled around and grabbed the inset ring that lifted the door. Everyone pulled at once. The door gave way a little.

"Again!" Harris called.

They all reset their grip on the ring and pulled again. The ring was cold now, and it tore their hands to pull on it, but no one stopped. The door gave a little more. They reset and pulled again. This time Quince and Dogg got their hands up under the trap door and helped to pull it up. The trap door gave some more. Dogg stood up, Quince joined him. They each gripped the trap door again and pulled it up some more. It was almost free, but ice kept forming over the sides, making their hands slip when they tugged now. It seemed like a lost cause. The ice was forming too quickly.

Harris joined Quince and Vincent to pull the door one last time. Ethan slipped past them and slid down between the trap door and the floor. He struggled to get through, but he got under the trap door somehow.

"PULL!" he yelled as he pushed up from underneath the door. It gave way with a terrible crack as the ice split.

"Way to go, Ethan!" Quince yelled as he scrambled down the hole and joined him in the crawl space under the house. "Hey, I think we might be able to get out from down here." He crawled off out of sight. Vincent climbed into the crawl space as well and headed in a different direction from Quince.

The ghost of Claire's father pointed to the sand under the trap door.

"It's under the sand," Claire yelled.

Ethan frantically dug at the sand. Claire climbed into the space and pulled sand behind her to help him search for the chest with the Book of Deaths in it.

Harris stayed at the hole in the floor watching over them. Dogg and Grace moved out of sight. Elizabeth kept beating Harris on the back with a broom. Claire kept digging. Sand filled in the hole as soon as she pulled it out. This didn't seem to slow Ethan down. He was on a mission and couldn't seem to dig fast enough. His lap was full of sand.

The house groaned above them as it started to shake. Bits of dirt fell from the floorboards overhead as wooden pegs worked themselves free from the wood they held in place. Quince came back, and Claire let him slip past her back inside the house. She could only make out bits of what he was saying to Harris.

"No go. No way out," he yelled.

Vincent came back next, and he slipped by shaking his head no. Apparently there was no exit from under the house either. She and Ethan kept on digging. The ghosts were gone, perhaps hiding, as a power bigger than them inside the house took over shaking the very foundation of the house.

CHAPTER EIGHTY NINE

The sun was setting when Rory went to the Shady Lady Restaurant to meet with the rest of the mob. Trucks lined both sides of the street now and the parking lot to the rear of the restaurant was full of vehicles as well. He parked his truck in the center of the road and got out.

"You boys ready?" he asked the men waiting in their trucks. Everyone said yes at once.

Inside, the restaurant was packed with people waiting for him to arrive. The chatter around the room was almost deafening. Everyone cheered as Rory entered.

He stopped to speak to Caroline Laws and her husband. "You ready to get your hands dirty, Councilman?" he asked Jeremy Laws. He seemed hesitant, but nodded yes.

"How 'bout you? You understand the plan?" he asked Caroline. She just gave him a huge smile that let him know he didn't even have to ask.

He walked up to the counter and blew the whistle around his neck to silence everyone. This brought Lila out of the kitchen.

"Rory, what the hell is going on here?" she asked.

"Just a little business," he said as he turned to the crowd. "We'll be loading up here in just a few minutes," he told the crowd. He grabbed Lila's hand as she came after him. She tried to pull away. "And don't think you can call that son of yours cause he's out there with that little runt right now," he told her. Her eyes grew wide with surprise and fear.

"Johnny," he called to John Walker, the Post Master, "Watch her and make sure she don't call that son of hers." He released her arm. Johnny took her over to a chair and sat her down. He pulled her hands behind her back, and Sam duct taped them together behind the seat. Then they duct taped each foot to a leg of the chair. She struggled, but she could not prevent them from tying her down.

"I have food cooking on the stove. It will burn and catch fire." she told Rory.

"That ain't the only fire there'll be 'round here," he said. "Beth Ann, turn it all off." His face grew an ugly smirk. Beth Ann ran into the kitchen.

"Did anybody bring some marshmallows?" he asked as a joke. Several people raised bags of marshmallows into the air. He chuckled. This was his kind of mob. His daddy would have been proud.

"Let's get to it then."

"You won't get away with this, Rory. Raymond and Robert will stop you!" Lila screamed at him.

"They might be able to stop me," he said as he pointed out the window. Several more trucks pulled up behind Rory's pick-up truck. "But he sure as hell ain't gonna be able to stop all of them." Rory grinned as he watched even more people show up on foot, torches in their hands, ready for the signal to light up. Rory strolled out of the restaurant like a king about to address his masses.

At the truck he lowered the tail gate. The bed of the truck was full of Kerosene. People swarmed around him to put fuel on their torches. Those that had their own gas prepared their torches as well.

"Light 'em up!" Rory yelled as he lit the first torch. A loud whoosh sound filled the air as torches were lit all around him. The buildings around him were bathed in the yellow light. Any-one who didn't have a ride jumped into the first available truck. Rory threw his keys to Sam Sharp and jumped in the passenger side of his truck. He climbed up so he was sitting out the passenger window to rally the crowd, lit torch in hand, as seventeen trucks and five cars headed for Templeton House. Behind the cars were the rest of the town—men, women, and children marched, torches in hand. At the back of the pack, Madeline and Herbert walked side-by-side with their own torches aflame.

"Slow her down," Rory told Sam as he admired the sea of torches that made their way toward Templeton House. He made sure that Sam kept the pace slow enough that the folks on foot showed up at the house at the same time as the rest of them. He wanted to savor this moment.

Sam parked the truck in the driveway, blocking the police cruisers. He motioned for the crowd to follow him toward the house. Yesterday he had made a plan with Caroline Laws that she and her husband would cover the back door and he would cover the side by the ocean. When he blew the whistle he wore around his neck, it meant the house was clear of people and they should set the house on fire.

A crowd stormed up the porch behind Rory. He could see movement behind the glass of the door, but all the windows were fogged up.

"Come'n out of there or you're going to die 'cause we are gonna set the place on fire!" he yelled. There was frantic movement behind the glass, but no one came out or answered him. Rory could hear voices, loud voices. They were in there alright and they were talking. They were ignoring him. If there was one thing he hated most, it was to be ignored.

"One last time, Chief, bring those folks out or you all are going to die in there," he yelled. Still there was no response. The house sounded like it was coming apart. Rory was damned if something other than his people was going to bring down this house tonight. He blew his whistle setting his plan in motion.

Several men marched up the stairs behind Rory carrying tanks of gas. They doused the house with the fuel. Rory made sure his was the first torch to set fire to the house. He put his torch to the door with a wild yell.

By now a circle had been formed around the house. The crowd made the same wild yell as they set fire to the rest of the house. Flames lapped at the clapboards. There was a sizzling, screaming sort of sound escaping from the house as it burned. The house was bathed in the light of the fire; it glowed in the dark, starless night. The circle of people widened as they pulled back from the tremendous heat that burned at their faces. Once at a safe distance, the mob waited and watched the house burn from all sides.

Rory was sorry there were people still inside, but he had done all he could to get them out. If they burned to death, it was their own fault.

CHAPTER NINETY

Ethan was buried to his waist in sand as he and Claire dug beneath the house to find the chest. Dogg and Grace came back to the hole in the floor where Harris, Vincent and Quince were waiting and watching. They were talking about something. Grace was waving her arms around and dragging Harris away from the hole.

"Quince! What's going on?" Claire called to him as she continued to pull sand out of the hole. Her left side and leg ached now from sitting in the cramped space and pulling at the sand.

"Not much. An angry mob has just set fire to the house, that's all," he yelled down to her. He was trembling from the cold.

"A warm fire sounds nice!" she called up, trying to remain calm.

"Yeah, except that we're still inside," Ethan hollered.

"Where's my mother?"

"In the living room. She is scolding the house for falling apart. Wooden pegs are flying out of the walls all over the place. We don't have much time!"

The thought of becoming bar-b-que gave Claire a chill, even though she was frozen to the bone. She dug faster. She and Ethan reached in the hole and grabbed sand at the same time. They looked at each other and laughed then reached in the hole and grabbed each other again, pulling sand away to reveal a hint of wood. They looked at each other with wide eyes. They dug faster.

The house shook harder causing in her a terrible need to flee, but Claire and Ethan stayed in the hole and dug the chest out of the sand. The terrible ripping sound made the house feel like it was just inches from her ears. She could practically feel the wooden pegs being drawn out of the wood above her. Inside the house she could hear boards crashing to the floor. Just as they were about to get the chest free, an arm reached down into the hole and grabbed her. It was the Chief.

"Door is open. The ice melted. We can get the hell out of here," he pulled her arm.

"No! I have to finish this. Go! Get my mother out of here!"

"Don't be stupid. The house will burn down. The ghosts will leave."

259

"What if they don't? What if they get trapped on the peninsula forever? I have to find the key to getting them out of here for good."

Ethan dug around the box freeing it from the sand.

"Ethan, you can go. This is something I have to do. You don't."

"Yes, I do. That guy was in me. I could feel his pain and anguish. He has to be set free. I'm not leaving until he can go, too."

Harris left the hole, and Claire prayed that he was getting everyone else out of the house. She and Ethan dug the box free. Claire stared at it for a minute and took a deep breath. The box was old and the wood was worn. A metal band around the box had rusted part of the way off, but the clasp was still solid.

"What do we do now?" Ethan asked.

"Take it in the house. Find a hammer or something," she yelled back. The house trembled, and she was sure it would crash around their heads at any moment.

"Okay," Ethan's eyes were huge and he shook from more than just the cold.

"Help me get it up there."

The box was heavy and it took both of them to lift it. Claire thought she was not strong enough to raise the box out of the hole. Her arms ached and her ribs were on fire.

"I can't do it," she yelled to Ethan.

"Yes you can. We're almost there," Ethan yelled at her. As she gave a final push the chest flew out of her hands. Then an arm reached down and pulled her out of the hole. It was Chief Harris again. When he pulled her free, Dogg grabbed Ethan and pulled him up from the space below the house.

"We can't get it open," she yelled above the noise of the house. While they were in the hole, entire boards had fallen out of the ceiling and off the walls. Wooden pegs littered the floor. The place looked like a disaster area. The ice was melting and dripping down the walls and from the ceiling, as fire licked around the window frame, eager to penetrate the house. Smoke filled the air making it hard to breathe.

"Where is my mother?"

"She's outside with the others. We should join her."

"Not until we open the chest. Whatever it is might need to be done in here!" she yelled as another board fell out of the ceiling, almost hitting Dogg.

"Alright, move," Harris grabbed the box and moved it away from them. Then he took out his revolver and shot the lock off the box. Claire thought she could hear Ethan, Quince and Dogg cheer over the noise of the house.

She dashed to the chest, removed the broken lock, and opened the box. It was empty except for a large, leather-bound book. The leather was old and moldy. Claire picked up the book and gently opened the cover. The pages were frail, molded on the edges. She read the first page out loud.

"Here be the Book of Deaths. All those written within have perished either at sea or within these walls. Every soul herein is bound to this house forever. Release can only come by the calling of the names of the dead."

"What does that mean?" Quince asked.

"I don't know." Claire yelled back. She leafed through the pages, running her fingers over the names of each soul listed. Each name was written in red ink.

"Blood!" Ethan yelled at her. She yanked her hand from the book and wiped it on her sweat pants. "We have to read them, out loud!" Ethan said as another board crashed down from above their heads.

The book was thick and it was half full of names.

"That will take too long," Claire yelled.

Harris grabbed the book from her hands and tore it into sections.

"READ!" he yelled as he handed each of them a section from the book. The temperature was rising as the fire worked its way into the house. The damp ceiling and walls slowed it down, but only a little. The heat from the fire dried the area closest to it, allowing the fire to work its way deeper into the house.

"Davy Thompson," Claire read as a shrill scream was emitted from the walls. Claire hoped that meant he had moved on.

"Richard Levers," Ethan yelled. Another shrill scream came out of the walls.

Dogg, Harris and Quince joined Claire and Ethan in reading the names from the Book of Deaths out loud. The house seemed to scream from every crevice. The entire building shook, bringing down another board from the floor above. Harris left the group. They kept on reading. After a minute he returned.

"We have to get out while we still can."

"But we have to finish."

"It will take too long. Take it outside. If it doesn't work, we can come back in" he yelled, pulling Claire by her arm. He was not taking no for an answer this time. The others followed close behind her. In the living room Harris ducked under a huge ceiling beam that had fallen and was on fire.

"Stay low," he called to Claire as he took the book from her hands. She crawled under the beam and reached for Ethan's pages. He passed them to her, and he came under the beam. Then Quince and Dogg climbed through. They fought their way to the door around fallen beams and wooden pegs. The door frame was a wall of fire.

"The fire is thin. Just run outside quickly. Roll in the sand in case you catch fire on the way through." Harris hollered to them. He took everyone's pages and stuffed them inside his shirt.

"GO!" he yelled. Claire hesitated, but Ethan ran past her and out the door. Quince was right behind him.

"Go now!" he called to Claire.

As Claire went to run out the door a mist appeared behind her and yanked her back inside the house.

"Be stronger than the house Claire," Harris yelled to her. A huge ceiling beam fell from above and knocked Harris to his knees. Pages from the book fell around him onto the floor. One of the pages caught fire. Claire pulled herself free from the pirate ghost and stomped the fire out. Dogg grabbed Harris, and Claire scooped up the fallen pages. They all ran through the burning door. The heat was as overwhelming as the cold had been. Even though she was not on fire, the heat given off by the house seemed to burn her flesh.

Quince rushed up the stairs to help Dogg with Harris, who was bent over and not walking on his own. They dragged him off the porch, away from the house, toward the beach. The house was surrounded by hundreds of people who cheered when they cleared the porch, every one, that is, except for Rory Lynch.

Claire noticed the cool temperature of the air as soon as she cleared the door. The impending storm had chilled the night air. She prayed the storm would hold off until all the spirits were released from the house and the house itself had been destroyed.

"Is he alright?" Claire asked, as Grace gave Harris a once over.

"He needs a doctor."

A man stepped out of the crowd and came over to them. It was one of the paramedics that helped with Chambers on the night of the séance. The man looked in Harris' eyes. He felt his pulse. Then he felt around his body.

"It may be a fractured collar bone. Possible cracked ribs. At the very least, he has had the wind knocked out of him."

"Read!" Harris yelled at them, but the sound barely came out.

Claire passed around the sections of the book to all her friends. They called out each name. The house screamed, and flames shot higher into the night sky. As Claire read the names from the Book of Deaths, Caroline Laws walked out of the crowd and reached out her hand. Claire was dumbfounded, but she tore her section in half and handed it to Caroline, who started to read the names out loud. Madeline stepped out of the crowd next and reached for some of the pages. Grace broke her section in half and handed it to her. She too began to read. Suddenly many people stepped out from the crowd that had made a line around the house. They each took pages and went back to the circle. They in turn passed half of their section to the person next to them. Claire was amazed, but she kept reading. She felt they had to finish the Book of Deaths before the house burned completely down or the rain came and put the fire out.

Claire's mother refused to help them read from the book or to help clear the ghosts in any way. Claire understood and did not force her to help. She knew that to her mother these ghosts had been companions. To her mother this was a tragic loss, her home awash with flames.

The house squealed and screamed as each ghost was released. It moaned and groaned as beams caved in and the house fell in upon itself. Claire's mother wailed with it. The fire grew brighter and seemed to change colors from yellow to blue to red with each name that was called out.

Harris refused to leave for the hospital until they had finished reading all the names from the book. Someone in the crowd had passed a jacket to him and Grace put it under his head. He watched the mob that had come together to take down the house, come together to clear as many spirits as possible before the house burned to the ground.

"Henry?" Elizabeth called out, causing Claire to stop reading. She looked at her mother who was staring at the house. On the porch a man stood motioning to her mother to come up the stairs and join him. He looked like her Dad, but something was wrong.

"What? Mom, no! It's a trick!" she called and reached for her mother as she got up and headed for the house. Quince and Dogg grabbed her mother and held her back. She fought against them, dragging them forward.

"Man, she is strong," Quince said.

"Or strong willed," Dogg added.

"Henry!" Elizabeth fought against them and then she fell to her knees. She grabbed her chest and went limp. The boys laid her gently on the ground. Claire knelt beside her mother.

"Mom? Mom!," she shook her mother hard, but there was no response. Dogg felt for a pulse. He shook his head.

"She's gone," he said and wrapped his arms around Claire, holding her tightly. Claire watched as a misty figure of her mother stood up.

"Mom?"

The ghost of her mother walked toward the house.

"Wait, Mom, no. It's not Dad. It's a trick. He's not Dad. No!" Claire screamed as she tried to break free and keep her mother from entering the house. Dogg squeezed her tighter. She fought against his grip, the pain in her left side blazing with pain. "Mom, don't go in there!" Her mother walked up the steps and joined the ghostly figure of her father. Before he turned and walked Elizabeth into the house, he winked at Claire.

"You son of a bitch!" Claire screamed at him, pulling against Dogg.

While Dogg held her, she wept.

The crowd around the house continued to read the names from the Book of Deaths.

Still weeping Claire pulled against Dogg again.

"Relax, calm down."

"I have to help them finish the book."

"You can take a minute and pull yourself together. My god, your mother just died."

"There is no time for that right now. We have to finish the book before the house burns down."

Dogg released her, and she grabbed her pages from the book. Before she started reading she took a chance to release her mother from the house's grip.

"Elizabeth Templeton!" She screamed her mothers' name at the house as if she had read it from the pages of the book. The house screamed back. Claire forced herself to believe that her mother was released from the house, but she had no way to know as the house was screaming every time a name was read from the book, and the entire town was reading off names simultaneously. But Claire refused to believe any different. Her mother was not going to be trapped inside that house forever.

They were still reading names from the book of deaths as the sun rose in the morning. The last embers of the house glowed in a charred heap. The storm that hovered over them throughout the night kicked into high gear with the coming of the dawn. The wind picked up a single page from the Book of Deaths. It had been dropped while being passed from hand to hand, and the names on the page were never read out loud. The page spiraled up, away from the house, as it was carried down the beach. Huge rain drops began to fall. The blood written names began to wash away without being read out loud.

CHAPTER NINETY ONE

The sign outside of the shop on Boardwalk Boulevard read 'Claire's Boutique'. Inside people had gathered to celebrate the grand opening of her new store. Dogg admired Claire from across the room. He thought she looked sexy in her bright, gypsy attire. Her eyes seemed to light up when people asked her about her new line of clothing.

"Guess I had better get used to you and her together," Lila told him as she sipped some of her famous coffee, catered to the event.

"Guess so," he said. He smiled, but he knew his mother was a hard sell. It would take some time, but he felt like he had all the time in the world.

"Finally got Rory to stop belly aching so I could come over," Chief Harris said, as he and his wife Becky entered the store and joined Dogg and Lila. Rory had been placed under arrest pending a trial of his peers. Harris knew he would get off easy enough since everyone had a hand in the fire, but he needed Rory to know he was wrong about setting fire to a house with people in it, so he made sure the trial was delayed as long as possible.

He looked around the shop admiring what Claire had done with the place in such a short amount of time. It had only been a few short weeks since the fire and the burial of her mother. Claire excused herself from the crowd and came over and hugged Becky.

"Those sheers look great!" Becky told her. She had given the sheers to Claire to use in the display window. Becky looked around admiring how bright and colorful the place was, just like Claire.

"Looks like quite a success. The town seems to be accepting you," Harris told her. She beamed.

"Yes they are. I was afraid people wouldn't shop here anymore once I took it over. But they were my designs she was selling before. With some simple changes to bring the styles up to date, things are flying off the racks!"

"What will you do during the off season, dear?" Lila asked. "I could use some help at the restaurant."

"Well, I can use the winter months to start working on the next year's fashions. Also I have opened a storefront online and I'll be selling my clothing year round from there."

"It sounds like you have a head for business," Lila stated.

"Are you completely moved in?" Harris asked her.

"Yep. Raymond helped me finish moving upstairs last night. The space is perfect for just one or two people," Claire blushed as she sipped her cinnamon coffee.

Cheers went up around the room as Grace and the boys entered the shop. Claire ran to Grace and hugged her. She began to show her around the shop. Quince, Vincent and Ethan joined Harris and Dogg.

"Wow, she really did it," Ethan said, feeling the fabric of a colorful summer dress on a manikin next to him.

"Yes, she did," Dogg said. "I hear congratulations are in order," he said to Quince.

"Yes. We are officially engaged," he said.

Madeline came in the open door with a huge plate full of tarts and cookies.

"Fresh goodies from my new Bake Shop," she said, as she passed the plate around.

"These are really good," Ethan said around a mouthful of cookie. Lila agreed.

"So, no more Deputy Dogg?" Vincent asked.

"Nope. He was promoted to Inspector Dogg. Starts his training next week," Claire said proudly as she joined them, wrapping her arms around Dogg's waist. His heart melted as her eyes finally lit up when she looked at him.

"Looks like congratulations are in order for everyone," Harris said.

"Cheers," they all clanked their coffee mugs together.

Down the street an almost blank piece of paper fluttered around a support under the boardwalk. It used to carry the last of the names from the Book of Deaths that were never read out loud. Now only a few letters remain. They were H__ry Tem_____ton and __ber_ C__mbers. The rain had completely washed the rest of the names away.

THE END

Here is a sneak peek at the next book in the Butcher Harbor Series...coming soon!

PIRATES COVE

Butcher Harbor Series

Book Two

CHAPTER ONE

Claire Templeton walked up the beach toward the charred remains of what used to be her family home on Butcher Harbor Peninsula. Her white gauze gypsy outfit fluttered in the sea breeze, whipping lightly around her well-formed calves. Her feet were bare. In her hands she carried a pair of beaded sandals. She stared at what was left of her home and shivered when she remembered what had happened here. It had been an entire year since the town mob came and burned her house to the ground. It was a desperate attempt by the town to rid the ghost house with its hundreds of ghosts. The only problem was that Claire, her friends and the Chief and Deputy of police were all trapped inside the house at the time.

The mob had been instigated by Rory Lynch. Rory came from one of the oldest fishing families on Butcher Harbor. His family had been here almost as long as the Templeton House had been terrorizing the harbor town. Caroline Laws, the local realtor for the harbor assisted Rory in his devilish plans. Claire used to date her son Julian during his senior year of high school. Julian died in a tragic accident during a graduation party held at the beach. Julian challenged Claire to ride the waves from a storm and Claire took him up on it. Riding the ferocious wave Claire got slammed and was churning around under water. Julian bailed from his board to save her, but hit his head on a rock and died later at the hospital. Caroline blamed Claire for her son's untimely death.

Between Rory and Caroline the entire town, including the tourists who spent their summers on the harbor, came to Claire's house with torches and set the home on fire after a séance had gone terribly wrong taking the life of Robert Chambers from the Paranormal Research Institute. His death had been ruled as a heart attack caused by high cholesterol, but Claire knew the horrible truth. The ghosts of Templeton House had taken the life of the paranormal researcher.

What was left of the house still stunk like fire and to Claire's surprise parts of the rubble still released tiny columns of smoke. Claire knew this was unusual, but did not dare to investigate. The house had been cleared by the mob. Not by their fire but by everyone pitching in and reading the names of the dead from the Book of Deaths found under Templeton House. Butcher Harbor residents had tried to get rid of the house for over a century. It wasn't until they all pulled together along with the Book of Deaths that they were able to release the souls of those taken by the vicious pirates that built Templeton House.

The sea grass behind her moved and she turned to see who was approaching her house. No one ever came out to see this house. This had been her first trip back to the peninsula since the fire Looking through the grass she could see there was no one there. She searched the grass toward the ocean when someone walked up behind her and grabbed her from behind. Prepared to defend herself at all cost, she drew her fist back as she swung around to face her assailant.

CHAPTER TWO

Before she could release her arm to swing a punch at her attacker, Claire's forearm was snatched up and held in place. Struggling against her assailant was useless; he had a firm grip on her. To her relief she found him to be the incredibly handsome Inspector Dogg of the Butcher Harbor Police Department. Since being promoted to Inspector he no longer wore the Butcher Harbor police uniform. Instead he was dressed in khaki pants and a light blue sports shirt with the BHPD shield logo embroidered across his heart. Claire starred into his eyes and got lost in them. She had to blink several times to bring her mind back into focus.

"What the? What are you doing here?" she asked.

"I could ask you the same question."

"It's been a year. I thought it was time to check out the what was left of the house."

"Ah. You know I would've come with you."

"I was just something I wanted to do on my own. So what are you doing here?"

"I was chasing a gnome."

In anyone else's world that would not make sense, but in her life anything was possible.

"A gnome?" she asked.

"Yeah, this little man that I have seen wandering around town. I chased him out here and lost him in the sea grass."

"So he's not from here? A tourist maybe?"

"No one in town knows anything about a short man staying in town."

"What has he done?"

"Nothing that I know of, but he keeps sneaking around and whenever I call to him he runs off."

"So you saw him out here?" Claire remembered she had heard something in the sea grass but hadn't seen anything. If it was a small man then that would explain why she hadn't seen him.

"Well I did hear something, but I didn't see anyone."

"Hmm. He's pretty short. You probably wouldn't see him above the grass."

They both surveyed the surrounding sea grass but it just waved gently in the breeze. There was no sign of manmade movement anywhere. Their attentions turned back to the scorched remains of the house. Neither one spoke for a few moments.

"Hard to believe that happened a year ago." Dogg commented.

"A lot has happened since then."

"Yeah," Dogg said pulling Claire closer to him and kissing her hard on the mouth. "Great things!"

Claire tried to catch her breath. Raymond Dogg had a way of sweeping her off her feet. She felt faint and was glad he had a firm grip on her waist. Feeling faint should have made her feel stupid and silly, but with Raymond it just made her happy.

He released her and walked over to the black mark left by the house. He kicked a few charred pieces of wood around with his boot. Claire came and stood beside him.

"Strange? It's still smoldering. That can't be right." He said and moved around the remains of the house for a different view.

"That was what I thought too. Seems like it should have gone out by now. Maybe it was struck by lightning or kids coming out and starting little fires at night." Claire tried to convince herself, but she knew that Raymond wouldn't buy it, and neither did she.

"Well, I'll have the night patrol keep an eye on it and see if it flares up. Check and see if anyone is coming out here at night. Come on, I'll walk you back to the shop."

Claire had purchased the boutique directly off the boardwalk with its shop downstairs and an apartment above it. She lived above the shop. Off the top floor was a roof top deck that afforded her a view of the ocean and surrounding town. Claire liked to spend most of her time up there and even installed a hammock so she and Dogg could lay outside and watch the stars on nights when he came over, which was pretty much every night now.

They walked down the beach hand in hand. Dogg had slipped off his shoes and socks, rolled up the bottoms of his pants and walked with her at the edge of the surf. Bubbly water raced in and out of their toes and made a small hissing sound as it retreated back into the sea. It was dusk now and the sun would set soon. Halfway back to the boardwalk Dogg stopped and turned to face Claire.

"I was going to do this later with candle light and all, but this seems like a perfect time. I won't kneel down in the water, but," he pulled a tiny black box out of his khaki pants pocket. "Claire Templeton, would you do me the honor of being my wife?"

Claire stood dumbfounded unable to speak. She stared into his beautiful eyes and could not imagine that he would ever want to be her husband and thrilled that he did.

"Okay, this is not how I imagined this happening," he said.

"Sorry, you caught me off guard. I had no idea…"

"So is that a yes or a no?" Dogg looked nervous.

"YES! Of course I would love to be your wife!"

Dogg scooped her up and carried her into the surf.

"What are you doing? Are you crazy?"

"Yes, I am crazy in love with you!" he said as a wave crashed at their hips pushing them toward the beach. Claire laughed and grabbed Dogg around his neck. He swept her up in his arms and tumbled into the surf as they kissed while the sun set around them.

CHAPTER THREE

Claire and Dogg ran back to her apartment and changed. Dogg kept a clean set of clothes in case of emergency in Claire's closet. He joked about how it looked pressed because it was smashed in between all of her gypsy outfits. The girl had clothes. He had to give her that. Once they had cleaned up they headed over to The Shady Lady to meet his mother for dinner. He called Chief Harris to make sure that he and Becky would be coming by the restaurant for dinner as well. Harris knew that Dogg had planned to pop the question and was finding it hard to keep that to himself. He would be glad to know the deed was done.

When they arrived at the restaurant owned by Raymond's mother Lila Dogg, they walked past their usual seats at the counter and took a table in the back of the restaurant used for special occasions and parties. Lila tilted her head as she watched her son sit down in the party room. She followed them over the table he had chosen in the center of the unused room. She carried two glasses and a pitcher of water with her.

"Something special occasion I've forgotten about?" she asked.

"Could be." Dogg said as he held Claire's left hand under the table to hide the surprise. Claire was beaming and he was afraid his mother would still be able to guess the surprise but he didn't care. Claire had said yes and that was all that matter to him right now.

Lila placed the glasses on the table and poured each of them a glass of water giving them both the evil eye trying to discern what was going on. She knew it was the anniversary of the fire. She expected the two of them to be moping around. In fact she hadn't expected to see either one of them tonight. It made her think back to last year. Rory and his crew of misfits had tied her up in her own restaurant to prevent her from alerting her son and the Chief of his torching plans. She could not believe that the entire town, even the tourists had torched that house while they were still inside. It made her shiver thinking about it. Tonight, she thought, I am going to put that out of my mind.

"The usual?" Lila asked. Dogg loved her pot roast and she cooked it often for him. The customers seemed to like it as much as he did so no one ever complained.

"Actually we are going to wait for the Chief and Becky if you don't mind. Maybe a few rolls and butter for now," he said.

Now Lila was really sure something was up.

"Should I have dressed for this occasion?" She asked smoothing her apron worn over a white tee-shirt and black jeans.

"Nope," was all he said. Something was up. She was sure of it. Lila turned and walked back into the kitchen to get them some rolls.

Claire giggled and found it hard to sit still. She kept rubbing the ring with her right hand. Dogg still held her left hand in his. It seemed like an eternity before the Chief showed up with Becky who appeared surprised to see that they were eating in the party room, but then that explained why her husband had purchased a huge bouquet of flowers on the walk over to the restaurant.

"Okay," Becky said, "What is the big occasion?"

"Nothing," everyone sort of said at once.

Lila returned with rolls and extra glasses for everyone. She brought a large ceramic pot full of roast and set it in the middle of the table.

"Flowers for me Chief? You shouldn't have," Lila said hoping to tip someone's hand. The suspense was killing her.

"Take off your apron Ma and join us. This is important." Raymond had never asked her to take off her apron when she joined them to eat. Stunned she did as requested, placed her apron over the back of the chair and took a seat across from her son.

"Okay, what is going on?"

Raymond had no idea how to tell them and he gulped down half a glass of water trying to figure it out. When he slammed his glass down hard he pulled Claire's hand out from under the table and showed her ring to everyone. Becky burst out in tears and raced around the table to embrace Claire. Harris rose to his feet and shook Dogg's hand. Lila sat in shock just staring at the ring.

"You okay Ma," Dogg asked as he slid around the table to hug his mother. She stood slowly and looked at him like he was a stranger. "Mom, hey, are you okay?"

"Yeah, sure son. I'm happy for you," she seemed to perk up a bit, "I'm happy for the both of you." Dogg was not convinced. He knew she would have trouble letting go of her baby boy since he was an only child, and she didn't care much for Claire, but he thought she would at least be happy for him.

"So when's the big date?" Harris asked to relieve some of the tension.

"We haven't really set a date yet. It's something we will have to think about." Dogg said. Claire nodded in agreement.

"Oh a spring wedding before all the tourists show up!" Becky was about to burst at the seams with joy for them both. Dogg wished his own mother could feel the same way. "Or perhaps this fall when they all go home, but before it gets too cold. A beach wedding. Or maybe on the boardwalk?"

"Slow down, Becky. Let them figure out what is best for them."

"Oh I know, but there is so much to do. Plans to be made. Who will be the best man? Flower arrangements, invitations have to be ordered. These things take time. We really should get started right away."

"In time, Mrs. Becky, in time," Dogg said. Then he turned to Harris, "Chief would you do me the honor of being my best man?"

Before he finished getting the words out Claire slapped him across his arm. "I had planned to ask him to give me away Raymond," she said obviously stunned.

"Oh, I never thought about that," he said surprised by the turn of events. He had always planned for the Chief to be his best man. Now he would have to find another. He stood in the awkward silence considering who else he could agree on for a best man. Harris stood silent letting them work this out amongst themselves. "Of course he should give you away. I don't know what I was thinking." He saw the relief in his fiancé's face. His mother on the other hand glared at Claire for a moment and left the table.

"I'll go get some plates and silver," she said as she walked away.

Dogg followed her into the kitchen.

"You okay? I thought you would be happy for me."

"I would be happy for you if you would have married a local girl."

"Claire is a local girl Ma."

"You know what I mean. She fled this town and moved to New York City to become some big shot fashion designer."

"She lives here now. Her business and her life are here. And she was raised here."

"If that is what you call what her mother did for her. And what about the Chief? I know you wanted him to be your best man if you ever married. You have felt that way ever since he took you under his wing and brought you onto the police force."

"I know, but Harris thinks of Claire as his daughter even though she isn't. And her father passed away. What am I supposed to do?"

"Think of yourself for once Raymond. Stop putting the world ahead of you. She could get one of her friends to give her away."

"It's not the same. It will be fine. I promise."

Lila handed him a stack of plates and she grabbed some silverware. They headed back to the dining room and joined the others. Harris had given Claire the flowers and Becky hadn't stopped going on about wedding plans throughout the entire meal. Once dinner was over and all the congratulations were done Dogg walked Claire back to her apartment. Neither of them noticed the gnome-like man that trailed behind them, dodging in and out of the shadows, trying not to be seen.

CHAPTER FOUR

"Hey, I hear congratulations are in order," said Deputy Craig Henderson when Raymond Dogg reported to the police station for work in the morning.

"Yeah, she said yes!" Dogg beamed. He had no idea how happy this would make him. He found himself singing in the shower, whistling on his walk to work, and generally feeling like he was floating on air. He hoped he would be able to concentrate on work today. Maybe it would be an easy day and no one would notice he could not seem to focus on anything but Claire's lips as she said she would be his wife.

The phone rang and Henderson answered it. He seemed to snap to attention as the person on the other end of the line spoke. "Harris! Chief! Pick up line one!"

The Chief picked up the phone in his office and started to scribble information on a pad. Then he hung up. Dogg and Henderson looked at each other for a second then back to the Chief. Harris picked up the scrap of paper and headed to the outer office.

"Dogg and Henderson- grab the boat keys and head out to these coordinates. Coast Guard says there is a distress signal, but they are afraid they may be too far out to be of any assistance. They have dispatched a cruiser and a helicopter but they think you guys might be able to get there sooner."

"What is the nature of the distress signal?" Henderson asked as Dogg grabbed the police boat keys from the key rack.

"They are not sure. The officer who heard the ping only got bits and pieces. Take your firearms. He did understand the word: Pirates! You had better hurry."

Dogg and Henderson ran down to the docks. Henderson untied the boat while Dogg jumped in and fired up the motor. This boat was used to patrol the coast on high use days at the beach. Usually the only excitement this boat saw was dragging people out of the water that had fallen asleep on a raft or had gotten dragged out too far by the undertow. It had never seen anything dramatic or life threatening. Now for the first time the boat was needed in an urgent situation. Urgent was not anything that ever happened on the Harbor. Their adrenaline was pumping at full speed. Dogg checked the coordinates while Henderson jumped aboard. They took off for the high seas for the first time in their careers.

The water was choppy today and their little boat was not made for ocean travel, just border patrol. Still the men made due. About a mile out from their destination they saw a plume of smoke and expected the worst. As they drew closer to the vessel their hearts sunk. It was a sail-boat, sails down and she was stopped in the water. The boat was called the Lazy Daze. It was on fire and there was no sign of people on board.

"Attention, attention, is there anyone aboard this vessel," Henderson called over the boats built-in PA system. Dogg maneuvered the police cruiser closer to the sailboat.

"This is the Butcher Harbor Police Department. We have received your distress signal and are coming aboard."

Dogg pulled the boat alongside and Henderson tied them loosely to the sailboat in case they had to leave in a big hurry. Dogg climbed on board first followed very closely by Henderson who went aft to search for survivors. Dogg went below, gun drawn, and didn't like what he saw. Blood covered the table, the wall and the floor. Some blood was smeared as if someone had been dragged back to the sleeper berth. Cautiously Dogg moved toward the berth, checking the bathroom and closets on the way for intruders or victims that were hiding away. He pushed the compartment door open with his gun. His other had held his polo shirt over his mouth to keep out the smoke coming from the room.

A large man and a tiny woman lay across the bed. He was sure that they would have succumbed to smoke inhalation by now if it were not for the gunshot wounds in their heads and chest.

"Henderson! Down here! Grab the fire extinguisher!"

Henderson came down and squeezed past Dogg shooting the extinguisher at the base of the fire. Dogg had grabbed another extinguisher and took Henderson's place when his extinguisher ran dry. Overhead they could hear the coast guard helicopter arrive at the scene.

Dogg uncovered his mouth for a moment to tell Henderson to go above deck and signal the helicopter. The fire was out now, but the boat could reignite from smoldering ambers at any time. Dogg checked each victim for a pulse, but he knew he would not find any. A glance around the compartment showed evidence of a disturbance. In fact the entire cabin was strewn with their belongings tossed around as if the boat had been ransacked. Someone was looking for something or just looting the couple. But why kill them?

Henderson came below deck with a short man in a wet suit. Dogg appraised him of the situation Henderson had most likely explained above deck.

"Looks like a robbery maybe. They are both dead. Smoke inhalation if not from the gunshot wounds." He had to yell to be heard above the helicopter. "I think the fire is out for now, but the smoke and dust from the fire extinguisher are deadly. We should get out of here quickly."

The CG officer went above deck and made hand signals to the helicopter, then he went back below deck. He snapped a few photos with a waterproof camera then turned to the two police officers.

"Help me get them out of here!" he yelled above the helicopter whooping above deck.

Dogg and Henderson grabbed the big man and the man in the wetsuit grabbed the tiny woman. They dragged the bodies up on deck. The helicopter was already lowering a basket to airlift the bodies from the boat. They sent the man up first, then the woman behind him. Meanwhile a coast guard cruiser arrived and other men were coming on board. The man in the wetsuit spoke to the man in charge from the cruiser and then hooked himself to the line from the helicopter and was pulled off the boat to the crew waiting above.

The man in charge waited until the helicopter was away before he tried to speak.

"I am Captain Howard Cutty of the United States Coast Guard. What is the nature of the situation?" He wore an solid dark blue uniform with shirt tucked in and pant tucked in at his boots. His shirt and pants carried the coast guard insignia. On his head he wore a dark blue ball cap with the same coast guard insignia on it. He was taller than Dogg and had a commanding presence about him.

"We have two Caucasians one male one female found below deck with gunshot wounds to the head and chest. The boat was discovered adrift and on fire. The fire seems to have been started in the sleeping compartment below deck where the victims were found. The boat seems to have been ransacked as if someone were looking for something in particular or just generally looting," Dogg reported to the officer.

"Let's go below and investigate," the man said as he was already halfway below deck. Dogg followed him and Henderson stayed above deck with several petty officers from the coast guard cutter.

Cutty took a quick look around assessing the situation. Then he turned his attention to the radio where the distress signal was sent from. Only broken off wires remained in the cubby hole where the radio should have been. It appeared that all electrical equipment had been raided. Anything of value seemed to be gone from the compartment.

A cursory look into the sleeping compartment showed the victims belongings strewn about the room. Cutty picked up some jewelry off the bed and dropped it down again.

"Costume jewelry. Whoever was here knew the difference between the good stuff and junk."

"I was told the distress signal mentioned pirates. Is that what you think this is all about?"

"We have been tracking a particularly ruthless band of pirates that seem to be based out of this area. They are in and out before we can get out here, if the victim is even able to get a call out. The woman reported the distress signal. I think her husband must have been above deck and she was still down here, undetected until the middle of her call when the line went dead."

"So there is a group operating out of my area?"

"We have been tracking them for several years. This year they have amped up their terror and their terrain. They are probably not out of your harbor, but are operating in this vicinity. We would like to bring you on board this operation since you have a quicker response time then we have. Your boat will not do for this type of work. I take it you do not have a larger vessel or you would have brought that instead."

"No, this is our only boat at the moment."

"That will not due. I will check into this when I get back to base. We'll tow this boat in and do a thorough investigation. Finger printing, the works. Try to catalog what might have been taken. Identify the victims. They most likely are rich, on vacation and flaunted their wealth at their last port of call. Someone took notice and came to get some of it for themselves. Meanwhile return to your base and we will be in touch with your Chief. It would be good if we could coordinate a defense against these pirates and put them out of commission. They are a dangerous bunch that are not afraid to commit murder as you can see."

"Very well. We will return to base and await contact from you." Dogg said as he went above deck to join Henderson. The petty officers already had a tow line secured from the eighty-seven foot long coast guard cruiser. Henderson said his goodbyes and the two of them boarded the tiny police cruiser and headed back to base. Less than a half mile from the Lazy Daze Dogg noticed the Wayward headed toward the harbor.

"What do you suppose Rory is doing out here?" Dogg shouted over the noise of the boat.

"This is not his usual fishing ground," Henderson yelled back.

They took a detour and drove the boat around the Wayward, giving Rory a wide berth, but letting him know they saw him. Then they headed back to the harbor.

CHAPTER FIVE

Claire busied herself at work in the boutique. She straightened out some of the outfits customers had stuck here or there when they decided on other purchases. She made an order for more sunglasses and sunscreen. It was impossible to keep them in the shop even though the customers could pick them up cheaper at the market or on the main boardwalk just a block down the street.

Even though it was only midmorning she felt lonely already. Dogg had left this morning for a briefing and training with the Coast Guard in Massachusetts. He was on special assignment with the them until the pirates were captured. Who even knew how long that would take? But he assured her he would be working out of the harbor after this brief training mission. She had never seen him so excited except for when she agreed to marry him.

Lila, on the other hand, seemed dead set against it. Claire knew that she would have trouble where Lila was concerned. Lila hated Claire's family and their old house. She disliked Claire as a person and really hated that she could see dead people. This is not the kind of wife Lila had wanted for her son. Claire suspected that she had planned on a cheer leader or pageant queen on the arm of her handsome son. He was in line for Chief of Police and would have great standing in the town. Lila did not want a clairvoyant troublemaker for her son's bride.

Becky Harris, on the other hand, thought of Claire as her daughter. Unable to have children of her own she had taken Claire on after Claire's real mother died in the fire at the house last year. Today already Becky had called to see if Claire could come by around one o'clock to the florist to look at some bouquets and flower arrangement for the wedding. Claire told her that she had no idea when or where the wedding would be held so she didn't know how she could possibly pick flowers right now. Becky assured her they would just window shop and see what was available and at what time of the year.

The doorbell jingled and in walked the mailman, or woman in this case. Angela Davenport had delivered mail as long as Claire had lived on the peninsula. She used to heave the heavy mailbag over her shoulder but now she had a Tricycle with a huge mailbag attached to the back of the bike.

Usually you could set your clock by Angela. Today she was early.

"Thanks Angela," Claire said as the lady placed the mail on the counter.

"I hear the deputy is off on a mission with the Coast Guard. Something to do with pirates?" Claire knew Angela was fishing for gossip to spread to the rest of the town on her route. That explained why she had delivered Claire's mail first today.

"Yes, he is away for training and on special assignment with the Coast Guard. He will be back in a few days."

"Such a pity leaving so soon after popping the question. Had you even had time to set the date yet?" she inquired.

"Not yet. Perhaps when he returns we will have time to discuss it. Right now he has more important things on his mind."

"Dangerous work this pirate hunting. He could get injured or even die in the line of duty. It would be a shame if you two hadn't even tied the knot yet."

What a horrible thing to say. Claire realized that Angela was just an old gossip and was looking for something juicy to deliver along with the daily mail, so she forgave her and let the comment slide.

"Dogg knows how to take care of himself. He will be alright," Claire said, not wanting to feed her own fears and doubts into the gossip that would no doubt be going around town.

"Okay, well I have to get back on route. I will see you again to-morrow," Angela reassured her. Great, I can't wait.

When Angela left Claire walked over to see what kind of goodies came in the mail today. She was sure she had seen Angela set down a manila envelope. It could be that catalog of fabrics she was waiting for. The catalog would contain all the latest fabrics for this season as well as the fall. Claire couldn't wait to get started on some new outfits she had designed.

The manila envelope was a disappointment. It wasn't the fabric catalog after all. Instead it was addressed from the Paranormal Research Institute. This was the place that Robert Chambers had come from. He was the man Madeline had enlisted to assist her with the séance at Templeton House. This guy came with an RV full of equipment and wired her house for the big event. When nothing came of the séance, Chambers threw Madeline out of her chair and took over the séance. He brought out the woman with the knife and all hell broke loose ending in Chambers' death.

She wondered what they wanted. Perhaps they planned to sue her over his death. She hoped not because her mother did not appear to have any insurance for the house and if she did, any information about it burned up inside the house.

Gingerly she opened the envelope and pulled out the letter inside. It was on Institute leader head. It was signed by Dilbert Daley, Research Coordinator. Claire began to read the letter. It appeared that the institute was taking full responsibility for the burning of her house due to Chambers careless actions. There was an offer to rebuilt Templeton House as long as Claire agreed to stay on an agreed budget of $950,000. To ensure the budget was maintained and to avoid Claire any undue stress the institute had a contractor that they used to build the institute and could offer his services to rebuild her home. It seemed they offered to rebuild the house as it was or to create a new more modern design for Claire.

For a brief moment she considered the offer. Her apartment was ridiculously small. Dogg had never stayed overnight because there was barely room for her let alone him. Often they slept in the hammock until the wee hours of the morning out on the top deck under the stars before Dogg would head home to change or work.

Of course there was always Dogg's house. He had a cottage in the middle of town. His little one bedroom home was comfortable for him, but for the two of them it could get messy. There was no closet space for all her clothes. The kitchen was so tiny compared to the one at Templeton House with the big island, all the cabinets, its. Hundreds of ghosts. She could not believe she had allowed herself to miss that place. But it was more spacious.

Besides, Dogg would never allow them to rebuild on that land. Even though the house had been cleared, anything could go wrong. No, she was not interested in this offer. She and Dogg would figure out their living arrangements some other way.

Outside the door the little gnome-like man peered in through the window. He watched as Claire curled the letter up into a ball and threw it in the trash can. Before she or anyone else could see him, he scurried away.

Pick   up   your   copy   of   Pirates   Cove   Butcher   Harbor   Two   soon!

ABOUT THE AUTHOR

Previously Lisa was the Thorsby Community Columnist for the Clanton Advertiser. She stopped working with the Advertiser to concentrate on writing her novels. At the request of her fans, a second book in the Butcher Harbor series is being written at this time. Book Two is called Pirates Cove.

She has also written several poems under her maiden name: Lisa Lewis. Remembering You was published in 1984 by World of Poetry Press. Nightmares, a poem written in memory of James Dallas Egbert III was also published by World of Poetry Press 1986. Ms. Moon has won several Golden and Silver Poet Awards.

When not writing, Lisa is an avid photographer and has shown her Waterfalls of Alabama collection January 2009 and April 2010.

Those interested in writing a novel can follow her on facebook at Writers Clubhouse:
https://www.facebook.com/lisalewismoon#!/groups/30471812962626 6/

You may contact the author at:

http://www.houseonbutcherharbor.blogspot.com

http://www.butcherharbor@yahoo.com

You may also find her on twitter @lisalewismoon and on facebook at Lisa Lewis Moon

The author encourages comments and will try to respond to every inquiry if possible.

REVIEWS FOR HOUSE ON BUTCHER HARBOR

Chris T.:
"Totally hooked. This is as good as, if not better than any Dean Koontz book!!!"

Julia H. :
"Amazing book hope there's a second one to go with the first!!! Intense and a great page turner!!!"

Sharon K.: "House on Butcher Harbor keeps you in suspense throughout.....had a hard time putting it down. Keeps me wanting more!!"